THE BROTHERS' KEEPERS

THE BROTHERS' KEEPERS

A NOVEL OF SUSPENSE

NLB Horton

This is a work of fiction. Names, characters, places, and incidents either are the product of the author's imagination or are used fictitiously. Any resemblance to actual persons, living or dead, events or locales, is entirely coincidental.

Copyright © 2014 by NLBHorton

RidgeRoute Press trade paperback edition 2014

All rights reserved. Printed in the United States of America. No part of this product may be reproduced, scanned, or distributed in any printed or electronic form without permission, except in the case of brief quotations embodied in reviews.

Editing by Jamie Chavez and Ginger Kolbaba
Cover Design by Rebecca Lown
Author representation by Mary G. Keeley, Books & Such Literary Management

ISBN 978-0-9914017-3-4 (trade)

For the unflappable young man whose Mandarin bravely rescued Chinese tourists, huddled in a Parisian elevator, after having lost the Louvre earlier in the day

DAY ONE
CHAPTER ONE

Brussels

Grace Madison, PhD.
Four A.M.
The ringing phone interrupted my first good night's sleep in two weeks. My heart raced, and the Sixth Commandment echoed through my groggy brain.

I am archaeologist Grace Madison, and I do not typically kill people.

"The shot shattered the window inches from her head." My son was on the other end of the line, referring to Becca, his bride. "I'm checking in with everybody. Dad was plowing snow off the road to the ranch house. You're obviously fine in Belgium. Where's Maggie? I can't find her."

"Your sister's in Paris, Jeff. Preparing for a conference in the south."

"You sure about that, Mom? She's proven to be a missing target before."

"I'll confirm and get back to you. Give me an hour."

The line went dead. Swatting at the light switch above the nightstand, I knocked over the water carafe, then left a caring tirade in Maggie's voice mail. After speed-dialing my husband, Mark, in Colorado, I yanked open heavy brocade draperies and nearly pulled a gilt bracket out of the wall.

I released the wadded fabric as I gazed eastward, at a clementine line gripping the horizon.

...

Five A.M.
"I can't find your sister. Your dad is working his way to Paris. Can you meet us there?" I was lucid now, paying attention.

FedPol, the Swiss national police force, would want to question Jeff and Becca, and try to prevent them from leaving the country. He was a war correspondent for the BBC, and she was retooling her career after her cover as an MI6 agent had been blown last year. They might have the contacts to flee the bed-and-breakfast high in the Swiss Alps, where I hoped things had been perfect until the glass exploded.

"Honeymoon, Mom."

"What's left of it, dear." I prodded him, picturing his coppery unibrow spiking above his glasses frame as he fumed. He loved and respected his sister, but would perceive her disappearance during his belated honeymoon as her epic failure. "I checked with her security team. Last they heard, she was swinging through Paris before heading to the water conference in Marseilles." When he didn't respond, I continued. "Jeff." My tone conveyed the Mom Look of Death, but he didn't give up.

"Why was she in Paris? Coax another proposal from Cliff?"

I tried to be patient. "Cliff doesn't require coaxing. She won't accept his offer anyway. *Can you leave Switzerland?*"

Quiet conversation preceded a rustling *thud*.

Becca's clear voice meant she snatched the phone. "Dr. M., we'll be there later today. Is that soon enough? You're at—your normal location?"

I admired her caution, still delighted my son had the sense to marry this formidable young woman. "Yes. Looking forward to seeing you, Becca. Thank you."

CHAPTER TWO

Swiss Alps

Fat snow squirted through the broken window, swirling past billowing draperies. Its wetness strengthened the piney scent of the forest surrounding the chalet. The sniper had hidden in the trees, and the hole in the floor indicated a perch at least halfway up the mountainside.

Becca's dark features contrasted with the snow and heavy lace dominating the Alpine décor—something Jeff was studying when the glass disintegrated. He hugged her, nesting his beard into her black hair.

"The good news is that I don't think Mossad is involved," she said into his chest.

"How do you know?"

"A chopper would be landing in the courtyard. Those cliffs look ripe for an avalanche. Flapping rotors might not be a good call." She nodded toward the mountains as she smiled up at him. "Or do you think they just haven't surfaced?"

"The shot and Maggie's disappearance make me nervous. She's probably not having a spa day." He did not want to think about Mossad, or specifically, Retired Commander Abraham ben-Dove Cyril. "I *always* expect Mossad."

THE BROTHERS' KEEPERS

They turned sideways, squeezing into the temporary room. Police were on the roof and in the courtyard, not bothering to hide. One call to the Wedding Cake on the Thames, as Londoners called MI6 offices, freed the couple. During the conversation, she did not mention that the bullet barely missed her.

"I'll let the front desk know we're checking out early," he said. "Then arrange train tickets. We'll have a couple of connections. Let's pack. Given that this is Switzerland, I'm sure we're safe now that the police are in place . . ."

" . . . and the shooter is long gone, having skied or snowmobiled into freedom."

Jeff nodded at an agent, rigid as the wall she abutted, and reached beyond Becca to close the door. They would be in Paris by mid-afternoon.

"FedPol and the police will follow the tracks, but no one will strike here again. You and I both know that was a warning. No sniper would miss your silhouette in the window."

"Which is why I feel perfectly safe going to Paris. And your sister might be in trouble."

"You think?"

CHAPTER THREE

Brussels — Paris

Grace

The bullet train blasted through coastal scud strangling Belgium and soaking western France, heading toward Paris. I tried not to hyperventilate and thought about the little I had learned from Cliff, my former teaching assistant at seminary. He now was acting director at the Kinneret archaeological site above the Sea of Galilee in Israel. I spent each summer digging and researching there. My winters were spent teaching, and at our family ranch in Colorado. Occasional forays led to major antiquities fairs like BRAFA in Brussels, where I exposed looted antiquities for a division of UNESCO.

Cliff waited in Paris to propose again to my daughter, as was his habit. I had called him shortly after I hung up with my son.

I tried to appear calm so I wouldn't frighten other passengers, but suspected my face was as distorted as the wrinkled, hard-cider apples piled in pyramids throughout the countryside in early February. I rubbed my forehead to smooth worried creases as the train slid into the *Gare du Nord* before noon.

After he lobbed my scarred suitcase into the trunk, I instructed the taxi driver to take me straightaway to where Cliff said my daughter was last heading on the Left Bank. Cracking a window, I dodged second-hand lung cancer from his nicotine-infused clothing.

I hoped Maggie had left a clue. She would leave a trail if she could. There would be no question we would attempt to find her. Her position as president of MBM (Margaret Bennett Madison) Hydrology took her to the world's most dangerous places. I had benefitted from her intelligence and survival training after shooting her abductor in the Judean desert last year. Even then, we suspected the evil behind her kidnapping wasn't finished.

Sprinting through puddles, and up the American Church steps, I cinched my thick overcoat to repel an Arctic gale buffeting down the Seine a hundred yards away. I shuddered in the slender narthex, as if tossing off dread. With opposing motions—tugging *cloche* down to brows and scarf up to earlobes—I created an Elizabethan ruff of brown hair that became curlier as it grayed.

I entered the nave, my wet footsteps slapping softly on the pale limestone. A chilly chancel gust brushed my face, sharing musty sweetness from last Sunday's roses. *Aromatherapy on better days*, I thought.

In my gut, I knew she was in trouble. We were close and stayed in touch, and could always locate each other in a few hours.

Her vulnerability made me sob. My maternal instincts locked into overdrive, distracting me from thinking clearly. I forced myself to be logical. When I realized I was failing, I dropped to a pew, exhausted.

Cathedrals triggered my prayer response, as intended by tall, narrow spaces pulling a worshiper's view heavenward.

At that moment, I chose to think first and pray later—never wise—and noted my prideful practicality sometimes complicated my lifelong faith. So I abandoned reliance on God to dissect my environment.

Shoving gloved hands deep into my coat pockets, I searched for anything unusual in the grainy light of a wintry day. Mark often said, "The nut didn't fall far from the tree" when describing my daughter's similarities to me, so I needed to think like her. How would she have left a clue?

She would sit roughly here, the pew we always chose, two rows behind Louis Comfort Tiffany's 1901 stained-glass windows. She was a creature of habit, like me, and those windows added an element of tranquility to our worship.

Pew backs for five rows in front of and behind me appeared normal. Their trays contained faded Bibles and well-thumbed hymnals, with pencils—one broken—upright in bored holes. I shook the books violently, holding them upside down by their covers, to dislodge anything. They were empty. I eased onto my knees, too boney and old for a frigid encounter, and looked for bits of paper. The floor was spotless. I groaned in pain and disappointment.

Then I did what I should have done: prayed. For wisdom. Enlightenment. Cunning. Maggie's life. As expected, I didn't hear the booming or still, small voice of Divine revelation. But after ten minutes of selfish pleading, I calmly turned, my unsteady steps leaving hallowed ground behind.

CHAPTER FOUR

Switzerland — Paris

Becca split a *pain au chocolat,* shooting crumb shrapnel across the narrow table onto Jeff's jeans. She dipped the pastry into a frothy *café crème* as they sped through Switzerland on their last leg of today's journey—the three-and-a-half hour train ride from Zurich to Paris via the *Lyria SAS.*

"What did you discover?" she asked after she swallowed.

"I'm not sure yet." He had been glued to his e-tablet since they left the hotel, and his *cappuccino* cup contained nothing more than stains. He was crabby, suffering caffeine withdrawal in a coffee-scented railcar. "Except I need to stay in touch with my sister better, and Mom was right. Maggie's scheduled to present the keynote speech at a conference late this week."

"Topic?"

"King Solomon's Treasure: Then and Now."

"What does that mean? She's a hydrologist."

"Beats me. I think the wise king's water would be long gone after three thousand years, wouldn't you?"

"Unless it's part of an old aquifer. Then even she can't tell which is his water and which is . . . " She paused. "You don't believe . . . "

9

"I never know what to think about Maggie. But she has a nasty habit of uncovering things that almost get us killed."

"And *my* work is supposed to be dangerous."

Jeff smiled grimly at the thought of his bride's career as an MI6 agent, and nodded as he picked up a newspaper. Ignoring pastries and unflavored yogurt littering the space between them, he began scanning *The Financial Times, Neue Zurcher Zeitung,* and *La Figaro,* retrieved from a tubular rack screwed to the carriage front.

"So I add German to your languages?" Her comment preceded a delicate *slurp*, onyx eyes unblinking over the rim of the white cup.

"Once you become fluent in one, related languages are easy." He set *Neue Zurcher Zeitung* on the table before contorting to thrust a plug into an outlet. "The first can be tough. Particularly if it's dead."

When her head jerked, he clarified. "Dead *language*."

She smiled. "Which language is related to Ugaritic? That's been extinct for a few thousand years." When his brows bobbled, questioning, she continued. "Dr. M. told me."

His midnight translation in Herodium last year revealed to his family unusual aspects of his life. "All of the northwest Semitic languages," he said.

Jeff did not like talking about himself, and struggled to morph from committed loner to intimate partner. Maggie and he were raised with the Bible verse, "From those to whom much is given, much is expected." His linguistic skills, a gift from God cultivated by hard work, had triggered recruitment by agencies on both sides of the Atlantic. He eventually chose to *broadcast* war, rather than make it.

Leaning across the table, propped on an elbow, he spoke quietly. "Hebrew, Aramaic, and Phoenician. Grammatically, Ugaritic is similar to Arabic and Akkadian. I don't mean to be short, Becca, but my languages don't seem important right now."

He gently wiped her chin, and she finished the job before dropping the soiled napkin into her lap. He stood, reaching into his bag on the overhead shelf and canvassing the aisle to see an attendant pushing the trolley their direction. Jeff ordered two *espressos*.

They had walked through the cars twice. Becca's training, and his experiences on rickety transports in war-torn countries, made them cautious. Reserved seats are suggestions at best on European trains, and they had assessed passengers before settling on this location. He moved around the table to sit next to her, taking his steaming cup with him, and typed into the tablet before sliding it across her abdomen.

> *People either love her or hate her, depending on if they're trying to get enough water to live, or enough to control the world.*

She erased before handing the tablet to him. "I figured. How bad?"

He typed again, sitting as close as possible on a public train while respecting that his mother raised a gentleman.

> *In Israel, they left a trail Girl Scouts could follow through the woods on a moonless night. These people are much more sophisticated.*

After erasing, he tucked her hand in his coat pocket and stroked her index—trigger—finger, calloused by target practice.

She leaned against him. "Do you want me to involve London? We're off-grid now, and can stay that way for the next two weeks since I'm on personal leave."

"I'd rather talk to Mom and Dad first."

"Let's ask the driver to drop us across the Tuileries. We can walk through the garden."

"I'd like that. Mom's car—you know she ordered one—can take the luggage to the hotel. A driver will be holding a sign with our names in the arrival hall." He whispered in her ear like a man in love. "The Tuileries are more consistent with my honeymoon plans than a kidnapping intervention."

"And the gardens are adjacent to her hotel. I would have found them one of the hardest things to give up if I were Marie Antoinette fleeing the Louvre. The flowers must have been breathtaking when it was her palace."

"All the women in my life love gardens," he said. "Kind of contrasts with your ability to get yourselves shot at. Kidnapped . . ."

"Married." She poked his ribs, then snuggled against him.

Brown hills and plowed fields rolled outside the broad window. As they crossed into Alsace-Lorraine in northeastern France, he kissed her lightly, continuing a border-crossing tradition of celebratory kisses. Despite a sturdy heating system designed to conquer winter in the Alps, the carriage was cold. The coffee cart passed again, its attendant doubtlessly recognizing Jeff's habit. Jeff noted the tight, thin-lipped smile of the Swiss, and shook his head.

Scattered farms and hamlets, tree lines resembling inverted push brooms, and scruffy Alsatian cows punctuated land cultivated by the same families for generations.

"You think he's a spy?" she asked jokingly, nodding at the server's back.

"Isn't everyone?" was Jeff's serious reply.

CHAPTER FIVE

Paris

Grace

A balm to internal panic, this Right Bank spot was my Parisian home before children. At *rues de* Rivoli and Castiglione, the arcaded structure was built for the French Ministry of Finance, then transformed into the most luxurious hotel—the Continental—in Paris before eventually becoming the Westin. From the train, I had booked a room overlooking the Tuileries gardens.

After my unsuccessful visit to the American Church, I planned to spend the afternoon wandering the neighborhood. Unfortunately, Mark urged me to stay safely at the hotel until he arrived tomorrow. So I sat and waited for what was left of my family.

While he was at Denver International Airport, we discussed alerting the American Embassy two blocks to the west, but decided contacting officials could further endanger all of us until we knew more. My intuition—something I attributed to or blamed on the Holy Spirit, depending on circumstances— also said we should talk with Jeff and Becca before doing anything. I planned to contact my seminary professors as soon as we discussed our situation thoroughly and privately, and developed a plan. They helped us find Maggie last year, after we discovered that they were old pros at the spy game.

With each hour, I was more confident she had been abducted, although I still didn't know why.

...

Jeff and Becca rang my room a little past 3:00 p.m., and we agreed to dine at The First, the Westin restaurant named after the *arrondissement*—neighborhood—surrounding the hotel. We spoke little during an early dinner of seared tuna and couscous, exhausted from stress and travel. We then walked as far as the *Rond Pont*—a beautiful traffic circle—discussing Maggie's recent activities and speculating about the content of her keynote speech. We turned back toward the Tuileries knowing no more than when we left the Westin.

Groundskeepers locked the garden gates as we ambled by, the Beau-Arts-era streetlights sealing Paris in a classic-movie glow. In front of a bouquet separating the hotel entry from its now-damp courtyard, one that offered elegant dining when weather permitted, we agreed we needed to be fresh and rested for Mark, so went to bed. We could do nothing more.

DAY TWO
CHAPTER SIX

Place Vendome, Paris

Grace

My third pot of *Mariage Freres Roi des Earl Grey*—the strongest tea in the history of the universe—was cold by the time his muscular shape swung through the quadrant of sliding doors at noon. He glanced at the crowd while circling the atrium, then stopped at the gent's room opposite. He was reconnoitering.

When he emerged into the quiet hum of the lobby, he turned toward me with a swagger produced by ranch horses, exhibiting street creds for well-fitted jeans and boots on a man who knew how to get both dirty. His navy blazer was Continental, but he was the quintessential Western American Male at the top of his game. *Be still my heart.*

For thirty-four years the sight of him had made me catch my breath. More than one perfectly veneered French woman—how do they *do* it?—glanced seductively as he passed. He ignored them, as well as dozens of white Dendrobium orchids floating like butterflies above a green-marble-topped table.

I was proud he strode to *me*. My husband was a rancher and former CIA operative. He traveled with ease, looking better when he deplaned than before boarding. I disembarked looking as if the craft had crashed *en route*.

He dropped his leather bag at my feet as I stood.

"We meet in the most romantic places under the worst circumstances," I whispered into his lapel. My charcoal pants fitted through narrow cuffs; a hand-knit cashmere sweater in cobalt (one of my best colors); and black, thick-soled loafers engineered to withstand any surface this elegant city threw under them, were deliberate and pleasing choices. A plaid pashmina flirtatiously rimmed the collar of my alpaca coat.

"When we find her, I'm going to hogtie her. Then take her home for good." His body didn't relax. "Any more news on the shooting? Jeff and Becca here?"

I tilted my head to answer. "She's almost thirty. Except for the fact that we love her and she is our child, our ability to control her ended long ago." I held his gaze. "They arrived yesterday. They were babysitting me until I told them to go wander around. That I'd wait for you, and we'd get down to business when you arrived. They're more than capable of taking care of themselves. I called them when you walked in. They're on their way back. And thank you, yes. I do look lovely. How nice of you to notice."

"Sorry. New outfit?" He bent, kissing my forehead. "Can we threaten to disinherit her if she doesn't move home? Why do the young women in this family attract trouble?"

"I attracted you in my youth, and you certainly proved to be trouble," I said as I smiled at him. "And this is not the heartfelt greeting I hoped for, handsome." Laying my cheek against him, I realized I hadn't taken a deep breath all morning. "Care to try again? We can't disinherit her. The entire younger generation seems troublesome. Jeff's not easy, you know."

His squeeze was reassuring. "Right. I love you. It's good to see you, Gracie. Where is she?"

"I have no idea, Mark." Italian Cypress—his scent, so my favorite—warmed me as we walked arm-in-arm toward the elevators. "Did you bring it?"

He acknowledged having the item I requested from the ranch, waiting until the elevator doors closed to shake his bag to indicate it was inside. We zigzagged through a labyrinth of hallways carpeted so thickly our footfalls were silent.

I slid the card through the key slot. "Expect a monologue about Jeff's interrupted honeymoon." My comment teased a chuckle from him.

In front of the window, a bamboo trellis supported three perfect hothouse peonies, the blooming tower mimicking the Eiffel a mile southwest in the Champs du Mars, and that had been delivered when I was in the lobby. Their pearl-tipped coral petals glowed in the darkly contemporary Asian décor. I didn't need to look at a card to know who sent them. Mark and I were rediscovering each other after last year's near-death experiences in Israel, and the journey sparked renewed courtship. His gift of my favorite blossoms was a tender touch, and I smiled at him. I was falling in love with this man again.

Flopping on the bed, he stretched a six-foot-plus frame cramped during flight. "In which language do I expect Jeff's diatribe? Find out how many he speaks?"

Jeff had mastered *Academie français* French in high school, and added Mandarin and Arabic during economic studies at St. Andrews, where he met Becca. When he began interpreting

Aramaic, Syrian, and Ugaritic, we wondered—about a lot of things.

Mark's voice gently tugged me back. "What do you think happened, Gracie?"

"Maggie would never stand up anyone. Certainly not Cliff. She doesn't love him, but wouldn't be rude. Or disappear without telling me. He thought she might have gotten busy—he's so besotted he makes excuses. But when I checked with him after Jeff's call, and told him about the shot at Becca, we decided she'd been . . . "

I was unable to finish the thought. At the window with my arms crossed angrily over my chest, I watched joggers and dog walkers through leafless plane trees, marveling at their commitment in winter drizzle. My cluelessness about her current projects was worrisome, and I frowned. Thinking of the flawless faces in the lobby, I wondered who did their cosmetic work, and turned to my husband. "I went to the American Church yesterday, but didn't find anything. She told Cliff she was planning to attend services last Sunday. That's as far as I can trace her. I think we should get in touch with Dr. Steele."

Dr. Stanley Augustus Steele was one of my favorite seminary professors, an eighty-seven-year-old wonder who had spied for Mossad during the formation of Israel. He and his associates and friends were instrumental in preventing the deaths of my husband and daughter in the Middle East months ago.

"I'm sure you and the kids talked about this last night. Assuming you didn't come up with anything . . . "

"We didn't. Talk or come up with anything. They think Maggie's conference topic, something about Solomon's water, is weird. They can't pinpoint why, though."

"We should talk with them. Then contact Drs. Steele and Merrit. If Maggie's disappearance and the shot are related, as I assume they are, then your professors are probably in danger again. Although they might not know it yet."

My mind wandered, and I took another deep breath. A faint peony scent reached my nose, and I touched a petal, then noticed a slip of paper tucked under the vase edge. I handed the printed message to Mark after reading it.

We have her. We can find you. Keep quiet or she's dead.

"Good to know the florist wasn't the only person in your room while you waited for me." His voice dropped with the scrap as he hugged me, his arms encircling my waist from behind. "That clears everything up, doesn't it? And eliminates contacting the authorities."

"I feel safer already. And regardless of your CIA and Becca's MI6 associations, we're not equipped to deal with this, Mark. *I'm* not. I can't play spy again. Not with her in danger."

"Are you prepared to risk her by contacting the embassy, or the French police?"

I unclenched my jaw to save tooth enamel, then ran my fingertips across my forehead. I would resemble an aging Shar Pei by the weekend. "No."

"We could, very carefully, utilize strategic assets at both agencies. Remain invisible. That's what I'd like to do. We need help, Gracie. Use all our options."

Taking a deep breath in an attempt to slow a heartbeat well beyond my healthy cardio zone, I struggled to balance the note and world-class intelligence agencies at our fingertips. I leaned my head to the left as he nuzzled the right side of my neck.

" . . . honeymoon." Mark attempted to distract me. "This can be part of renewing our marriage now that we're empty nesters. If you marry me again, we can have another honeymoon, albeit an adventurous one. Or we can just live in sin until Jeff and Becca knock. Not that anything can distract us from worrying about Maggie."

I looked forward to the rest of my life with this man. Somewhat half-heartedly, we picked up where we left off in the lobby.

CHAPTER SEVEN

Tuileries Bar, Paris

Grace

A demonstration by underpaid dentists clogged streets around the Louvre, and Metro drivers had walked out to protest thirty-five-hour workweeks they deemed too long. At least the dentists were polite enough to schedule their protest, even if I hadn't read about it in *Le Monde*. These examples of free speech delayed Jeff and Becca's return by three hours, and Mark and I made good use of our time.

...

"S'il vous plait, une kir royale," I replied to the vested waiter's query. Of the four bars I visited as a near teetotaler, this hotel bar was my favorite because it was classy and beautiful. Oxblood velvet walls and romantic lighting necessitated stronger reading glasses than I carried, so I ordered my one drink without glancing at the menu.

Other women's size-zero backsides were cosseted in tufted banquettes so deep they required an abdominal crunch to exit. My US size 12 was firmly planted in a chair in the darkest corner. Jeff and Becca faced us, and a heavily whiskered monsieur, whose medal-laden coat sagged down a back arced by scoliosis, beamed from his portrait above Mark's head.

We were hidden by the bartender's kingdom, a peninsula that was the center of the universe thanks to a young woman with legs twice as long as mine wearing a skirt the size of a doily.

Becca squeezed lemon into a gin and tonic. Mark poured Jeff a glass from the split—half bottle—of Barolo, a tannin-rich Italian wine I couldn't get past my nose.

My cultivated son paused his review of lethal matters to swirl wine in the broad balloon. "Do we know anything else? Other than what Mom shared?"

"No. This is our last respite for a while." Mark referred to Maggie's absence. "I don't know about your mother, but this disappearance hit me out of the blue. I thought Maggie was finished being WaterWonderWoman."

The waiter brought mixed nuts with wasabi peas, and set my flute of champagne, in which scarlet cassis pooled, on the table. A bright twist of lime peel, chicly Parisian, balanced on the crystal lip, then took a bubble bath the moment I nudged the glass stem. I sipped, then spoke. "I doubt she chose to be kidnapped, dear."

He took my hand.

Using a towel tucked into his white apron, the waiter dabbed at the wine that had corkscrewed out of Jeff's glass during his swirl. Sniffing, he muttered, "*Maladroite.*" Clumsy.

"*Vous avez manqué un point.*" Jeff didn't miss a beat, nor did he glance at the man. "You missed a spot," he translated since his dad didn't understand a word of French.

The waiter scowled, and I reminded myself that traveling with Jeff was revelatory.

"Did you have any trouble with your carry-ons?" Becca's question referenced what Mark brought from the Man Cave at the ranch. She, Jeff, and I had discussed my request for the laptop, and my brief conversation with Maggie several days ago, which led me to ask for everything she had sent to the ranch in the past month.

"I travel lightly, with things less alarming to TSA than sneakers worn through their cattle chute." He leaned back to recite his list. "Disks of data and a pink laptop. I was memorable pulling *that* out of my bag, entertaining the rest of the PreCheck line. Zip drives of references from extra-biblical sources dating to the Old Testament. Recent deliveries from her to the ranch, all of which made no sense to me. Normal oddities, considering it was hers." Mark chugged his Barolo as the waiter rolled his eyes. "I'd like to share some of these items with you after a walk to clear our heads."

Jeff poured the nut-and-pea mixture into a zip-lock bag tugged from his pocket. "You never know when you're going to get a good meal on these family outings."

Becca and I abandoned our drinks, respecting the steps and cobbled pavement we were about to traverse.

...

Mark took my hand before turning toward the taxi queue.

"I thought you said we were walking." I slowed down. Ours was a complicated, mature marriage between complicated, sometimes immature individuals. Recent surprises—his CIA affiliation, and my extracurricular archaeological work quietly policing looted antiquities for UNESCO—demanded transparency if the marriage was to survive. "Where are we going, Mark?"

"There's a concert at the American Church." He nodded at the doorman, who whistled for the cab swerving next to the curb. The driver wore ear buds as he jammed out to Johnny Hallyday's *"L'envie,"* so couldn't hear Mark's whispered statement as we slid across the seat. "Six more eyes on the spot can't hurt, and I agree she'd try to contact us."

Jeff tapped the driver. *"Autour du Pont Rond deux pas de l'Arc de Triomphe."* Around the Round Point twice, then to the Arch de Triomphe—the circuitous route. "My sister would be suspicious," Jeff said of the young woman he had rediscovered in Israel, who was an exponential extension of the stubborn girl from their youth.

"Agreed," Mark replied. "Plus, the waiter was too attentive. Let him think we're walking somewhere." Mark studied the flier pulled from his sport-jacket pocket, and pointed to the schedule of weekly concerts like those in churches throughout Europe. "Classical concert Sunday evening. Happy Hour Chamber music Thursday. Hip-and-trendy Fridays, with burgers in the courtyard. Thank God it's Thursday." He shoved the paper into his pocket. "I picked up the brochure from the concierge. We may as well contribute to kingdom work. Keep the doors open." Donations at mid-week concerts generated essential funds for the Christian faith dying in the European Union.

Brake lights blinked in a tangled mass on the Champs-Élysées, and I wiggled as I looked uphill. Apparently I wasn't the only impatient person in the cab because halfway to Napoleon's triumphal arch, Jeff tapped the driver. He instructed the man to cut past *Marius et Jannette*, a seafood restaurant near the arch base, then deliver us to the American Church on the quay. Jeff monitored the headlights and traffic behind, Becca studied surrounding vehicles, and Mark returned his attention to the brochure—in a language he didn't read.

My husband listened exclusively to songs about stolen beer, shot horses, and ex-wives who ran off with pickup trucks—themes often combined in the same song. Occasionally, he would risk seventies rock. Chamber music was a stretch, but a great opportunity to snoop.

...

American Church, Paris

Before the first notes, Mark peered from the hundred-capacity balcony. Jeff and Becca enquired about Sunday services with the rector. Never once running his fingertip beneath his starched collar, I assumed the cleric enjoyed the couple acting interested. My husband then stalked the eighteen-ton wood, lead, and copper instrument whose three thousand pipes lend dignity to traditional worship.

Out-of-tune guitars and pierced, soul-patched believers must have been relegated to the contemporary service and burger extravaganza, because this crowd looked reverent. Not knowing what else to do, I sat on the family pew and prayed until my tribe settled next to and in front of me. For these things I was thankful.

When the music began, I hoped someday artists performing in St. Chappelle, St. Severin, and the American Church would expand beyond Pachelbel's "Canon in D Major," a masterpiece of Baroque that was now fast food for tourist ears. Today was not the day.

I love every type of music *except* country western, but after two of the subtle movements from the composition, I couldn't remain still. I needed to find my daughter. Absentmindedly, I scanned a hymnal, as Jeff did in front of me. Embarrassed myself by knocking the broken pencil onto the floor with a clatter. Silently flipped the pages. Reached for the book he handed over his shoulder as Becca picked up for her handbag.

I flipped the hymnal open where his thumb marked the spot. Squinted at handwriting in the margin of "Be Thou My Vision"—Maggie's favorite hymn. Affirmed my belief in guardian angels. Mark leaned in to read.

> *If you find this, I'm in trouble. Two guys have been following me, and I just got a look at their faces. It's the guys who tried to kidnap me in Bethlehem. They're three rows behind me. Start with the Elf's gift to the Grasshopper, then the Man-Cave missive, red leather shoes, and lion that roared at them. Love you, Mama.*

I snapped the hymnal shut. We marched indiscreetly up the aisle and out the door. Mark dropped a fifty-euro note in the tithe basket to atone for our disruptive rudeness.

Dashing into dusk, we were illuminated.

CHAPTER EIGHT

Tuileries Gardens, Paris

Grace

We convened a tight circle near the dry fountain at the west end of the park. The Louvre towered on one side, and the Eiffel and Place de la Concorde glowed distantly on the other. Part of our configuration was for privacy, part an attempt at warmth, and the rest a ruse to resemble tourists huddled over a guidebook we didn't have.

"Let's remember to keep our voices low and speak facing the ground." Jeff warned. "As I told Dad on the ridge at Kinneret . . ."

"Devices can hear even the quietest conversations." Mark turned to me as he finished Jeff's sentence. "Why did you ask me to bring her old laptop?" He leaned in to hold my arm affectionately. I was not deceived. He was hot natured and freezing, so I put my arms around him. This was Paris, after all.

"When I spoke with her, she mentioned leaving files at home. In her old laptop. She worked on it off and on during the wedding week. She also mentioned sending mail to you, with other things she might retrieve later." A mother's near-perfect knowledge of her children is a spiritual gift, even if early biblical translators made a patristic effort to overlook maternal influence. "The laptop is a technological dinosaur, so a brilliant place to hide information. She would think that way. And she wouldn't alert me if she were doing something dangerous because she wouldn't want me to worry, or try to stop her. But she would drop hints, knowing I'd remember."

"It's all at the hotel." Mark's hands were free since I was hugging him. He retrieved his wallet, and handed Jeff a scrap from the leather bi-fold. "Speaking of valuable, this might be. I can't read it—one of your weird languages. It was wedged in the laptop, and I pried it out. I think I got the whole thing." Jeff examined the paper as Mark explained. "I couldn't open the computer. We need help."

"TQRB.AH{H,,,}/W.ARGMK, W.ARGNK." Jeff splattered us while choking to death. "'She approaches her brother and cries out, for a message I have, and I will recount to you.'" Seeing our confusion, he continued. "It's Ugaritic. *Epic of Baal*." He looked at the wording again. "{.}MBKNHRM, QRB/{A} PG, THMTH." He pulled it closer, appearing puzzled. "'At the springs of the rivers, amid the streams of the deep.' Then she continues with something about wilderness and mountains. Her Ugaritic is weak."

"Strong enough, apparently." Mark rocked to encourage circulation in his extremities while the drizzle matured into a sleety rain. Cowboy boots were poorly insulated, never waterproof.

"Impressive." Becca's tone was sincere. "Very smart of Maggie."

"Any more?" I focused on retrieving my errant daughter, who wasn't clever to me now.

"Clues about mountains. Rivers or springs in the deep. The wilderness. In ancient context. *Epic of Baal* dates to BC 1350 as part of the *Cycle of Baal*. Rough-and-tumble stuff. Extremely explicit. The message is intended for me, since she is 'approaching her brother and crying out.' She's covering her tracks in case this falls into the wrong hands. Although anyone with ill intent toward us would know *brother* and *me* were the same person. But few people read Ugaritic. Even fewer *bad* Ugaritic." He looped like I did, surrounding the problem to reveal any weird trajectories.

We didn't have the time. "And how did she know weeks ago she'd need our help?" I nudged him to focus, but he brought the paper to his nose.

"*LHT*," he read.

"Excuse yourself?" Mark was a stickler for manners.

"'Tablet.'" Jeff looked from the paper to his dad. "She's scribbled the word *tablet* at the bottom, separate from the rest of the writing. Possibly telling us to look at it."

We stood silently, a rare occurrence. I thought about the cuneiform tablet Dr. Steele gave Jeff and Becca in Israel as a wedding present.

Traffic built, its ever-present roar punctuated by honks. Frying onions, probably from a Castiglione *brasserie*, infused the heavy air. Arcades protected shoppers now, but would soon fill with Parisians going home, or meeting friends or lovers. *L'heure bleu*, the Parisians called it. *The blue hour.*

Jeff fished through the tattered backpack he swung off his shoulder. It had traveled the world with him, although it now resided with him and Becca in England. His hand moved from its interior to his pocket quickly, covering whatever he retrieved. Then he angled toward us to reveal a tip of the ancient clay tablet, the cuneiform mentioned in Maggie's note. She also referred to its giver—the Elf, my esteemed professor, Dr. Steele—and my son by his nickname, Grasshopper.

"At the wedding, I promised you a look, Mom, and we were taking it back to London. I'm glad it isn't in the luggage at the hotel. Dad, I hope you hid the envelope."

Mark nodded as I secured the top button of my coat, tightened the scarf around my neck in a most un-*Parisienne* way—I lacked French scarf-tying genes—and checked my phone for a text from my daughter. Two of the three moves were successful. My head receded into my collar, and I looked like a turtle.

"So we have The Man Cave missive, which is the package she sent to the ranch a week and a half ago. The laptop and cuneiform tablet—'the Elf's gift to the Grasshopper.' But red leather shoes and the lion that roared at them?" I asked.

"The Wicked Witch of the West comes to mind," Jeff replied. "But Toto's not in Kansas anymore." He was not being irreverent, just airing a spiraling mind.

Becca shook her head as church bells pealed. "And Maggie's not there, either. You'd better think before Dr. M. gets unhappy." She smiled at me as I glared at him. She was aware of the Southern phrase the family often quoted: if Mama ain't happy, ain't nobody happy.

The bells scrambled tones from Notre Dame, Eglise Saint-Germain l'Auxerrois, and a cathedral in the direction of La Madeleine. Indistinguishable above the traffic and echoing against architecture a thousand years old, they merged into a melodious epiphany.

"That's it," I said into my scarf. "That's what she meant."

"What?" they asked.

"The red leather shoes refer to the Vatican. The Pope wears red leather shoes. Until this Pope, red-leather *Prada* shoes. The lion that roared is Venice. The lion is the Venetian mascot. Rome and Venice locked up throughout history. The lion roared at the red leather shoes." I leaned into Mark, trying to get warm, and he held me against his side. "That's the best I have. Any other ideas?"

"Makes some sense." Mark spoke slowly to consider the suggestion. "Particularly in context."

"But how do we fold in the cuneiform tablet? And her Ugaritic notes to Jeff?" Becca pulled us along, knotting threads into a rescue mission, keeping us focused.

Stress made me short-tempered. "We need someone who knows what they're doing." I sounded harsh, a conclusion confirmed by their startled looks. I placed my hand on Jeff's lapel. "I'm sorry. You're doing a good job with the tablet, Jeff. But we're overlooking something. Aside from the Louvre, the best place would be the *Antiquaires*. Beyond that, dealers at the *Puces*, but they aren't open until Saturday morning. The Antiquaires closes at seven, so we have time." I looked doubtfully southwest, toward the building housing the consortium of dealers.

The three-story *Louvre des Antiquaires* was across the rue de Castiglione from the museum. They were half of a perfectly proportioned cream-and-gray square that included the Palais Royale and four-star Hotel de la Place du Louvre.

In good economic times, the Antiquaires burst from basement to ceiling with world-class artifacts. Ancient and medieval rings and prayer books, armory from the Middle Ages, Renaissance tapestries, and jewels changed hands in discreet sales that kept dethroned royal families afloat. Every trip to Paris meant a visit for me because I considered its contents museum-worthy, and I was always on the lookout for ancient pieces that might have been looted.

"Good idea, Dr. M.," Becca said as she turned to the Louvre. "High-end dealers have few customers. They love to chat."

"Especially to my wife." Mark loosened his arm, then bent his elbow as a crook for my hand. "A woman of impeccable and educated taste . . . "

We crossed the road, vehicles drowning his sweet speech. Passed Hotel Lotti and splashed across the Place du Louvre, where a drenched, silver-painted, bed-sheet-wrapped human depicted the Statue of Liberty. A tambourine floated at his or her feet, bereft of tips.

Jeff took Becca's hand. "Do you remember Laura McAlex?"

"You mean gorgeous, redheaded, curvaceous Laura McAlex with an unhealthy interest in you at St. Andrews?"

He ignored her tone. "She landed a research job at the Louvre straight out of school . . . "

"Daddy is a clan chief, dear groom. Although miniscule, Clan McAlex is loaded. She has *connections*."

"Regardless of Daddy McAlex—" Jeff tried again "—she had to resign. A dealer here hired her. An article in the hotel magazine mentioned her shop. She might be able to help."

"She won't help *me*." Becca's voice could have sliced a week-old baguette.

We entered the foyer through dark glass doors, tinted to protect the treasures within. Jeff studied, I thought harder than necessary, the directory of dealers while a shiver coursed down my back.

CHAPTER NINE

Louvre des Antiquaires, Paris

"Jeff*rrr*ey." Laura McAlex purred as she reached toward him. Her brogue was as rich as forty-year-old scotch.

"You're in big trouble," Becca whispered while he looked innocent.

"It's been too long." McAlex nested back in her chair, crossing her legs in a skirt so tight the seams squealed.

Jeff and Mark had paused by a chain-mail coat of armor for an elephant, and arrived a minute after Becca. Grace stood beside a display of illustrated medieval manuscript pages six dealers down, fishing for information via cell phone from the director of security at MBM Hydrology.

Danger lurked in the Louvre des Antiquaires.

Mark cleared his throat. "Why don't you ask Ms. McAlex about the tablet? We have dinner reservations soon," he said to his son in an effort to prevent the hostility becoming physical.

Becca was twisting the yellow diamond on her left hand, sitting in front of the ormolu-laden desk, picking at the high-carat filigree with her fingernails. Her unfinished business with McAlex, who *owned* McAlex Fine Antiques, would have to wait.

"Mark Madison, Ms. McAlex." Mark's voice boomed. He pumped his hand between Laura and his son, emphasizing separation.

"You have something of interest?" Laura ignored Mark. "I have an appointment in twenty minutes, so apologize for rushing you, Jeff*rrr*ey." She did not glance at anyone else as she moved a candle around her desk methodically.

Jeff sniffed. "Whiskey?"

"Peat," she replied.

"I could use a shot," Jeff said.

"Drinks some evening after work?" Laura smiled at Becca.

Jeff cleared his throat. "Would you take a look at this?" From his pocket, he handed her—using two fingers—the cuneiform tablet.

She studied the taupe-tan block, cradling it as a child would an Easter egg. It fit perfectly in her petite palm. Retrieving a microscope from the credenza, she placed the incised tablet on a petri dish, raising and lowering the dish to focus. Her performance was deliberate.

"Fairly common tablet. Semitic, I think. Several have come to market since graduation. What am I looking for?" As she spoke, she rubbed her forefinger lightly across the tablet, looking at Jeff through lashes clearly not her own. "Aren't you the language expert?"

His level tone sounded sincere. "I'm unsure about the dialect. Probably Semitic. We remembered you were here, so dropped by to see if you could enlighten us. A lot of unusual relics roll through these halls."

She seemed to weigh his words, tilting her head to one side so that her coppery coils of hair clashed against the red-and-white toile walls. She fondled the cuneiform, not looking at it, as if she were reading Braille. "I think it's standard issue. I don't mind having one of our experts have a go at it, or can walk it to a friend at the Louvre if you can leave it for a couple of days. Becca's language skills don't help?"

"It was a gift, and I'd hate for something to happen to it. We were curious," Jeff said, preparing to duck.

"A gift from whom?" She had not leaned forward with the tablet.

"An old family friend," Becca said, holding out her hand. "We need to get Dr. M., so may I have the tablet?"

Laura handed it to Jeff as she spoke. "Now if you'll excuse me. I need to prepare for my meeting. Such a pleasure, Jeff*rrr*ey. Mark, Becca." She gave Mark a cursory nod, and spat Becca's name.

They survived the brush off, although Jeff thought the worst was to come as they walked toward the central stairwell.

"Someone was about to get hurt back there," Mark said, glancing at his daughter-in-law.

"I'm sure she has health insurance." Becca looked straight ahead.

Jeff slipped the cuneiform tablet into his trouser pocket. His fingers explored its surface, while the other hand reassuringly clasped Becca's. He almost skipped down the stairs, meriting his nickname, Grasshopper. They emancipated Grace as her phone call ended, and updated her as they exited past the Place du Louvre, down the Castiglione, and toward the Westin.

Jeff was excited. And almost glad his bride was so angry she did not speak and distract him. Two blocks later, Mark did.

"What is it, son?" He led the way as they trotted to La Fountaine de Mars at the Place de Concorde, dodging Parisians and tourists flowing under the arcade.

"A seam," was Jeff's puzzled reply.

CHAPTER TEN

1st Arrondissement, Paris

Grace

"Jeff!" My lunge garbled my scream, which morphed into a squawk. I tripped over the curb, arms flapping, flat onto the sidewalk in a vivid impersonation of a dancing chicken. Proving once again that my given name is a misnomer.

The dark Peugeot missed Jeff, bounced off the mini-median bordering the bike path, and veered east toward the Champs-Élysées in a controlled motion unrelated to lost traction on wet roads. Dinner—Bresse *poulet, pommes frites, haricots verts, tart tartine,* or chicken, French fries, green beans, apple tart—attempted an uprising.

It was miraculous Jeff wasn't seriously injured. Or worse.

"You are alive, Grasshopper." Mark helped him up after peeling me from the pavement. I appeared to rearrange my clothes to become decent, but really recomposed a shattered psyche after seeing a child almost killed—again.

Becca, shaken if you knew where to look, leaned against a window displaying lacy pillows stenciled with Eiffel and Arc. She was farthest from the street, her hand at the small of her back. She carried the Walther P99 lightweight standard-issue firearm of MI6, and her stance and scanning vision made me feel safer.

Passersby cut a broad berth as traffic roared onward. Jeff brushed debris collected during his jump-and-roll, and I was thankful that *merde*—dog poop—no longer decorated Parisian sidewalks. He checked his pocket, nodding to confirm the cuneiform was there.

"We need to get our stuff and get out of here." I evolved from a dancing chicken to Captain Obvious. Things were looking up.

"Where to?" Becca monitored our surroundings.

"There's something wrong with this cuneiform." Jeff's pocket pulsated as he fondled the clay tablet, then pulled only half to the folded edge.

"It's broken," his dad said.

Thank you, Mark.

"We know," the three of us stated loudly.

"I mean it's strange. Where can we look at it privately?" Jeff turned to his dad. "We can't stay here."

"Follow me." Mark pivoted to the rue Saint-Honoré. Hearing no other suggestions, we followed him. Up the hotel steps, into the antechamber outside the men's restroom next to the bar we left a couple of hours earlier. Becca and I stopped. He held the door. "Come on. No time to be girly."

Jeff and Mark checked stalls, which were empty. *God answers prayers.* Becca pulled from her purse a multi-purpose tool that looked like an impulse buy from a rack at a Home Depot register. She ejected slim blades, popping them in and out of the lock until one stuck.

"Thank you." I patted my daughter-in-law on the back. "Yours is an usual, but welcome, skill set, my dear."

"Any time, Dr. M. And no, Jeff, you can't have it." After only months of marriage, she knew the Madison males' genetic predisposition to tool obsession.

We clustered at the changing table, a politically correct addition to men's rooms in developed countries. I moved two bitter-orange infusers in front of us, under the wide mirror. Jeff hovered over the cuneiform halves to inspect a protrusion like a metal cigarette. As his thin fingers twisted it, the tube glinted in light from a bright overhead fixture.

"Well, well." Mark leaned in. "That what I think it is?"

"Looks like it," I replied. "A scroll?"

"Believe so." Jeff muttered, steadily torqueing the rolled metal. "Copper."

Becca ensured her tool wedged as far into the lock as possible. "How tiny is the inscription, Jeff?" She eased between the men. Since the purpose of scrolls was to convey information, it had to be inscribed.

These relics were notoriously fragile. It may have appeared a relief, but archaeological experience led me to believe our troubles were beginning if we planned to unfurl it. Jeff slipped it from the tablet.

"May I see it?" I shifted under the light, pulled my jeweler's loupe—I don't leave home without it—to my eye. "It's been opened. Recently. Erratic oxidation. Normally I'd say take it to a pro. Since Maggie's missing, I say we do it. It's soft." I poked the artifact, feeling thin metal give under pressure.

"Semitic." Jeff squinted at it now. "Possibly Aramaic, or Egyptian, on the reverse side."

"Here we go." Mark rolled his eyes and joined Becca as she examined the cuneiform, his frame dwarfing her petite self. Jeff and I stepped back as the restroom door rattled. Becca handed the scroll to Mark, and pushed the tool to ensure it held until matters outside became urgent.

"*Momento, por favor.*" Mark called at the door. "Housekeeping."

"We're in *Francccccce*," I hissed.

With his fingernail, Jeff loosened the scroll edge. It didn't crack, so he continued delicately, murmuring to himself. "We'll have questions once we see what's here. Who opened it recently? Dr. Steele? Is this what makes the cuneiform special?"

The scroll, now flat, was incomplete. I handed him the loupe as the noises became more insistent. "Quickly."

"I've seen this before." Jeff turned it this way and that.

"May I?" I asked. He laid the scroll in my hand. The language was beyond me. But I recognized the illustration. "Madaba?"

"*Yes.*" His blue eyes twinkled victoriously. The rest of his face remained stiff. "The mosaic map of the known world. St George's Chapel, Jordan. AD five to six hundred? Unless there's a similar one still hidden somewhere, which I doubt."

"So that's where we're headed?" Becca spoke to us, but her hand was against the thumping door. Animated French accompanied keys rattling in the lock as the tool tilted toward the floor. "What's our story?"

"Nonsense." Mark lifted the door lever. "We don't need a story."

Her hand was at her back now, and I clutched the scroll flat against my thigh through my coat pocket. Jeff stepped behind his father, in front of Becca and me.

"We're in *Francccccce*," Mark teased. "They're liberal-minded. I'll bet women are in the men's room all the time." He opened the door and probably thought he was funny.

I did not.

"Few places even have segregated water closets, remember Mom?" Jeff used the Continental name for a restroom. Panic made me forget things like modesty.

A perplexed concierge and two distressed bar patrons pushed in, unconcerned about Becca and me. The concierge focused on the lock, the patrons on the facilities. No one waited for us to leave before tending to business.

Becca and I hurried out.

"Assume the luggage is compromised." She thought aloud as we bisected the atrium, looking nonchalant except for my bug-eyed face. "Leave it."

"I need to get Maggie's laptop." Mark entered an elevator and punched buttons with more force than necessary. "And the package she sent."

"They will have found them in the room." She was stern. "Leave them."

"I didn't hide them in the room."

The doors closed.

"Go after your dad. We travel in multiples now." I nudged Jeff toward doors opening across the bay. "We'll wait at the concierge desk." My stomach churned, either because of the kir royale, or implication that Madaba would lead us to the Middle East, which might create another confrontation with Spigot, the power behind last year's water theft. I breathed deeply, braced for another "misdirected" Peugeot in the lobby, and remembered Maggie's words in Jerusalem, "We Madison women aren't given to hysterics."

Maybe we weren't hysterical in Israel, but I might be in *Francccccce*.

Three minutes later, Mark carried a plastic bag emblazoned with *LAUNDRY, Westin Vendome*. He explained it contained the hotel magazine ("reading material for our trip"); items Maggie referenced in her mail; and a pink, moss-littered laptop.

"Plan?" I picked vegetation from the crevice between screen and keyboard as we headed to the revolving doors. He must have stuffed the device in the potted plant in the hallway, which was clever.

"First Galleries Lafayette. Buy what we need since we're leaving our things. Only the basics. No time for stylish choices. They close in twenty minutes." Jeff had devised the plan, then shared it with Mark in the elevator. I was happy to leave it to them. "We missed the last direct commercial flight to Amman."

"Just wait a minute," I said, pulling my antiquated Droid Incredible 3 from my pant pocket. Jeff raised his eyebrows to ask the question, *What the heck are you doing?*

I texted. Almost immediately, my phone emitted the response sound, followed closely by a second parlay. Satisfied the correspondence was complete, I passed the phone to Jeff, who stood between Mark and Becca.

> **ME:** *Elf, need help. Going to George's mosaic. Lost her again. Thoughts?*
> **SS:** *Know nothing. Give me time.*
> **ME:** *Instructions?*
> **SS:** *Stay put for now. Back to you tomorrow.*

SS was my beloved elderly professor, Dr. Stanley Steele.

"Let the first two cabs go. Take the third." Becca watched the vehicles pull in. "This one."

We did as she said.

"Where to?" I asked. "We're not supposed to leave Paris."

"I know just the place," Mark replied.

CHAPTER ELEVEN

St. Mark's Square, Venice

Canal water lapped against the ashen stones of the wharf, continuing a nine-century assault on Piazza San Marco, or St. Mark's Square. Sky and water almost matched, a hazy phenomenon Venetians knew meant perfect weather. So Steven Steele strutted a little with each step through his adopted hometown.

The Doge's Palace, built to impress merchants trading with *La Serenissima*, as Venetians called their city-state, sat between the lagoon and unorthodox pastiche of St. Mark's Basilica. Its rosy complexion and structural grace resembled the interior of a conch shell.

The basilica was named for the evangelist's remains—"relocated" by two wily traders in AD 828 in an attempt to repair Venice's compromised credibility with the Vatican. Built of remnants stolen from Constantinople during the Fourth Crusade, its hodgepodge style was condemned by the beauty around it.

"The Venetians made a sow's ear from a silk purse," he said as he did each time he saw the church.

Venice in winter was sometimes flooded (the *aqua alta*) so deeply that skiffs ferried through the piazza. Elevated boardwalks enabled tourists and residents to continue adventures and lives during these deluges, although photographs of luggage carried overhead through thigh-deep water peppered the Internet. This year, the water had reached Steele's waist, marking the sixth highest flood in history.

To make environmental matters drearier, sea-level Venice was humid year-round, an island laced by canals that sometimes reeked of sewage.

He loved it here.

This evening, overcoming melancholy winter-weather odds, the city basked in a warm setting sun. A breeze brought ocean freshness, and La Serenissima was *La Bellisima*—The Beautiful.

Antiquarian Steven Anthony Steele, twin of theologian Stanley Augustus Steele, PhD., tossed a vintage Burberry overcoat on the metal café chair, and carefully balanced a loden-felt fedora on the top rail. Six outdoor tables testified to vacation weather in the offseason. His beeping phone telegraphed business.

"Antico Privato." He listened. "I'm at the Florian. Walk toward the basilica from the museum. On your right. A gelato? I'll choose. Look for the dapper old gentleman."

He chuckled. *Every* elderly Venetian gentleman was fashionable.

The overpriced Florian was *the* place to people watch in the summer, when only the glamorous secured a table. As the waiter delivered the menu, Steele talked to himself about a Parisian dealer who just landed at the airport, and a scroll listed at auction four years ago.

Carnevale tourists, loudly drunk, distracted him from his thoughts. The ruffians reminded everyone the pre-Lenten festival was reaching full swing.

"I didn't know where I'd settle after Stan and I argued about the estate," he said after requesting two glasses of water. Moments later, a voice spoke from behind him.

"Antico Privato?" The redhead theatrically peeled off sapphire leather gloves with lilac lacings, and dropped them on the table. She extended a pale hand. "I'm Laura McAlex."

As he had done for decades, he stood, although less easily now. He bent over her manicured fingertips while introducing himself. "Steven Steele. Proprietor of Antico Privato."

In a practiced way, she crossed a leg over the other so a high slit exposed one glorious thigh. Old men seldom openly gazed at a woman without developing a lecherous reputation, but it would have been odd for him to be the only man at the Florian averting his eyes.

"I hope we can come to terms on your cuneiform tablet. My client is very interested." She leaned in, stretching her purple sweater across prominent assets, and spoke with a cultivated lilt.

"I made it quite clear in my texts that I *might* know where it is, but that I don't possess it any longer, Miss McAlex."

She adjusted the shoe strap encircling a slim ankle. The heel rocketed like a dagger from a red sole. A cold gust picked up dried leaves and pigeon feathers. It slapped his face, and he jumped.

"I could place a few calls if you'd like." He smiled, and looked dotty. "I haven't heard the fragment sold again and often hear about paths of unusual pieces after they've left my possession."

"I am *so* disappointed." Her abundant eyelashes fluttered like wings. "My client is eager to complete his set."

He wiped his mouth, hiding a smile with his napkin. The waiter leaned over to refill her water glass, getting a better look at that purple sweater. The old man's chin bobbled before he spoke. "It's a rare collector with sets of these tablets. This piece was snapped up immediately after the catalog was mailed."

"My client is—unusual. Here's my card, although you know how to find me. Please let me know if the owner is interested. I can offer you a generous commission." She stood and smoothed her skirt, ignoring the impact she had on the wait staff as she bent for her handbag. "I like to reward those who help me."

"I should spend more time in Paris," he said with a smile he didn't bother to hide. "But your gelato! A winter gelato is a privilege accorded few, young lady!"

She adjusted her scarf and slipped on her gloves. Then looked at him dismissively, the way most young women did. "I'm sure you'll enjoy it more than I would. Thank you for any help in tracking the artifact." As she sashayed toward the basilica, her hips swung in a rhythm that made the waiter take a seat at the next table, his chin cupped in his palm.

Steven Steele nudged him, and tossed him a napkin. The waiter looked offended, then theatrically wiped his neck before handing the antiquarian the coupe containing three scoops of melting pumpkin gelato. It was Steele's favorite, available only when housewives tired of making *zucca* risotto. He let the first sweet, salty dollop sit on his tongue, then placed the call.

"Stan? She wants it badly. Let's move."

He left a two-Euro tip and slung the unneeded overcoat across his arm. Walking at an age-appropriate pace toward St. Mark's and home, he twirled his hat on his fingertips. As he passed the northwest corner of the basilica, he glanced at the Triumphal Quadriga on the upper register. Masterpieces from Classical Antiquity, that ten-century period with a mid-point at Christ's birth, the sculpture is commonly called the Four Horses of St. Marks. They were carted from Constantinople with other plunder in 1204. Then marched to France with Napoleon in

1797, and returned to Venice in 1815. The originals had been in the basilica museum since 1994.

"Or so they say," he said. Humming Verdi's "Rigoletto," he smiled at every pretty girl he passed as he crossed the formal square.

CHAPTER TWELVE

Wittenberg, Germany

Protestant Reformer Martin Luther was a barbarically ill-mannered, theologically enlightened freethinker with distinguished taste in places to stage a protest.

Wittenberg was a picturesque Utopia in north-central Germany on the lolling river Elbe. Evenly paved streets and canal-side flowerboxes, watered via a pulley-and-bucket system hundreds of years old, perfectly merged contemporary life with tradition.

Luther's academic festival at his Augustinian monastery a half-mile southwest of the square, down the *Collegienstraße*, occurred every three years. The festival united scholarly theologians from around the world, who discussed Luther the man and rebel, the Protestant Reformation, trends in Christendom, and families and careers.

In the midst of attendees walking from the monastery uphill to *Thesentur*—pilgrims had notched into oblivion the door on which Luther nailed his theses, so this was a reproduction—Dr. Stanley Steele cleared a gravely throat.

"We're aware Luther might not have actually *nailed* his theses, although within seventy-five years, the Catholic Church condemned the manifesto as heretical, documenting its existence. Because he used academic Latin, we can assume he wasn't trying to start a revolution." His friends and colleagues—and if you were one, you were the other—murmured. "I think we agree he protested the sale of indulgences, rather than tried to restructure Christianity."

Stereotypically in tweeds and glasses, this dull-looking flock was engrossed in the analysis of Luther's motives. The florist on the left carted blooms inside. Backpack-laden children scuffled onto the sidewalk from the doorway of the chocolatier on the right. The *plat du jour* of the bar ahead was schnitzel and fried rice because those smells drifted toward the plaza.

The dark young man crossing the street was just another Wittenberg University student in jeans and puffer coat. He was unnoticed, except by Steele and every young woman he passed. Grace had mentioned more than once his leading-man good looks. Nearing the Best Western Stadtpalais, he angled into the front door.

Steele moved slowly because of a limp from a childhood accident, so motioned everyone to go ahead without him. He entered the electronically controlled vestibule, pushed through the second doors, and crossed a poorly lit lobby in time to see the student take the stairwell. Steele passed into the elevator. They met at the theologian's room, and he locked the door behind them.

"Matthew, good to see you. But I doubt your arrival bodes well." Steele clapped the young man's shoulder in grandfatherly fondness. "I received a text from Grace an hour ago, but haven't had a moment to myself. What's wrong?"

Matthew Peter, a Mossad operative, smiled shyly. He moved his hands in a small circle above his head and pointed to his ears.

"Of course." Steele used the scanner from his inner breast pocket to sweep the room, holding it in the air as he circled slowly. The tiny box, the size of a dental-floss container, flashed green. "It's clean. Speak, son."

"Dr. Steele. Good to see you. I was visiting my father in Switzerland when Cyril contacted me. I'm on my way to Paris. Maggie's missing, and word is she was about to present something radical at a conference. The Madisons are in Paris. They don't expect me but are going to need my help."

"Spigot?"

"Apparently the deaths on the Temple Mount didn't end it, sir. Commander Cyril respectfully requests you reassemble as many of your friends as you can, and await his contact this evening. I'm leaving immediately, and will be in Paris before midnight."

Steele thought of his conversation with Steven, and knew this was the crisis they had feared all their adult lives.

...

On a Germanic-scaled sofa near a pianist inexplicably devoted to Barry Manilow, Steele's feet dangled above the carpet. He greeted colleagues returning from dinner, and stared at his suede Hush Puppy chukka boots, which he waterproofed before leaving the States. The joke of the day had been that Noah's Ark could have floated through Wittenberg, so he was thankful for dry socks.

He told Matthew he wanted to rush to Grace. Matthew advised good sense, and suggested that he should talk with the retired Israeli commander before doing anything. At eighty-seven, Steele was first to retire each night, so he was concerned about doing something unusual, such as sitting in the lobby into the evening if treachery was afoot. But Matthew asked him to wait there, so wait there he would.

Steele had met Cyril, from Mossad, as an archaeologist in the 1940s. The commander was recruiting spies for the nascent Sovereign State of Israel, and knew archaeologists employing locals would be excellent sources of information and reconnaissance around their sites. He blackmailed Steele and his friends in exchange for dig permits. No one relished their work with a group now called **MOSES**, but they acted scrupulously by creatively conducting covert tasks. The few remaining members were in their seventies and eighties, but no death had been as devastating as that of a young professor who had been killed with Spigot operatives last year. When MOSES helped rescue Grace and Maggie to keep water flowing through the Middle East, and oil everywhere else. David Spiedel had been a casualty of war.

"I am too old for this spy nonsense," he said to his root beer float.

A bearded man in cap and glasses sat next to him, shaking rain from his umbrella onto Steele's corduroys.

"Good evening." Steele spoke loudly to the man he had noticed moments ago, through windows overlooking the street. He was pleased that his surveillance skills weren't obsolete. "I did not expect you in person." This last bit was quiet so that no one else would hear.

Cyril laughed, and replied something about the weather getting worse. They looked like strangers chatting amiably. But looks can be deceiving.

"I seldom leave Israel." Cyril spoke under his breath, with a smile to which his face was unaccustomed. Its muscles could not grasping the concept of merry wrinkles. "Follow me in two minutes. Say something about fresh air to settle your stomach. You're not young anymore, and can't eat rich German food. I'll be at the pharmacy in the next block on the left, toward your fabled door."

Steele replied, as Cyril stood, that the weather did appear to be worsening. "When did we become old enough to use a pharmacy as cover?" Steele asked, facing the floor to brush beaded raindrops from his chukkas. Apparently Cyril thought the door was a fable, and didn't recognize Luther the Reformer any more than Jesus the Messiah.

The commander chuckled. "Quite a while ago. But at least I'm asking you to meet near the medicines for an upset stomach, and not in the incontinence aisle."

"God is good to me," the professor said. He checked his watch, a gift from his late wife, and reluctantly awaited his evening stroll.

CHAPTER THIRTEEN

Wittenberg and Jerusalem

George Wesley Merrit, PhD. was ending his fifty-eighth summer dig, preparing for another year of teaching seminarians.

When Steele's number appeared on his phone screen, he answered expecting conference news. His huge hands dwarfed the phone, and his physique, honed by service in the precursor to the Navy SEALS, overshadowed anything smaller than a pyramid in the Valley of the Kings in Egypt. "Steele! How is everyone in Wittenberg?"

"The young reinterpret Luther. The old are bridges to tradition. Nothing's changed. And the truth is somewhere in between."

"The truth is the Cross, but you know that."

"Correct, my friend. How was the dig?"

They discussed summer archaeological work, and plans for the semester starting in days. Merrit asked about Cliff Anderson, who had replaced Grace's dig director David Spiedel after the young professor plunged from the Temple Mount last year. Cliff was on sabbatical to "get his life together," which meant continuing to propose to Maggie.

"Interrupted," Steele replied obliquely.

Merrit paused. "She didn't turn him down again, did she?"

"Didn't have the chance."

Merrit remained silent, organizing a response. Decades as a linguistic analyst and paramilitary strategist, as well as four doctorates, powered a mind like an Ouija board. "Where are you? They?"

"Wittenberg and Paris. Respectively. Can we talk?" Steele referred to the line encryption while walking to the pharmacy.

"Yes. After last year, I'm afraid to deactivate the security package."

"According to Matthew and the commander, some things survived the fiasco above the Triple Gate. Maggie's at the center. I've been asked to regroup." Steele could picture Merrit twirling a shirt button. He was famous for this habit that arose when he struggled through a dilemma.

Yards from the pharmacy, Steele realized its bright interior lights made him an easy target. He stepped into shadows around the corner after ensuring the alleyway was clear, to a private spot where he could concentrate on Merrit's responses.

"When and where?" Merrit was cryptic.

"I don't know yet. But stay there until you hear from me. Who's with you?"

"Kreips and Thornton left yesterday for the States. Flately and I are dining on the beach in Tel Aviv tomorrow to celebrate another season. Each year is a gift from God."

Steele needed to finish the conversation before entering the pharmacy. "I'll get more facts in a moment, when I meet the commander."

Merrit's voice rose from the bass pitch normal from a man his size. "He's *there*? He never leaves . . . "

"Surprised me too."

"Why did he leave?" Merrit articulated Steele's thought, then sighed. "That bad. I'll wait, and we'll be ready. Any idea which direction?"

"No idea. Put the button in your pants pocket," Steele said, knowing his friend sighed when it popped free. "School starts soon, and seminarians will need funds." Merrit paid spouses of impoverished students to reattach his buttons, increasing his already-universal popularity.

"I found two more there. Did anyone ever get to the bottom of Cyril and Jeff's problem?"

"No clue about those two, either. She's been missing for eighteen hours." Steele stood on the top pharmacy step, flapping the automatic doors. "I'll call as soon as I know anything."

...

Cyril studied a box of antacids. Steele's full head of white hair bobbed in the shampoo aisle. He then moved to the toothbrushes. At last he walked past the commander for a bottle of aspirins. "Do you have any experience with that brand? This German food is so rich." He pointed at a box in Cyril's hand.

"Yes. This is the brand I buy. All over the world." Cyril nudged a small Star of David hand-drawn in pencil on the box top. "It's sold throughout Europe and the Middle East."

Steele saw the hole, toward the back of the shelf, from which the box had been taken. And tapped the box to acknowledge he knew for what, and where, to look. "Any contraindications?" He maintained the ruse, aware the clerk headed their way, but dropped his voice. "Speaking of Europe and the

Middle East, two friends have already left. Three remain in the region."

Cyril nodded, then moved toward the candy display. "We can work with that." Then he spoke loudly. "Digene is harmless as Alka-Seltzer. Easier to swallow because bubbles don't invade your nose."

Steele took the box to the register, holding his thumb over the altered spot, and the clerk followed him. The commander was gone when the exchange was finished.

Steele entered his room five minutes later, and swept it before opening the package. Words in classic Greek were written on a slip of paper folded into the dosage instructions.

Madaba, Rome, Venice.

Addresses, in scholarly Hebrew, were printed beneath these names. Online research revealed a pharmacy at each.

He called Merrit. "I don't have much. Three potential locations. Madaba, Rome, and Venice. I have addresses. Pharmacies. Look for boxes of Digene, marked with the Star of David, toward the back of the stock."

"What's Digene?"

"Antacid. And everyone needs to read Greek. Maybe biblical Hebrew."

"Classic or modern Greek?"

"Classical, although there's no guarantee the language won't shift."

"Shifts only worry me if Jeff's involved. Not many of us work with Ugaritic."

"Don't worry about Jeff. I'm pretty certain we can handle anything he generates. If you get something linguistically creative beyond your four, send it my way."

Although Steele couldn't imagine rocking chairs on a retirement-home porch, the thought crossed his mind. And he was glad they were not being asked to conduct covert ops by purchasing boxes of Depends.

DAY THREE
CHAPTER FOURTEEN

Latin Quarter, Paris

Grace

The three-star Hôtel Eugénie, which we checked into at 11:30 last night, was a sweet hideaway. The close call outside the Westin brought us here, where Mark knew the proprietress. I thought it best not to ask.

We had agreed we couldn't maintain this pace, and that the worst was probably ahead. I passed out sleeping pills, and we set cell-phone alarms for 7:00 a.m. We would contact Dr. Steele at breakfast if he didn't contact us before.

Aside from raucous students in the streets of the Latin Quarter, I slept well enough, curled beside Mark. An incoming text awakened me at 8:00 a.m., long after sunshine had slipped between the curtain and windowsill. Mark's note said he was eating downstairs, and had turned off my alarm since we didn't know anything when he left.

I focused on the screen.

SS: *Royal Jordanian #118; departs 12:45.*
ME: *Tickets?*
SS: *At the gate. Daylight.*

The first thing I told the family was that we were running daylight, which in spy language was the highest level of danger. I had done my homework, and the day wasn't starting well.

...

Charles de Gaulle Airport, Paris

We joined swaying humanity awaiting agent instructions in the avant-garde—*ugly*—circa 1970s terminal. Our stop yesterday at Galleries Lafayette yielded a mismatched style that looked authentically French.

Cliff, per Jeff's instructions, stood across the crowd, peering curiously. Because of the bodies, I didn't notice a subtle tap until it became a persistent assault. I pivoted, ready to unleash the Wrath of Mom.

Matthew Peter, the deliriously handsome Mossad agent who saved us after I rescued Maggie in Israel last year, stood next to me. Maggie and I privately referred to him as WadiMan, and his insincere smile indicated he was as worried as the rest of us.

I tilted back an inch so Mark, Becca, and Jeff could see him. He was the object of Cliff's stare, just as he complicated Cliff's conquest of Maggie's heart. Matthew's presence, despite its damage to Cliff, meant Mossad was a step ahead of us.

My shoulders sagged.

Matthew worked toward the perimeter of the gate crowd. Mark inclined his head to mean I was to follow the slim young man escaping down a linoleum-tiled hallway. We extricated from passengers boarding the Amman flight. Followed up the stairs leading to elite-flyer lounges. Matthew disappeared through an unmarked door in the back wall of the snack bar.

The door was unlocked. Matthew stood inside with three men.

"Mossad searched manifests, so knew you were headed to Amman. Commander Cyril has arranged seats to Jordan on an Israeli cargo plane operated by Tel Aviv Transport. We'll get everyone up to speed in the four-hour flight, and you can get some rest." He looked at me as *everything* drooped.

"Madaba," I said.

"I'll arrange a transfer, Dr. Madison. We'll be landing at the cargo terminal, and you need to be ready to hit the ground at a run."

Jeff stood hesitantly at the door. He and the commander shared an unstable history, revealed by a brutal fistfight in the Israeli desert. My son had covered a covert op in which Cyril's daughter was killed, and as Jeff said, Jews never forget. *Would their animosity prevent him from trying to find his sister?*

"Jeff?" I asked.

"They don't know." He turned to me although he spoke to Matthew. "I'm taking a flight to London. I need to visit a contact about the scroll. The whole cuneiform business. I'll catch you tomorrow night, wherever Matthew tells me you are."

Becca's heavy brows, hallmarks of Portuguese ancestry, collided over the bridge of her nose. "Who is it? And where? And no, you're not going alone."

I admired her protective style.

"A bird." He referred to an informant. "At Bermondsey. And yes, I'm going alone. We don't have much time, and I can move faster by myself. I wouldn't split up if it weren't necessary. Send back up if I don't return. There's your trail."

She didn't like his plan, and her fists-on-hipbones stance was implacable. She struggled to reorient from personal to professional, a battle played out on her face. His departure was as difficult for her as it was for me.

"You'll stay in touch?" She didn't move. "When tomorrow night will you join us?"

Jeff nodded. "I'll stay in touch. This is pretty straightforward. I need to ask some questions, in person. After they open, around 4:30." He meant morning because vendors arrived at this parking-lot flea market at 4:00 a.m. "I'll text Matthew to find you."

"I don't like it." She hugged him. I resisted the urge, recognizing my reassigned place. "But I understand. Don't blame me if someone tails you."

He shook his head. "Just make sure MI6 is discreet." Then he looked at us, kissed my cheek, and nodded before shutting the door behind him.

CHAPTER FIFTEEN

Paris — Amman, Jordan

Grace

Matthew gave us the option of briefing first and resting last, or vice versa. Mark's questions began before we were wheels up from French soil, making the choice. I tried to strap myself into a harness designed for someone tougher, and more delicately boned.

"No one knows what's going on? MOSES is reassembling. Cyril is involved. Maggie was about to turn the world on its ear at some summit. Jeff's mysteriously departed for London." Mark scowled. "Don't you know *anything*?" He leaned toward Matthew to repeat this monologue three times. "I thought Mossad ended our problems back there on the Temple Mount summer before last."

I sipped a bottle of water that Matthew handed me after buckling me in. I did not think we were going to solve anything during the flight, so inserted foam earplugs and focused on useless windows across the hold. A year older than on our last adventure, and at an age where every year counted more than the previous, I didn't relish another chase. I pulled the cargo blanket around my shoulders, hoping it would melt the chill I had carried since that early-morning call in Brussels.

...

I awakened to find Becca locking up with Mark, calmly trying to avoid one of the angry exchanges common between my husband and son. The men's relationship was improving, and I suspected she wanted to maintain peace.

Cliff whispered that we neared Jordan, and Mark had been impossible during my three-hour nap.

Then Becca held high the magazine from Mark's hotel laundry bag, and Matthew looked at her gratefully. "Mark, where did you say you got this?"

Mark glared, exasperated. *"From the hotel,"* he answered before returning to the Matthew Inquisition.

So much for making the daughter-in-law feel welcome.

"Where in the hotel?" she persisted.

"From inside the only hotel we've been in during the past twenty-four hours!" Mark shouted before correcting himself. "Sorry. I'm frustrated." His chin dropped to his chest.

"We all are." She cut him no slack, reminding him that bad behavior didn't accomplish anything. "Frustrated." His breathing slowed, and she tried again. "I have a reason for asking. Did you get it from your room?"

He looked disoriented. "Well, no. I picked it up from the table near the elevators. Near the oriental-looking vase of red flowers. Where I stuffed the laptop."

She peered at the index, then cover. "The article about Laura's antique shop isn't here, and it *was* in the magazine in our room." She rubbed the spine. "It wasn't torn out of this copy, either. Why was our room copy different from this one? Someone directed us to Laura McAlex."

"And why did she know enough about the cuneiform tablet to finger it?" I asked as Becca leaned sideways, over her tote.

"Dr. Steele's cuneiform tablet?" Although Matthew was happy to remain invisible, and that Mark's attention was elsewhere, he still had a job to do. "And a scroll?"

"It's technically a copper *fragment*," I said. "Not a whole scroll."

"It appears to be inscribed in Aramaic and depicts the Madaba mosaic. Like Dr. M. says, it's a broken bit," Becca said.

"How do you break copper?" Matthew's question stopped us. "Is the tear intentional? Is it a tear or a cut? Can you tell?"

I was embarrassed we hadn't paid attention to the abrupt edge. Mark's experience with metal work at the ranch should have triggered questions, but the concierge and bar guests' interruption in the men's room shortened our study of the scroll. In our eagerness to find Maggie, we stopped the minute we recognized Madaba.

I got my loupe as Becca pulled the flattened artifact from her e-reader case, our choice as safest travel storage. Reexamining the scroll, and oxidation surrounding and in etched marks, it clearly was cut long ago. The rough edge was a crude gash.

We banked downward, landing gear emitting a harsh grind as it dropped from its bay.

"So Madaba directly from the Amman airport." Mark made his statement of intent.

"Yes." Matthew confirmed our destination over the phone, and briefed the person on the other end about the cuneiform and scroll. My money was on Cyril.

"And does anyone know where Dr. Steele is getting these cuneiforms?" Matthew asked.

"He collects them," I answered. "He has a shelf full in his office."

...

Amman

The van was standard government issue—black, with tinted windows. Except for a glowing strip of yellow running lights, it appeared abandoned. As we left the plane, the vehicle side door slid open while the driver stayed behind the wheel. Dr. Steele's head was illuminated with a halo from the dome light.

"*DUMU.MES DUG.GA-YA.*" I spoke Ugaritic, the Hittite language.

"My dear son," he translated. I couldn't think of the word for *daughter* quickly enough to insert it. "To Madaba. Hurry," he said as he patted my shoulder. "Your Ugaritic has improved, Grace. Sorry about the circumstances. Did you rest?"

I must look terrifying, I thought as I climbed in, then crouched to the back row. I stopped. My tattered gardening hat, whose brim and crown were connected by duct tape, waited at the end of the bench seat. Underneath, my safari-vest pockets were carefully positioned so their contents didn't spill. I sorted and rearranged talismans of archaeological life, pondering the location of my Glock.

Dr. Steele was last to board as I donned my gear, and he smiled at me. "I've kept them for you."

I straightened the vest over my shirt and tied the rawhide strips under my chin so that the pink-beribboned hat rode across my shoulders. Even facing disaster, I needed to be tidy.

Mark pulled my sunglasses from the top pocket, nervously cleaning them with my bandana as he looked at my familiar accessories. "I would almost say all was right with the world now."

Taking the hand returning my glasses, I kept my voice steady. "It will be when we find our daughter."

A lavender dusk peculiar to the Middle East settled into the eastern hills.

DAY FOUR
CHAPTER SIXTEEN

Borgo neighborhood, Rome

The cab skirted the seventeen-hundred-year-old Aurelian wall, followed by a young cleric gripping the steering wheel of a battered brown Lancia coupe.

Seven minutes later, the cabdriver careened around the first-century Coliseum thrice, in the Roman tradition of extending the ride for a bigger fare. Then the vehicle straightened into the web of streets and shadows marking central Rome—the *Centro Storico*.

"Christian Dior, Piazza del Popolo. Via Condotti," the young man said into his cell phone.

Laura McAlex's first stop was the city's most expensive shopping district, between the Piazza di Spagna—Spanish Steps—and the Corso. Before the Lancia had left for the airport shortly after dawn, Monsignor Pietro Agnelli instructed his assistant to report her positions. Agnelli continued to work on the fragile parchment in his apartment near the Vatican, his gloved hands touching only edges. In ten minutes, he heard a crackling transmission.

"Gucci," the young priest said.

"Moving up," Agnelli muttered. "Just as I did." The photo underneath his desk blotter was of a skinny boy, with dirty ankles exposed by hand-me-downs three inches too short. *"Pantiloni Corti." Short Pants*—the nickname with which his classmates had taunted him. Destitution was cruel.

Agnelli returned his focus to the mosaic depictions. Twenty silent minutes passed.

"Bulgari," the cleric reported.

Agnelli raised his brows. After ten minutes, he wondered how much she could spend. When incense preceded the vesper call, he stared at his phone as if mental telepathy would trigger an update.

"McAlex Palazzo," his assistant said before the line fell silent.

This heart-stopping real estate capped the Steps. It wedged between the Hassler—one of Rome's most expensive hotels—and Medici Gardens—one of the city's most beautiful public spaces. She could have walked from Bulgari, but he suspected purchases prevented a pedestrian climb of the largest outdoor staircase in Europe. Honestly, gypsies would have targeted her carrying bags with expensive labels, so it was just as well she rode. Then there was the matter of luggage, since his man reported four large pieces.

After slipping the parchment into its protective sleeve, Agnelli reviewed papers about the palazzo, one of several McAlex properties. Winter warmth made Rome a frequent stop for the Paris-based heiress. God bless the spoiled brat.

She worked efficiently, despite the disadvantages of youth and gender. They would meet this evening so she could summarize her time with the Madisons. He had directed them to her via the Westin magazine. Briefed her on what to do. Was disappointed she could not secure the cuneiform. Hated that he wasted church funds on an exact duplicate, costly because only one hamlet in southern Italy created perfect counterfeits behind a veil of expensively insured silence. It would have been so easy to switch the relic for the copy.

But no matter. Almighty God would take care of His children.

And when He failed, Mother Church and Agnelli were prepared to take over.

CHAPTER SEVENTEEN

Above the Mediterranean

Sniff. "A sarcophagus. *Nas*-tee." *Sniff.* "Or it might be me."

Before Maggie opened her eyes, she smelled decay from organic pigment as many as six millennia old, mixed with odors emanating from her person. She flashed back to the vast Egyptian collection, which she and her mother passed on lost adventures while mastering the Gallic shrug of indifference, at the Louvre.

What? Us lost? Mais non!

Her voice was slurred, and the base of her skull ached.

"Drugs," she said, trying to clear her head by forcing her mind and mouth to interact.

But aches were better than being dead. If whomever had her—boss of the Bethlehem Boys with a failed conversion at The American Church—wanted her dead, she would be. Being alive indicated she possessed something of value.

No surprise there.

She had been in Paris to talk sense into Cliff, who was in the French capital soliciting funds for the Kinneret dig. She wanted, once again, to make it clear that as wonderful as he was, she was not the right woman for him. Then she planned to go to the Water Summit in Marseille. She was committed to women's roles in the provision, management, and conservation of water, pivotal responsibilities which had been recognized since the 1992 Rio Summit.

"If I start thinking about what I'm missing, I'm going to distract myself from getting out of this coffin." She realized talking to herself was a sign of insanity, then added, "I wonder how long I was unconscious?"

Roaring aircraft engines and the familiar quiver of flight meant she had moved farther from places anyone would think to look for her. Her shoulders pressed the sides of the box. By rolling left, then right, she brought her hands atop her body with only scraped knuckles to show for the effort. Her wrists were unrestricted, so she pushed with flat palms on the lid.

Nothing happened, except she discovered she could move, so was not badly hurt.

She pushed harder, creating scattered slits of light where the halves met. Sarcophagus lids and bases were aligned via tongue-and-groove systems, and pegs were visible when she exerted pressure on the top. This was not an upper-class sarcophagus because the lid was light enough to budge, unlike the thick, so heavy coffins of wealthy or noble Egyptians.

"*Viva la bourgeoisie!*"

She steadied her breathing to maintain enough mental focus to prevent claustrophobia. Groping the perimeter, she found two places opposite each other that would not yield to pressure, so pushed hard to connect the points. Something like a mover's strap secured the top and bottom.

When Maggie was young, Grace had given her a pocket-knife exactly like her own. A red-and-white, floral-cased Swiss army knife with two blades, nail scissors, and a file. Mark kept Grace's dangerously sharp, and taught Maggie to do the same. She slid this knife from an interior pocket, pulling evenly on the metal loop hooking the knife to a quarter-sized penlight.

"Observant Muslims. Anyone else would have found this, but someone was afraid of defiling himself." She pivoted the blade. "I'm glad I spotted those two creeps at church. I wouldn't have been unprepared."

Clutching the knife, she sawed in a restricted motion until the strap snapped.

"Thank God for religious diversity."

In the freezing, pressurized belly of a thundering transport plane, the light was so weak she could barely discern angular shapes of crates stacked toward the cockpit and distributed toward the tail. Mounds of fabric, wood shards, and bubble wrap littered the floor. She climbed out of the box, dodged sticky tendrils of duct tape, and plucked particularly aggressive pieces from her hiking boots and cargo pants. She assessed her health, which seemed good enough. Her hygiene and clothing were another matter.

Sniff.

Her skull throbbed with every step. She remembered changing from a silk dress at church before heading for an afternoon of research in the Byzantine Library at the College of France. On the Avenue Sully-Prudhomme, she plunged farther into the Seventh Arrondissement toward the rue de l'Universite, staying dry by tucking under awnings and crisscrossing streets. It had been a Victor Hugo day, medieval and gloomy.

She bought a Nutella-filled crepe from the stand near the Eglise de St.-Germaine-des-Pres, and continued east, to the rue de Cardinal-Lemoine in the Latin Quartier's Fifth Arrondissement. Someone grabbed her when she passed an alley near the Place des Invalides. Her memory stopped there. Then picked up again, off and on, in a warehouse.

Finding nothing of note in her capture, she turned to investigate the hold. Mummies—well-wrapped legs to her right emerged at burlesque angles—were actively engaged in the afterlife. Labels indicated antiquities were being repatriated to Egypt, Jordan, and Iran.

Repatriation was big business, particularly for unstable governments from which antiquities were plundered during colonial times. Museums "owning" items of questionable provenance were pressured to return—*repatriate*—them while curators argued that the world's shared cultural heritage could not be protected by brigands in Kabul and Islamabad. They were, unfortunately, correct. But museums depended on tax-deductible donations that evaporated when collections were perceived as stolen.

She picked through the hull. Hers wasn't the only uncrated sarcophagus, and she was relieved to find only persons dead for thousands of years.

Maggie assumed her note about the Bethlehem Boys at the American Church was not found, and she was on her own to affect a rescue. With barely enough oxygen to think, and approaching hypothermia, there would be no heroics. Parachuting was out of the question.

"Egypt will be Cairo. Iran will be Tehran. Jordan will be Amman."

These cities had large airports and curated museums able to receive the plane and cargo. She had work contacts in each. Her strongest allies were in Cairo until the Muslim Brotherhood had forced them out, but it was important to escape the plane as soon as possible. If she interpreted her discoveries correctly, it would not be long until war erupted over an ancient water source in the petroleum-producing world, causing the rest of the world to run out of oil.

"Since we started in Paris, we'll move west to east. That means Amman, then Cairo, then Tehran. So I repack that sarcophagus to feel as if I'm still there, then find a container going to Amman. Replace its contents with myself."

She sifted, taking one or two pieces from open boxes, and filled her sarcophagus with incised tablets and random *ostracon* to approximate her mass. Using moving straps dangling along the hull perimeter, she rebound the box.

The floor tilted dramatically, and the hot-dog pilot cut the engines and adjusted flaps.

"On a commercial liner, I'd have thirty minutes. I'll assume fifteen on a transport flown by the Red Baron."

She searched for a hiding place, finding a crate of dusty textiles addressed to the Museum of Popular Traditions and Jordan Folklore Museum. The institutions shared the foundation of a Roman amphitheater along busy Quraysh Road in Amman. They were small, dark, and sparsely populated. And unguarded—the perfect place to escape unseen. She could disappear into the few shouting tourists exploring the famous acoustics of the site.

Even better, this crate was centered amidst others from which straps were removed. Nothing on its exterior would attract attention or indicate its contents were compromised, and her captors would likely pilfer those easier to reach.

Maggie dug a hole in the textiles and climbed in. She pulled them around her while praying dust did not trigger her asthma. Leveraging from the waist while tugging the shipping-crate top, Maggie shimmied down. She positioned the slab, but needed to move the last few inches from underneath. Yanking it roughly across the box, she finally dropped it into place with a *thud* drowned by keeling engines.

Burrowing into sophisticated depictions of the ancient world—people, ibex, and one menorah—she was sad the remnants were not well preserved so that generations could enjoy their heritage. Then the camel blankets gagged her.

"These smell a lot worse than I do."

She pressed her nose to a crack between slats as the descent increased. Her heart hammered, and breathing was difficult. In minutes, wheels screeched on the tarmac in a jarring landing at, she prayed, Queen Alia International Airport in Amman.

...

Amman

Forklifts have a distinct sound, a high-pitched whining of shifting gears and moving mechanisms. Maggie's box was loaded into a truck bed, untouched during three stops, and deposited. Men discussed many things during this journey, the foremost being whether to steal more. She hoped her crate was not a target because her pocketknife was not a combat weapon, and *krav maga* from a knitted position would prove fatal—at least for her.

The Roman amphitheater was twenty miles from Madaba, the Queen Alia Airport ten to the north. The documents she mailed two weeks ago to the ranch were insurance in case her discovery endangered her—as it had. They would lead the family to Madaba.

Grace was known throughout Jordan and would dine at Haret Jdoudna near St. George's chapel. It was tradition.

At the thought of her mother, Maggie's heart ached. Grace would be desperate by now. Maggie had to get to Haret, a cluster of late Ottoman houses in village style. See if her mother had been there. Leave a message that she was alive. Check the chapel floor for the clue.

"Most people would just have the embassy find their family. But most people wouldn't be working here in the first place, and wouldn't be hot on Solomon's trail. Besides, Haret isn't far away, and I can come back to the officials after I've looked for signs of Mama and checked that chapel floor." She whispered, fairly certain she was still sane, as she peeped into the storeroom from the safety of her crate.

The coast was clear. She slipped into the Folklore Museum, and from the museum onto Quraysh Road. From the position of the sun, and smells from neighborhood *shwarma* restaurants, it was early afternoon. She chose a cab over the oft-stopping bus. It was unusual to find an available cab, and she was thankful for her good fortune or God's grace.

CHAPTER EIGHTEEN

Madaba, Jordan

Grace

"So it was there after all." Dr. Steele caressed the scroll as gently as he would have the Christ child.

Despite a searing afternoon sun, dark windows dimmed the van interior and blurred the pale buildings on the outskirts of Madaba. The beam from his battered flashlight enabled him to inspect the antique. Hands whose blue veins formed a topographical map of life probed carefully after more than a half-century of archaeological discovery.

"Dr. Steele, what exactly is important about this piece of clay?" Becca's question verged on respectful, and Jeff's absence weighed as heavily on her as it did me. "And if the cuneiform tablet was so important, why did you give it to us?"

"First things first, my dear. This copper scroll is the important element. Not the tablet." He shifted. "How much do you know about the Crusades?"

"Not much." She and Jeff had met in economics classes, a course of study leaving little time for liberal arts. "History is an abyss in my otherwise fine education."

He shifted to look back at her. "This scroll fragment gets interesting in the Fourth Crusade. But Jeff . . . " He caught himself, and glanced at Becca and me. "Its origins are Christian, and it's inscribed in Aramaic." Shifting into lecturer mode, he continued. "The Emperor Constantine led the Holy Roman Empire for the first half of the third century. The empire was based in Constantinople. Istanbul.

"As a Christian, he legalized Christianity before making it *the* religion of the largest dominion in the world—Byzantium. His impact on our faith was incalculable for many reasons, not the least of which is that it became expedient to be a Christian. His mother, the Empress Helena, identified most of the early holy sites Christian pilgrims visit today. Another formidable woman and devoted scholar." He winked at me before returning his attention to the scroll.

Mark coughed. "Five minutes to St. George's, Dr. Steele."

"Yes. Thank you. By the crusade, roughly AD 1200, Constantine amassed treasures in Constantinople. Not only temporal treasures lie gold and precious jewels. Christian treasures. Parts of Christ's crown of thorns. Constantine's hoard of religious relics was the greatest ever."

"Aside from sheer power, how did he do that?" History was not Mark's strong suit, either.

"Constantinople was *the* trade crossroads for east and west. Straddling Europe and Asia, separated only by the easily navigable Bosphorus. Positioned to become wealthy. Empowered by the geographic and military dominance of the Holy Roman Empire. This fragment is one of Christendom's early treasures from Constantine's stash."

"If I may interrupt, what are we looking for at the chapel?" My staccato tones were intentional. Our priority was Maggie. And I knew all this.

"We study the mosaic," Dr. Steele replied kindly, holding the scroll high. "Compare it to this fragment."

"I've never heard of the scroll. Is it a gap in my education or is the scroll obscure?" Cliff startled me. He had been silent since Paris.

"Most people aware of the scroll legend believe it's myth. But someone believes it's fact, or Maggie wouldn't have disappeared. And the Madisons wouldn't have been sent to Ms. McAlex by the bogus magazine." Dr. Steele patted its glossy cover on the console.

We were discussing the magazine when the van pulled to the chapel courtyard. A contorted olive tree and the stone plaque to the right of the door were familiar friends in the soft light of dawn.

"So what is the point of the scroll?" I turned my attention from one of my favorite places, and asked for clarification.

Dr. Steele was gathering his belongings. "Well, first note it is incomplete. According to legend, the other half is in the Vatican vaults."

"The Red Shoes." Mark referred to Maggie's cryptic hymnal note. "And the Lion? Grace's guess was Venice."

"Right again, Grace," Dr. Steele replied. "A team positioned there last night. One in Rome, too. Both cities are important. But I'm unconvinced the Vatican possesses the other half any longer. For now, we focus on the chapel. They're opening it for us, but this is an active commercial district, and we'll be seen. Cliff, I'd like you to guard the entrance.

"And one last thing," Dr. Steele said as he touched Mark's shoulder, then opened the door. "We're comparing this scroll fragment, on which nearly three-quarters of the mosaic is depicted, to the one-third left embedded in the floor. The original mosaic was defaced in AD 600 by Muslims at any spot where Christ was depicted as the Son of God, so be aware of that inconsistency."

Three quarters! I hadn't studied the scroll in the men's room in Paris because we were interrupted by visitors, so hadn't noticed an almost complete Madaba mosaic. Dr. Steele had my attention, as would the more than two million tiles creating artwork that depicted two hundred early Christian sites—regarded as the Michelin map of its time. "The scroll could provide historic proof of the biblical record," I said, gasping. "It documents biblical history?"

He hesitated. "I think more, Grace."

"What's on the other piece of the scroll?" Becca asked. "Why don't you think it's at the Vatican?"

"The index, or a sort of key to this half. Any Catholic curate aware of the legend knows what's supposed to be on the map, but he won't know where the places are. This half makes sense of the other. Many spots are of historic importance, but at least one could change the future. Honestly, I suspect Maggie, with her hydrology, can tell you more about the critical location than I can."

Dr. Steele stepped from the van, invigorated by the treasure in his hands. He didn't tell us why he suspected the second piece left the Vatican, but I wondered if the Holy See could be behind the wheel of the speeding Peugeot in Paris.

"And you gave it to us why?" Becca called after him.

He paused, then turned around to her. "Because it was just too dangerous for an old man to keep." He walked through the gates, toward the front door.

Becca held her hand out to me as I took the big step from the running board. I smiled my thanks, walking toward the church complex with more questions than answers.

...

The chapel that withstood assault for almost a hundred twenty years held firm, protecting the ancient relic inside. The cross-embellished double door was bolted securely, despite everything five overt Westerners and one local-looking guy could do to it. Becca attempted to pick the lock while Mark proposed a Zacchaeus-worthy climb of the olive tree to reach the upper-story windows. Cliff and Matthew applied another dose of brute force while Dr. Steele prayed. I tested the side door, cursing unhappily out of range.

Dr. Steele was gone when I returned to the courtyard.

"We tried to stop him, but he's looking for the priest." Mark explained while circling a pine tree, no doubt looking at its branches to see if he could scale it.

"You're telling me you couldn't stop an eighty-seven-year-old man?" *Ridiculous.* "What happened?" Turning to Becca, I hoped she would throw in her lot with me, but she watched to see if Mark would respond. When he didn't, she moved to my side.

"He insisted on going alone, Dr. M. Apparently, the father—Silvius, I think—lives nearby. As a Christian cleric, he is doing us a favor by opening the chapel, which was supposed to be unlocked. Dr. Steele was concerned about him."

He still should not have wandered off alone. "When did he think he'd return?" I asked.

"All he said was 'shortly.'" Matthew answered as he and Cliff joined us. "There's a teahouse in the next block. It's a small tourist place, so won't be crowded with locals preferring coffee. You'll be comfortable. And less obvious."

I waved toward the gate. "Lead the way."

Mark was triangulating between olive tree, pine tree, and a tower barely deep enough to accommodate six mismatched bells forming a carillon. I dragged him across King Talal Street, toward the four-story balconied buildings. "Give it up, Ranchman. You'll have the chance to be a hero later."

We passed the shoebox-sized Treasure Center, and an ice cream parlor that would be packed until well after *isha*, the last call to prayer. A beady-eyed Arab in a drooping *kaffiyeh*, the braided rope loosely knotted around his head as if secured in a hurry, was rearranging rotating carrels on the sidewalk. When the second sideswiped me, Mark shoved it fifteen feet with one push. He and the Arab glared until it crashed against the back wall of the shop, and we slipped into the teahouse next door.

Matthew spoke with a man behind the tin counter, and a young woman placed a samovar on a window table where our group waited. A view of the traffic island dominated the prospect, where a billboard depicted Queen Rania in Chanel sunglasses, King Abdullah in white robes, and crown prince Hussein—all three scaled larger than life.

The window table was a poor choice, but the only seating. Matthew watched the door. I watched him, bracing for news that wasn't good.

"They haven't seen the priest in a couple of days. Shops around here appear to be under surveillance," he said. When Mark raised his eyebrows and ticked his head toward the proprietor, Matthew nodded once. "A *sayan*."

"A Jew who helps Mossad as an act of patriotism," I explained to no one. "Mossad wouldn't function well without them, and they number in the thousands across the globe."

"Patriotism or revenge motivates sayan. And thousands is low, Dr. Madison. But the rest of your information is correct."

Matthew tilted the samovar, pouring a green stream into six jiggers. Of course it was mint. "He suggests we enjoy our tea, then circle the block. I'll do a double loop, but if we can get to his back door unseen, we can wait in the upper room to watch the church courtyard until Dr. Steele shows."

"We're not safe here?" Becca asked, then held up her index finger to make a point. "Correction. We're not safe anywhere."

"Bad things happen in upper rooms in these parts." Cliff was right.

I chuckled before noticing he was not smiling.

"Let's split into two groups. Mark and Dr. M in one. Becca with Matthew and me." Cliff glanced both ways down the street, which split into a Y at the island, as he spoke. "Go opposite directions. Our group will do the double loop. Matthew can act as decoy if necessary. You two go the other direction and meet us upstairs, where we'll wait for him. If something happens, get to the van. If that doesn't work, return here."

The proprietor wiped the countertop, periodically disappearing with plates of food through a door behind the counter. A Justin Bieber song cranked up next door, which made me feel worse.

"I'm good with that," I said. "As long as I can escape the noise."

Everyone agreed. Cliff dropped five dinars on the table.

"Ask him to watch the man with the carrels on the sidewalk," Mark said to Matthew. "My concern has nothing to do with his poor taste in singers."

Matthew spoke to the proprietor, whose face immediately looked worried. He shook his head vigorously, slapped his cheek twice, and gestured toward the souvenir shop.

"He has no idea who that guy is," Matthew advised Mark. "The owner hasn't been seen for three days."

We hurried to the sidewalk. Shading my eyes with my hand to minimize reflection off the chalky chapel stone, I remembered morning broke with a blast here. Sunglasses from my frayed safari-vest pocket soon perched on my nose. My floppy gardening hat, recently re-taped, soon shielded sun-damaged skin.

"Should some of us head around the New Orthodox School?" I referred to the spit-and-polish academic institution abutting the chapel. "Or do we stay on the same block?"

"Same block," Matthew replied. He watched working-class men, as did the rest of us, and I knew we categorized each one. Becca walked next to him, Cliff followed, and Mark and I turned in the opposite direction, up a slight hill. We reached an alleyway that emptied into a street behind the teashop. We cut right, then right again, then up the delivery-door stairs.

In a room that once was part of a home, Mark filled a plate—lamb and pilaf, hummus and flatbread, cucumbers and onions, dates and almonds. I stood, a sentinel at the window, as I had in Paris. Scents from coffee and baking filled thin desert air. My mouth was sour from the tea, and I needed to eat. But I wasn't hungry, and my stomach churned. Mark handed the first plate to me, indicating the table.

Five minutes later, footfalls preceded Becca and Cliff.

"Matthew took a longer walk," Becca said as she filled her plate. "I didn't see anyone suspicious, but it's been a while since I was a jumper."

Jumpers are active field agents. I had studied terminology after discovering my daughter-in-law's association with British Intelligence, and not knowing if Cliff or Matthew, himself Mossad, would be my son-in-law. I tried to be prepared, like a good Boy Scout, but wasn't prepared for Dr. Steele and Matthew to disappear.

CHAPTER NINETEEN

Madaba

Grace

Two hours after Mark sent coded messages to "the Office" (CIA headquarters in Langley, Virginia) and Becca apprised MI6, Matthew and Dr. Steele were still missing. And so were my daughter and son.

The CIA was "in touch with Mossad unofficially." Mossad was not forthcoming. MI6 told Becca they had not heard from Jeff. Mark threatened to restrain me, an act necessary in moments.

"I'm serious about the upper room." Cliff fixated, and did not touch his food. "Political alliances shift hourly here. What if they don't show? Something could've happened. And Maggie's still missing—" he patted my hand to keep me from smacking him with it "—which you know too well, Dr. M."

"Are you suggesting Matthew or Dr. Steele is a mole?" I snatched my hand from his.

"I am not suggesting Dr. Steele is a mole. I don't trust Matthew." He rocked to balance on the back legs of his chair, crossing arms over chest to look too much like Mark to be believed. "I'd like to be out of here before the work day ends. We're trapped if things go wrong."

"No." I peeped out again, struggling to maintain evaporating composure. "Period. About Matthew. I agree about not staying here longer than necessary."

He had a point, but I was not going to admit it yet. Dr. Steele could lay dead, his murderer taking the fragment with him (or her). It was unlikely, but possible, that Matthew was a problem. We needed a plan uncomplicated by pilgrim crowds disembarking a tourist bus across the street, in front of the chapel. They would be disappointed the door was locked. Go to lunch. Guides would call tour companies, who in turn would call the Orthodox Patriarchate. We had an hour, perhaps two, before our opportunity to study the mosaic privately ended.

But we had much bigger issues, which I decided to hammer home. "Every hour that goes by lessens the chance that Maggie will survive this. That's my primary concern. Not Dr. Steele or Matthew, or this scroll business. And we can only hope Jeff is safe."

Becca put her arm around my shoulders to speak. "We have the van and driver. At the end of the street. We need a reasonable deadline of maybe fifteen minutes. If it passes without resolution, we take the van. I agree with your priorities, Dr. M."

I thought her suggestion was fair. The other option was to break into the church in broad daylight on a crowded street, in a place where we looked nothing like the natives. Probably get arrested, then be unable to help either child.

"Where to?" Becca gazed out the window.

"I have no clue. But I can't stay in this room much longer," I said.

Cliff and Mark exchanged complicit glances before Mark spoke. "I agree about the kids."

He had a strong survival instinct.

"And I think that's generally a good plan, but we need a destination, Gracie. Dr. Steele mentioned Madaba, Venice, and Rome. We're in Madaba, so do you think Venice or Rome is a better probability?"

I turned, prepared to negotiate.

Becca's fingers grazed my arm. "Dr. M."

Her stare was fixed on something, so I looked over her shoulder. An old beggar, little more than a moving mass of dirty rags, limped down the sidewalk while leaning on the arm of a man dressed in the uniform of the local poor—rumpled, ill-fitting pants under a nondescript *djellabah*, or tunic. The beggar's crippled gait was familiar, as was the man's elegant stride.

At least we hadn't lost everyone—yet.

...

We bolted down the stairs, colliding with Matthew and Dr. Steele. Before they could explain, the proprietor wedged us into three rolling carts from the bakery, propelled them into a commercial van, and spirited us two blocks to the delivery door at the back of the chapel. His gesture indicated we should wait, and Matthew and Dr. Steele left with him.

I patted down my vest for the fourth time, seeking my missing Glock. We huddled at a sunken door lower than the alley pavement, hidden behind a half wall covered with a rambunctious pomegranate bush. Two minutes passed, then scraping drew our attention to a turning knob. Matthew stood inside the chapel, a finger to his lips. We scooted low, past him.

Dr. Steele, holding an ancient key, studied the mosaic. I patted his bony shoulder. He didn't look from the floor, but placed the key in his robes while stating the priest was believed dead.

I decided to wait to ask how he got the key, although was certain he didn't kill for it. And I wanted to know how he and Matthew found each other, and where they got disguises. An animated game of Twenty Questions lay ahead.

"I'll explain it later, Grace," Dr. Steele said. My professor knew me well.

When I realized I stared at him instead of the mosaic, I moved to the other side of the artifact for an unimpeded view.

...

We were front and center in the Greek Orthodox Chapel of St. George. Crystal chandeliers hung above two central aisles separating rows of six hewn pews. The mosaic anchored the space between the nave where people worshiped, and the spot where the *templon*—dividing wall—should stand. St. George's was the only Greek Orthodox Church I knew of that lacked this design standard, but its absence revealed the architectural theology in its fullness, and the mosaic as a whole.

Matthew climbed to the left mezzanine, watching through clerestory windows well above the pedestrian pathway paralleling the chapel. Cliff stood at the front door, mindful as guard. We studied scroll and mosaic, paying more attention to the former than the latter in our eagerness to understand their differences.

Finally Matthew spoke. "Drs. Steele and Madison. Something doesn't make sense from here."

We moved to the staircase before crowding the mezzanine, nearly spilling over an ethereal iron balustrade. I wondered if any governmental entity in Madaba did safety inspections.

"See where the figure of Christ approaches Peter to make him a 'fisher of men'? The Sea of Galilee, where the Bible says Peter's recruitment occurred? If you block out the perimeter of the mosaic there, does it look like a flower?" Matthew pointed.

Before we could answer, Mark responded. "Even I see that." Mark was remarkable, but graphic detail was not his strength.

"Yes." Dr. Steele chortled. "It looks like a flower." Color flooded his cheeks, and I thought he might start dancing in a space dangerously small to boogie. "It looks specifically like a crude Luther Rose."

"But Luther was hundreds of years *after* the mosaic was created. This doesn't make sense." Mark sounded irritable, but at least we knew he was listening.

"A fire charred the mosaic." I thought aloud. "We believe it was looted at least twice. More significantly, repaired. All sorts of things could happen in fifteen hundred years."

"So what does it mean?" Becca asked. *Had she acquired a linear dislike of rabbit trails from my missing son?* "Assuming we're not hallucinating or believing something we want to believe, why would a Luther Rose appear on the Madaba mosaic?"

"And what's the Luther Rose?" Mark asked. "It looks like a daisy to me."

Before anyone could respond, Cliff shouted. "Company!"

We reached the floor as something exploded against the wooden front doors, almost flattening Cliff. I hoped the four-foot-tall inserts of brass crosses and fittings held long enough for our escape.

Mark and Matthew shoved two flimsy pews, one atop the other, under the handles. Braced the blockade with an enormous candelabrum. Wedged its base against a stone pillar. Becca and I huddled at the back door, which led through an alley to Haret Jdoudna. Her gun was drawn. Cliff was a sentinel between the fracas and us.

"Out!" Mark yelled as he waved toward Haret. He and Cliff picked up Dr. Steele by the armpits and dashed the length of the chapel ahead of Matthew. The theologian's legs moved in a running motion even though his feet were nine inches above the ground. He held the fragment in front of his face as if reading the Torah.

...

We careened into the covered market of Haret. The village-like complex was Mecca for pilgrim busses because food and facilities were clean, and souvenirs affordable. Pita and homemade hummus compensated for roasted rubber chickens purchased by comedians worldwide. Jordanian silver jewelry and costumes tempted patrons waiting for much-appreciated Western restrooms—with toilet paper!

Dr. Steele was dropped between a stack of camel blankets and a wall.

Matthew pulled a Berber robe over his head. Grabbed a tray from a confused waiter. Trotted into the restaurant looking authentic, thanks to Lebanese genes.

Becca and I pushed past an offended queue of women. Toward the only stall in the door-less ladies' room. Mark, across the passageway, tossed a prayer rug on top of Dr. Steele. Ducked into the kitchen with Cliff.

Shouts and crashes made me peep over the stall wall. Armed men pushed through religious tourists in a land where holy war can erupt before flights depart for home. As their sound became distant, I counted to fifty. Becca flushed. I opened the swinging door.

Maggie faced us.

I yelped, and we flew at each other.

"I saw your hat race by right before Dr. Steele landed on me," she said as we hugged. "The only duct-taped gardening hat with pink ribbons in this part of the world." I patted her, checking to ensure she was all right. "I knew you'd be here if you or Dad got my messages."

"You're okay? We need to talk about this kidnapping nonsense, Maggie." I tried to control my breathing so I would stop sobbing. She hiccupped. A crash from the kitchen meant we were still in danger. I tried to cram the three of us into the stall, which didn't work.

"Let's get out of here. You have a lot of explaining to do, young lady." I tightened my hold on her, and tried to focus on escape to prevent hysteria. The smell of warm pita reminded me we hadn't eaten for hours. Then I realized I smelled *her*. "Good grief. I have Wet Wipes in the van. Plus a perfume pen of Chanel No. 5 in my vest from Israel."

"That bad?"

"Because both your beaux are here to rescue you, yes." I was *not* thinking clearly. "You sure you're okay?"

"I'm okay. Both of them?"

I nodded as I peeked around the doorframe. Assured the danger had passed and there were multiple places to hide, I hugged her and we exited the ladies' room in a movement resembling a three-legged race. Becca, gun drawn, tailed us. Maggie looked over her shoulder, watching Matthew assist Dr. Steele from his nook, the scroll pressed flat between his palms. Finally, before we burst through the hanging kitchen doors to find roadies, Dr. Steele asked if introductions were necessary.

"Rescuing you is becoming habit-forming, Ms. Madison," Matthew called. "Maggie."

"We have to stop meeting like this, Matthew," she replied loudly. "People will talk."

"I suspect they already are." He smiled, nodded as he spoke, and hurried Dr. Steele to the exit.

The door to the walk-in refrigerator flew open, crashing into the wall. Mark ran out, spotted Maggie, and dropped a case of water. He locked her in a bear hug, said something about revoking her passport, and then pushed us—I had not let go of her—toward the exit.

Cliff, frozen behind Mark, looked ready to embrace my daughter, but I was not finished. He had to wait his turn. I handed him bulging bags of food, and we fled toward the street, Cliff in hot pursuit.

"Wipes and perfume as soon as we hit that van, Mama," she huffed as we dashed.

"Count on it, baby. But if you don't tell me what this is all about, you're going to need a lot more than Wet Wipes to clean up the mess."

CHAPTER TWENTY

Haret Jdoudna, Madaba

Grace

We raced past huddled tourists whose bus drivers were unconcerned and on prayer break. Scurried in a wide lump toward the van, up the hill and around the corner, tucked from sight. I never released Maggie's arm. Mark and Cliff were front and rear. Becca wove among us, prepared to shoot.

"You're all right?" Matthew asked too casually as the van doors slid closed.

She nodded. "Uninjured."

"I haven't been all right in days," I started. "Weeks, months, or years. Maggie, what happened?"

She twisted, scratching her neck. "I managed to escape." She shrugged. "Knew you'd come through Haret if you and Dad made it as far as St. George's. Tried to get here in time."

I cleared my throat to ask more questions, but Matthew spoke before I could.

"Do you know who kidnapped you? Names? Anything?"

"They were from Bethlehem, like I said in my note. That's all I know."

He hooked his fingers over the back lip of the gearbox to twist toward us from the front seat. She patted my free hand since the other still held hers.

"How did you get here?" he asked.

"Cargo plane. Broke out of a sarcophagus—" *that explained the stench* "—to hide in a crate labeled for the Folklore Museum in Amman. Caught a taxi."

"Were there any names that . . . "

"The crates were being sent to museums, Matthew. I would have told you immediately if there were names. Note that I didn't read all of them because we started to land. And I needed to escape. I don't know much."

Their relationship was as vibrant as ever.

He pursed his lips. "So we can assume this relates to last year." I opened my mouth to question her, but he continued. "Let's keep moving. The difference in scroll and mosaic is intentional?"

"A little backstory might help, Matthew. Both hers, and yours with Dr. Steele," I said. "Where were you for two hours? We were about to leave. Who attacked us in Haret?"

Dr. Steele looked at Matthew. "I told you we were almost out of time, son. Grace, I couldn't find the priest, then Matthew showed up with the disguises . . . "

"Sayan," Matthew explained where he got them.

"We were heading back when we thought it best to lose our tails. There were three of them." He patted Maggie's shoulder. "They followed us to the chapel, though."

That explained who attacked us. "Where did you get the key?" I asked, not letting him off easily.

"A *balder*—courier—had a replacement in a drop spot within thirty minutes of my request." Matthew peeled his djellabah over his head.

THE BROTHERS' KEEPERS

"Why do you think the priest is dead?" Mark's hand on my forearm reminded me we had more important matters. If Matthew would stop asking questions, Maggie would get her chance to explain to me why she had been kidnapped again.

"Blood at his house, and a garrote tangled in the rosemary bush by the door, Dr. Madison." Matthew's visual shut me up, and I gulped. He instructed the driver to head to the border.

"I don't know who the men were," Matthew said as he texted. "As to your question, I don't think we're the only group after the scroll. I don't know who the men were at Haret, either, but got some photos, which I just sent to Tel Aviv. They could have been the same group." He showed his phone screen to the driver. "Or not."

I distributed food and tried to forget the assassin's wire used to strangle the priest. God rest his soul. Matthew requested that someone—I assumed Mossad—check on Jeff, and Maggie dropped her trash in a bag after inhaling two pitas.

"Returning to your earlier question, Matthew," she said, "I believe the difference between the map in the mosaic, and the map on the scroll, is intentional. The rose 'mistake' on the map draws attention to Luther and the Sea of Galilee story, but also marks the Dead Sea. In terms of Scripture and church history, the Dead Sea is not a major player. The mosaic throws off anyone without the complete scroll, and highlights the correct area if someone *does* have the scroll.

"Dad, did you bring the stuff I sent to the Man Cave?"

Mark handed her the laundry bag.

She plucked moss out of the laptop edge. "Were you able to open it?" Mark shook his head. "It should still have a charge, then." She handed the computer to Matthew, who inserted into a slot a wafer-thin metal file from his wallet. He turned the computer on and began to work.

Maggie explained. "Matthew and I have been consulting on this project for a while." She smiled at her dad and me, pointedly ignoring her associate.

During her computer speech, Cliff looked between she and Matthew before stiffly removing his arm from her shoulders. She didn't seem to notice.

"Matthew is Cyril's personal assistant, even though the commander is retired." Dr. Steele tried to help. "Neither of us is a model retiree. To quote Jeff, *epic failures*. By the way, where *is* he?"

"I was hoping you or Matthew could tell me." Becca peered out the window as she spoke the toneless words.

"We're checking," Matthew said.

"I don't know, child," my professor answered her. "But he is in God's hands."

She smirked.

"Focusing on what we can *try* to control, is anyone qualified to summarize?" Mark's question was a demand again.

"I took a plane ride in a sarcophagus surrounded by looted antiquities being repatriated to museums in three Middle Eastern countries." Maggie answered evasively.

I interceded in my role as peacemaker. "We found a map on half a copper scroll hidden in the cuneiform tablet. It doesn't match the Madaba mosaic on which we *think* we're finding the Luther Rose near the Sea of Galilee. Mark, I agree it looks like a daisy."

"I don't know much more than you do, Mama," Maggie replied. "Dr. Steele, how was the Luther conference?"

"Reforming in some ways." He loved theological jokes. Bless his heart. "Then our young friend Matthew appeared, triggering a clandestine meeting with Cyril in the local drugstore."

"I'm still waiting for an answer, Maggie," Mark said.

With a nod to Matthew, Maggie began. "It's Spigot. And water. The story originates with Solomon, flares in the Fourth Crusade, turns during the Reformation. Dr. Steele, how did you get this cuneiform?"

We stared at him. Our silence made it clear he was at bat. The seat dwarfed him, and he tried to disappear in it.

"At the street market in Wittenberg four years ago, a dealer selling Luther memorabilia had the tablet. It looked right. Was well enough priced for a seminarian's salary. So I bought it for my office collection." He shifted, reaching for a napkin to wipe hummus from his hands. "There are so many stories about first- and second-generation Reformers. It's hard to determine what's true." He cleaned his glasses and pinched the bridge of his nose like I did to relieve a headache. "Given his fondness for languages, I thought it would be the perfect gift for Jeff and Becca."

"But you said it was too dangerous for an old man to keep," Becca reminded him.

"So I did. And it is. When the Calvin quincentennial was celebrated a decade ago, someone mentioned a cuneiform tablet Luther received on his unwilling pilgrimage to Rome. Supposedly, Venetians looted it from Constantinople during the Fourth Crusade. Crusaders, and Venetians who sold ships and supplies to them, looted the city to enrich themselves."

"But who gave it to Luther? And why?" Cliff's hands were shoved to the bottom of his khaki pockets. "Is the cuneiform with the scroll *your* cuneiform?"

"In a moment, Cliff. The story says the son of a sixteenth-century doge named Loredano gave Luther the cuneiform. Pope

Julius II made Loredano's tenure miserable and had to pay the family an enormous sum because of fabricated territorial disputes. Loredano's son sought revenge. Family lore was that the tablet could destroy the Catholic Church. Obviously, no one could figure out how or why, or they'd have used it to do just that. They didn't know about the scroll inside."

He appeared to catch his breath. Tires sang on hot asphalt, and a refreshing level-five hurricane buffeted from the air conditioner.

"So it *is* your cuneiform. And the scroll is the relic?" Matthew held it in the air.

"*Biblical Archeology Review* ran a story last year on the Luther fable," he began again.

Would he please get to the point? I was running for my life!

"It mentioned the cuneiform. The information clicked. I consulted an—antiquarian." He squirmed. "We determined that my cuneiform might be the missing one. Before we could do anything, he heard that less-than-savory characters wanted a scroll inside the cuneiform, which I hadn't discovered, of course, because the clay tablet was intact. We decided I should give it to Becca and Jeff for safekeeping. No one could trace it to them. They could protect it better than anyone else.

"The scroll is the *valuable* part of the relic," Dr. Steele's words were quiet. "Maggie, would you care to explain why this scroll is important?" His shoulders dropped, shrinking the enthusiastic man who had recently cradled the antiquity.

"Of course, Dr. Steele. The Venetians tried to shortchange the Pope after the Fourth Crusade, which preceded Loredano's territorial problems by three hundred years," she said. "The Pope during that crusade, Innocent III, excommunicated all of

Venice—including the animals—when he heard they had plundered the city."

"I'm confused," Cliff said. "I didn't think the Church cared about people then. Ethics aside, why did Innocent make a fuss about the attack? Why is the scroll so important?"

"And why do you know all this? It's seminary-geek stuff. You're a hydrologist!" I was dazed and confused. And getting angry. *Angrier*.

Maggie frowned. "The Venetians purchased the greatest indulgence ever. They bribed the Pope with looted treasure so he would lift the ban, but cheated him by keeping a few things. One was this cuneiform tablet." She worked through her theory, repeatedly turning the scroll like a flapjack. "It's unclear whether they knew the scroll was inside, or whether they thought it worthless. I suspect it was just forgotten, and considered unimportant."

She scratched her neck. "As to the Pope's concern for Constantinople, think of the money the city generated for the Vatican. The seat of the Holy Roman Empire was a papal cash cow. A holy treasure chest. Ransacking it created powerful ramifications and cash-flow problems."

"And the scroll is special why?" Becca asked while rolling up her shirtsleeves.

"Solomon. The scroll, when united with its other half, depicts Solomon's treasure." Maggie was so matter of fact that her explanation didn't sound preposterous.

I was disinterested in Solomon's fable. "You mean his *mythical* treasure? The historic record is clear, Maggie. Did a Sunday School lesson create this life-threatening boondoggle?"

"You're assuming the treasure was something like gold and pearls. It's infinitely more valuable, Mama."

"Copper!" Mark interjected vigorously. "Everyone knows Solomon's treasure was copper from his mines."

"Most people believe that, Dad. It's what those who knew the truth *want* people to believe. For four thousand years. You know those mines in the desert near Timna?"

We visited them in mid-June fifteen years ago, when they didn't need a smelter to melt everything. Including me.

"What do you need to mine copper? Or anything else?" Maggie led us.

The answer dawned simultaneously, but Cliff responded first. "Water. That scroll, when united with its other half, shows the location of the water powering Solomon's mines."

"Exactly. And I think the water could still be there," Maggie continued. "If my research is correct, a perpetual spring. We're discovering karstic structures under Israel, where calcite dissolves as water tables evolve. Holes, or karsts, form as the rock erodes. The table was higher in Solomon's time. But the spring could still be producing, just at different levels."

"So is it an underground river?" I remembered shifting water tables during drought years at the ranch. "Has the river dropped?"

She shook her head. "Technically, it's not a river. Ground water following a topographically determined path. I suspect the Vatican or Venetians want this half of the scroll, and have worked out as much as I have. Someone has the other half. I was kidnapped because I was asking the right questions, doing the right research, about potential waterways. Or it's Spigot." Her mouth hung open as we pulled into the Amman airport. "Perhaps all three? Vatican, Venice, and Spigot. That's a triumvirate!"

While she was postulating, Matthew and Dr. Steele conferred so quietly that no one could overhear.

"I thought we were crossing at the Allenby," Mark said as he peered out the window. The Allenby Bridge connects Israel to Jordan via the Jordan River. It's one of the most closely guarded, complicated border crossings in the world.

"Where's Jeff? Why isn't he here?" Maggie asked as she unbuckled her seatbelt.

"London," Becca said.

"As to why *we're* here, I'm afraid it's my fault." Dr. Steele's rare *non sequitur* was shared in a confidential tone. "We are going to Rome to meet a friend. And Venice to meet enemies." With those words, he stepped from the van. "We're going to wait in that hangar—" he gestured toward a steel building "—for our flight, which has been delayed. Please get comfortable."

Matthew confirmed our destination with a nod, and led us across the tarmac.

The empty structure contained two rooms outfitted for quick stops. One had rows of cots, which those less inclined to hygiene or chatting—namely, Mark and Dr. Steele—claimed.

Becca handed Maggie flip-flops from her tote, followed by pajama bottoms and a tee shirt that she unwound from the e-reader containing the scroll fragment. I pointed at the shower door with the Wet Wipes from my vest, then handed her the perfume pen and my tube of lip gloss.

The second room contained a coffee maker. Tea, bread, and cheese. Figs dating to the time of Christ, and inedible olives found in a jar excavated at a dig. My guess was the eight-thousand-year-old round tower at tel Sultan in Jericho.

Some of us dozed in this second room, and we discussed what Dr. Steele could be doing. Becca wanted to awaken him with questions, reflecting fear for Jeff. We convinced her that he needed rest—he looked like death when he left the van—and that we could trust him a little longer.

Three hours later, Matthew walked along the nearest set of bi-fold hangar doors while chatting on his phone, the roar of a jet causing him to stick a finger in the unoccupied ear. A Cessna Citation pulled beneath blazing floodlights. We were going to Rome as discreetly as possible, so not commercially.

Whatever Cyril was trying to do, this plane beat the cargo transport to pieces, and I decided I could suffer during the too-short flight. I popped in foam earplugs, and when the pilot cut the interior lights, fell asleep.

CHAPTER TWENTY-ONE

St. Peter's Square, Rome

"Steele warned us about the redhead," Merrit muttered in the crosscurrent of Vatican frankincense and Roman pizza. Aromas washing over St. Peter's Square—one distinctly Eastern, the other stereotypically Western—represented the ongoing conflict between church and state.

She had entered the pharmacy across the Via de Portia Angelica two hours after it closed. Merrit had retrieved the box of Digene earlier, where instructions in Greek were precise.

The glowing basilica beckoned the faithful, who were oblivious to sketchy activities—drug deals, fist fights, sex—in the shadows by those disinclined to holiness. Tourists streamed west of the square, along the Angelica, the Leone IV, past the Borgo Pio, Vittorio, an Angelico, and at last to the Viale Vaticano. Two thousand feet up the Vaticano, they entered a private portal for after-hours tours of Michelangelo's Sistine Chapel. Hundreds of dollars per head ensured a visit without the crushing company of as many as thirty thousand strangers who visit the Papal See every day.

Merrit's bulk was hidden in the northern arches, meditating as becomes a priest. He faced the kneeling nun two hundred sixty yards south, in the opposing colonnade near the Petrine Museum. He peered vaguely as if contemplating eternity. In reality, he surveyed the elliptical space, which in ten hours would teem with snaking human lines.

John Flately's Benedictine habit was as cavernous as the burkha he had worn in Israel to stop Spigot. His wimple covered a blazing red buzz cut, almost certainly dyed. Merrit suspected the nun wore kneepads to protect his eighty-something-year-old joints during prolonged contact with stone.

He checked the safety on his pistol, and knew the nun's Kareen M-92 was loaded.

"Anything?" Flately prayed humbly into clasped hands.

"No, but keep looking. Steele's note said he thought it would be tonight. They're running out of time. She's still in the pharmacy."

"What exactly are we looking *for*?" The nun's penitent position did not change. "Was he specific?"

"Something out of the ordinary. Although most things are out of the ordinary here, so I'm unsure how we're to tell."

Rattling plates and raucous laughter heralded the dinner hour at restaurants nearby. Acrid cigarettes polluted the brisk air, and *la dolce vita* infused the Roman collective memory so that her occupants forgot their trials of the day.

A couple of hundred yards away, a priest descended the basilica steps that Martin Luther crawled on all fours more than five hundred years ago. Priests were rare outside Vatican City late at night, and Merrit and Flately perked up.

"A little unusual." Merrit stroked the rosary in no particular fashion because he was Protestant and did not know what to do with it. "Geriatric-looking priest at eleven o'clock."

The stooped cleric crossed the square close to Merrit, bisected an empty taxi queue, and entered the pharmacy. He reemerged moments later with the woman.

"That's it, then." Flately twisted as he stood, squishing his head covering toward his face to ensure his sideburns were hidden. "And what constitutes *geriatric*?" He moved toward the couple.

"I don't know any more." Merrit followed, toward the Borgo Angelica and around the corner. "I guess anyone older than us. Let's get a photo when they cross under the streetlights. We'll lose them if they enter Vatican City."

"People older than us are dead." The nun moved into position, *flapping* his habit as he lifted his hands in supplication toward the dome. The camera between his palms zoomed in for successive shots. The men tailed for five minutes, until the couple disappeared into the custody of the Papal state.

"Got it." Flately slipped his hands beneath the white scapular to hide his technology, and checked his wimple again to ensure hair that inspired his nickname, Fiery Flately, was covered.

Then the priest and nun strolled discreetly on opposite sides of the street, and continued uphill into a civilized Roman night.

CHAPTER TWENTY-TWO

Borgo, Rome

"I'm certain," Laura McAlex said to the cleric who had not introduced himself. Their communication had been electronic. The face-to-face meeting was a first.

Monsignor Agnelli had not spoken since they left the pharmacy. She had followed him in one Vatican entry and out another, finally weaving through the Borgo, past shops and services that ensured the Holy See functioned efficiently.

He gestured to the most uncomfortable chair in the *trattoria* beneath his apartment just outside St. Anne's Gate.

"I offered to have an expert look at the tablet, but they didn't want to let go of it. I don't think they know what they have, but they're suspicious. And Jeff*rrr*ey's no fool. Everything about the cuneiform appeared authentic."

The cleric opened a book from the Papal archives, and poked a page with a stubby finger on a hand disfigured by hard labor. She reached for her throat, laying her palm on her chest as if protecting it.

"Did it look like this, *signorina?*" He swiveled a light so the beam fell in an oval on the page.

She reached for the drawing, but he shook his head. Leaning forward, she confirmed the illustration was of the cuneiform.

"It is unwise to be too curious." His tone was harsh, his weathered face impassive as he returned the book to the top of a literary Tower of Pisa.

"Your family has served the Holy Father and Mother Church for generations, and we thank you for your help and devotion. We will be in touch if your services are needed again."

The interview was over. He gestured toward an unlit alley that emptied into a turn leading toward the Spanish Steps. As she walked to her palazzo, she knew her plan was working. The magazine had directed the Madisons to her, and she confirmed they possessed the cuneiform. For now.

She and the cleric would sort through who worked for whom soon enough.

...

Agnelli reentered Vatican City, split the Raphael rooms, crossed the atrium of sarcophagi and statues, and entered the Pinecone Courtyard opposite the tourist arch. As was his custom, he sat at the closed café outside the Braccio Nuovo, sorting his thoughts in the blessed void created by the end of tourist hours. Staring at the gigantic first- or second-century bronze pinecone carved by Salvius, he marveled that the man inscribed his name on its bottom.

"Imagine being remembered for a giant reproductive organ," he said, too weary for contempt.

Looking north, toward Innocent XIII's Palazzetto, he remembered the young man who dreamt of a cardinalship or papal appointment. Then his Vatican Bank work provided insight into church finance, and he recalibrated his goals, choosing earthly riches instead of heavenly promises. As determination to become wealthy increased, prospects of clerical greatness diminished. To line his pockets, he researched whispers within Vatican City, or surrounding those trying to approach its epicenter, the Pope.

The gravel crunched behind him. Agnelli nodded to a guard. He wondered about the young man's dreams—would they become as corrosive as his? No matter. His dreams were within reach, and he needed to finish.

During a research expedition years ago, he had uncovered a reference to the scroll. Its story was strange enough to be true, and the documentation clear. The scroll was Solomon's, moved from Constantine to Luther. It was the Reformer's gift to the world, which, Agnelli had to admit, beat Salvius's pinecone.

The scroll became his obsession. Although it was supposed to be in Vatican City, he could not find it. He courted a dozen Swiss Guards—an organization whose criteria included physical attractiveness—assigned to the vaults, and found nothing during the years they were lovers.

He watched antique markets, and attended auctions whenever church business could support a trip to the bigger shows in Paris, Brussels, or London. During this process, he encountered professionals in every facet of the arts and antiquities world. From low-level thugs fencing stolen goods, to agents of collectors bidding via phone from private jets, Agnelli cultivated a network he hoped would serve him well.

He also became aware that two people searched for his treasure, always ahead of him.

THE BROTHERS' KEEPERS

One was Dr. Stanley Augustus Steele, a protestant theologian of impeccable reputation. The other he knew only as leading something less noble than a seminary class.

Agnelli joined forces with the latter when an auction catalog listed a cuneiform matching the description of the one he sought, and he realized the dealer was Stanley Steele's brother.

DAY FIVE
CHAPTER TWENTY-THREE

Borgo

Early the next morning, Agnelli walked the quarter mile to Vatican City, murmuring about the coming days. Priests had populated the Borgo for centuries, so everyone ignored a cleric talking to himself as he strolled to work, hands clasped behind his back.

"The Church has held the keys since St. Peter. Across the front line stands the world. Regardless of the inclusiveness of this Pope. Or his reckless liberation theology. We've lost the battle. It's time to cut my losses."

He walked to the end of the street, past a shoemaker who resoled the red Papal slippers, and crossed near the shop selling linen undergarments for high-ranking prelates. Entered Vatican grounds through St. Anne's, then St. Peter's Basilica through a door for Vatican personnel.

"How could Mossad place an impenetrable wall around them?" He searched for answers about the Madisons and their friends while ascending three hundred twenty steps to the top of the dome. Aromas became stronger as his legs weakened.

The coffee shop atop St. Peter's was closed to the public. Residents and employees of Vatican City could slake their thirst thanks to the Disciples of the Divine Master, a contemplative congregation of near-extinct nuns helping priests in parish work.

"*Un cafe, per favor. Grazie,*" he said to the *barrista,* a kindly woman clutching the largest hearing horn ever made. He repeated himself four times and received a *macchiato* from the crepey dear.

He sat on a spindly stool by the window. Rome spread over seven hills—Capitoline, Palatine, Aventine, Caelian, Esquiline, Viminal, *Quirinal—as it had since BC 753.*

"For decades, I've called your names as I fell asleep."

When he had discovered Steele also searched for the scroll, he uncovered references to archaeological theologians recruited by Mossad during the formation of Israel in the forties. Some still lived, like Steele. Surely men his age didn't threaten his endeavor? He needed information on survivors from this group, so sent a text.

Future plans included renouncing his vocation, and moving to Provence, or Monte Carlo, or both. He considered seeking the office of Pope, which he believed he could attain once he possessed the scroll, but decided he had wasted enough of this life sacrificing for the next. Although the Church brought Pantiloni Corti from the sticks of Padua to the metropolis of Rome, and taught him the supreme value of self-interest, it was time to write his own ticket.

First class. In long trousers. Custom made in Milano.

His days in Rome were numbered. Just like those of any impediment between him and that scroll.

CHAPTER TWENTY-FOUR

Bermondsey Square, London

4:45 A.M.

A hodgepodge of outdoor stalls sagged in sleet trapping exhaust at nose level. To paraphrase W. C. Fields, it was not a fit night out for man or beast. Both species surrounded Jeff as closely as the pre-dawn fog leeching down the Thames.

Parking for the antiques market was nonexistent, and the London Underground provided shelter from elements in the cover of crowds, so he arrived via Tube. His black fleece hoodie under a rain jacket, with low-slung jeans and plastic sneakers, balanced a street-wise haze on his pasty jawline. He would have looked tough had his beard not screamed *orange*!

Becca's call to headquarters confirmed his flat was watched, so he stayed at a grotty hotel near the market square. Travel clothes were rolled in the backpack slung over his left shoulder, leaving his right hand free for the Walther. The spare magazine hung heavily in the front pocket of his baggy jeans.

Originally named the New Caledonia Market, Bermondsey was a commercial venture borne of an archaic law stating that anything sold between dawn and dusk in one day was provenance free. Many sellers were thieves, or fronts fencing stolen goods. Buyers were legally indemnified against their purchases, even if snagging Axminster rugs lifted from the Queen's bedroom at Buckingham Palace the night before.

Forgeries were plentiful, but treasures could be found. Stories of the grimy vase hidden under a rag and bought for five pounds, that sold as a Ming for eight million ten years ago, were true.

Through the mid-nineties, Bermondsey was a rough-and-tumble place where you walked *across* from dark alleyways, using the street as a buffer between you and what lurked therein. You did not pop into a pub to use the loo, but followed your besieged nose to a wall. You paid in small bills after shoving your stash down your shirt before leaving your flat or hotel room.

Recent development, here on the far side of Tower Bridge, sanitized the neighborhood. Police patrolled places that they used to leave to locals, particularly after sundown.

Jeff gazed at apartment blocks surrounding the square. How much longer would the legendary market survive encroaching gentrification by oligarchs, despots, and foreigners needing hideaways for mistresses and millions?

He surveyed the space, and walked its circumference twice to ensure he was not followed. Shuffling between tables, he swung his flashlight back and forth, and stopped to inspect toy trucks and Edwardian mourning pins encasing braided hair of the deceased.

The man set up on the erratic perimeter, Jeff assumed to facilitate escape if things got rough. Sloshing toward the table, he regarded a cheap brass ashtray inscribed to Allah while waiting for the Arab to acknowledge him.

"My brother." The brusque greeting in thickly slurred English made Jeff laugh. His contact covered a Cambridge education with faux-Syrian inflections, and could easily adapt to a more-convenient tongue. He was the only person Jeff knew with language skills as extensive as his own.

"My brother." Jeff mimicked the Arab's accent perfectly, evoking a mercenary chuckle.

Jeff glanced at the junk. Moved to other tables. The Arab's money did not come from selling trinkets, but MI6 kept him safely operational despite dealing. Accurate information about his homeland was too valuable to extradite for a few grams of cocaine.

This was the dance—look at everything, then return to bargain. Feign increasing indifference. Do it all again.

He flitted through a dozen displays, getting colder at each. It was not 5:00 a.m., yet Bermondsey was packed. Serious dealers would be gone in thirty minutes, leaving only tourist dregs. Jeff needed information before rejoining the chase for Maggie.

Picking up the ashtray, he shone his light on it while keeping his face in shadows. "Any news?" He turned the tray over, looking for a signature he knew he would not find.

"I hear many things. Their value varies."

"They are all of one value to me." Jeff referred to their usual fee. He had cultivated the Arab for years, and some of his best BBC scoops started here.

"The value increases when the subject is beloved."

Jeff put down the item and turned to leave. *So he knows about Maggie.* He would confirm his suspicions through another source, but hated to rejoin the family without information.

"My brother." The voice was sarcastic. He held out a copper plate as temptation, should someone be watching. A German couple moved their direction, still two stalls away.

The Arab looked at the plate and spoke downwards. "I am weary of the West. I want to go home. Can you get me there?"

"Not my call," Jeff responded.

A folded slip of paper slid from under the Arab's thumb into the plate as Jeff took it. While the BBC was careful about keeping tabs on informants, MI6 was obsessive. He doubted they would let someone as valuable as this man, disappear. Psychopaths returned in catastrophic ways.

But Jeff needed to know what the man knew, so thumbed the paper into his palm. "I can ask. No guarantees."

"What is it you want, my brother?"

"Information on the location of the beloved, and a missing fragment." Jeff cut his eyes toward the Germans. "The holy half." He referred to the Vatican. "And any admirers it might have."

The Arab nodded. Hummed something in a minor key. Handed Jeff an ivory-inlaid curio box after sliding a scrap inside. "I was expecting you."

Jeff wanted to ask how, but knew information was knotted within the Internet. Hidden in innocuous chat rooms and on message boards. The German couple trolled toward them, laughing at the collections. Jeff was getting anxious. Needed to conclude the transaction.

The Arab opened a thermos. Turkish coffee laced with cardamom and cinnamon taunted Jeff. "I need a guarantee, my brother."

"I need information." Jeff opened the box. Inspected it. Snatched the paper. Put the scrap in a pocket with the other. Glanced both directions uneasily.

The Arab poured coffee into the metal cap, then into the paper cup he handed Jeff. Jeff waited for him to sip from the cap. Pressed the cup rim to his lips. Feigned a swallow.

"Part of what you seek has been found. But we are a needy couple of . . . "

A split-second after the *pop*, a bullet destroyed the Arab's forehead.

Jeff rolled under the table, pulling the plastic cloth with him. Tripped the German woman, who tumbled into falling trinkets. She upturned the table. Screamed nonsense about anti-Aryan sentiment.

He kept rolling. Off the curb, into a flowing gutter. Next to the car whose driver's window was blown out by a second shot. Crept around the back bumper. Zigzagged, crouched, along the vehicles. Headed for the Borough tube station, staying low.

Scooting quickly past post-blitzkrieg structures, he flew along dour redbrick public housing where thugs ruled. Picked up Abbey Street, then Long Lane. Incoming sirens pushed him to the smaller Elim Street, through the once-elegant estate across a cricket field. He cut into Tabard Gardens at the tennis courts. Jogged through the Green past Rochester House and St. George's Rectory. Once far enough away to be disassociated from the attack, he walked Great Dover Street to the Underground, and picked up the next Piccadilly line train to Heathrow.

He would read the slips of paper, clasped in the fist thrust in his pocket, at the airport. As to the murder, he needed to figure out if he had made a mistake. And what had been found? He prayed it was Maggie.

CHAPTER TWENTY-FIVE

Fiumicino Airport, Rome

Grace

Our descent awakened me. Everyone was stretching and yawning, so I was not the only person whose in-flight entertainment had been of the shut-eye variety.

Dr. Merrit waited near a van on the tarmac, in the glow from a bank of REIL (runway end identifier lights) three hundred yards away. He boarded with hands cupped over his ears because the pilot didn't cut the engines, and we took off for the thirty-minute flight to Marco Polo in Venice.

Darkness outside made the cabin lighting seem harsh, so perfect for cross-examination.

"Dr. Steele?" Maggie began. When he looked at her, she continued with a smile. "Story time."

He innocently adjusted his hearing aids. Then slumped when he realized she wasn't giving up. "When we land in Venice, we go to an antiquarian shop near St. Mark's," he said.

Thirty seconds later, I pushed. "What can you tell us about the scroll? A spring powerful enough to support Solomon's mining?" I glanced to Maggie for confirmation. "Where is the water if the spring is active?"

He shifted thick-soled orthopedic shoes, and fiddled with his glasses. Continually adjusting how they sat on his ears, he created tufts of hair resembling horns—an alarming look for a theologian. Then he took a deep breath before speaking.

"Luther wasn't interested in harming the Church, but protested indulgences impoverishing parishioners while enriching the religious establishment. Clerical corruption was another issue. The cuneiform and scroll weren't important, and for all we know, he put them in a drawer and forgot about them." He paused, as if awaiting more questions.

"What's going on, Steele?" Dr. Merrit leaned toward his friend.

"You're going to have to trust me a little longer, Merrit. I promise to tell you everything when we get to Venice. I think much of the story will become apparent there." By the time he stopped speaking, he had two left horns and one right one.

I hoped they weren't omens.

...

Venice

My positive review of Venice began and ended with her embellished Moorish and Baroque architecture, and whitish-teal lagoon water.

Life intricately snarled in her passages. Buildings obscured the rest of the world. I couldn't discern where the sun rose or set. Landmarks were hidden, so strolling was a blind man's bluff ending in a living Gordian knot. I detested her humidity because I didn't feel clean when clothes clung to my body—a bad look for lumpy me.

To continue, the canals inconvenienced me, which meant I missed the point.

I once jumped four vertical feet *in a dress*, from a boat to a rocking dining terrace, because of rapidly rising tides. Saw a terrier strangled by its collar when its leash caught between gondola and pier. Hit my head on the underneath side of the stone Bridge of Sighs, scandalously renaming it Bridge of Swears.

These memories put me in a bad mood before we crossed St. Mark's basin. From the airport to the island, early morning scud lay like a soggy blanket. I wanted to leave immediately. And there was the matter of my missing son.

A wood-trimmed water taxi—the sleek limousine of Venice—surged directly into a bracing squall for the three-mile trip to the San Marco pier. Dr. Steele led us across the piazza at a clip possible because revelers were still passed out from last night's orgy. Venetians moved purposefully, ignoring rain that would sprout umbrellas within hours.

We cut into Calle de Peregrin—dark even on sunny days— immediately left of St Mark's Basilica. Walked single-file down a passage not five feet wide, between a Murano glass emporium and an "American" bar. As rain and rent increased, spaces shrank near stores like Max Mara and Cartier.

Dr. Steele's last left, into a sheltered alley so short we ran into each other, brought us to a door with a tiny sign. *Antico Privato*. He rang the bell. A click indicated the door had been unlocked. Movement of a security camera behind a windowsill flower box caught my attention.

Was security because of treasures within, or intrigue outside?

I lagged behind in the musty-smelling space, afraid we headed for a trap. At the apex of a miniscule hallway whose low ceiling distributed Venetian plaster across the floor—the price for constant dampness—a room overlooked a private garden. When Mark and I crossed the threshold, we found our party in an arc.

"May I present my twin, Steven?" Dr. Steele gestured to his mirror image on his right. His brother pressed a revolver to my professor's temple.

. . .

"It's not right to leave him with that lunatic. Brother or not." Dr. Merrit huffed up and over one of the more than four hundred pedestrian bridges linking man-made islands into the Venetian city-state. Step treads were consistent only in that no two were alike, although most required a couple of stuttering footfalls. Locals moved to the center of each bridge, away from the well-worn banisters he gripped to cross safely in the drizzle.

We reviewed in a logjam, partially sheltered by an awning a shopkeeper neglected to crank down the night before. Steven Steele had explained the brothers had a score to settle, which he preferred to do amicably. He would kill Dr. Steele if we didn't leave.

We could probably have overtaken Steven, but did not want to risk an eighty-seven-year-old-finger on the trigger of a gun held against the head of someone we loved. Or really, holding any gun, anywhere, at any time, against anything.

Assuring us he would be fine, Dr. Steele had pointed to the front door and said he would contact us. He sent us to a vessel, one he said we would recognize, in the private taxi queue across the piazza. He stressed we were not to call the *Carabinieri*—police.

"I'll be in touch. My contact will get everything to you," he said as we filed out.

I tripped near the door, distracted by hoping his faith was well founded. I shared this thought with Mark as he helped me up.

"Do we just leave him there?" Becca asked.

"I think so." Everyone looked at me, mouths open and eyebrows raised. "Dr. Steele has always known what he was doing or wouldn't have lasted this long. Besides, he had a reason for telling us *exactly* what to do. Am I the only person wondering how much he knows? Dr. Merrit?"

"He's been cryptic since he called Tel Aviv. Sent Flately and me to Rome for reconnaissance, but gave us little to go on. It's very unlike him." He gazed toward the Antico Privato sign. "I'm waiting here to see if they leave. Someone has to stop Steven and . . . "

"Merrit." Mark startled the man he always referred to by professional title. "Grace is right. Go with her to find the boat. Grace, let me know where you end up. I'll keep an eye on things here, then join you." Turning to Becca, he continued. "Have you heard from Jeff?"

Her eyes went flat, like obsidian marbles. "No."

He squeezed her shoulder. "He knows what he's doing. Best thing we can do is our jobs well until he returns."

Mark was broad and strong at the shoulders, thick through the chest, agile as a cat, and powerfully fast when necessary. They say love is blind, but I knew I was not. He caught my eye and nodded, indicating we were to go on. Then stepped into a gelato shop. I pulled my daughter, and motioned at my daughter-in-law. We started toward the piazza and water taxis, leading Dr. Merrit, Matthew, and Cliff.

Tucking under the length of loggia outside the Doge's Palace, we peered through rain toward the queue. My heart sank. Early morning rush hour was underway, the service industry piling into Venice for the fortune that is made during Carnevale.

We dispersed along the quay. I combed my fingers from forehead to crown, tugging flat, wet curls from my eyes. All I needed was shampoo because the rain was now steady as a shower.

"Here," Cliff said, stepping aboard an average-looking craft near the end of the line. He pointed to the name, *Katharina von Bora*, with a miniscule Luther Rose dotting the *i*.

We boarded without question, ignoring the protocol of asking permission from the captain. Ducked into the cabin where lace café curtains were drawn for privacy. Slid onto upholstered benches, drenching them. A chest of bottled water anchored steps to the bridge. Engines revved in reverse, then forward, propelling us into the lagoon without asking our destination. I smelled strong coffee.

"Luther's wife's name. Clever of you to recognize it," Matthew said.

"Not what I recognized first." Cliff cocked his head toward the bridge as the *Katharina* moved from lagoon to Grand Canal.

I started up the stairway. Matthew was ahead of me. He pulled a Beretta 9mm from his back holster, motioned respectfully—there *are* other ways to make the gesture—for me to sit, and peered up the shaft. He stiffened, then turned to us and grinned. We lunged and craned, but he pulled Becca to the front.

Abraham ben-Dove Cyril looked seaworthy in a captain's hat and starched white shirt. He greeted us with a cocky salute before sliding the craft under the Rialto Bridge in a monsoon.

Jeff stood beside him, lips set in a firm frown, holding espresso in a paper cup.

...

Ca' Sagredo sat across the Grand Canal from the Rialto Market, next to the Ca' D'Oro waterbus stop. The five-star hotel was an odd hideout for our traveling troupe, and I was beginning to wonder how wise it was for spies to travel *en masse*.

We didn't check in or use the monumental split staircase, but piled into a tiny elevator—in threes—near the terrace to which I leapt years ago. I wondered how well orchestrated our journey had been. And by whom.

Cyril led us to unoccupied quarters on the top floor. We convened in a ballroom whose obelisk windows provided inadequate light for all but the slowest dancing. I was not in the mood.

"I know." Cyril's words hung between aubergine-and-gray terrazzo floors and brooding floral panels inset in *boiserie*. "Only they can resolve their acrimony. I believe he is safe, though."

"We need to get Steele." Dr. Merrit spoke forcefully, and flushed. The air was the bone-penetrating cold of the ranch meat locker, so my professor should not have been scarlet.

The commander shook his head. "He and his brother have already left Venice. Mark is on his way here."

I turned to Jeff, who spoke for the first time since rejoining us.

"I'll update you when Dad arrives," he said. He clung to his wife, and she to him.

...

From the center of three Moorish windows, I watched for my husband. *We're as clueless as two days ago.* I clutched the stone frame to lean over the brackish water, worried about Jeff's silence. *Dr. Steele is almost a father to me, and he's in danger. Again. The rascal.* I looked up at the peaked arch, and prayed.

Then reminded myself that we do what we teach. I taught the children to do the right thing—always—so had to do the right thing now. Which was to help Dr. Steele.

Mark hopped off the Number One waterbus and took the steps two—or possibly three—at a time, slapping the marble with each step. We met at the landing, which smelled of fish. My mouth was watering because of the food scents, something it always did in Italy and France. He misunderstood.

"Glad to see me?" He scowled.

"Always. And Jeff's back." The escape of two octogenarians in a city riddled with canals and bridges was inconceivable. As a long-married woman, I ignored his black mood as we walked to our quarters. "How?"

"Long story. I'd like to tell it only once, though." He kissed me on the forehead. "Jeff know anything new?"

"He won't share until you're there." I mentioned this before knocking on the locked door.

"Thank God he's here. Nothing is as it seems."

"Nothing is ever as it seems, Mark. Except Maggie and Cliff just brought in a feast. We're all hungry. Let's talk over dinner."

The lime-green linen cloth was laden with platters of food representing the Italian flag—red tomatoes, green basil and parsley, and white pasta. Mark helped himself to the *antipasto misto di pesce*—a salty, mixed-fried-fish appetizer—while the others raved about *spaghetti con moeche*—spaghetti . . . *al dente,* of course . . . with soft-shell crab. Salad would be Continental style—after dinner—and then we would revel in the Promised Land, *tiramisu,* the coffee/chocolate/cream pinnacle of Italian gastronomy.

"I told Jeff, while waiting in the water taxi, everything. I forgot to mention that the garden opened onto a side canal," Cyril said before my husband exploded.

Mark surveyed a steaming mound of spaghetti. "Would've been helpful to know *everything.*" He loved food as much as our son, and checked his anger by filling a plate. "When I went to the apartment, which had become quiet, they were gone." He trapped the tine tips of a noodle-wound fork in his spoon. "They didn't leave through the front door." He twirled.

"Signs of a struggle? Or worse?" Maggie asked. When Mark shook his head, she grasped the neck of the wine carafe. "Everything look orderly? Were the doors locked?"

He nodded while bringing pasta to his mouth. She poured *chianti.* He stopped her at half a glass, flipped spaghetti off his fork, and splattered his shirt in a Rorschach dot pattern.

"Does this strike you as suspicious?" I dabbed an ice-water-soaked napkin on the tomato confetti, giving him a lead.

He set down his fork, and took a salad plate from Maggie. "Yes. The entire thing strikes me as off. One of the most irregular aspects is an ex-commander of Mossad didn't mention a back canal and post Matthew there." He stared at Cyril for twenty seconds, then turned to Matthew. "People should be covering every exit larger than a mouse hole."

Cyril assaulted his greens by marching them around his plate until they wilted, and sopped bread through the balsamic vinegar dressing.

Maggie slid a mound of Tiramisu toward Jeff. He pushed it back and spoke.

"Commander, we had this problem in Israel and Jordan. Constantly being played. Almost cost Maggie's life. I was nearly killed in London yesterday. I won't do this again." He dropped his napkin on the table to signal the end of his meal. "You have one opportunity to convince me to remain. I believe I speak for Becca. I hope I speak for my family."

Cyril mounded tiramisu on a plate, chewing and talking with his mouth full. "I didn't think you would prevent their escape, Mark. They safely left Venice. Through the back door." He swallowed, then turned to Jeff. "What happened?"

"You first, commander," was Jeff's reply.

CHAPTER TWENTY-SIX

Ca' Sagredo, Venice

Grace

"Dr. Steele suspected this was the mythic Luther cuneiform. Shortly after purchasing it, he contacted his brother." Cyril reviewed for us, clustered around a table littered with noodles and sauce, resembling a war zone. "They discussed the Luther angle. Dr. Steele laid out proof. They agreed to list the piece in a catalog to see if it generated interest."

Jeff was half-lidded, his arm around Becca. Maggie sat between Cliff and Matthew, leaning up while they leaned back. Mark held my hand tensely while Dr. Merrit twirled a button.

"The brothers decided it was safest with you, Jeff, until they decided what to do. Your engagement provided an opportunity." He cleared his throat and finished an after-dinner espresso in one gulp.

"How do you know all this?" Mark asked, placing his fisted hand in the center of the table, more than halfway between himself and the commander.

"Six months ago, an intermediary contacted Steven. The opening offer was four hundred thousand Euros, 20 percent more than the auction estimate. Steven contacted his brother.

Both believed the offer validated Dr. Steele's Luther assumption. Then Steven met the dealer. The offer doubled."

"Your source?" Mark's hand was still fisted.

"The Steeles have been under surveillance since Spigot."

"My water address?" Maggie grasped both ends of her twisted napkin. "The title was published only two months ago. I thought I had time."

"Mossad has continued to investigate Spigot after Rosenthal and al-Jafar flew off the wall on the Temple Mount. The organization has ties everywhere. Even here." Cyril held her gaze. "Because of your hydraulic and site knowledge, Ms. Madison, the skills of this group, and our Spigot experience, we're a threat to their acquisition of both halves. Your paper led them to believe you had the scroll. *Half* of which I believe your brother possesses." He looked at Jeff, whose eyes were closed, and waited for my son to acknowledge the gift from Dr. Steele.

"Where are the halves?" Jeff's question ignored the scroll fragment in Becca's e-reader. He hadn't mentally left for parts unknown, so Cyril's answers must have satisfied him so far.

"Legend has it the other piece is in the Vatican vaults." The commander turned his espresso cup in its saucer, his fingertips placed lightly on its rim.

"That's the second time we've received a non-answer," Becca said. "I don't care where legend says it is. Where *is* it?"

Cyril smiled. "I'll note MI6 still recruits the best and brightest."

"Where *IS* it?" Mark slammed his fist with this question. "And where are the Steeles?"

"We believe its location is tied to the mosaic in Madaba. There's a lot of encoded chatter right now. Some of it is about your morning at Bermondsey." He nodded at Jeff. "A package of research is in each bedroom for review."

"In other words, you really don't know where it is." Cliff leaned up with Maggie.

"Where do you *think* it is?" Matthew scooted his chair nearer the table to match Cliff's closeness to my daughter. She rocked back after shooting disgusted glances at them.

Cyril motioned for Matthew to join him at the door, his other hand resting on the knob. "We don't know. And I don't have time to play games." He glared at Jeff. "But we're hoping you'll use *your* half to prevent Spigot from getting its hands on that water. Or whatever it is. Be prepared to leave within fifteen minutes after I hear from Dr. Steele." He stalked out.

"Where are we headed?" I called after him.

"Germany or Switzerland." His voice was so quiet it was hard to hear.

"Reformation country," I responded.

We remained at the table.

"I still don't like it," Dr. Merrit said, holding a button in his palm.

"Neither do I," Mark replied.

Becca's expressionless face prevented her mouth from moving much as she spoke. "He issued a command."

I wondered if anyone else noticed.

"Nasty habit of his," I said. "None of us reports to him."

"But I'm committed to fair use of water, which directly impacts this spring problem. And we need to help Dr. Steele, which means Cyril at least *thinking* we work with him," Maggie said. "Not for. *With*. I know how much Dr. Steele means to you, Mama. And honestly, he means a lot to the rest of us." She squeezed my hand, then tossed the distorted napkin, which resembled a piece of Fortuny fabric—eternally wrinkled, like my forehead—on the table.

"We *are* the brothers' keepers." My voice revealed strain I couldn't hide. "Genesis 4. I would never forgive myself if something happened to Dr. Steele. Cyril is obviously only in this for the sake of the Sovereign State of Israel. And I'm not leaving you alone to solve this, Maggie. We are a team."

"Of which I am a part," Mark stated gallantly. When Jeff snorted, Mark continued. "Sometimes reluctantly, I admit it. And there's the issue that you keep getting kidnapped, Maggie. And someone shot at Becca." Maggie jumped, and looked at her sister-in-law.

He stared at our daughter. "The time will come when we *won't* be in time, and the strain of your activities is showing on all of us, Maggie. I don't see how we can stop this, if it's Spigot or something else, without continuing to help Dr. Steele."

"And whoever is after Maggie is clearly after Dr. Steele, regardless of Steven's behavior," Becca concluded. "I'm fine, Maggie. Really. They missed."

"Only because they meant to," Jeff replied.

"Then let's address our involvement once we hear from MI6 and the Office," Mark suggested. "But I agree we have to help, Gracie. And that we need to end this."

He didn't trust the commander, who managed to tell only as much of any story as necessary. A major contention was his secrecy, a second his attitude, which wasn't of a *retired* commander. Mark and I had discussed our problems with Cyril at length. But I wasn't sure I trusted MI6 and "the Office." I held a grudge.

"I'm going to contact Flately." Dr. Merrit blotted his blotchy face as he stood, then swayed toward his room. "I left him in Rome. He's using contacts from his Shroud of Turin work to investigate a priest Steele had us keep an eye on."

"We need to watch Dr. Merrit's health," I said under my breath.

"Why did you ruin my honeymoon?" Jeff turned to his sister, leaning into her face. His unrelated question startled me.

"Don't start with me," she responded. "I didn't exactly enjoy my time in Paris."

"You have the gift of involving us in compromising situations, Sis." Jeff tried his half-lidded stare. "What's going on?"

"Just water again. Lots of it."

"You believe it's tied to Solomon's treasure story? That's a fable." His ears turned red. "If every shred of evidence didn't support the seriousness of this situation, I'd say it's horse feathers."

Nothing like a little argument to aid dinner digestion.

"So . . . " Jeff's voice persisted, and I prepared to intervene. "Dad's waiting for Langley. Becca and I expect data from London. Dr. Merrit is contacting Dr. Flately. We need to work through Cyril's documents before we take off for parts unknown . . . "

"And you still haven't told us what happened at Bermondsey." I wasn't going to let him slip away without an explanation. "I haven't pushed because we had company, and you were the least of our problems now that you're safe."

"Coffee?" He held his forefinger to his lips.

Of course the apartment was wired. "Okay. My treat." I scooted my chair back. At the door, I stopped. "It's probably locked, you know."

"Devices exist that can pick locks," Jeff said. "And if we don't have one, Becca has radical skills."

No one mentioned her failure to get us into the Chapel of St. George.

"I'd love a coffee and a stroll," she said.

"Will the material be safe here?" I asked.

"You know Mossad is watching the building. Let security be *Cyril's* problem," Mark said.

We found the door unlocked, probably because Cyril knew we would pick it anyway.

Tourists normally ate earlier than Italians. The restaurant, buoyed over the Grand Canal, didn't open for dinner for another hour. The rain had stopped. People sipping coffee in late-afternoon sun occupied two tables.

The large corner table was empty, and five espressos and my club soda appeared in minutes, followed by a platter of buttery cookies. Jeff's coffee was a double. Becca and Maggie played soft, disruptive music from their phones to prevent our being overheard. We huddled toward the cookies, and Jeff downed his first cup before he spoke.

"This will be quick and cryptic. I don't expect information to leave the table." *Sip.* "My contact at Bermondsey was killed in front of me." *Sip.* Cookie-plate slide. *Munch.* "He slipped me two notes. One indicates intelligence operations—plural—are tailing us." *Sip.* "The other implicates Mossad in ways I don't understand." *Slurp* and *drain.* "That's it." *Clatter* on the table. "So to address your earlier concern, I'm not safe, Mother. None of us are."

A member of the Rolling Stones disembarked fifty feet behind us, and we turned so paparazzi wouldn't photograph our faces. Because of Maggie's unsettled heart, I wondered if Jeff's Mossad mistrust extended to Matthew. I would ask him privately.

"I have to ask if you suspect Matthew," Maggie blurted.

Cliff shoved two cookies in his mouth, and scooted back his chair, scraping noisily.

"I would like to know sooner rather than later," she said.

"Not directly," Jeff replied. "Although I'm having a hard time getting a read on him."

Mark cleared his throat. "Let's get some exercise. Walk around and look at Carnevale-goers. Keep an eye on each other. Then return to review what we have. See if we have more from MI6 and the CIA. And the BBC." He nodded at Jeff. "If we're lucky, we won't hear from Cyril anytime soon. Might even get a night's sleep, instead of these three- and four-hour naps."

After two hours of dodging revelers, we returned to a Cyril-free zone. We picked through leftovers, and retired to our rooms to study the material after Mark, Jeff, and Becca shared the little intel from their sources.

Only Mark knew I had alerted UNESCO, the cultural division of the United Nations, on the boat from the airport to St. Mark's. I would head to the Cyclades, and through Greece and Turkey, in late summer to check on compromised digs after my work at tel Kinneret near the Sea of Galilee. Then I was off to Machu Picchu in Peru to assist in its transition from tourist attraction to scholarly institute. I reported to the Assistant Director-General at UNESCO. My requested reconnaissance appeared in files on my phone twenty minutes ago.

I, too, was a spy of sorts.

CHAPTER TWENTY-SEVEN

Venice

Steven, the antiquarian, was more rotund than Stanley, the theologian.

The former avoided barber shops visited by men fortunate enough to be hairy into their eighties. His ponytail also distinguished him from his neatly trimmed sibling. Before they crept out the back door, Steven's three-inch braid, faded jeans, walnut leather bomber commemorating a raucous youth, and baggy, white button-down looked bohemian. He was the stylish twin.

Dr. Steele's Harris Tweed jacket over argyle vest and rumpled khakis were professorial, his snowy head enveloped in Steven's felt fedora.

"A pair of twins is always noteworthy, but ancient twins would be remarked upon for days." Dr. Steele stepped into the rocking launch, oddly named *The Whinny*, and they powered toward Santa Lucia station in Venice. Today's catch at the Rialto assaulted him, and he smiled at small green crabs spastically choosing life by racing down a table skirt dangling over the three-hundred-foot-wide canal. "You smell oddly of mothballs, Steven. Or it's the market. Pungent, even."

"Both. I have cultivated an image ever since we 'agreed to disagree.' The ponytail is strange enough to be written off as an idiosyncrasy at my age. *Our* age. A well-dressed old dealer can go a lot of places this jacket can't, even in artsy-fartsy Venice. It's been stored."

"Obviously. Since the '70s?"

"How'd you know?"

"I'm the observant twin."

They puttered forward, waves from the tide slapping the metal bow in a way that threatened to destabilize the small craft.

"What's he going to do when he finds we didn't use the car?" Steven referred to a silver Audi that Cyril had left at Mestre, the industrial spot on the mainland where Venetians stored their wheels. He had told them where to find it, and exactly what to look for. "How much of a head start will the train give us? He's going to be royally . . . "

"Yes. *Upset*. He will be." Pinching the hat as wind picked up through the broadening tidewater, Dr. Steele contemplated how long it would take Cyril to find them. Of course Cyril bugged the car and planned to follow. The theologian appreciated Mossad support, but was repulsed by endangering friends. He filled his lungs with fresh ocean air delivered by westerly gusts portending a storm, and tried to figure out how to answer Steven's question.

When Steven cut the motor in front of the station, his brother's answer was thorough. "Two or three days at most. Mossad and their sayan are everywhere. He'll issue an alert within the hour. The rest depends on how long it takes him to pin down the train. Closed circuit in a train station is less high-definition than in an airport. No central security checkpoint at the station, either. Trains aren't as glamorous to bomb as airplanes, I guess, so security is comparatively lax."

Steven lifted 1980s aviator sunglasses, and leaned from one side to the other, peering to park the floating box precisely. "We could have taken another car."

"Too easy to track. Rental cars require IDs, credit card, and international driver's license." Dr. Steele paused. "You have one?" Steven's could delay Mossad until it appeared empty somewhere.

"Not here. And not common-looking," Steven said, fishing in a pocket for the ticket he handed his brother, who adjusted the hat. They strode up the urine-drenched ramp to the right of the main entrance, and turned left into a reception hall so generic that it could have been anywhere in Europe.

When Dr. Steele had called a week ago, after Maggie's disappearance, he asked Steven to handle arrangements. The train to Zurich was in queue three, departing within moments of the Venice-Simplon Orient Express to Paris. Swelling platform crowds, dressed differently for each journey, would make the brothers harder to pick out when a speckled feed was reviewed.

Steven ignored the line to Zurich. "I got these tickets through a friend. They're not in our names," he explained while walking to queue five. Handing his brother a passport not his own, he checked in with the spiffy female attendant stationed outside the car with *Vera* scrolled next to the door. The discreet gold lettering was as effective as a florescent *No Trespassing* sign, and her dark-blue uniform complimented the vintage carriage. Both were polished like Southern sterling spread for an after-church supper.

"Shady characters in antiquities make a lot of money?" Dr. Steele asked.

THE BROTHERS' KEEPERS

"You have no idea," Steven replied, taking the first large step onto the carriage ladder. He had chosen an indirect route to Switzerland, knowing security footage would eventually reveal the man in a fedora and his pony-tailed friend in retro aviators boarding the train against which all others are judged.

...

Dr. Steele grinned at his surroundings. Glowing wood and gentrified brass represented the pinnacle of the Deco period. In an Hercule Poirot moment, the brothers' liveried steward presented champagne on a tray. The theologian wallowed into the leather bench, supple from beeswax buffing, and sniffed flowers and polish in uncirculated air. "So, antiquities pay well?" he asked.

Steven yanked papers from the backpack, a genius accessory to post-hippie chic, before dropping the twill bag on the carpeted floor. "It does pay well, actually. One of the reasons those shady characters are attracted to it." He flipped through papers. "I also invested a hunk of my inheritance in Microsoft when it went public in '86." Rattling the documents while separating them, he shoved a stack at his brother. "We get off at Innsbruck. My car is there. A three-hour drive to Zurich. Maybe longer in winter." Steven peered at the dirty glass roof of the station. "Although the weather's finally cooperating. Glad I covered *The Whinny* last night. We'd still be bailing her out."

Dr. Steele took the documents as the door opened, and informed the steward they would dine privately. Fewer people would see them if they stayed in their compartment. Chronologically sorting material, which began with a summary of paperwork, he remembered their agreement. He would cover

Solomon to the Fourth Crusade, then skip to Luther. Steven's responsibility started with a pre-Dante piece composed around the time contemporary Italian developed in the eleventh century. It included papal writs, Swiss Reformation references, little-known notes from Zwingli.

Steven plopped a Zwingli document atop his brother's stack, out of order. "I left my car at the Innsbruck station last week. I paid cash and used a borrowed ID for the ticket home. We should hit Zurich before nine, and I have a room. I hope our switching from train to car will slow Cyril down, although another train would be more expedient." He pointed to a photo of doors at Zwingli's church, the Grossmunster.

Dr. Steele looked from the photo to his brother. "Zwingli takes us to Zurich. But I thought we eliminated the doors, Steven."

"I did too. But we're back to Munch's art."

The monumental Otto Munch bronze works depicted Bible stories on panels in the north portal, and Reformation milestones on the southern doors.

Steven crossed his legs, creating room for spreading files. "We looked at the wrong one. Probably because the south doors aren't as famous. We should've known better. Look at Luther." He tapped a panel.

"A senior moment?" Dr. Steele bent over an image of the south-portal photo enlarged to fuzziness. "You took this? When?"

"Last week."

"What am I looking for?"

"What's he standing in, Stan?"

"A stream, I assume of living water. The Elbe. Wittenberg."

"Study the mountains behind him."

"Why would I . . . mountains behind him? Wittenberg is flat."

"Tell that to Munch."

The steward knocked. Dr. Steele moved papers aside, then peeped under sterling domes. Duo of salmon and crayfish parcel. Cream of pumpkin soup. Roasted stuffed quail with favas. Cheeseboard with homemade chutney and oat crackers. Chocolate lava cake.

After repeatedly assuring the man that hot tea would be fine—"We probably should have wine so we won't stand out as teetotalers in Italy," his brother said wishfully—Dr. Steele plucked a fork with one hand, paper still clasped in the other. He studied the mountains in the photograph and, after attributing the oversight to senility, said he felt stupid.

"Solomon's pillars. Timna." The theologian's face crumpled into a grimace. "Iconic."

Steven pushed away the soup bowl to accept the tea tray before the door closed again. He dissected the quail with clinical precision, buying time to phrase his response. "It was there all along. Somehow, from Zwingli to Munch, we're again tying Luther to Solomon. And water. Parallels your aquatic adventure in Israel last year, doesn't it?"

Neat piles of bird and beans adorned Dr. Steele's plate. He absentmindedly played with his food. "I'm afraid so. I thought it ended on the Temple Mount."

"Could have. Might not have. But the door requires more research," Steven said. "If Munch coded the Luther panel, he might have coded others as well. We'll see where he leads us. I have a hunch." Steven's hunches usually became fact, as did his suspicion decades ago that the brothers could achieve more if believed estranged. "There's not enough online documentation to do this long-distance, and I didn't photograph all the panels."

"Your hunch, brother?" Dr. Steele gazed lovingly at dessert. "Does it have anything to do with where you think we'll end up?"

Steven raised his brows and ate half his cake in one bite. "When I settled there decades ago, we both knew this ended in Venice."

CHAPTER TWENTY-EIGHT

Innsbruck, Austria — Zurich

Steven's car was a pristine 1961 Estate—station wagon—Citroen in larch green, with a white cap. Torpedo lights emerged from the lower edge of the front hood, resembling a crab's stemmed eyeballs. Quirky and uncommon, the vehicle attracted attention.

He was the flamboyant brother.

Dr. Steele ran a quick sweep to ensure it was not rigged with a tracker. He then carefully knelt to peer under the carriage. Given that few eighty-somethings are capable of getting on their knees, anyone hiding a bomb would not have bothered to hide it well.

"If you knew about the sophisticated security system, you wouldn't have bothered," his brother said. He handed Dr. Steele a threadbare lap robe from the back seat and said something about defective heating. "I should've told you before you worked so hard to get down. Sorry."

Dr. Steele prayed that the drive through the Tyrolean Alps, best suited to a sleigh in winter, would be uneventful. Steven kept the car on the road, using every ray of fading light. He navigated sloping turns around frozen lakes beneath frighteningly majestic mountains as his brother declared God's decoration of this sliver of earth overkill. After vehicular skiing for three hours in a westerly direction, punctuated by small talk when necessary, they began the slick slide into the Zurich valley.

"Would you summarize your research?" Dr. Steele poured hot chocolate from the VSOE courtesy thermos, and handed the capful to Steven. "We should review before we get there." Wishing for a cookie, he took the cup back as his brother prepared for another cocoa-curdling turn.

"I made an effort to learn about my new home. In thirty years, I've met neighbors who love Venetian history because their families *made* it. There are references, mostly in private letters loaned for my history of Venice—which I'm not writing—to a decision to withhold Constantinian treasure from the Vatican. Obscure things they didn't think the Pope would miss." He quit talking to slide at three miles an hour. "I know you're aware of some of this."

They had discussed a lot of suspicions.

"Some letters were specific, listing things undocumented elsewhere. The Venetians were proud of their deceit." He shifted for a steep pitch toward Lake Walensee, the last before Lake Zurich. They would parallel these watery fingers for miles.

The Citroen made a grinding sound as Steven downshifted. "Proud to cheat the Pope, whom they despised." Lights appeared, in towns scattered like phytoplankton.

"Did you find the cuneiform tablet on a list?" Dr. Steele asked.

"No. Not a cuneiform. Something called *carved rock*, measuring two by four inches, dated BC 1500." Steven focused on the road as the brothers settled into silence.

...

"The cuneiform. What then?" The Zurich marina was to the right, and Dr. Steele remembered elegant dinner cruises that began and ended there. "Where did it go?" The vineyards to the left, wrapping up and around gentle hills, looked skeletal, like arms and legs splayed on a cross.

"I returned the papers, asking where the family treasures went. Did they still own them? Had they been donated? The matriarch rattled animated answers. Extended branches of the family owned some, others rotated in a museum-loan program. When I asked about odd things, such as this rock, she had no idea." He held out his hand for the drink. "But she mentioned that when a despotic old patriarch had become Doge, some pieces were gifted to dignitaries. The family attributed missing items to his tenure in the powerless, ceremonial position that bankrupted more than one egomaniac and his heirs."

"Luther." Dr. Steele wiggled. Original seat springs were getting intimate by prodding his backside. "When was her relative Doge?"

"Around 1500."

"Perfect timing to support the *rock* passing to Luther in hopes he'd use it to undermine the Church. Luther died in . . . "

"Fifteen-forty-six. I did my homework."

"So the theory holds." Dr. Steele stretched his hands behind his head, reaching toward the tailgate to arch his back. "Solomon to Venice to Luther." He groaned.

"But there's something else. When I scanned Vatican documents, I started reading about a similar tablet. They keep a pretty thorough register in the vaults, and I . . . "

"*You* were in the Vaults?" *No one got into the Vatican Vaults!* "Really? What I'd give to spend a week in those vaults."

"Focus, Stan. And it would be a Faustian bargain. I've been curating for the past few years, although I don't know why they need me. You'd be amazed at the world-class antiquarians wearing vestments. Nonetheless, Venice is small. Once you're known, a lot of doors open. But yes. I was briefly in the Vaults. And the Library, if you really want to hurt."

His brother sighed. "The Papal Library. Sin. I'm jealous. Take me now, Lord."

"What I am trying to say is they keep a register. Someone in the Vatican is looking for this cuneiform. Has been for years. Actually—" he paused, tapping his fingers on the wheel as if counting "—about since the time they started using my services."

"Neither you nor I believe in coincidence," Dr. Steele said, reading Steven's mind.

They were quiet until Zurich proper. Although the hotel offered complimentary valet, the vehicle was so memorable they stopped in a corner of a nearby car park. Using a sheet from the trunk, they covered the car after tucking it between concrete pillars.

"Who is it?" Dr. Steele stepped to the stairs, analyzing the blob. He decided the shape was undoubtedly Citroen, but the opaque cover should buy time. "Looking for the cuneiform."

"A Monsignor Pietro Agnelli. I asked around. He's dabbled. Never trading. Attending shows and receptions. Mingling, asking questions. For five years. Most consider him a professional snoop. But he's interested in cuneiforms and scrolls. I think he's trouble."

Interesting, Dr. Steele thought as they walked toward the bright Altstadt sign four short blocks ahead. The Zwingli statue and Limmet River were behind to the left, the twin towers of the Grossmunster three blocks northwest.

"What does the good monsignor do in the Vatican?" Dr. Steele asked. They approached the hotel in a night so cold it ignited arthritis in his knees, and he reminded himself this was not the time to feel old.

Dr. Steele braced as Steven's brow wrinkled, and he cut his eyes to his brother.

"Vatican Bank. Understands the value of things. Is undoubtedly immersed in fraternal intrigue." Steven jerked his shoulder upward to settle the backpack over his spine, but did not move toward the door leading to hotel reception. "They all are engaged in intrigue, and he's looking for you, asking questions."

The theologian peered at the dark sky. "I was hoping to visit the Grossmunster tomorrow. After a good night's sleep." He paused at the base of the steps, then walked past Steven toward the cathedral. "My flashlight can show us those door panels right now."

CHAPTER TWENTY-NINE

The Grossmunster, Zurich

Even in the dark, Dr. Steele could see the doors were gone. "I refuse to believe these are missing because of us," he said to Steven, who resembled Methuselah.

The theologian hobbled up seven demilune treads to the portal, peered at the Alpha and Omega reference—*Revelation 1:8*—carved into arches high above his short self, and confirmed they were in the right place. The second time he made the trek, he believed what he saw. The architecture was as it should be, except Munch's Reformation doors were missing.

"They were here last week." Steven plopped onto a snow-covered rock wall, and slumped.

"Most poorly timed restoration in church history." Dr. Steele leaned against a doorframe, losing the battle of denial to fatigue, muttering. "We can't break into wherever they are . . . "

"We could've in the old days," his brother said.

"Even if we had time to find them. Is there a photo of the Reformation panels? I couldn't find a clear one using obscure academic databases from the seminary."

"I didn't think to photograph the entire doors." Steven's voice rose defensively.

THE BROTHERS' KEEPERS

"Who'd have thought they'd vanish? Now what?"

They helped each other down the steps and around the end of the building, toward slope and street. Limp, age, and hour compromised a safe descent, so they moved cautiously to the hotel. The twin towers of the church were Zurich's most famous landmark, and they shot like festive bottle rockets piercing navy sky. Mocking the siblings' depression.

"Getting old stinks." Dr. Steele spoke for both. His mouth tasted like stale chocolate, and he realized there was a reason cocoa, unlike wine, was not marketed as improving with age. "But it's reality." He straightened himself. "Sleep. Be out before dawn. With missing doors, we're going to have to work harder to follow a five-hundred-year-old trail. We need to respect our physical limitations."

"I feel like Joshua."

"What?"

"You know. Armed with a trumpet, trying to conquer Jericho."

"Well, he did it, didn't he?"

"Sure. But I don't feel lucky."

"You don't need luck. You need God."

"Well, He's not telling me where to go next."

Dr. Steele sighed, unwilling to launch a theological discussion on a hellish night. "We can't stop now. Out by five? Cyril might not miss us yet, but between now and then, he'll start looking." Resettling the too-large fedora on his head, he walked a few paces before pausing. "'Here I stand. I can do no more.'"

They made the last left, and would cross the Altstadt threshold in moments.

"Luther at the Diet of Worms?" Steven guessed. "I'm not too good on his quotes."

His brother pulled the hat lower, obscuring their resemblance and preventing the hat from blowing into Limmet. He kept his head down, and shuffled. "Unless you're ready to gamble on Venice, it's the best guess I have. Or at least that's what God just told me."

DAY SIX
CHAPTER THIRTY

Ca Sagredo

Grace

Maggie and I rose with the sun. From our rooms, we walked a hundred steps right on Strada Nuova, to Pasticceria Bar Martini di Palombella Lorenzo, to purchase breakfast.

"A neighborhood pastry shop owned by Lorenzo, who liked stiff drinks and had a girlfriend he called Beautiful Dove." I had the Simples, a genetic predisposition to giggle stupidly under stress, so I quoted Ferdinand Foch. "'We're surrounded. That simplifies the problem.'"

"Spare me French military history," she complained. "And your barmy Italian translations." Sniffing, she continued in her role as Little Miss Sunshine. "Venice always smells moldy."

"Not in a pastry shop." I waited for another revelation. With none forthcoming, I decided to explain things to her. "It's *sinking*. Have you noticed the bridges? The water? You know—hydrology impacting a city built on piers stuck into the sandy bottom of a lagoon?"

She poked me, and moments later, we returned to Ca' Sagredo arm-in-arm, our free limbs clutching bags of carby goodness. We brewed tea, a twenty-five-year mother-daughter ritual. When the others joined us in the steel-and-glass kitchen, Mark and Jeff assaulted the espresso maker, determined to unleash its nectar.

We heard him coming.

"I don't care where they are. I don't care how they did it. *Find them.*" Cyril, cell phone plastered against his left ear, burst through the door. He snorted. "They're gone."

"Yes, commander." Jeff, maniacally caffeine-deprived, did not abandon his two-fisted grip on the machine. "You shared that gem yesterday." The contraption spit viscous grounds on his sleeves and the counter as he said something offensive.

"No. They're *totally* gone. Even I don't know where they are." Cyril's shoulders hunched forward and his brows were flat. I put my hand on Mark's in hopes of keeping him seated. Almost gagged as burning-coffee smoke enveloped the utilitarian space. Becca rushed to open a window.

"Meaning you did yesterday? How do you know they're gone?" Maggie sipped her French Breakfast tea, admirably combining suspicion and innocence. "More mold," she said under her breath as she wiped a tissue beneath her nose.

"The car I left for them hasn't moved." He lifted his chin, and reminded me of a Pekinese with an under-bite. "Be ready to leave when I find where they went." The chair he upset clattered off the floor and against a tile wall. "I expect within the hour."

"Wonderful," Jeff said. "Can't freakin' wait."

"He doesn't have a clue," Maggie said to the slamming door.

"He's a jerk," Cliff said. "Why do we need him? Can't we find them ourselves?"

"He represents one of the world's most sophisticated intelligence agencies. Add that to what we bring to the table . . . " Mark trailed off, shrugging.

"CIA, MI6." Jeff extracted a thimble of espresso from two cups of grounds. "Even BBC."

I wondered about his central nervous system. We might need to do an intervention someday. Before I could suggest it, he turned to Cliff.

"Your affiliation?" Jeff asked.

"Unattached," was Cliff's immediate rely.

Maggie arched an eyebrow. "And likely to stay that way if you don't explain yourself. I don't understand why you keep popping up."

He ignored her, surely a deal-breaking mistake, until Jeff responded. "Add Mossad to what Dad, Becca, and I access, and we should be ahead of everyone. Jerk or not, he's valuable. 'Keep your enemies close . . . '" He picked through *brioches* and *bombolones*—small croissants and doughnuts. Venetians ate light, sweet breakfasts. Ranch eggs were not an option. "And we need to keep watch on him because information from Bermondsey has never been wrong." He talked in circles in case of bugs.

"Speaking of which?" I began.

Mark glanced at me, using the telepathy created by decades of marriage to indicate this wasn't the time to prod Jeff, or share news of my clandestine work. "I think he's of more use to us than he is a pain. Although I'll grant he could have ulterior motives."

Maggie cocked an eyebrow when she saw the glance between us. "Mama and I have things to tell you," she said. Everyone focused on her even though I knew she would question me later. She typed on her tablet, and slid it to the center of the table.

> *We think we know what's going on.*

She pulled dark blonde hair into a ponytail and slid a hair band down her wrist to contain the heavy waves.

"Do tell," Mark requested as he brewed a cup of espresso. Jeff growled. She typed again.

> *Obviously, they're after Luther. That means north, probably Germany.*

She picked a tangerine from the platter. Pinched the peel so the citrus scent cut Jeff's burning grounds and diluted the odor from the Rialto, where the morning catch was being unloaded.

"Becca." Mark drew his phone from his pocket, and held up a finger for Maggie to wait. He and Becca texted requests for passenger manifests from German-bound trains and planes.

I reached for the tablet.

> *I'd add Switzerland. Look beyond Luther. Reformers communicated—well documented—to spread the revolution. Zwingli, Calvin, Bullinger. All <u>Swiss</u> Reformers. At least two wrote to and met with Luther.*

Mark and Becca added Switzerland. Cliff reached for the tablet.

Won't Mossad be doing the same thing? Checking?

He poured hot water into Maggie's teapot. She offered a scant nod of thanks, still irritated by his refusal to talk about his intelligence affiliation. Dropping another muslin-wrapped bag tea into the steaming pot, she took the tablet from Becca.

> *They've probably already reviewed the manifests. We shouldn't forget those agencies Jeff says are tailing everyone and everything. Particularly the Middle Eastern corps.*

Dr. Merrit entered standing straight. Jeff jumped to get an espresso for him, and Becca handed him the tablet to review. After reading, he typed.

> *I want Flately to meet us wherever we end up. We need him.*

I nodded. He was part of the group that helped stop the water theft in Israel. And Spigot, the organization behind it. I still unearthed mission shenanigans through Jeff and Mark. With the addition of Dr. Flately, we became an unconventional assault team. *That* thought thrilled me to pieces.

"I'd like to continue. We probably don't have much time." Maggie scratched her neck, an ill-bred habit that made me frown. "Mama's right. We can't just focus on you-know-who yet. Matthew . . . "

"Is AWOL," Cliff said happily, but unhelpfully, to the woman he loved. "MIA. I ask again, can we trust him?"

Maggie grabbed the tablet.

> *He broke through firewalls in Dr. Steele's e-mail accounts. The crafty old fellow had several. In one, we found he and Steven have worked on this cuneiform thing for years. They are, to use one of his favorite phrases, 'in cahoots.'*

No one responded, so she let the information sink in before continuing to type.

> *We should assume this is not a kidnapping. From the e-mails, they were never estranged.*

"I object to the word *cahoots*," Dr. Merrit asserted, forgetting our careful use of technology to avoid being overheard. He looked at her in a way that forced doctoral students under desks. Realizing what he had done by speaking, he took the tablet.

> *And what about Steven holding a gun to his brother's head?*

"Dr. Merrit." Her tone was patient, and I wondered if I could prevent two of my favorite people getting crossways. "I am not casting aspersions." It was her turn to type.

I believe he has noble reasons for wanting us to think he's been kidnapped. And my bet is the gun wasn't loaded. We are certain of our facts, sir. I think in ways we don't understand, Dr. Steele and Steven's careers have been symbiotic.

"Grace?" He needed confirmation, and looked at me.

I paused. "I love them both, Dr. Merrit, but don't think Maggie would make these statements without excellent reasons. The documents seem conclusive."

He reluctantly nodded at Maggie to continue.

I believe, and Mama does too, the brothers know a lot more than we do, including the location of the rest of the scroll. They at least have a strong hunch, which is driving their flight. I think they're tying up loose ends in their theory, hitting some of Luther's historic locations . . .

"And possibly other sites," I added.

"To follow the trail. With us *safely*—" she looked at Dr. Merrit "—twiddling thumbs as they chase the thing. Possibly getting killed in the process."

"But how do we know where to go?" Becca asked. "Can we whittle enough locations down to split up if necessary?"

I held out my hand for the tablet.

I do not want to split up, and we need to pack because Cyril will explode here soon. Three possibilities: Wittenberg for Luther. Zurich for Zwingli,

> since their correspondence is well documented. Bullinger was there too, but later. He's less likely. Geneva for Calvin. There are lesser sites, relating to Luther in Germany. But I'd start with these three. Wittenberg, Zurich, and Geneva. In that order.

A group of children must have gathered outside because whoops and racket filtered from the passageway. Jeff walked to the window, then handled his phone as he surveyed the Calle D'Oro. We overlooked an alley to the Line One waterbus and *vaporetto* stop. He moved the lace curtain an inch left and right. I assumed he tried not to disturb us as he motioned for his dad.

"So do we take off without him?" Cliff asked, referring to Cyril. "Or is it wiser to wait to see what he comes up with?"

"I'd vote for the latter," Becca said.

Jeff inspected the cabinet contents, retrieved a can of cashews, and took the tablet.

> *I agree, but my sources say two gentlemen matching the Steeles' description boarded the Orient Express to Paris yesterday, getting off in Innsbruck. Can you make sense of that?*

Mark stood behind me, his hand on my shoulder. "I'll pull up a map."

"No need," I said, on the familiar ground of church history. I took the tablet.

> *If they got off in Innsbruck, they're deliberately trying to lose us. Nothing happened there—the*

> *Austrians ate strudel and waltzed through the Reformation. My bet is Zurich, loaded with relevant history, and close. An easy connection, then westward. Can you see if they boarded a train to Zurich? I'd go there.*

Jeff slid the nuts into a zip-lock bag, and I decided he was a squirrel. "Better hurry. Cyril entered the building with Matthew in tow. Neither looked happy," he said, pocketing his lunch.

...

Mossad entered a kitchen reeking of coffee—some burned—and baked goods. My daughter-in-law dunked a doughnut. My son rhapsodized about cardamom-infused Turkish brews. My daughter nibbled a tiny croissant laden with tablespoons of chunky apricot jam that drained down her hand in a near-steady stream. I hid the narrow tablet under my womanly thighs.

"Any news?" Mark asked.

Cyril accosted the espresso machine, splashing now-thick liquid into a bar glass. No one stopped him before he gulped it down. And choked.

He cleared gummy grounds from his throat with a gravelly grind. "We believe they're heading north. Germany. Luther. They were at the train station yesterday, poorly disguised." His manner was more abrupt than earlier, something I would have guessed impossible.

I chose not to mention they were disguised well enough to escape Mossad. "Which train?" I asked.

"Innsbruck."

Merrit offered a pastry, which the commander dismissed with a rude cut of his hand.

"So we head there?" Jeff took his cup to the sink.

"You do. I've been called to Jerusalem. Matthew will accompany you."

"He isn't needed, you know," Cliff replied too quickly. "We can handle this ourselves and keep in touch."

Matthew wisely stayed out of the discussion. Jeff's shoulders bounced.

"If Matthew's with you, I can send aid. He stays." Cyril turned to his assistant. "You know what to do and how to reach me. I want to hear from you every couple of hours. Find the Steeles." He left, much to our delight.

I was afraid someone would applaud. "Doughnut?" I passed the platter to the young man no one fully trusted. He declined.

"We're going north by train. We leave in forty-five minutes, so please get your things and meet at the waiting water taxi. Five minutes?" He spoke formally, avoiding eye contact. Did he believe he was in command? Before I could correct his misconception, Maggie did.

"Ten at least." She rose slowly, her eyes never leaving his face.

...

Mark closed the door. "That's weird," he said, throwing clothes into his tooled leather bag, then holding it open for my excess. "What do you think's going on?"

I dropped the last rolled sweater into my orange nylon carry-on. "You felt it too? Maybe Hamas is bombing the North again. Or rebels are flooding in from Damascus. What did Jeff want you to see out the window?"

Mark wheeled both bags to the door. "A priest."

"Jeff is finding religion?" I teased. Although my kids were believers, they wrestled with the mystic parts of Christianity, such as the virgin birth and Christ's dry stroll across the Sea of Galilee. I kept explaining these events were why it's called *faith*. "What's up with the priest?"

He held me tightly, I hoped to be a romantic fool. He really just wanted to whisper in my ear so no one could hear. "He thinks the guy's been following us. Says he saw him in Madaba." He kissed the top of my head. "I questioned him pretty hard, but with Jeff's memory, I believe him. We're checking to see if we can track him. He got a decent photo."

He rocked me in a country two-step, humming an off-key Waylon Jennings' waltz. "Most priests in Venice are old enough to be on a first-name basis with Saint Pete. This one was young. He leaned against the wall, not moving toward the vaporetto or waterbus. Priests always have things to do. They don't *dawdle*. At least not in public."

"Talk to Maggie at the end of this dance. Remember—" I whispered "—'the red shoes and the lion that roared at them'? Maybe we don't have all her story yet. Can we find secure seats on the train?"

He kissed my forehead before letting go. "If Mossad hasn't requisitioned the entire thing."

"They're known for subtlety." I stopped him with my hand on his arm, and stood on tiptoe to kiss his stubbly cheek. "Do you have any idea where this will lead?"

He rested his chin on my head, hugging me. "No, Gracie. But I think we need to hurry and find those brothers."

CHAPTER THIRTY-ONE

Venice

Grace

We met Maggie in the hallway. She was packed before we picked up breakfast, so her ten-minute delay made a point.

"*By the way of deception, thou shalt do war,*" she said as the elevator dropped.

"Mossad." I was familiar with their motto.

"We need to distrust everyone outside of our gene pool. Becca excepted."

Mark looked at her. "What about Cliff and the theologians?"

"Trust no one," she replied firmly.

"You know something we don't, baby?" I asked. She was unusually agitated.

"No. But I've never been this uneasy." Given her work in some of the most dangerous places on the planet, her instinct was good enough for me. "You remember the GPR—ground-penetrating radar—Israel used to stumble on the filling cisterns last year? They have a trove of unclassified data. Without contacts, it's buried under layers of bureaucracy. Matthew easily helped me access it. Which makes me wonder even more about his role."

The unspoken comment was that she was wondering about *him*.

We were last to board. The ten-minute trip to the station took five because we ignored a speed limit set to prevent water from lapping onto terraces and docks of hotels and *palazzos*. Matthew led to a Eurostar City train—*frecciabianca*—to Milan. He told us we would change to a tilting train—*pendalino*—to speed along angled track over the Gotthard Pass. Given their reputation for breaking down mid-journey, I hoped we made it to wherever we headed, and decided to ask where that was.

"What's our destination, Matthew?"

He acted as if he didn't hear me.

We entered an almost-empty Car One, a first-class cabin. Mark grumbled about rudeness. Our seats were in the middle, three on each side of a central aisle. Four casually dressed men sat two rows in front and back of our seats. Luggage and freight covered the row between. I glanced at Mark, and he mouthed *Mossad*.

Passengers moved through the railcar, attempting to occupy open seats. Europeans were determined to beat the system by sitting in a better class than the tickets they purchased. I had never seen an official question seating, but today, a steward greeted—*intercepted*—passengers, checked seating assignments, and ushered people to other cars.

I tapped Maggie's arm before she could sit with Becca and Jeff, who watched something on the platform. "Join your dad and me?"

"What is it, Mama?"

With our heads close, I spoke softly so the passing parade of aspiring first-class passengers holding second- and third-class tickets couldn't overhear. "How do the Red Shoes tie into this thing? Your dad said Jeff spotted a priest he thinks has followed us since Madaba. He was standing across the Calle D'Oro this morning."

The train eased smoothly through the industrial park. Jeff and Becca whispered, and he glanced our direction. He motioned for Mark, who crossed the aisle. They pressed noses on a window, craning their necks to look toward the caboose.

Maggie fiddled with her iPod. "There's a guy at the Vatican looking for the cuneiform and scroll. My original reference, in the note, was about the scroll withheld from loot Venice used to lift a ban. The Vatican is involved somehow. Or at least this guy keeps popping up."

"Do you know who he is? Or anything about him? What he looks like?"

"Agnelli. He attends conferences, a geezer in a collar."

"But he's old? Because the man on the Calle was young."

"Definitely old. But young priests work with old priests. So don't discount a young one. Or that he and Agnelli are connected."

We rode, accompanied by James Taylor through Maggie's ear buds. I tugged one out. "Why is he creepy?" Her well-developed ability to spot creeps was an asset for a beautiful young woman.

"Honestly, his facade is working-class, which has probably limited him in an organization that values good looks as much as the Vatican. Remember the Swiss Guard criterion for handsomeness? Everything about him is beige. Hair, eyes, skin. Teeth, even. He's not the stereotypic kind-old-man cleric, but an aggressive persona curbed by a collar. Street tough."

Mark moved behind us in time to hear her last words, relocating a pile of luggage to lean up. "The priest boarded. The good father tried to travel with us, but was sent to the far end of second class. Definitely being followed by a guy in robes." He sat back.

We crossed the milky finger of the Laguna Veneta, where it turned aquamarine as it bled toward the Adriatic. Rolled onto the sunbaked mainland, building speed toward Milan.

I worried about our findings in Zurich. Tried to dissect the wily Steele brothers. Prayed for safety. Practiced Lamaze breathing to calm myself. Glanced at red-tile Mediterranean roofs. Ignored Mossad's burly presence.

I needed a good book to distract me. It wasn't destined to be a light-reading day.

The explosion rocked the train. Screaming metal-on-metal overwhelmed everything. I thought it would never stop. Maggie pitched onto me. We tumbled into the floor between seats. Jeff *thudded* across the aisle. Ugaritic from a four-thousand-year-old bathroom wall spewed from his mouth as he articulated my thoughts. Becca grazed her cheekbone on a lightly padded armrest.

Our carriage leaned precariously. Skewed like a teeter-totter across electrified tracks. The end of the train was an inferno. Black smoke billowed past our windows. Obscured my vision. When the cacophony stopped, the screams began.

Tomorrow, papers would report a young priest among the dead. Mossad said his cell detonated with a call from a burn phone in Vatican City.

CHAPTER THIRTY-TWO

Mestre, Italy — Switzerland

Grace

The dwarf-sized red hammer I yanked from beneath the window had been only one object shattering glass. Suitcases and duffels were mounded against the far wall of the car, having broken windows by bouncing off of them. Matthew's call was outbound before the keel of warping metal drowned shouts of instruction.

Our fellow travelers—confirmed as Mossad from their heroics—smashed shards from the frames. They eased over and out, and dropped to the ground at Mestre, the mainland closest to Venice, and where her airport is located. Mindful of the imbalanced car, they moved delicately. Coats over lower window edges ensured we didn't scrape, while strong arms helped me—age before beauty—Maggie, and Becca, then the men, from the railcar.

Window to earth was an eight-foot drop, and sod rolled another two feet down from the raised tracks creating an unreasonably small target. My leap was a prayer-powered act of faith, even though I flapped my arms until two strong Mossad agents placed my feet on crunching pebbles.

Once stable, I ensured we were unharmed. Mentally, I had gone off the tracks in a wadi somewhere in north-central Israel last year.

The most difficult extraction was Dr. Merrit, who insisted on going last. When it became apparent he wasn't leaving until everyone was safe, we preserved his dignity. I tried not to watch as he stepped down a staircase of agent bodies, helped on both sides by Jeff, Cliff, and Mark. Our security detail returned for luggage before anyone arrived to prevent it.

I tried not to breathe chemical-laden smoke, and ignored bodies charred beyond recognition two hundred yards away. All total, our extraction from the train took almost an hour.

Cliff insisted we move from the wreckage, and a possible second explosion. Our guards told Mark and Jeff to stay put, so Mark paced while Jeff stared toward the still-active inferno. Both men were temperamentally predisposed to help.

Emergency vehicles took another half hour to reach the train. Two-note sirens grew louder, their high-low tones blending with the escalating cries and sizzles. Flashing lights pinpointed the ambulances and police as they threaded the rugged railway embankment.

A gale shifting from the Italian Alps pulled heavy fumes from us to the south, shrouding the scene. I thanked God for His windy breath of kindness, and turned from the carnage. I gazed up the tracks. The easement, a red-poppy zipper in late spring, was littered with debris. Becca and Maggie trailed me as I walked to a rock propping a distorted pine seventy-five feet north, toward Switzerland. Looking back at the young women, I wondered where I could find ice for a bruise on Becca's face.

The ridiculous thought didn't disguise my certainty that the bomb was intended for us.

"Alternative transport is on its way." Matthew zipped his phone in the vertical pocket of his down jacket, then walked to an officer heading to us. They consulted, and he returned. "Our statements will be handled by Mossad. We're clear to leave.

...

Umbrian hill towns look easy to breech from a Eurocopter EC635, their defensive postures weakened by an eagle's perspective and my late-in-life espionage experiences. I knew every wall could be scaled with determination and the right equipment.

We swerved toward Zurich in two black transport aircraft. Avalanches clung to each north-facing slope. Headphones, which I was unsure how to operate without conversing with everyone aboard and possibly on the ground, protected my ears from rotor noise. I gazed at the landscape, and heard we clipped the northwest corner of Liechtenstein before slipping into Swiss airspace.

I wanted to run away. *Would it be wrong to abandon Dr. Steele since he had deceived us? Why weren't professionals handling this mission?* I walked the happy trail of rationalization and denial, and wallowed in self-pity fueled by fear.

I reminded myself Mark was a retired professional, as were Dr. Steele and Cyril. Becca was retooling, while Matthew and, we all suspected, Cliff, were active. Jeff had yet to share his experiences, but they appeared significant.

Only Maggie and I were amateurs, and she had to be at least half-crazy because of risks she took in her work. The question was, did *I* want to help? I was outnumbered, so resigned myself to volley between snow-capped peaks, gazing at God's creation. Airsick.

We arrived in Zurich on a crystalline day around noon. The word for it was *pure*. Given our activities, we were not. Matthew removed his headset, and wrapped adapter wires round ear covers the moment wheels touched ground at Zurich-Kloten Airport.

"A team is meeting us," he said as he unbuckled his harness.

The airport, seven miles north of town, was not surrounded by anything that would divert gusts from Lake Zurich. The moment the doors opened, icy wind barreled into the cabin, whipped unrestrained hair, and flapped unzipped puffer coats that were quickly secured. Matthew leapt to the tarmac with ease, demonstrating the athleticism that enabled his wadi jump after I shot Maggie's kidnapper in Israel.

He turned to us as guards unloaded the cargo bay. "The Steeles were here last night, although we're unable to find them now. I would like to sweep through spots they visited . . . "

"Grossmunster." I couldn't stop myself in time.

Matthew raised his eyebrows. "Yes, Dr. Madison. Grossmunster. How did you know?"

"It's where I would have gone," I replied truthfully, although I wanted to lie as a matter of principle.

"Why?" His question meant our good relationship had evaporated, and he was now as wary of me as we were of him. "What's at the Grossmunster?"

I thought before replying. Familial eyes burnt a hole in my back. "History," I replied. I stood in the chopper doorway, one arm reaching to each side of the opening, looking as if I were about to do a skydiving free fall five feet to the cement. Face first, of course. A Mossad guard set a metal ladder at my feet, and offered his hand. I glared at Matthew, whose impeccable manners failed him as a four-car caravan sped to us.

"*What* history?" Matthew didn't move.

"*My* history, Matthew. As a Gentile, Protestant Christian. If you can't figure it out, then you and Mossad need to research."

I walked to a vehicle—the middle one for safety—and climbed into the back seat, breathing fir-scented wind I hoped would cure airsickness. Maggie followed, while Mark walked to the other side, sandwiching me in.

Maggie nudged and whispered. "Well done. He deserved that."

Mark's elbow poked my other side. "I'm sorry I wasn't ahead of you. I would've helped you out."

I squeezed his hand as an alarming thought invaded my head. *Could we not trust anyone?*

CHAPTER THIRTY-THREE

Zurich — Worms, Germany

His brother could not drive a canvas-covered car. Dr. Steele would like him to have tried. The Citroen was a Babe Magnet.

Before leaving the car park, two young women and someone of undeterminable gender with a nickel-sized green cork in a hairy earlobe approached the brothers with admiring questions.

"Just don't stop again," Dr. Steele instructed Steven, who enjoyed the attention. A lovely girl wearing a mini skirt turned from her car, smiling at them. "We are invisible."

Less than fifteen minutes later, after winding through the Old City of Zurich and almost flattening a dozen pedestrians and three moseying swans, the brothers turned north toward Worms. Despite generations of sophomoric jokes, it was pronounced *Verms*.

Steven worked with the heater until the smell of warm electrical wires filled the car. "North on eight, west on six, ending in Worms after a left south of Nuremburg. Less than three hundred fifty miles, but a full day. Especially in winter. Even on the Autobahn."

"Have a fire extinguisher?" Dr. Steele asked as he sniffed, and reached for lap robes while praying for no obstacles—feathered, furred, or frauleined—and no embers.

The German road system, a wonderland of petrol stations and restaurants built into bridges suspended above highways, was an efficient infrastructure for voyeuristic observation by *der grobe Bruder*—Big Brother. They would be seen.

"Anything caffeinated in that thermos?" Steven asked.

Dr. Steele retrieved the Orient Express freebie thermos, filled with coffee two shops north of the Aldstadt, where they also bought bread, cheese, and jam for a traditional breakfast. Propped between uncooperative knees still battling shrapnel from an arthritic flare, caffeine access was a production. He longed for a Spanish omelet, unscrewed the lid, breathed coffee that fogged his glasses and left his skin damp, poured a cup for Steven, and offered advice.

"Mindful of our age, I would suggest limiting caffeine until Worms. It necessitates frequent rest stops, as does scatterbrained driving. Coffee is a diuretic. Try to keep us on the road, Mario."

Then the cup slipped. Although most of its contents landed on a blanket, enough hit Steven's jeans to merit a quick left cut into a service station. Vehicles scattered like minnows during the wet-road maneuver, and a silver Renault mirrored their three-lane, suicidal dart.

"You okay?" Dr. Steele asked in a voice shaking more vigorously than usual.

Steven stood in a persistent snizzle—snowy drizzle—and shook the blanket. "Fine." He dusted his pants and glanced around, indicating he had seen the car follow them. It sat on the far side of the fuel pumps, engine running. "Company so soon? Mossad?"

"Who else?" Dr. Steele thought it could be quite a few people, but would not share this opinion yet. "Change of plans?"

"I don't think so. But we *are* alone. Is that wise? Honestly, I thought we'd have a little more time." Steven gunned the car into the traffic as one wiper blade made the seesawing sound of a child's first session on a violin.

"Cyril's one day faster than I thought he'd be," Dr. Steele said as he handed his brother a half-cup. Worse people than Cyril could be in that sedan. The Madisons would require a couple of cars or a minivan.

They streaked through southeast Germany. Bavarian topography was heavily wooded, craggy mountains settling into hillocks subdued by the meticulous German mind-set. After Bavaria, they moved west into the Rhineland, toward Heidelberg. Wine-country pruning created wildly absurd topiaries.

Hunting stands, everything from slabs of timber riddled with bullet holes to an elegantly constructed mini-*haus* on stilts with glass windows, peppered the landscape. Fields not committed to grapes were neatly fenced or designated by clipped rows of trees. Towers, mostly hidden by groves, alluded to power and wealth. The winter landscape was post-apocalyptic.

The sedan followed. They acted unaware. When they stopped for gas or to stretch, it stopped. But no one ever left the vehicle. Unless it had an extra tank, it would require filling before Worms, and Dr. Steele expressed this thought to Steven. Their last turn north, for a twenty-two-mile jaunt, was less than a kilometer away.

"I'm inclined to run until it has to stop, even if that means a scenic tour of the countryside between Heidelberg and Worms. Those Renaults can get forty miles to the gallon." Steven pushed the Citroen, which purred loudly at higher speed. "We'll have to fuel once more, but can wait until north of Heidelberg. Any thoughts as to what's going on?"

His brother nodded. "The Cyril group, which includes the Madisons, would have stopped us long ago. Cyril would confront us, and Grace would lecture about foolhardiness. They would also require a larger vehicle. The person in the sedan wants to see where we're going and, at this point, doesn't mean us harm. We're followed for information. Which means it's whomever else is after the scroll."

"You know, multiple groups might be after it." Steven drove aggressively and evasively as the sedan struggled to keep up.

"I suspect we'll know soon enough. Where do you think it is in Venice?"

"St. Mark's Square. A stone's throw from Antico Privato."

"Why?"

Steven, acting professionally schooled in vehicular matters, navigated a congested pod. "Because that's the best place to hide it." He swung into a convenience stop, between petrol and diesel banks. The sedan pulled to the far side again, its driver pumping fuel at last. "I've always thought it was there, but getting to it wasn't worth the risk until this venture confirmed the spot.

"I'm going to take care of the car. Why don't you see what you can find out about our friend over there? Your tweeds look more harmless than my biker jacket." Grinning at his jibe, he popped the gas cap, and stretched broadly.

Dr. Steele hoped his inflamed knees would go the distance. To his brother's surprise, he walked straight to the sedan. "Hello, my friend. I see you've been with us since Zurich. May I help you?"

The driver squirted fuel on the rear quarter panel of the car, and rammed the nozzle in the tank opening. Dr. Steele engaged a novice at the spy game, an observation that generated another thought.

The young man was immaculately clean cut, simply dressed, and refined. Dark hair and eyes punctuated an olive complexion deepening the longer the men stared at each other. His appearance supported the theologian's suspicion. He muttered something in Italian, then corrected to German, and essentially told the elderly gent to buzz off. Dr. Steele could not resist the urge to bid him a good day—in seven languages, one after the other, before returning to the Citroen.

"Bold move, Stan."

The theologian babied his knees by carefully folding into his seat. Their pursuer rushed to replace the nozzle, cap the tank, and follow. Steven was not going to make it easy. He gunned the Citroen, which roared onto the Autobahn. He circled, returning to the far side of the station as the sedan shot northbound in the direction Steven first took.

"You have a strong sin nature, don't you?" Dr. Steele chuckled, and massaged his knees. Steven grinned manically. "He's an Italian cleric, Steven."

"How do you know?"

"In this business for decades, you know how to spot a cleric. And he has the accent. Do you really want the details?"

He nodded.

"Okay, but first is there any way we can lose your wheels? We are beyond obvious in this noteworthy machine."

At some point, the young man would wise up and return, so they needed an unrecognizable replacement vehicle. They entered the highway toward Worms while Steven listened to his brother explain the man's vocation.

"He's frail and excessively neat. His hair was trimmed within an inch of its life. He was pale, indicating academia. A slight tan line appeared above where his collar normally rides. The leather cord around his neck meant a wooden cross at the bottom. Given his coloring, I'd say Italian, which is also the language he spoke before correcting to German."

They barreled off an exit ramp and into a roundabout. "You thinking Agnelli?" Steven asked as he wheeled under the Autobahn.

They crisscrossed rapeseed fields flooding the German economy with Euros, and whose seeds invade agriculture in surrounding countries. Rapeseed yields canola oil.

"What's the deal with Germans always conquering other lands, even if by agriculture?" Dr. Steele asked before answering Steven's question. "No. Not Agnelli. Agnelli sounds seasoned, and this young man made a silly mistake by getting caught and speaking Italian. If I'm right and he's Vatican, he's in for a hard time when he returns empty handed."

They arrived in Worms in minutes. Steven knew where he was going, although his brother could have directed him. They approached the city center, a small area with a good drug store—not again—excellent restaurants, and clothing shops. The Reformation statue dominated a park at one end of a pedestrian zone, but Steven pulled into an alley to park in a garage with open doors.

Dr. Steele tapped his shoulder. "Okay. What?"

Steven turned off the engine and reached into the back seat for his jacket. "Let's hit the statue, see what we can discover, grab some food, and press on. I'm uncomfortable about the guy in the sedan. Not to mention Cyril and Mossad."

"But your car. We can't just leave it in someone's garage."

"Why not? At our ages, we can say we got the wrong house. Anybody would believe that. We can return for it if we don't find a better option. I think we should hurry, though."

...

The square used for *al fresco* dining was empty in sprinkling snow. On their way back toward the Citroen, they would swing through the cafe for savory pastries and coffee. Dr. Steele saw the glass displays still contained breakfast baked goods.

The piercing *Lutherdenkmal* dominated the view forty yards ahead. Bronze statues formed a spiky crown around the figure of a standing Martin Luther. Frederick the Wise of Saxony and Philip of Hesse, important political players in the turbulent Reformation scene, stood front and center, while Reuchlin, Melanchthon, Waldo, Wycliffe, Hus, and Savonarola completed the well-dressed party at Luther's feet. The edifice was a Reformation "who's who" on the site of the long-demolished Town Hall.

A tour bus disgorged between the brothers and the statue, and the Steeles crossed diagonally to arrive first. Both knew the guide would gather her flock, orient, then lead—if they were lucky—to a pre-arranged meal. Unfortunately, they heard the group would look at the statue first, then dine on schnitzel and potatoes.

The park was wedged into a strolling zone to the south, and shops and residences to the east. Beyond the park and through leafless limbs, the Bishop's Palace, where Luther's plaque lay in the garden, was abandoned. He uttered, "Here I stand. I can do no other" there.

Steven was up the steps, peering at Luther. Thirty Americans discussed staying warm as they approached the monument, and their comments indicated they were Minnesota Lutherans hardy enough to withstand forlorn weather.

Steven straightened to look at his brother, whose face indicated he had not found anything either. The Lutherans gathered at the statue base for a lecture, then started up the steps as the brothers descended the right side.

"Ideas?" Steven tipped his beret at a lovely old lady who twinkled at him. Dr. Steele touched the front lip of the fedora.

"Not the ones you're having." The theologian tugged his brother toward Luther's plaque. "I want to check the Bishop's yard, then we can leave. Try not to be obvious, Don Juan. We're hiding, remember?"

On the last turn in a three-block walk, a shot blew out the street light nearest them. They ran—a speedy amble—across the street and into the oldest Jewish cemetery in Europe.

Steven breathed so hard that he could not smell anything, and he mentioned his nasal cavities were frozen. "No one fires guns in Germany," he huffed as they jogged a brown, trodden ribbon through the snow.

Dr. Steele missed the leafy cover of summer and noted the oldest tombstone, dating to 1076, which he had studied in June on a seminary tour. "Right. Another problem. Now . . . need to hide. Tall markers . . . knoll. Shields until . . . figure what to do."

Even in winter, gravesites were littered with written prayers weighted by stones or scattered like leaves. On the perimeter, tablets incised with the Ten Commandments honored the dead. Marble obelisks carved in Hebrew comprised the middle ring. Registers inlaid with black onyx surrounded by fruit and floral carvings signified the top tier of eternal class distinction.

The Steeles hid in the midst of these ornate artworks, footsteps leading directly to them.

They listened, and filled burning lungs with frigid air as old bodies stiffened. After five minutes that seemed fifteen, Steven suggested they escape through the back gate.

Dr. Steele offered to go first. "I don't think I can drive your Citroen, and someone needs to alert the Madisons. Cyril, too." He eased from the stony barricade, turned to the gate, and shuffled.

He heard the shot before he felt it. Tumbled in the snow. Searing pain confused senses overloaded by the snowy roll.

CHAPTER THIRTY-FOUR

Grossmunster

Grace
"What do we look for?" No one answered Mark.

After swinging by the goliath Zwingli statue, we trotted up seventy frozen steps to the Grossmunster north portal, shrouded in winter mist. Turning the corner to face the deeply inset doorway, we encountered a robed seminarian droning at a crowd blocking the entrance.

The University of Zurich Graduate School of Theology was housed on cathedral grounds.

"Penance," Jeff muttered, his bearded chin shoved beneath a muffler festively decorated by icy spikes.

"Listening to him is too high a price for sin," Becca said. She nudged through huddled pilgrims awaiting lecture salvation, and we followed in an unholy conga line, past biblical scenes under a vibrant geode transom. The sincere young man was still talking when the doors closed behind the security detail we picked up with the choppers.

European cathedrals are unheated, but the Grossmunster interior was partially insulated from a bone-penetrating chill rising from the Limmet River a hundred fifty yards east.

Matthew stepped in front of me, threateningly close. My body tensed until Mark cupped my elbow.

"What are we looking for?" Matthew asked.

I bit my tongue to prevent inquiring why our fearless leader didn't know. Dr. Merrit sat on a wooden pew worn butter-smooth, forty feet beyond Matthew. A thick scarf covered his graying chins, his felt hat in gloved hands. He winked while patting the bench next to him. I decided to behave until I joined him.

"I'm not sure, Matthew. I suggest we fan out, look for anything suspicious. I'm going to recuperate from those stairs. My lungs are seared." It was the best I could do short of taking him by his collar to shake him senseless.

I sat next to my professor. He placed a gloved hand on mine, and dropped his head as if to pray.

"I think it's the other doors, Grace. The set where the unfortunate crowd waits is Biblical, but the other is Reformation. Stan had a file last semester. And related reference books on his desk. They're being refurbished. The doors. They're not here. They're what we're after."

I bowed piously, confident faked prayer was not heretical in this situation. "What was he looking at?"

"There were a lot of Luther books in the stack, so I guess something Luther." Leaning forward, he balanced his forehead on his fists, and strangled the hat. "Maybe find a photo?"

"Out of my technological league. Let me turn the kids loose on it." I dropped the kneeler with a *crack* and hit my knees.

Maggie stood at the pulpit, scratching her head in a most uncivilized way. She looked toward my noise. She acknowledged my nod, and directed Jeff and Becca toward me. Matthew, Cliff, and Mark were forward in the chancel, studying three stained-glass windows emitting no light above the altar. Mark saw my motion too, and I believed he would keep Matthew busy. He pointed at a window farthest from me, doubtlessly expounding creative theology. Or a theory about metal and liquid glass, and the creation of the window.

"Mama?" Maggie whispered, slipping into the pew ahead. "What's up?"

"We need a photo of Luther on the doors from the south portal. Dr. Steele studied them. They're Reformation. Can you help? With your phones? More detailed, the better."

My young brood walked through arches to the narthex behind me, toward another set of geode windows glowing from meager afternoon sunlight. Color streaked across the floor like a rainbow, reminding me of God's faithfulness in keeping promises. I assumed the young people sought stronger cell service near the windows, instead of in the center of a stone edifice.

Turning to the front, I nodded when Mark caught my eye. He extricated himself from Matthew and Cliff, who appeared to disagree, and joined Dr. Merrit and me.

"We're looking for images of the other doors. Being refurbished. Dr. Merrit thinks Dr. Steele came here for them. I have Maggie, Jeff, and Becca sourcing images online."

"You okay, Dr. Merrit?" Mark touched his shoulder. I hoped he was breathing.

"Yes," he said, raising his head after a few moments. "I was really praying this time."

...

Matthew stepped outside to take a call as the seminarian's audience filled the cathedral. We quickly convened.

THE BROTHERS' KEEPERS

"Maggie nailed it when I showed her the image. Which, by the way, is impossible to find. A friend in London had to help." Becca displayed the doors on her phone screen. "Luther's background is Solomon's Pillars in Timna."

"Dear Lord, I hoped never to return to Timna," was all I managed. Southern Israel induced menopausal overheating on a scale contributing to global warming. I hated Timna. "Is that all?" I was now toasty from memories of that God-forsaken place.

"No. It looks as if a stream flows from the pillars, which supports Maggie's thesis about Solomon's water source," Becca said. "Solomon's mythical treasure might not be a wild goose chase after all."

Jeff narrowed his eyes at his sister, then his bride, who nudged him. He snickered at his shoes. "Horse feathers."

Before we could continue, Matthew approached as if something were wrong. "Shots in Worms. Tourists identified the Steeles. We need to go."

...

"Matthew, it's time we chatted," I yelled.

Jeff glanced at Maggie. Escalating rotor noise made listening difficult. Soon the aviation headset would restrain me, and I suspected the children knew what was coming. "Exactly what is your role in this endeavor?"

I longed for a jet. Motion sickness was not a graceful thing, and Maggie and I abhorred helicopters because they made us ill in messy, public ways.

Matthew stared out the windshield. The craft slid forward to rise in the nose-down position, just like a camel when it stands. Mark, sitting directly behind Matthew, yanked off the young man's headphones and waited for him to turn, which he did angrily.

"When Grace asks a question, I expect you to respond with the respect she deserves." My husband yelled for reasons unrelated to slapping blades. Everyone except Mossad cocked an earpiece out to listen. "Either that, or we're outta this bird at the next stop, and your team can continue alone. Know you'll be *competing* with us, not aided by us. When I say 'us,' I mean MI6 and the CIA. And the BBC. As good as Mossad is, you are exponentially stronger with our help. Do you understand me?"

Mark crimped Matthew's headset, the veins on his hands bulging from a high-pressure grip on sturdy metal and plastic. He was gallantly outraged, and I appreciated his intercession. We long ago mastered the good cop/bad cop routine.

Matthew pivoted to me, holding his hand palm-up toward Mark. "I apologize." Mark passed the headset. "I do not intend to be rude. But am not at liberty to tell you why Cyril was called to Jerusalem. I'm trying to manage different tasks in several locations at once. Probably not doing any of it well."

"Then let us help you." Holding Becca's hand, Jeff yelled for their two-person team.

Cliff looked at the couple, then at Maggie, who watched Matthew. I hoped the three resolved their differences soon because Cliff's hurt-puppy look was beginning to grate on me. The Mossad agents looked out the windows, as if they didn't hear what was being said. They probably didn't since their headsets stayed put.

Jeff wasn't finished. "Your top-down management technique is an epic failure."

Matthew repositioned his headphones and sat quietly during the forty-five-minute flight to Worms.

...

Heiliger Sands, Worms

On the five-minute walk to the Jewish Cemetery, or *Heiliger Sands*, we passed a green-and-white Citroen surrounded by police tape, a sight that made me smile. I had a weakness for classic cars—the quirkier, the better. I was thinking about it when I saw Cyril, the last person I wanted to see.

Standing across the memorial park, I recognized the bundled stump near the far gate. German police inspected shoulder-high tombstones on the knoll to the left, gesturing from us to Cyril. Matthew trotted to his supervisor. The rest of us took our sweet time.

Cyril stomped snow from his boots when we approached him. We stood in a cluster of family sites to the right of a much-used footpath.

"We're going after them. We assume they've been abducted, based on footprints and eyewitness accounts." After this encouraging news, he walked to the police, who immediately cordoned off the knoll.

"Ya gotta love this guy," Jeff said without a shred of sincerity. "Okay, Matthew. What do *you* plan to do?" This was a test.

Matthew inclined his head. "I don't know yet." He passed. We valued humility. "But while you're here and Mossad is there, let me mention everything I say in front of my team is repeated to Tel Aviv. If you have issues, share them privately. I'll try to address them when I can." Tugging a scarf from his throat, he walked to Cyril, leaving us ankle deep in snow.

"Was that a concession?" Mark offered an arm to me, and the other to Dr. Merrit. We walked the slushy path carefully, heading to the gate. "I don't envy his position."

After six minutes of being ignored, Mark handed Dr. Merrit and me to Cliff. Then assaulted the police tape, yanking it above his head with a *snap*. Talked down—literally, even though Germans are tall—an irate police officer. And said *something* to Cyril before leading us away.

CHAPTER THIRTY-FIVE

Worms

Grace

Mark had informed Cyril there was no need for us to freeze to death, particularly since the snow intensified when Cyril joined the officers. Mark triumphantly relayed that Mossad would meet us at the bakery.

I nursed a *café au lait* strong enough to keep me awake for eternity, which might be a good thing. Cyril was unhappy about Mark's declaration of independence, but could not have him arrested in Germany. The shop was glassy and brassy, warmed by a wood-burning fireplace and serving good food. I was unsure which was most welcome.

Jeff, Becca, and Maggie made a table; Mark, Dr. Merrit, and I another; and two Mossad agents that Cyril insisted accompany us were at the third, leaving a table for locals. Jeff consumed enough to make our siege worth the owner's while. We ate silently. Matthew's warning about other agents worried me, and his admonition seemed to weigh heavily on the others as well.

After fifteen minutes, during which I thanked Mark twice for insisting on shelter, Matthew entered. He told the agents to wait outside, taking a chair between our tables.

"They've disappeared. We believe they've been taken to Wittenberg. Don't ask how I know." A server brought a mug of steaming coffee, and he responded with *danke*. He sipped with closed eyes, leaning back. "Commander Cyril is organizing a rescue, which may or may not work. That opinion is classified. It's late, and he wants you out of Worms. We're going to Rothenberg for the night, which is touristy enough we should blend in. Tomorrow, we head south to await Cyril's rescue team."

"Why are we not a part of the team?" Mark's napkin was wadded on a plate, and he waved away the server when she tried to clear it. "Cyril getting territorial?"

"And why Rothenberg?" I asked. "Nothing happened there, Reformation-wise."

Matthew smiled weakly. His eyes were framed by crow's-feet, and I realized even olive complexions could develop under-eye circles. He looked at me. "That's exactly why he wants you there. Nothing happened."

Turning to Mark, he began again. "He figures you wouldn't split up, and needs Maggie intact. We're certain it's water-based, and she's the resident hydrologist. The one that keeps getting kidnapped and hurt. Which, by the way, is something we need to stop." He gazed at her and waited, but she offered nothing. "The one who probably hasn't told us everything. It's as simple as that."

With his last statement, he looked at me. "I regret being rude to you, Dr. Madison. I have a lot of respect for you and your family."

I patted his shoulder despite misgivings, and asked for a paper cup. The server gladly reheated drinks to go. Jeff purchased everything from the morning baking, telling his dad he was committed to eliminating starvation, starting with his own. Mark contributed to Jeff's purchase since it looked as if we would spend dinnertime on the road.

We massed outside. Mark's arm around my shoulder was warm. Jeff and Becca hugged like honeymooners. Cliff and Maggie stood awkwardly until Dr. Merrit stepped between them to start a conversation. About predestination. Bless his heart.

When Matthew returned with the Mossad guards, we walked past the Citroen.

"Sweet wheels," Jeff said, admiring the classic station wagon.

"We believe it belonged to Steven Steele." Matthew extended his hand to help Maggie into a van. He followed suit with me, and we started our drive of less than a hundred miles east, to one of Europe's most intact medieval centers.

I found a black plastic case on the back seat. My name was written on masking tape slapped diagonally across its top. I recognized the case immediately. Sliding clasps, I exposed bubbled foam nesting a matte-black Glock G32, a semi-automatic .357 magnum with distended slide. Two magazines holding fifteen bullets each, and a silencer, lay next to this hand-held cannon with a slim grip for a small hand.

Matthew was either brilliant at throwing someone off his trail, or our evil assumptions about him were wrong. No one would arm an enemy with a bazooka.

Mark's eyes bugged out. He ferreted on the floor and found a box containing a black-and-silver Glock 17L GEN 4 identical to the weapon I had surrendered when leaving Israel last year.

"Looks like you got an upgrade," he said, referring to the more powerful firearm in my hand. We used this model at the ranch, populated with mountain lion and bear, and I was already worried about recoil.

"Trade? I'm more comfortable with that one." I held the pistol toward him.

"Love to," was his reply.

Maggie looked over her shoulder and mouthed *wow*. She pointed to herself as if to ask, "Where's mine?" I nodded toward the floor, and she shuffled enthusiastically. I shoved a third box to her after finding it near the outer wall. Jeff and Becca had been armed since Paris, and I hoped Cliff was.

Mark moved to the bench center as she joined us. Her Glock 17L was like mine. I was thankful for years of target practice, both at Middle-Eastern digs and during Maggie's ranch-based training for Olympic gold.

We were armed and dangerous.

...

Rothenberg, Germany

Two busses of chirping Japanese tourists disembarked next to us at the brick-and-timber hotel.

Jeff groaned. "You must be kidding me."

Cliff snorted. "I would say we blend right into this crowd, Matthew. *Bonzai*."

"I suspect you would prefer *sayonara*," Matthew replied without looking his direction.

Maggie and I glanced at each other. Their animosity increased our risk.

Raucous, probably drunken youth cavorted on the wall walk inside the rampart encircling the old city. The defensive structure was almost adjacent to the hotel, and their noisy antics did not entertain me.

"I hope they shut up or pass out in a stupor." My verbal filters were *gone*.

We moved quickly to our third-floor rooms, fortunately in the remodeled wing of the U-shaped building. Mark and I centered the room configuration, facing the party wall. Maggie was next to us, Jeff and Becca beyond her, Dr. Merrit on our other side. Mossad completed our seven circles of protection.

The room was funky German contemporary. Almost Bauhaus, a style better in summer, when geraniums drooped from window boxes at each multi-paned aperture—according to a photo on the desk. Mark answered a knock, which interrupted his loving gaze at the bed.

"We're out at 7:00. There's a buffet downstairs at 6:00." Matthew's face broke into a grin. "I hope you and Jeff don't clean it out before I get there."

"I heard that." Jeff said, he and Becca leaning from their doorway. Maggie's head poked into the hall, and Cliff and Dr. Merrit's doors opened. "I'll be there at 5:45," Jeff said. "Hungry."

"Breakfast at 6:00. Pull out at 7:00. Get there before Mark and Jeff," Matthew repeated before disappearing down the stairwell.

We bid our goodnights, and I dozed within minutes.

DAY SEVEN
CHAPTER THIRTY-SIX

Rothenberg

Grace

I stirred. My heart was racing, and I was strangling the pillow. *Did I hear noise? Was it mother's intuition?*

"Something's wrong," I whispered, shaking his shoulder. "I feel it."

He rolled over, struggling to surface from deep sleep. "What? What time is it?"

"I don't know. I want to check the kids." I slipped from bed, threw on a bathrobe I had draped across a bench, and tiptoed to the door.

"Let me." Cutting in front, he reached for the door with one hand while struggling to don his robe with the other. Transferring his Glock from the nightstand to his robe pocket, he turned the knob.

A rifle shot cracked nearby. We dropped. Then were up and out, colliding with unrobed Mossad and semi-clad Matthew, well armed in every sense.

THE BROTHERS' KEEPERS

Jeff and Becca flew into the hallway a second later, with Walther P99s—40SW—ready. Screams in the old wing interrupted Cliff's furious banging on Maggie's door. Matthew put a silenced round into the lock. Before they could enter, Mark blasted through, with me in his wake.

Draperies billowed in a breeze careening from frigid Bavaria one hundred fifty miles south, past Munich. The body in the bed didn't move. Images of the Negev flashed in my mind, and I imagined blood. I bound past Mark with a cry. Reached to turn her . . .

"Mama," she said from behind me. "Took you long enough." She smiled in the doorway before staring at Matthew evenly. Cliff rushed her, stopping short. She had emerged from a room across the hall.

I pivoted, tangled in sheets, and would have fallen if not for Mark's catch. Pillows in my hands were warm. A human-shaped wad of bedclothes lay where her body should have been. Heating pads were plugged into an outlet behind the nightstand.

She pointed at the hole in the wall, where the bullet entered just above the pillow. Where her head would have lain. Jeff and Becca moved to my sides.

"We figured they'd use heat-seeking technology. I'm sorry, Mama. But we needed them to think I was dead. If you'd known, you'd have hidden behind the drapes or something. Gotten *yourself* killed."

"It was my idea," Jeff said. "Blame me, Mother."

I looked at my children and vacillated between relief and rage. Everyone with a will to live stood quietly.

Maggie hugged me. "I couldn't sleep anyway because of insomnia. Genetically, *yours*."

Gibberish in the hall meant Matthew spoke with Cyril. Chirping in the parking lot meant other guests were gathering near their buses. I held my daughter at arm's length, finally managing to speak through a bone-dry throat. "You're all right?"

"Yes."

I looked at Jeff and Becca. "I understand." I didn't. "I'll deal with you later, Jeff." I wanted to smack him. Hug him for saving her life.

Sirens became louder.

"How?" Mark asked as Matthew rushed in, trying to get past Cliff to her.

"Wait there. You can hear fine." My voice frightened even me, and I found myself pointing my finger at Matthew as if I would shoot him with it. He and Cliff edged behind Mark.

"Becca received input from MI6 very late. Chatter ran high on monitored sites, implicating us. *They* actually called *her*. She told the front desk she needed heating pads for a sore back." Maggie explained step-by-step to calm my nerves. "We put together this plan after you went to bed. We weren't sure they were going to try, so didn't worry you. Becca picked the lock across the hall so I could stay there. We waited. I heard the shot. Figured it would take you less than a minute to break through the door." She smiled. "You beat my estimate considerably."

"Your mother's *instinct* awakened her seconds before the shot," Mark rumbled volcanically. I pictured his face standing above a dying Maggie in Israel, and knew he would not risk losing her again. "No more single rooms." He turned her toward our room, her arm around his waist. "I'll take the single."

He knew someone wouldn't try a second time tonight, so whirled to unleash on Matthew, breaking free of Maggie's grip. *"How did this happen?"*

"I'll hear from Cyril within ten minutes as to what to do next." Matthew's ringing phone created an excuse to step into the hall.

"To . . . *forget Cyril*!" Mark yelled, aborting profanity. "My family is out of here!"

"I'd prefer a double." Maggie rubbed her head as she returned to the subject of accommodations. Her father stared, dumbfounded. "And I'm not out of here. We don't need to go through this again, Dad. There's a job to be done. I need to help do it." She tugged at her scalp while referring to an argument with her dad, and her refusal to leave Israel, during a midnight camel caravan on the Ascent of Adumim.

I knew I was cross, but I couldn't stand the scratching any more. "What is up with the scratching? Why are you always messing with your hair?" I was ashamed of my inane questions, but couldn't erase them. "You've been scratching since Madaba."

"It itches."

"Let me see. You probably have a bug bite." I sounded stupid, and everyone in the room gaped as if we were the village idiots. I marched her to the vanity, turned on the light, pulled her hair up, and froze.

"Mark." His name also attracted Jeff and Becca. Cliff blocked Matthew from the cramped bath. I turned her to face me and clamped the ponytail on top of her head. When they saw my discovery, woven into her hairline, they gasped.

Our daughter was being tracked.

CHAPTER THIRTY-SEVEN

Rothenberg

Grace

"Why do they keep missing?" Dr. Merrit asked. He held a freshly plucked button in his right hand, and an assortment, fished from his jacket pocket, in his left palm. But his coloring was good.

"I don't believe this miss was intentional. The simple answer is that tracker. They follow us to the scroll," Jeff explained as Becca texted.

We had cut the chip from Maggie's hair and sent images to MI6, arranging a brush pass—spy lingo for a hand-off—to a London-bound courier.

"It's an old tactic," Becca explained. "Every bomb maker leaves an identifying fingerprint that pinpoints his or her region. Chipmakers do, too." She glared at Matthew. "I'm tired of knowing less than the other side."

Matthew looked at me, silently appealing for help. He could forget about it.

"And the tracker might explain why you found that note under the peonies at the Westin, Mom. Telling you someone had abducted Maggie." Jeff handed the phone to Becca, and she murmured something about confidential protocols to send the text. "Whoever's after this knew you'd involve MOSES and try to tap the Steeles. None of this has really made sense until now. We're being used."

"But if they've already kidnapped the Steeles, why would they need to kill Maggie?" Dr. Merrit's voice rose with his coloring. I followed him to the empty window frame, patting his back between his shoulder blades.

Mossad agents with flashlights bobbled along the wall walk. They moved up and down irregular stone stairs that I have almost used as a slide—but *that* can be said about staircases around the globe. These are, in my defense, particularly dangerous and uneven.

As I considered the agents canvassing the rampart, I knew it was hard not to leave a trail in the dark, but perhaps more difficult to follow one. "Maybe the group that kidnapped the Steeles isn't the group that fired at Maggie or planted the chip? Maybe there are *two* groups?"

This was my best idea. I would find later I was almost right.

. . .

"My mission is to protect her . . . sir, do you want me to do my job or not?"

Before the call started, Matthew sent two Mossad agents to the hotel front and back doors, ostensibly to watch. Given the tone of the conversation, he really wanted to confront the commander without his boss's witnesses.

His tone remained respectful. "I understand, but you can't guarantee her safety like he can . . . we're followed or attacked at every turn, sir . . . " His rigid body, clad only in pajama bottoms, faced away from us. Slim though he was, the fairer sex now appreciated that he was ripped, his bronze gorgeousness not stopping at his collarbone.

As I told Maggie frequently, I might be old, but I was not blind.

He spoke forcefully, words wadi-crisp, voice unnervingly quiet. "You've tasked me with it. I think it's the best thing to do . . . you have . . . you have easy access via the heliport and we can meet . . . there. Remember, I was there when you sent me to Paris. It's secure."

He turned, eyes hard on Maggie. She looked at her toes, which curled under in a peculiar fashion. "That's my plan, Commander. You know where to find us . . . yes, a new vehicle . . . fifteen minutes. I'll keep her alive. Sir."

The conversation appeared to end.

"One other thing. I'm sending the agents to you." He held the phone two inches from his ear, commotion audible from three feet away. When the screaming stopped, he returned the phone to his ear. "They make us too large a party, hard to transport without detection . . . once we arrive, we'll be safe . . . I've already called . . . they're ready . . . I understand."

His jaw clamped hard at whatever Cyril said next. Then he didn't give the commander a chance to interrupt. "Four of the seven of us have intelligence training, Commander. The three remaining are equally proficient. Two additional Mossad aren't worth the inconvenience, and the chateau is impregnable.

"Yes, you can track me." He grimaced. "I realize I'm assuming . . . yes, full responsibility . . . I hope to see you in two days as well." His face conveyed he lied. He poked the phone, and I assumed the end-call button was now recessed permanently.

He didn't mention the tracker we were sending to London.

"Put your luggage in the elevator. Please." It was the size of a dumb waiter, which he acknowledged next. "Cliff, if you straddle a suitcase, you can ride down with Dr. Merrit. We'll stay together and meet in reception." He nodded at Cliff.

We crept downstairs three minutes later. Since it was after 10:00 p.m., the kitchen staff was gone.

"Father, forgive me." After shaking it to hear the slosh, I stole a coffee server heavy enough to be full from last night. Jeff stole dinner rolls and fruit.

"Better than nothing." Mark left a twenty-euro note on the counter.

Matthew instructed Mr. Back-Door Mossad to fetch his associate, and told them they could check, but were reassigned to Cyril's rescue. They disappeared. German filtered from the delivery entry, where authorities talked with someone in Israel. I thought of the horrific history between the countries, hoping it wouldn't impede our escape.

Matthew looked at his watch. "In five minutes, we're out the kitchen door. Our agents did a night-vision scope and can't find anyone else. Dr. Madison, you'll be delighted to know there are four drunks within range, safely comatose." I was only a little ashamed. "We're going to move uphill, under the wall walk instead of between buildings on the street."

"Easy target," I muttered, *so* disgusted with my life.

"Exactly. At the gate, we'll turn right, leave the old city, and there better be a Mossad vehicle waiting. Once we're out, I'll explain the rest. As best I can."

"What's going on?" Maggie's athletic stance—feet planted wide, arms crossed over her bosom—was combative. At that moment, I saw the perfect contradiction that appealed to Cliff and Matthew. Behind Grace Kelly's beauty lay the shrewdness of Golda Mier, the heart of Mother Theresa, and the fierceness of Eleanor Roosevelt. "Should we ditch agents assigned to protect us? Doesn't this place too much responsibility on you? Aren't you asking us to trust you too completely?" Given their focus, Matthew and Maggie were the only people in Rothenberg for the last eight centuries, although Cliff looked euphoric as she cross-examined his rival.

I was proud that Matthew held her gaze as he tried to figure out how to answer her, or avoid it. "'Yes.' To all your questions. One of the Steeles is injured. Before you ask—" he looked at me "—don't know which. Despite Cyril's misgivings, I'm taking you to the safest place I know. I trust our host. He's known Cyril since his MOSES days. Since before, actually."

CHAPTER THIRTY-EIGHT

Old City, Rothenberg

Grace

Ten minutes later, long enough for Jeff to brew coffee after spewing soapy water almost swallowed from my stolen thermos, we crept out the back door. Matthew led, Jeff and Becca followed. Maggie, Dr. Merrit, and Cliff—each young person took an arm—were next, and Mark and I were last. A five-minute, uphill, slickly cobbled hike ended through the vehicular gate.

A car whipped in front of us, closely followed by a van.

I started to speak. "That's not big . . ."

Mark shoved me out of the way. "Drop!" His yell scattered us. He pointed his Glock at the armed sedan driver preparing to shoot.

The man's body reacted to a half-dozen silenced rounds—staccato *poofs*—from Mark, Becca, Matthew, or the driver of the van behind the sedan. As I scrambled up, weapon drawn, I remembered the large Jewish population in Rothenberg, which explained the Mossad vehicle now waiting beyond the corpse and running car.

In haste to react, Jeff dropped the coffee, and didn't get off a shot. "What the . . . " he began, correcting himself when he saw

Dr. Merrit. My son did a three-sixty to check the family. Then ran to assist the professor.

Matthew spoke to the Mossad driver, who evaporated into an alley. We clambered in, eager to leave a medieval city joining Timna and Jericho on my least-favorite list. A list that grew with each covert endeavor.

Matthew checked our attacker's body to ensure he was dead, jogged to the van while on his cell, and addressed us from the driver's seat. "Before I explain, or try to, is everyone okay?"

We were, thanks to the three-foot-thick rock walls we dove behind. Not all of us had happy landings. My throbbing shoulder meant I had ricocheted off something that didn't welcome me.

"Does filthy count?" I asked. I had rolled through wetness whose nasty origin I suspected was related to too much beer, and remembered doing the same thing in the Jericho marketplace with a burkhaed Maggie at my side. "But physically, I think I'm okay."

"Mama," she said, patting my knee. "You're eternal. And I love you for it."

"Well, theologically, kind of." I had unlimited faith in my next life.

Mark coughed. "We're fine, Matthew. Just dirty and bruised. I think it's time you explained yourself." He held his hand toward my Glock, still in a ready-to-fire death grip.

"Sorry," I whispered. "Amateur."

"You're doing just fine." He kissed my forehead, checked the pistol to ensure I wasn't about to shoot someone I loved, and returned it.

Matthew relied on the dash GPS panel. Jeff, in the passenger seat with his Walther in his right hand, watched.

"A heliport?" my son asked, tapping the screen where a green button flashed close to our moving red dot.

"This was going to be a drive, but not any more. We're airborne. Out of this rat hole."

We would arrive soon, according to the display. Curiosity and survival got the better of me. "Matthew, where are we going?"

He sighed. "I never know how to explain this, Dr. Madison, although I seldom need to. We're going to the Swiss side of the Swiss-Italian border. The accommodations are very safe, will accommodate us, and most importantly for you—" his eyes twinkled and teeth flashed in the rear-view mirror "—has laundry facilities."

That sealed the deal. Anyone who appreciated my need for clean clothes was trustworthy.

"It's also en route from Wittenberg to Venice, where Cyril's information says we'll go next. I'm expecting documents from Mossad. He tells me MI6 and the CIA are sending intelligence as well, not having known where to contact you." He looked at Mark and Becca. "We'll be there a night or two. You'll be able to review everything. Trust me when I say the chateau is comfortable."

He wheeled into a parking lot as a fishtailing EuroCopter, deep silver with a red tail number, landed. It looked corporate, not military or covert. Rotors idled as protracted steps dropped. I was *overjoyed* this bird had steps. The Middle-Eastern men that descended wore suits and exchanged the customary shoulder slap of welcome with Matthew.

Maggie nudged me and mouthed, *Chateau?*

"I caught that too," I replied.

"Interesting," Jeff said.

"Agreed." Mark offered me his hand as he spoke.

"Is that an AK47?" Maggie squinted at a three-foot black weapon in one man's hand. "Is this a rescue or a kidnapping?"

"I think it's an Uzi, my dear." Dr. Merrit said from a window seat. "And if they want to kidnap us, I doubt we can stop them."

Matthew motioned for us as the armed men moved to each side of the craft.

Although the snow fell heavily again, I sweated. Then reminded myself that a chateau, particularly one with a washer and dryer, had certain appeal.

CHAPTER THIRTY-NINE

The Autobahn, Germany

He breathed, and thanked God for that. But he hurt. Poking, he remembered the shot.

"Stan." Steven sounded close. "We're on our way to Wittenberg."

Dr. Steele focused, puzzled by cartons stacked to the tailgate of a musty box truck. The brothers were unrestrained behind the cab, held prisoner by thousands of crated potatoes.

"How's your shoulder?" the antiquarian asked.

"Not ideal, but manageable with God's grace."

"You've been shot."

"You were always sharp, Steven. You?"

Steven leaned against the exterior wall until he shivered, cold penetrating the cracking leather jacket. "I ran out when you went down. They were on me pronto. One guy was angry you'd been wounded. I assumed they drugged us because that's all I remember."

"I am thankful for good drugs. Who has us?"

"They speak Italian."

Gently prodding his shoulder, Dr. Steele decided the bullet grazed soft tissue. "Recognize a Roman dialect? Did they look priestly?"

"Definitely not priests. The dialect isn't Venetian. Maybe ghetto Roman, consistent with their personalities. I don't have your language ear, Stan. The guy was so enraged, he reminded the others we had to be alive in Wittenberg."

"What are we going to do?"

"No idea."

"They want the scroll. Help me up, please."

Steven was careful what parts he grabbed to upright his brother. Age, wound, and cold were a dangerous combo.

"Can you tell if I've lost a lot of blood? I don't feel weaker than usual."

"I don't think so." Steven peered at the bandage, found his brother's tweed coat stuffed between two boxes, and laid it over his shoulders. "They did a decent job of bandaging, although it isn't nice-looking."

"I'll take a competent woman over a beauty any day, Steven."

...

Wittenberg was two hundred fifty miles northeast, toward Poland. They would get colder. Dr. Steele pictured summer digs in Jordan, and the Jericho oasis where he had waited for Merrit and their friends last summer. Visualization encouraged his mind to think his body was warm.

From consistencies in the rattling motion of the truck, he suspected they traveled the Autobahn again. If correct, they would be in Wittenberg in less than three hours, minus whatever time he had lost to unconsciousness. "Any idea how long we've been here?"

Steven shook his head. "I came to almost an hour before you did."

They were close.

"We need a plan, Steven. What do you think they want in Wittenberg?"

"I'd want to know where you got that cuneiform."

"I bought it in a summer market. From a seasonal dealer who could be anywhere in Europe right now. I can't possibly find him again."

"Then you'd better make something up. These guys, at least two of them, don't want to play nice."

When the truck stopped twenty minutes later, the Steele twins were ready.

...

Wittenberg

The potato truck was parked in a loading zone that almost blocked the monastery portico.

"Near the Best Western at the other end of town," Dr. Steele said, gesturing with his good arm.

The surly one had asked where Dr. Steele bought the cuneiform. The theologian lied. He directed them to a tiny junk shop—cracked Bavarian plates, old Nazi helmets (from China), pressed-glass compotes—wedged between the Wittenberg square and the hotel, across from the florist.

Their abductors would find nothing. Then Dr. Steele would suggest Luther's monastery, several hundred feet toward the pedestrian-zone perimeter. He would try to slip a note scratched on a torn potato-crate label to someone he knew, hoping they would alert Merrit.

If the brothers were alive after the monastery, he would propose Veste Coburg, a castle southwest of Wittenberg, where Luther translated the Bible as a prisoner of John the Steadfast during the Diet of Augsburg. He knew the curator there. If they were alive after that, he would think of a reason to work toward Italy, giving their friends a chance to catch up. The Steeles assumed everyone knew they were missing now.

"Do you lie to us, old man?" The kidnapper's need for comprehensive dental surgery reinforced his treacherous sneer.

"No. You'll find the shop there. And—" he seized the opportunity "—we should try the monastery, check Katarina's bench. I have other ideas if we don't find what you're looking for."

They passed the Stadtpalais Best Western and the drugstore where Dr. Steele met Cyril only days ago, and arrived at the junk shop fifteen minutes after it closed.

Back at the monastery, which would close soon, they marched straight to the window where Luther built a seat for his beloved Katarina, high above the courtyard and with a view of children and garden. From this domestic perch, she listened to student discussions after dinner, contributed practical wisdom Luther valued, and knit for their growing family. Few contemporary pastors taught that Katarina was the fiscal engine keeping Luther's family afloat, but her business savvy and financial discipline enabled Martin to jumpstart the Reformation without the distraction of poverty—and *he* knew it.

Dr. Steele made a spectacle of inspecting the seat, humming as if discovering things while delaying long enough for someone to find them. When the director approached, having heard he was in the building, Dr. Steele accepted his friend's offer of completing the tour—and irritated their captors.

He slipped the note in the director's pocket during a painful, comradely shoulder hug.

...

"I didn't find what I was looking for," Dr. Steele said as the brothers were shoved in the jump seat of the cab. "I suggest we head to Coburg, where Luther wrote on the castle walls."

"This is your last chance." The driver snarled, which he did better than sneer because fewer decaying teeth were exposed. "Luther's graffiti doesn't interest me."

The brothers hoped Director Mauss called the number on the note.

CHAPTER FORTY

Southern Switzerland

Grace

We dropped over a cleft, in a shaft of moonlight piercing the border between Switzerland and Italy. Lights encircling the elliptical inner walls of the chateau blazed, casting shadows on ivory stone. I wondered if it was normally this bright in the middle of the night, or if we were special.

The isolated edifice was lakeside, kept company by glittering hamlets at water's edge. Tiled turrets, multiple round towers, crenelated ridges—our grim plot had a fairy-tale chapter after all.

The pilot quietly chattered into her headset during our approach, and Matthew watched the descent. He was silent through Swiss air space, body rigid as if steeling himself. I studied the gashes—spines of earth erupting from settled snow—and was relieved I wasn't airsick. Darkness neutralized my equilibrium.

We landed in the keep, the protected central yard. The rotors stopped, and staff unloaded our meager luggage. A man in a dark suit and regimental tie addressed Matthew, saying something about " . . . waiting in the library." Condensation clouds from each word hung in still air, and Matthew turned to us. The retainer seemed to watch Maggie.

"If you'll excuse me, I have a meeting," Matthew said formally. "You'll be shown your quarters. Food is in the dining hall, and someone will escort you if you'd like to eat there. In-room dining is available by dialing eight on your room phone."

They disappeared through a bright portal before we could follow. His associate stayed a step behind, to Matthew's left.

"You hear that?" Jeff asked. "The guy referred to Matthew as *amir*."

Becca took his arm. "Does that surprise you?" They walked toward the doorway, following the luggage-toting entourage. "He has *privilege* printed all over him. Note his reserved bearing. And fine bone structure, indicating a beautiful mother. Like yours." She winked at me.

A man shifted in windows roofing the portal just before we entered. Ceilings of coffered gilt, thick draperies, and books humanized the décor above us.

"Amir. *Prince*, right?" Maggie looked queasy, a condition probably not induced by the helicopter.

"Definitely," Jeff said, unwillingly handing Becca's bag to a man wrestling it from him before starting up a staircase spiraling three stories. "*Prince* in several languages. Dad, I know we checked him out last year, but I'd like more than a cursory dossier now."

"Anyone crazy enough to try in-room dining?" Maggie was not going to miss this meal.

Cliff cursed lightly, an appropriate response from a man discovering his chateau-inhabiting rival was of royal blood.

. . .

Dr. Merrit's phone rang on the second-floor landing, startling everyone except suits of armor propped on sticks in niches. He unbuttoned his coat, sport jacket, and pant pocket, then retrieved the phone as it fell silent. I was amazed he owned clothing with buttons still attached. He donned readers, hidden in the third pocket he patted down, and stared at the number. "Germany, but I don't recognize it."

"Call back," Mark said. "The Steeles were taken to Wittenberg, right?"

He pushed redial, and we waited. *"Guten abend,"* he said. My eyes wandered across Gothic arches punctured by an ocular window, and I was glad my stress level had dropped since my family was safe. *"Danke."* He turned to our escort. "We need to speak with Matthew. Immediately." He straightened to full height.

The man nodded, and liveried boys disappeared with our luggage. "Follow me, please," was his French-accented reply.

We hiked for four minutes on this level—not counting half staircases. Sconce-lit hallways with Persian runners over wide-planked oak floors led to two galleries adorned with paintings of mythic battles. Skirting a ballroom with no fewer than twelve—of course I counted—Murano-glass chandeliers, we finally stopped at walnut doors carved with boars and bears in a smack down. My money was on the bears.

A man outside conversed with our escort before cracking the doors, clearing his throat dramatically. He said something like "Elizabeth Reed," as if announcing whoever she was, although I was certain she wasn't with *our* group.

"Eza bet reed," Jeff translated. *"If you please.* Lebanese-Arabic dialect."

Matthew opened the doors. Our mouths dropped. Smaller than spaces we had toured during a world-class education for

Jeff and Maggie, this library was divine. Books covered twenty-foot walls served by a library ladder on wheels. I coveted that. A bank of windows overlooked the keep and mountains. Task lights beamed from the right spots, comfortable chairs grouped in corners.

"May I present my father, Bashir Cushan?" Matthew gestured to a handsome man at the windows. I still was not blind.

He walked past his son, around the endless library table, to us with a shy smile. Gray trousers and blue-and-gray cashmere sweater were understated. Matthew would age very well.

He started with Mark. "*Bienvenue*, M. Madison. Welcome to my home." Using the formal French of Lebanese society, something I had struggled with when archaeological digs took me to that country, he greeted Cliff, Jeff, and Becca before ending with Maggie and me.

"Dr. Madison." He bowed over my hand, and properly stopped three inches short. "My son speaks of his regard for you. My home is yours."

He turned to Maggie, took her hand, and stared at her. Then bowed. "You are Margaret. Very much your mother's daughter." Acknowledging our likeness, glancing between us, he looked at Matthew and chuckled. "You could not be more welcome here. Son, I would have known them anywhere."

"How should I address you, sir?" Maggie shifted into business behavior. It was obvious much had been shared between father and son. "*Amir* Cushan?"

"Please call me *Bayee*, Mademoiselle Madison."

Cliff gargled.

Turning to Dr. Merrit, he continued. "We have a problem, Dr. Merrit? How may I assist?" Pulling a chair from the table, Bashir helped my professor before taking the next one, leaning in conspiratorially. Matthew seated Maggie, Becca, and me, then gestured toward chairs for the men before seating himself behind his father.

Cliff nudged Jeff.

"*Father,*" Jeff whispered from the corner of his mouth.

"Thought so," Cliff sighed as he looked at his boots.

...

Bashir Cushan flipped his hand at his staff, dismissing them.

"Tell Cyril they're headed to Coburg," Dr. Merrit finished instructing Matthew. "Stan is wounded, so bring medical. He's old."

Matthew pressed a button on a switch panel near the windows, and closed the draperies with a *swoosh*. He pressed another, and a bookcase swiveled to reveal electronic equipment.

"Let me check with the commander before dinner, in case changes alter what we do tonight." He turned to a monitor that displayed Cyril's face. "You know where they are, commander?"

"Wittenberg. But they just left."

Matthew squared his shoulders. "Dr. Steele got a message to Dr. Merrit. He's leading them to Coburg. The castle. Three Italians captured the brothers. He's going to try to keep them in Luther's rooms near the gift shop. If the brothers escape, they're heading for sedan chairs under the armory. Look for the swan litter."

"The Reformation! The swan! Zurich! I give up!" Cyril threw his hands in the air.

"He's wounded." Matthew verbally slapped the commander.

"Stanley or Steven?" Cyril was serious again.

"Dr. Steele. He requests first aid." Matthew waited. "Did the agents find you?" He referred to the Mossad guards we ditched in Rothenberg.

"No." Cyril looked startled as he told someone to find them. He spoke Hebrew, but so did I.

"I didn't think they would. Thank you, sir." Matthew clicked out as Cyril's mouth opened, and the screen went black.

He swiveled his chair to face us. "Mossad agents rarely defect."

I liked his style. "You troubler of Israel." I quoted King Ahab in the Old Testament book of 1 Kings.

"Thank God I wasn't named Elijah," he said as I laughed. "Bayee, security is high?"

When his father nodded, Matthew continued. "I suggest we get some rest. Cyril will come here once the Steeles are safe." He smiled at me. "Dr. Madison, place your laundry outside the door. Feel free to use anything you find in your rooms, treating it as your own. I think the earliest we'll leave is tomorrow afternoon.

"And if you need to take a midnight stroll—" he cut his eyes toward Maggie "—the chateau is big enough for you to ramble *indoors*."

She blushed.

He and his father kissed each other's cheeks.

"My son is correct," Bashir said as Matthew left. "I will guard you as my children. Since we've been delayed by the information Dr. Merrit received about Dr. Steele, I have asked an informal dinner be served to each of you in your rooms."

Maggie's face fell, and he smiled at her.

"I will make it up to you, Margaret. When you awaken, please ring eight for coffee or tea. M. Madison—Jeff—I hear you are fond of Turkish coffee, and we will serve it. Breakfast will be buffet. Ring for an escort to the morning room. *Bonne nuit.*" He stood, indicating we should leave.

Traipsing through another set of rooms and more hallways, we eventually settled into bedroom suites I thought overlooked the lake. I couldn't wait to see the view, and tried to ignore a swaying stack of intelligence dossiers on the desk.

CHAPTER FORTY-ONE

Borgo

Agnelli paced because he could not sleep.

Yesterday in the vaults, he had found what he sought in a misfiled record. His novitiate's usefulness ended then. Agnelli placed the call that triggered the explosive in the young man's briefcase. He had planned for the blast to kill them all.

He cultivated more novitiates. One was en route to Coburg castle to relieve the punks of the Steeles, who were unwittingly leading him to the scroll.

He would leave for Venice in an hour, prepared for Carnevale festivities. Surging crowds and chaos would provide cover when he retrieved the scroll fragment, whose location he discovered in a cleverly mistranslated Latin copy of Luther's treatises, *Disputatio pro declaration virtutis indulgentiarum*.

Carnevale bacchanalia would be a perfect introduction to his next life. He could tolerate festival inconvenience.

DAY EIGHT
CHAPTER FORTY-TWO

Chateau Cushan, Switzerland

Intelligence reports teetered a foot-tall on the desk, yodeling Maggie's name at 6:10 a.m.

After showering, she donned twill cargo pants from the closet, cinching them with an edelweiss-embroidered belt. She grabbed the sage-and-apricot chair throw to wear over the billowing alpaca sweater from the armoire.

She convinced the burly female, who looked as if she had been outside Maggie's door all night, she would be safe in the library. The woman escorted her to a room Maggie could not have found on her own, and now waited outside.

Maggie walked to the switch bank near the windows and pressed buttons until the task lights turned on. In the process, she swung the rotating bookcase/command center twice, opened and closed the draperies, and dropped a mirrored disco ball from a ceiling compartment. When it twirled and flashed, she turned everything off before the Village People started singing "YMCA."

"That must have been some party."

She settled in to study a karstic system recently found under the City of David in Jerusalem. These underground caverns, which laced the globe and contained water during various geologic periods, were being discovered more frequently in the Middle East. She suspected this discovery, and research from the paper she did *not* present, triggered her kidnapping. Her work pinpointed a possible location of the water source strong enough to power Solomon's mines, and depicted on the scroll fragment tucked into Becca's e-reader.

Her research paper would have revealed this system. And preempt anyone from claiming it. Water was the most valuable commodity in the Middle East because it was most scarce.

Leaning back, she turned over the papers to ask herself questions. Could the geology near the Dead Sea support a system larger than she first thought? Was the Jerusalem karst random, or part of a series stacked south through the desert to the Gulf of Aqaba? This scenario would create a hydrology that could alter the balance of power in the region.

She reached for her documents again, wondering whom to trust with her theory.

Becca's late-night search in Venice had secured data from MI6, which filled blanks left by unreleased archaeological surveys of karsts in Turkey and Greece—the closest identified structures. Maggie would have asked Matthew for these files since Mossad knew everything, and he procured the GPR data so readily.

But he was an associate of Cyril's. Life-and-death experiences expedited the normal progression of friendship. She needed to be careful she did not reveal too much to someone about whom she knew little.

And Cliff worried her. He grew more erratic with every twist and turn.

She opened her laptop. Through **MBM** Hydrology remotely, she accessed software and sites to analyze Becca's data. Maggie trusted the **MBM** encryption department to keep her cyber visit secure.

A quiet knock startled her. "*Entrée*," she said, mimicking Bashir Cushan's French. She did not look from a screen depicting a possible trend along the Jordan Rift Valley, one she probably should have spotted long ago.

"I was informed you were working. Somehow, it doesn't surprise me. Matthew said you were determined and ambitious," Bashir said. "May I send for tea?"

She tilted the screen, a professional habit that made him smile. "If it doesn't inconvenience your staff, that would be welcome. *Merci,* Bashir."

He frowned at his given name, then spoke to someone outside the door. "Are you having any luck? Or would you prefer not to discuss your work?" A gentleman, he stood waiting for her to ask him to sit—in his own home.

She looked past him, at a bouquet of coral lilies, pinpointing the room fragrance. "*S'il vous plait,*" she said as she gestured to a chair, which he took. "I'd rather not share until I have something concrete." She waited for him to say why he was there. "Lovely lilies."

He nodded. "Lilies are one of my favorite flowers. The other is jasmine."

She remembered her nighttime stroll with Matthew along the Sea of Galilee, one that had unsettled her to the point of rudeness. He said jasmine was his mother's—Bashir's wife—favorite, and had spoken of her in the past tense.

She tapped a pen on the tabletop. "Bashir, I don't mean to be rude. But I have a lot to accomplish, a friend is wounded, and your home provides shelter to do things only I can. With respect, your point?"

He joined his fingertips in a teepee and stared at them. "My family helped govern Lebanon for generations. When Matthew was young, he and his mother were abducted. It was politically motivated, but also religious. We were Maronite Catholics, with a history dating to the fourth century. Matthew was raised a Christian. She was killed during the rescue led by a young Israeli friend."

He paused.

Her mind clicked. "Cyril?"

He didn't move. "Cyril's family expatriated to the States, then to Lebanon. They were waiting to return to 'their land,' an opportunity seized when the West created Israel. I trusted him. He did his best."

"Matthew's mother was martyred?" Her voice trembled. Pity was dangerous. Every time.

"Essentially." He folded his hands, slowly twisting an ancient gold ring. "When he was old enough, he asked permission to join Cyril at Mossad. I think Cyril almost views him as a son. I believed he was safer in Israel than in Lebanon, which I later abandoned for this chateau. This will never be home. But home is unsafe."

She was unsure how to respond, disconcerted about intimate details of Matthew's life. "Does he know you're telling me this?"

"No. He wouldn't be happy. But sometimes an old man does what he thinks is best." He stood, reaching to pat her hand. "She was very much like you. He's all I have."

Maggie was so dumbfounded that it barely registered he walked to the door. Matthew and she did not even *like* each other. Much. Then again, whom did she like? Or trust? When the door closed, she returned to work, planning to analyze Bashir's revelations when things settled down.

Thirty minutes later, Maggie decided they had forgotten her tea.

CHAPTER FORTY-THREE

Chateau Cushan

The karst theory was feasible, a conduit running along the Rift. As recently as ten thousand years ago, the region was verdant, supporting flora and fauna on ancient murals and mosaics in museums around the globe. Karsts could have moved Solomon's water independently of recognized sources such as Amu Darya, or the Euphrates, Indus, or Tigris Rivers.

It was possible Solomon's waterway functioned only when water tables were high. He lived seven thousand years *after* the verdant period peaked, when an arid environment replaced pre-agrarian abundance. Maggie knew she needed to move from contemporary science to historic references. For that, she needed Jeff's weird linguistic skills.

She stretched, twisting one way, then the other. Walked stiffly to the windows, rubbing her eyes, pressing fingertips to temples. A headache loomed, and she did not welcome the distracting throb as dawn cast a fire line on peaks several miles northeast, across the lake.

He slipped in, and she looked back when the tray slid on the table.

"My father suggested I bring your tea. May I join you?"

"Of course." She dropped her hands and returned to the documents, trying to look uninformed of Bashir's revelations. The proper English tea set, painted with tiny yellow rosebuds, was far from Bedouin. Neither type of service would have surprised her.

Straightening his cardigan hem, Matthew sat opposite. The fisherman's sweater of bubbly ivory wool highlighted his dark face. She stared. He grinned while waiting for her to stop.

Creep, she thought when she realized she was caught.

"You wear the furnishings well." He referred to the chair throw masquerading as her wrap.

She ignored him because he was acting ungentlemanly. "You do what you can with what you have, Matthew. Shall I pour?"

"Please." He scooted the tray within reach. "I keep clothes here, even though I don't get the chance to visit often. It's nice to have a change, particularly one so different from desert wear." He patted his forearm appreciatively. "So soft."

Maggie wanted to pat him appreciatively, then shook herself and reached for the teapot. She was thankful Mama taught her how to serve properly because Matthew assessed her performance as she assessed his totally unfair handsomeness.

Pick up saucer. Don't slide cup off. Ensure teapot lid is hooked on. Pour while holding pot and saucer off table. Repeat. Offer one lump or two. Cream. Lemon slices. *Whatever.*

"You insist on making my work difficult still." He angled in his chair, a long plank of crossed ankles and at-ease arms. He goaded her with fondness unseen since the shores of Galilee.

"Arnold Schwarzenegger's big sister still outside?" she asked.

He tossed his head back and laughed, saying she was.

She studied the changes in him. His hair was shorter than the shoulder-length locks from the wadi. The waves framed his face and curled around broad cheekbones. His heavy brows and thick lashes, firm chin, and the perfect nose were as beautiful as she remembered. His hair was wet, and she wondered if Bashir had awakened him to share that she was working in the library.

She was losing ground.

"She's more protection than I am. I don't know where Father found her, but she's a beast."

"Um-hum." Her mind returned to the guard.

He stirred. She splashed a spoon around in the cup.

"Matthew, I'm fine. Really. Go do what you need to do. I've been neglecting my work. Have some technical analysis to do." *Why did she flee into business?*

"You've not been neglecting it. You haven't had a chance to do it."

He was right.

"Do you always try to get rid of young men who bring your breakfast?" he asked.

Lor-Dee. He was adorable when he flirted. "Young men don't have the chance to bring me breakfast, Matthew. I'm the celibate type."

"And I appreciate that," he replied seriously. "Very few young women choose that path these days."

Another knock yielded a covered platter. A lifted lid released the yeastiness of fresh brioche. She breathed and giggled. She loved brioche.

"Well, haven't heard *that* sound before." He taunted her with the platter, finally holding it so she could select a pastry. "The way to Margaret Bennett Madison's giggle is through brioche."

She chose the biggest one.

He frowned. "A very large brioche." He arched toward her to inspect the roll. "*My* brioche."

"No. You need butter and delectable raspberry jam to induce another giggle."

"They're on their way. We had to churn one and seed the other." The condiments arrived too quickly for him to be serious. "*First she tries to get rid of me, then she takes my brioche. The woman is shameless.*"

Heat rose to her hairline as she stuffed half of the world's largest brioche in her mouth, puffing her cheeks unattractively while trying not to choke. She couldn't smile without revealing dough balls. So she chewed this bite for at least two minutes to masticate the floury delight, trying not to suffocate in the process.

He watched her, grinning. "I am eagerly prepared for the Heimlich."

Well, that has intimate potential.

They ate in silence, and she savored everything—*everything*—about the experience. She poured again, then rubbed her temples, hoping the caffeine would forestall the persistent ache. She stood, walking to the window with her back to him so she could run her tongue over her teeth to dislodge tenacious clumps.

"You well?" He followed her.

Her tongue cleaned faster.

"A headache, probably from lack of sleep. I don't know how everyone keeps this pace. And I'm the nut who willingly got up early, instead of enjoying that marvelous bed. That's the fluffiest down comforter ever."

"Many geese gave their feathers for you, Ms. Madison. They were honored." He bowed, and reached for her hand. "Give me your left hand."

She stiffened. "Why?" *Failure.*

"Just do it, Maggie."

After ensuring it was not jam-sticky, she placed her hand in his. He pulled her six inches from him, and she stared at his collarbone. Thanking God she had washed her hair, she noticed he smelled of sandalwood. Using the thumb and forefinger of his other hand, he gently pinched a tendon in the Y at the base of her thumb.

"Look up," he said, watching her. "Let me know if this is too much pressure." After a minute of steadily increasing force, he opened his fingers and laid his hand over hers. "How's that? Better?"

She had no idea how it was. She was not breathing. And her brain had left the building. She prepared to throw herself at him. Then she remembered she wore a chair throw. *Failure.*

"I think it's gone. The headache. Not the chair throw." *What was she doing?* "That's amazing."

"Acupressure. Works every time." He looked confused, probably about the chair throw, but did not let go of her hand.

What was she supposed to do now? She considered dropping the disco ball.

"So much good comes from these hands." He turned her palm over. He had expressed admiration for work he called "altruistic" last year in Galilee. Much remained unsaid during those early morning hours. They blew the moment before returning to their rooms—she angry, he clueless.

"I do what I can. It's a privilege." She needed a manicure, and would look for a file and emery board in her room.

He ran his forefinger from her wrist to her fingertips, drawing invisible lines to each pathetically ragged nail. Then he clasped his hand over hers firmly, and cleared his throat.

"One day, maybe we can just talk, get to know each other in a normal way. I would—enjoy that. I'm interested in your work, and admire your relationship with your family." He looked away.

She would not hyperventilate. Once certain her voice would not squeak, she replied. "I would like to make that a priority." *Was she structuring a business agenda?* "Really." *Crap.*

"Then it will happen. I suspect this will be over in a couple of days. Maybe we can find time then."

"Or we'll be dead." Her gift was not romantic encouragement.

He squeezed her hand hard, startling her so badly that she jumped. "I cannot let you die, Maggie. Remember, I'm to protect you. At all costs."

She flared. "Then we're in a bad way, Matthew, because I'm pretty determined to see you're not hurt either."

"Don't . . . " he said, ready to lecture.

"Exactly. *Don't.* I'm grown. I help those I can. Save your breath for things you can change. I'm not one of them." She wanted to stand there, holding his hand. *Help!* "This is lovely, but we need to work."

He let go.

She grabbed another brioche, and studied notes while trying not to dribble jam down her hand, onto her laptop. "Any news on the Steeles?" *And away she goes, into work again!*

He swallowed, and pressed to his lips a starched napkin with an embroidered crest.

Ah, his lips. She hiccupped.

"We won't hear for a couple of hours," he replied. "Cyril's ready. The Steeles are his job." He toasted her with his teacup. "You are mine."

"Back to work." She pushed away her plate to open her laptop wider. *Look! Faster than a speeding bullet! She hides behind responsibility again!* She eyed the pastry platter, so he placed the second-largest delicacy on her plate.

"Are you still trying to get rid of me?" His eyes were serious.

She longed for that disco ball. Pity was no reason to be attracted to someone. Someone beautiful. A prince. She would have been ashamed had she not enjoyed herself so much. So she hiccupped again.

"Always," she said, smiling. *Gorgeous man.*

He picked up tea and brioche, using the plate to point to the bookcase hiding the computers. "Would you mind if I worked here? I'm expecting a file on Spigot. Breakfast is out in thirty minutes. Not that you'll be hungry after your brioche."

"It's your house. I assume you can work anywhere you want." *She needed to see a shrink.*

She watched him power up the equipment, recognizing he equaled her ability, commitment, and expertise stroke for stroke. He was perfect.

"I'd like to return here with you when this is over," he said with his back to her.

"That would be lovely, Matthew," she replied, her screen swimming in front of her eyes.

CHAPTER FORTY-FOUR

Coburg Castle, Germany

Dr. Steele missed the *rosa rugosa* blooms that lined the steep brick driveway to Coburg Castle in the summer. Their scented shades of pink, red, and white sweetened the uphill haul, and were exquisite excuses to catch his breath by literally stopping to smell the roses.

Strudel, under a dollop of ice cream and served beneath an umbrella on the terrace, was added incentive to walk, rather than use the tram that dropped off visitors beyond the cafe.

The vehicular arms were closed at the drive base, although the sidewalk was unobstructed. They parked in the bottom lot to pant up the snowy slope. Mid-way, he decided the tram should run in winter. Technically, the castle should be closed. He hoped the gates in the castle wall were open, and that Director Mauss had reached someone who could save him and his brother.

Heavily mortared stone surrounded the Baroque entry. They crossed an anchored drawbridge in the upper bastion. Dr. Steele peered into the moat. Part of the Saxe-Coburg-Gotha ducal holdings, the builder was obsessed with security, a trait the wounded theologian appreciated more than ever. He was weakening, and reminded himself that his eternal security was absolute. But relaxed a little as they approached the open gates.

Walls twenty feet thick created a twenty-foot tunneled entrance. The gift shop and Luther rooms were ahead. The transportation museum and swan litter were left, down three flights, in a four-story structure where the last reigning duke, a grandson of Queen Victoria, had lived. A stony bower connected the buildings, and housed an extensive armory. Dr. Steele noted this collection should they need trebuchet or crossbow. He could shoot both.

This castle's nooks and crannies confused him, and he glanced around, struggling to keep his bearings in case the brothers needed to do something radically impossible. Like run.

Their Italian hosts were restless, the buildings dark. They crossed a five-hundred-foot-square central yard covered by six inches of snow, and angled right. Climbing broad, almost-black wooden stairs just left inside the door, they moved toward the Luther chapel.

The Steeles were sprightly, but their age delayed their captors.

"Where are we going, old man?" The tallest Italian, whom they had dubbed Sneerface since he didn't grasp enough English to be insulted, grabbed Dr. Steele's good shoulder and leaned into his face. Dr. Steele was about to answer when footsteps in the hall they had just cleared stopped him. Cyril led a couple around the blue-and-white *kachelofen* in the corner. Overadorned with frisky cupids, the refrigerator-sized porcelain heater could have kept barrels of ink warm for Luther while he translated the Latin Vulgate Bible into German.

"Doktor Steele." Cyril's accent was pathetic, and he wore the lanyard-draped plastic badge of Museum Director Frankel.

"So good to see you! I'm sure you remember Fraulein Erhardt." He gestured toward a female Mossad agent. "And this is Herr Schmidt, a curator helping us catalogue the Gotha jewels. We were working late, and I thought you might want to view them before we left, and they were returned to the vault."

He turned toward the Steeles' abductors. "We have a large banquet tonight, commandants from German Special Forces. It's in the Guest House, and we are instituting special security to impress them. Would you like to see the jewels before you begin your research, which we welcome?"

One thing appealing to crooks more than a scroll fragment is historic baubles outside a vault. Sneerface hesitated.

"You're welcome to return later, of course. Luther again, Doktor?" Cyril asked. His agents played along, chattering in German-accented Hebrew. The languages shared guttural tones, so one was as good as the other. The captors weren't well educated enough to understand either.

"We have time," Sneerface said, nodding eagerly. "Not much."

Dr. Steele put his hand on his shoulder, rotating the joint so the commander knew, when things got rough, where he was wounded.

Cyril led to the armory via the bower arch, accessing a ramp once used by carriages and riders. Towers thrust into roiling clouds resembling the contents of a bubbling witches' cauldron. The weather would be awful soon.

"We try to keep things authentic. They almost buried the *treasures*." Cyril shone a flashlight on the path as cold emanated from glistening rock walls and floors, and dampness cut through their clothes. Dr. Steele ignored his shoulder and arthritic knees to concentrate on balance.

THE BROTHERS' KEEPERS

Cyril retrieved keys before ascending three steps anchoring enormous bronze doors. They led to the stables. Each door sported three fluted-spade hinges that were wider than the commander's still-muscular arm. He had intentionally moved the group as far from castle occupants as possible, near the outer wall.

"They've been stored in the vault for generations," Cyril teased.

The jewels were scattered from Monte Carlo to Sweden in strongholds of royal houses, pawnshops masquerading as antique jewelers, and bank boxes. This was the ambush, and Dr. Steele nudged his brother, who blinked to acknowledge awareness. The Italians jittered nervously, eager for the glory beyond.

Cyril leaned against the left door, swinging it easily. Everything at Coburg was well maintained. The brothers followed, then their kidnappers. Dr. Steele immediately yanked Steven to the right. The Mossad couple was last, but never entered. Four operatives swarmed the Italians, disabling them.

In the scuffling and cursing, no one heard the scooter shoot up the ramp.

Its driver pulled even with the stable door. Leveled a semiautomatic weapon. Began strafing widely. He—or she—killed the Italians first.

Dr. Steele prayed he would live long enough to complain about the weather. He didn't see anyone else fall. He was in a stable, under a manger, seeing stars.

CHAPTER FORTY-FIVE

Chateau Cushan

"Here we go." Matthew's worried comment preceded chatter, then a static crackle from the screen.

Cyril's blood-splattered face was in a low-ceilinged, brightly lit room, consistent with Maggie's teenage memories of the utilitarian spaces in Veste Coburg. Grace had dragged her and Jeff everywhere, providing the academic credentials to see places hidden from tourists.

"Sir?" Matthew's tone was professional.

The commander said something to a medic running behind him before responding. "They're wounded. Both of them now. Stay there." Maggie moved into Cyril's view. "Ms. Madison, tell your family they're alive. And we're trying to beat more than one group to the fragment."

"Mama was right," she said. "She thought there were two."

Cyril grimaced. "It was difficult enough with one." He disappeared.

She stepped back when Matthew swiveled his chair to speak.

"I suggest breakfast, then work again. Whenever he gets here, we won't stop until we have the whole scroll." His lips smiled, but his eyes were pinched at the corners. "You think you can eat anything after the huge brioche? Correction—*brioches?*"

She turned to her laptop to hide a blush, but he caught her hand. "It's a joke, Maggie. I'm hungry. Are you? Served here or in the Morning Room?"

She tried to deactivate Herculean defense mechanisms. *What would a normal young woman do?* She didn't know, so she made something up.

"As lovely as the library is, I haven't seen much of your ancestral hovel. Do you think you can *find* breakfast?"

He laughed. "I'll follow Jeff." He password-protected the system, and they walked to breakfast hand-in-hand.

CHAPTER FORTY-SIX

Chateau Cushan

Grace
They were the last to enter. We turned to stare.
"We were in the library . . . " Maggie blurted. Even her hands turned scarlet.
"Working," Matthew finished.
"On what?" Jeff didn't miss a beat.
She said *karsts* as Matthew said *brioche*.
I laughed, and Mark raised his eyebrows. Becca elbowed Jeff in the ribs. Cliff stared at his muesli while Dr. Merrit grinned. Bashir nodded happily.
"Did someone say brioche?" Jeff asked, sipping from a tiny Turkish-coffee cup as he renewed childhood battles over the breakfast-pastry-of-choice during trips to France.
"Too late. She ate them all." Matthew filled a plate from a sideboard mounded with Continental—fruits, breads, eggs—and Middle Eastern—cheese, bagels, tomatoes—foods. "Every single one. Even the biggest, which was mine."
"No doubt. Where's my invitation to brioche?" Her brother persisted. "When were they served?"

"About 6:30," Matthew said.

"Awfully early to be working on karsts and brioche, don't you think?" Jeff would not give up.

"I'm throwing you under the next train," Maggie muttered.

"I'll be in the library, reviewing *intelligence*," Cliff, one of the most amiable people ever born, snapped. "Jeff, when you have the chance, I have questions."

Bashir motioned to a staffer to escort his son's rival to the library. "Have you heard anything of your friend, Ms. Madison? Dr. Steele?"

"Yes," Matthew and she answered.

"I believe I am Ms. Madison, Matthew," she said, unaccustomed to being spoken for in any sense. "Identity crisis?"

He inclined his head, embarrassed. "My apologies, *Ms. Madison*. Please continue."

Bashir chuckled.

She glanced at Matthew as she spoke. "I was in the library when Cyril told Matthew *both* Steele brothers were wounded." I gasped. "Nothing fatal, Mama. He'll let us know when they're ready to be moved, but we're to stay here until we hear from him."

Mark headed for the door. "I want to get into the Mossad packages again. In light of everything that's happened since Venice. Do we have anything new?"

Jeff and Becca were behind him.

"Don't think so," Becca said.

I was refreshed, but clean laundry did that for me. I suspected Matthew and Maggie of something interesting because they wouldn't look at me. She focused on Eggs Benedict and cheese blintzes topped with *crème fraiche* and raspberry jam—her favorite breakfast after brioche.

Her appetite was larger than usual, and I wondered if love did that for her. Or if it was nerves.

"I'll have updated information by the time I return to the computers," Matthew said, inverting his fork. "Reconvene in the library, spread out, and plow through this stuff until the commander gets here. As I told Maggie—" he nodded at her "—as she ate her *fifth* brioche. When he arrives, no one rests until this job is finished."

When kidding about her now-*dozen* brioches stopped, everyone except Matthew, Bashir, and she abandoned empty plates. She had eaten as quickly as etiquette allowed, downing a second pot of English Breakfast tea.

"She has a good appetite," Bashir stage-whispered.

Before she could protest, Matthew spoke. "Yes. And her bloodlines are strong. A line of champions. With good teeth." They compared her to a filly in Bedouin fashion. Then Matthew became grave. "She'll need that energy, based on Cyril's demeanor. Ready, Maggie?" He stood to assist her with her chair.

She took her last sip of tea. "Will we have more tea?"

"Headache still?" He tilted his head as he looked at her.

"Only slightly." She looked at her teacup. "Caffeine would help, though."

"I can arrange it," Bashir interjected. "Luncheon is at 1:00, tea at 4:00, and dinner at 8:00. Son . . . " He watched Matthew, who hadn't looked from Maggie's face. "*Son.*" Matthew turned toward him. "Please let me know Cyril's ETA when you can. I am happy to feed and shelter you, but need to apprise the staff so they can do their jobs." He slipped out the door.

"Let's go." Maggie followed him.

THE BROTHERS' KEEPERS

Matthew caught her in a few steps, and tugged on her hand. "This direction."

...

They took the long way.

"I'd rather enter separately," Maggie whispered, unaware I had just arrived and was studying books on the other side of the door.

"Courage, Ms. Madison," Matthew replied. "Although I understand it would be kinder to Cliff if we didn't walk in together, and that's important."

"I prefer to be kind. One of us should dawdle."

I held my breath.

"I need to change my socks?" he asked.

She entered the library, and jumped when she saw me smiling. I popped an eyebrow, and she giggled.

When Matthew joined us ten minutes later, Cliff and Jeff were discussing documents from Solomon's era, working forward in time. Dr. Merrit and I focused on Luther, working backward. Becca and Mark were a clearinghouse, charting possibilities on a spreadsheet, working with Mossad data preordered so the most valuable was first.

Maggie analyzed Z-SCANs again, having created a 3D model linking karsts in a low channel from Jerusalem to Timna. She told us it worked theoretically, thanks to cretaceous limestone. Geophysics supported her analysis, she said, and we wouldn't need to prove anything until we possessed both scroll halves. By then, we would investigate, under heavy security. If Mekorot—the national water company of Israel—didn't hijack the research.

When Matthew powered up, Cyril appeared.

"I can't transport them," he said. We gathered around a seated Matthew. "They're too fragile. Steele—Dr. Stanley—was shot in the shoulder yesterday. It wasn't professionally treated. He needs rest and antibiotics. Steven was hit in the calf today. I can't find a physician who'll clear them for travel."

"Where are the agents I sent to you from Rothenberg?" Matthew's question seemed incongruous.

Cyril's jaw twitched. "The body of one was found outside the Old City walls in Wittenberg this morning. You suspected?"

"Are you coming here? Or do we meet somewhere?" Matthew must have decided his answer was obvious. One agent killed the other. The killer's presence on our security detail, and tracker woven into Maggie's hair, explained how we were followed. "We should push on because the rogue officer could be aware I brought them here."

I leaned over Matthew's shoulder. "Commander, have you asked the brothers why they ran?" That information could expedite joining the scroll pieces, and they needed to come clean.

"No. Steven is still in surgery. And they sedated Dr. Steele. He should be lucid within the hour."

Jeff put his hand on my shoulder to break in. "We need everything."

"They're sitting on something," Mark added as he towered over Jeff.

"I don't know what it is, but I'll work on it." The commander's eyes cut to Matthew. "Be ready to move. I hope this evening. Tomorrow morning at the latest."

"Where to? What should we bring?"

"Venice. Everything you've got." The Israeli clicked off.

CHAPTER FORTY-SEVEN

Chateau Cushan

Grace

Maggie's voice interrupted us just before noon. "I have enough. Can we compare notes? Maybe you can fill in some gaps. Lunch still at 1:00?"

"Yes. Here or in the Morning Room, Maggie?" Matthew positioned her as chatelaine of the chateau, and ensured she had enough hot tea to float the Queen Mary 2 on a transatlantic crossing. "I could probably speed it up a little if you're hungry."

"I'm fine." Her voice was firm. "How about we cross-reference our research over lunch?" Her energetic look meant she had discovered something.

"I'm good with that." I was ready to return to the States, become a *hausfrau*, and get facials—which meant stress was deteriorating my mind. Standing to encourage circulation, I inspired a trend. Everyone shoved their things to one end of the table to mill about and look at books. It was a literate crowd. Before I could, Maggie scooted up the ladder, peering at the upper shelves.

When she descended, she slid straight to me. "You're not going to believe this, Mama, but even the top row is dusted."

Matthew watched her, then called for lunch early. The room became half library, half fine dining. He had closed the drapes when we started working, I thought to prevent glare on his screen or being overseen, and opened them now to fresh snow. It fell from clouds creating a foggy band obscuring the mountain peaks.

The first course was, according to Matthew, *bunder gerstensuppe*, a rustic barley soup with bacon and ham. He held Maggie's chair as he announced the ingredients, then sat next to her. Cliff took the chair on her other side.

I hoped nothing required knives.

When hot bread was given to Matthew as host, he passed opposite my daughter. Cliff offered the one remaining roll to Maggie, who made a production of splitting it with him. Reviewing the trajectory of the basket, I discovered Jeff had taken two. When he grinned, I knew he had intentionally provoked the interaction between his sister and Cliff. Family dynamics are eternal.

Maggie tucked her spoon between bowl and plate, freeing her hands to gesture as she talked. "I've a plausible karstic system from Jerusalem to Timna, and it could continue to Aqaba." She swirled bread around her bowl.

I raised my brows, and she continued. "I didn't mention it earlier because I didn't have the software to be sure, and it relates to the paper I was presenting in Marseilles. But I downloaded it through the office system this morning. Layered in the research from Mossad, MI6, and the CIA. And confirmed the topography and limestone make a system possible, if not probable, now that they've found one in Jerusalem." She popped the soggy bread into her mouth. "What do you have?"

"I'll go." Jeff blotted soup from his chin, leaning back in a *bergère* too short for the tabletop. "Solomon was cagey about water. Once again proving his wisdom. But water powered those mines, according to para-biblical records. So I searched for a text I read years ago. An Ethiopic script called the *Kebra Negast*. It tells about Menelik, son of Solomon and Sheba, who traveled to Jerusalem to meet his famous father. Mentored under him. Vaguely documented the water source."

Mark patted the table in front of Jeff. "The point, Son. Although I'm interested." He tried. "Just—later."

"Well, Sheba accompanied Menelik to Jerusalem, and would have known a lot of Solomon's secrets, right?" Jeff's eyes opened wider, animated carrot brows bouncing. "You need background, Dad. Scholars think Sheba used a language called First Tongue. Symbol-based and similar to hieroglyphics. They've found First-Tongue inscriptions in Yemen, where Sheba was from, and references to a great queen. Timing is right. Regardless of the Menelik angle, the Bible didn't document all children of Jewish kings, most of whom were illegitimate."

Mark nodded enthusiastically, totally faking it.

"Does it really look like hieroglyphics, Jeff?" I asked. Syncretism morphed beliefs across cultures, but I hadn't studied writing moving similarly.

"Generally. Anthropomorphic figures. Characters resembling doughnuts. Tedium aside, there's an inscription about the great queen's love, his wealth and prowess—on many levels, but this *is* Ancient Near Eastern. A passage about wealth mentions mines. Then Menelik is quoted about the 'mighty, invisible river' powering them. Was the river invisible because it was underground?"

"That all you have?" Cliff grinned. It was good to see his happy face.

"No," Jeff said, playing it straight. "There are similar references, without a queen, in New Kingdom Hittite . . . "

"I *knew* it!" Mark laughed. Jeff's love of obscure Akkadian lore made a lasting impression on his dad.

"Yeah," Jeff continued, "the Ammonites and the Sumerians. Egypt as well."

"Do you . . . " Mark asked incredulously.

"Once you know one of them, the rest are related," Becca interrupted, patting Jeff's forearm to slow him down before he launched the language Olympics.

"Yes." Jeff sat forward, curtailed.

"Why hasn't this been revealed before?" Cliff traced invisible lines on the table with a forefinger. "Certainly Solomon is a person of interest and subject of study."

"Probably because no one looked closely at the mechanics of his mines." Dr. Merrit's long silence made me wonder if he was worrying about Dr. Steele. "Scholars have been preoccupied with wealth, wisdom, and kingdom writings. Things with theological impact. And Jeff's right. The Bible is meant to tell the story of Christ, not record minutiae. I don't know anyone, or any institution, looking across civilizations, like we are, at something as specific as water for Solomon's mines. This is targeted cross-cultural research. Something Christendom should do more of."

A knock on the door announced the second course, grilled *Emmentaler* cheese-on-rye sandwiches, with berries over microgreens. We waited to continue until the staff closed the door, remembering the Mossad mole.

"Now, what's up with Luther?" Matthew asked.

"He's always driven me nuts," was my response. "But that's a lifestyle and manners issue. Dr. Merrit, will you do the honors?" I slid my hand across the table, as if introducing him.

"We're right about the cuneiform trajectory. Solomon to Constantine to Luther, generally. I do believe part of the scroll ended up in the Vatican, buying out excommunication, but then was moved elsewhere. I also believe the part about the Venetian doge's grandson carrying . . ."

"I have more," Cyril's disembodied voice said. We turned toward the monitors, where the commander appeared. "Check the encrypted files I'm sending. Normal code. Read them before I arrive. I plan to leave late afternoon. I want us in Venice at sunup."

The screen went black again.

"Your summary, Dr. Merrit?" Jeff retrieved files and laptop, and we returned to Luther.

"Bottom line is, we don't know where it went. Apparently Cyril thinks it went to Venice." He looked at me as I nodded. "There are a few annotations supporting this assumption, primarily in Venetian documents traced through the siblings' e-mails."

"How'd you do that?" Mark asked.

"God works in mysterious ways," Merrit said. "And so does MOSES. Specifically, I had the stateside MOSES members unravel the correspondence Maggie and Matthew hadn't had time to analyze."

"We can hope the location's in this." Matthew watched files download as he summoned staff to replace luncheon plates with a bubbling chocolate fondue, and enough fruit to serve Mossad. Skewers, upright in a silver tube, were seized.

"But there's something else." I drooled on a flawless strawberry so flavorful it must have been picked from an estate greenhouse. "Important. Cyril says we head to Venice. I think we go to Rome."

"Mama?" Maggie handed me another strawberry. "What did you find?"

"Here's my theory. Luther, despite boorish behavior, adored his wife and family. Doted on his kids. We're assuming he handed off the cuneiform in Rome when he crawled the steps of St. Peter's. What if he knew more than we think? What if intellectual defiance motivated his journey?"

"I don't understand," Mark said as Cliff agreed.

"Luther? Defiant?" Jeff joked, spiraling his strawberry and slinging chocolate ribbons all over himself.

"Dr. Merrit found passages referring to Solomon's living water in correspondence between Luther and Calvin. That's nothing new. Theologically, streams of living water refer to life in Christ. But Luther writes about things along stream banks in unusually bucolic terms—out-of-character prose for a ruffian, which he was. He says Roman streams are surrounded by death, and the key to life is death. Then he mentions death along Roman waterways."

"I am totally confused." Maggie set down her skewer. "I know about the Tiber."

Everyone stopped chewing. I sounded crazy, so tried to explain further. "Not the Tiber River. Scholars have interpreted this passage as Luther dissing the Catholic Church by saying the living water in Rome was dead. Meaning that the Catholic Church was spiritually dead." I watched my professor for guidance.

"Go on, Grace," Dr. Merrit said. "I don't understand, but I'm keeping an open mind. And you're beginning to make sense."

"Frightening," Jeff said.

I chose to ignore my son. "We've overlooked one consistent thread. The very simplistic Luther rose on the mosaic. Luther had a daughter named Margarete. Marguerites are referenced in the letter to Calvin. I looked at the Grossmunster doors, where small flowers touch Luther's feet. He stands in a field of what could very well be daisies. A marguerite is a daisy. Early Christian female leaders were named Margarita. Famous inscriptions appear, particularly in the Catacomb of Priscilla in Rome, about a woman named Margarita who is buried there. Photos of that burial chamber show frescoes depicting an unusual amount of water, and a damaged bit strongly resembling Timna.

"We have not addressed the flower that recurs *everywhere* in this chase. Maybe Luther is using it—particularly the tomb of Margarita in Rome—to direct us."

"Any flowers in the frescoes?" Maggie asked.

"Yes. And they look like daisies. In our pursuit of the other scroll half, we've ignored the flowers."

Bashir had entered moments ago, and waited for me to finish. "Son. A word?"

Matthew walked to his father as Mark spoke. "You're saying you think Luther hid the key to the scroll location in a Roman catacomb?"

"Plausible, Mama." Maggie nibbled a slice of apple. "I have some theories about the location of the . . . "

Matthew interrupted her, his dark face ashen. "Please go with staff to get your things. They will bring you to the carriage house. We need to hurry."

"What is it?" Maggie asked.

"The carriage house. Hurry, Maggie."

CHAPTER FORTY-EIGHT

Klinikim Coburg

Cyril's face confirmed that Dr. Steele was not in heaven. The theologian shut his eyes, as if to try again.

The window shades were down, with louvers tilted upward to filter light. Cyril was backlit.

"Ste . . . " Dr. Steele began.

"Is fine," the commander said. "Took a bullet in his calf, but they've extracted it. You'll both be here for several days. *Klinikim* Coburg, the finest medical facility in the city."

"The Madi . . . " He grimaced as he tugged his IV.

"I'm leaving soon to meet them. We have a dead agent, a rogue agent, something Spigot-related, and an unknown group in pursuit. Tell me all of it."

Dr. Steele took a deep breath, blowing out so his cheeks expanded like a puffer fish. Cyril adjusted the cannula squarely in both nostrils of the long-time operative, and laid the tube over the papery hospital gown.

"Pull . . . out in my sleep," Dr. Steele said, adjusting the cannula again. "In Venice."

"Where in Venice?" The commander rested his weight on the bed rails.

"Don't know. Steven does."

"Are you lying to me?"

"Wouldn't. Friends in danger."

"You'd lie if they weren't?"

"Probably not. Reserve the right to sin." He was tired already. "Where is Steven?"

"Across the hall."

"Conscious?"

"Not yet."

"Move him here . . . arrange it." He closed his eyes, turning from the commander.

Cyril stared at the frail body, wondering whether this would be the last time the brothers were together on this earth. Then left the room. When he returned, he told Dr. Steele the nurse would move Steven's bed as soon as he awakened. "He's sedated from the surgery. Now, tell me the rest of it. Slowly."

Dr. Steele smiled weakly. "Four-thousand-year-old tale? Two old men have time?"

. . .

Cyril shifted in the uncomfortable metal chair, his arms straight, with hands on his knees. His jaw hung slack. His mouth formed a dark ovoid in a grizzled face. Dr. Steele had not seen him speechless in fifty-plus years.

"When did they change it from Stahl to Steele?"

"Immigrated. German name a liability. English wasn't. Expedient."

The door across the hall opened, and he turned to look for his brother.

"So you've been after this most of your life?"

"After many things. This is one." He tried to raise his head. The bulk of the tale was finished. Bed brakes clacked as they were released.

"Stan?" Steven's voice was raspy. "Alive?"

"Vibrantly. You?"

"Eternal. 'Til God calls me home. Your line."

"Told him, Steven."

Silence.

"Madisons? Merrit?" Steven drew a laborious breath between every word.

"Great danger. No secret . . . worth innocent people."

"Understand. Not all innocent, Stan." Steven's eyes stayed closed. "Tell Commander . . . where?" Steven gave his brother the go ahead in case Cyril had not been informed.

"Venice?" Cyril asked from a hanging lunge over Steven's bed.

Steven did not answer. Dr. Steele started to speak, but Steven lifted an index finger to stop him.

"Where in Venice?" Cyril impatiently gripped the foot of the bed. "I'm leaving soon, picking them up, and we're heading there. I need to know where to look."

Steven shifted. "Hard to give up . . . heirloom."

A high-pitched squeal pierced the air. Dr. Steele tried to sit up. Nurses rushed in, a white flurry around Steven. Cyril backed away. The room filled with chatter. Shouting spilled into the hallway.

Stanley Augustus Steele groaned, and grasped his chest.

"Twins sometimes die in the same instant," Cyril said, walking from the room.

CHAPTER FORTY-NINE

Klinikim Coburg

Steven's flat-line episode sent him to intensive care, where he would stay for at least five days. He was in good hands. If not with the medical staff, then with God. There was nothing Dr. Steele could do in Coburg, other than recover from hospital-food-induced indigestion.

He also could not wheel his hospital bed to St. Mark's Square. Nor scale the basilica, where Steven thought the fragment hidden, in an open-backed hospital gown without getting arrested. Well, since it was Venice during Carnevale, he *might* be able to get away with flashing his bottom. But he preferred to dress properly.

Steven muttered the location after Cyril left, before being removed by a harried medical staff worried about wounds taken more seriously after government and intelligence inquiries. Fortunately, in their preoccupied state, the doctors and nurses thought Steven's words were the senseless babble of a dying man.

But Dr. Steele knew better.

"Luther's rose." He muttered Steven's whispered directions. "Horse's hoof."

He retrieved the Digene box purchased in Madaba during his solo stroll to find the dead priest. Plucked from it directions overwritten in Hebrew. Opened the metal cabinet in the room corner.

Staff had not taken his clothes. He had money. It was time for the afternoon shift change.

Stanley Augustus Steele, PhD., would escape!

CHAPTER FIFTY

Doge's Palace, Venice

Agnelli's prelate *cappa magna* costume expedited entry to the palace and allowed him to avoid the visitors wrapping helter-skelter to St. Mark's Square. There they entwined with tourists heading to the basilica, which was closing. More than one misguided soul had spent an eternity in the wrong queue.

The colorful regalia triggered bowing from Italians, and gawking photos from everyone else. He had upgraded his rank to that of a cardinal at the apartment, since it was Carnevale and he was leaving the service of the Vatican. The ceremonial robes were a costume to him now.

The aqua alta had subsided before he arrived, so he let the red cloak drag across courtyard tiles worn smooth by six hundred years of foot traffic. Residual dampness had altered the paver color, deepening it from bone to terra cotta.

A papal uniform simplified travel, especially at checkpoints where a look of loving forbearance opened pre-approved lines. More elegant than the silk cape—*ferraiuolo*—or red-tufted *biretta* that made him look like a Neapolitan pizza deliveryman, his costume was travel clothing *par excellence*.

Rather than use the private Bridge of Sighs entrance, he passed under the Great Counsel Room, picturing works therein by both Tintorettos and Giovane. The lagoon was at his back. The Loggias and Scala D'Oro were ahead.

He strode upstairs, between mammoth marble statues of Mars and Neptune. As a boy, he had climbed ladders to haylofts and slipped late into Sunday services, his hands grubby and hand-me-downs threadbare.

"Pantiloni Corti is dead," he muttered as this triumphal walk put his ascension in perspective.

The apartment reserved for Vatican use was a well-kept secret. It was not grand or beautiful. Those adjectives applied to public rooms in famous Venetian spaces. But it was free and secure. Hidden as part of a Byzantine pact between the Holy See and Venice to lift the ban involving the scroll.

The document Agnelli discovered yesterday led here. To St. Mark's Square.

Particularly during Carnevale, the area was busy. But if that scroll half was here, he would shake the earth to find it. He had already moved heaven.

CHAPTER FIFTY-ONE

Chateau Cushan

Grace

A dirt-streaked navy duffel lay between Becca and Jeff, abutting an industrial nylon carryon containing Dr. Merrit's things. Cliff capped a wheeled Tumi—Maggie's—with a tattered twill backpack assigned to him. Mark and I combined belongings into a zippered olive hanger bag, a slight tear in one corner.

Matthew had gathered the luggage while we chose clothing from extra garments at the chateau. I was thankful to be rid of my mismatched Galleries Lafayette wardrobe, but still looked sartorially challenged. From the looks of the bags he provided, he didn't expect them, or possibly us, to return.

Bashir gave instructions—in Lebanese, according to Jeff—to four armed men dressed in winter gear identical to the outerwear we just donned: white jumpsuits retrieved from a rolling rack.

I resembled a plus-sized Sta-Puft marshmallow. Round is a shape.

Matthew trotted into a space hewn from rock, laced by metal girders, and unforgivingly lit by banks of fluorescent bulbs. He followed Mark and me, a gray backpack slung over his shoulder. I didn't expect carriages in a carriage house, so four

Mercedes, the same color as the helicopter that brought us to the chateau, worked.

Snowmobiles, however, created serious misgivings. I refused to ride them at the ranch because I was not an adrenaline junky. And I hated their noise.

"We're under siege?" Jeff turned his half-lidded stare to Matthew, protectively putting his arm around Becca.

"Not quite. The chateau sits essentially on the property edge, which extends a half-mile into the lake. Two hundred acres are dangerously fenced and patrolled. Father has cameras throughout. Some obvious, some hidden."

Bashir stepped forward. "I discovered this morning someone tampered with the southern cameras, and feeds from the other units revealed visitors moving toward us." He seemed undisturbed.

Matthew handed his bag to a guard before continuing. "Father will successfully defend the estate. But this will delay our departure. Weather's moving in, possibly ice fog that can be impenetrable. We need to leave before everything breaks loose and before dark. While we can."

"What about Cyril coming here?" I mentioned the commander's edict.

"He's joining us in Venice. We can check your theory, Dr. Madison, in Rome." His tone was detached. "Father will send our things. Take only what is necessary. Strap it on. Put it in pockets that zip or button. These machines aren't fluid on cross-terrain rides. Especially at high speed.

"Routing through Rome will delay us a couple of hours." Matthew spoke to Maggie, his voice soft. "I remember your problem at Hezekiah's. We're trying to escape overland. But if that doesn't work, we're returning here, and you're going to have to trust me to do something you'll hate."

She frowned. Cliff put his arm lightly around her shoulders, tentatively emulating Jeff's pose. Score one for Cliff. She didn't shake him off, but didn't nestle into his chest, either. "What exactly is it, Matthew?" she asked.

"Let's cross the bridge if we come to it. Mark." He turned to my husband, who was watching men prep the machines. "I assume you can operate one of these? And you too, Jeff?"

"The ranch would be impossible without them." Mark's response was immediate. "Jeff, you rode one again two Christmases ago?"

Jeff said he had.

"Cliff, you ever driven one? Dr. Merrit?"

Dr. Merrit had not, and would lack the strength. But Cliff used them during adolescent winters in the Midwest.

"Deep snow makes them unwieldy. These commercial-grade machines are five hundred pounds," Matthew said as he strapped his pack on one. "I would advise you be a passenger, Dr. Merrit. Behind a guard. Cliff . . . "

He stiffened, and I hoped Matthew didn't demean him by assigning him to a guard.

"Would you take Maggie? Before you can say anything, Maggie," he interrupted her as her mouth opened, holding up a hand for silence. "I am certain you can drive like Danica Patrick. I also know you're a crack shot. You're most useful firing. I would like for you to sit in front of Cliff, facing him. But let him drive, and use his body as a shield." He handed her an Uzi from a waiting guard. "This is powerful and hard to shoot from that position. But you can do it. Shoot everybody except us. We're dressed identically, so easy to spot. Cliff?"

The men squared off as Matthew continued to speak. "My job is to protect her. I know you'll do that with your life. If anything happens to me, get her to Cyril. He'll wall her off with Mossad until this is finished." He hesitated. "Take care of her. Please."

My eyes filled with tears as Cliff extended his hand.

Matthew shook it while addressing the rest of us. "Dr. Madison behind Mark. Becca behind Jeff. Both women armed. Shoot to kill. Stay in the middle of our diamond formation. We'll break it only when the trail narrows at the tree line. Dr. Merrit, you and your guard go first, then machines carrying Maggie, Dr. Madison, and Becca. I'll be at the rear."

"The easiest to pick off," Maggie said. Her arms wrapped around her body, crossing so far she could have been in a straitjacket.

He placed his hands on her shoulders. "My job is to protect you. That makes me a target." They stared at each a second longer than necessary, until Bashir cleared his throat.

"Don't hesitate to return." He winked at Maggie, but heavy vertical creases ran between his brows. "She is tougher than she looks. Hers is a courageous bloodline, Son. It makes a difference at times such as this."

Matthew nodded at his father. Then he dropped his hands before continuing to explain what we were about to do. "The trail is marked. If I honk three times rapidly, return to the chateau. People here will know what to do, which is cross the border into Italy. Infra-red cameras indicate we'll move away from forces approaching the chateau."

"Shades of Bond," Jeff muttered. "James Bond."

"You should be used to this," I said to my son, referring to his off-grid BBC work.

"Which brings me to my last point. If you fall off a snowmobile, a guard will pick you up. Stay buried. Do *not* stand up.

Wait until the last minute, clasp the guard's arm, and swing on behind him."

Bashir distributed vests and helmets. "The vests are bulletproof, as are the helmets. The rest of your body is vulnerable."

"Let's do this." Matthew's gloved hand revved a throttle.

I reached for my daughter, and kissed her cheeks. "See you at the border, baby."

Jeff and Becca hugged me. I tried not to blubber, but believed we faced death.

Mark pulled me. "The sooner the better. We need a head start, Gracie."

I climbed on, adjusted my vest and helmet, then tugged on Mark's gear to protect him. Matthew raised his hand in a chopping motion. Bashir hit a button. Old doors swung nimbly open into a heavy snow, while a ramp on which we sat—I hadn't noticed it—tilted along invisible seams. My throat was parched.

The roar from rising RPMs reverberated through my helmet insulation. Unless our attackers were deaf, they would know what was happening, and where, in a heartbeat.

The machine pitched forward. I wrapped an arm around Mark's waist. The Glock 9mm was racked back, a bullet in the chamber. I prayed for ungodly things.

"Stay low, Gracie!" Mark yelled over his shoulder. He gunned through the snow, machine slides shooting left and right. Half stood on the running boards to leverage his body while I held onto his belt. The snowmobile nose shot through air. We cleared a mound. Settled four feet beyond the crest. *Yee haw?*

We followed Maggie and Cliff. A guard raced toward the forest ahead of them. We were almost obscured by dense flakes, which I knew would hurt my face had the helmet lacked a shield. Jeff and Becca tucked into our snowy rooster tail. Occasional backfires sounded like gunshots. With each one, I whirled on the seat. My elbow was propped on Mark's shoulder, my Glock ready.

Jeff and Becca were about to join us in the trees when Mark jumped. He looked up, and I did too.

A chopper raced toward us.

When Matthew's snowmobile—last in line—penetrated the forest, he talked into his helmet front. He circled, narrowly missing a pine while covering us with snow. Raised and lowered his hands, palms down, indicating we were to wait.

Could one chopper mean more? We needed to return to Bashir, but would be impossible to miss, flying over the snow beneath hovering sharpshooters.

Activity appeared on the upper-bastion wall of Chateau Cushan. Something—a large pipe—poked out and over. Bodies swarmed around the object. The chopper hung low, hidden by a canopy of old-growth spruce and conifers, perfectly pinpointing our location. Occasionally, landing skids cracked through the treetops, disturbing branches enough to reveal us while sprinkling us with needles and cones.

Matthew's mouth moved. He prostrated himself on the seat, pointing toward the chateau. We dropped. A flash preceded the explosion. Flaming shrapnel bounced through the evergreens. Becca, knocked from Jeff's machine, scrambled on. Matthew pointed again, honking three times. We broke for safety.

I heard the shot before I felt it. I would have sworn someone hit my back with a baseball bat. The force went through me, bumping Mark.

"You okay?" He yelled, dodging as sharpshooter rounds pinged divots around us.

"Faster!" My peripheral vision picked up two incoming machines—not ours—from opposite sides. Two more moved toward the front of our line. *Toward my daughter.* I shouted something profane.

"Do it, Gracie!" Mark yelled as the Glock muzzle passed his ear, and he maintained a constant speed.

I breathed out, steadying my chest so its rise and fall wouldn't corrupt my aim. My target was an unprotected armpit. My goal was to penetrate vital organs.

I pulled the trigger. Missed. The Glock rebounded high—I couldn't do a classic brace in this position. But I scared him or her. A weapon pointed at me, so I pulled the trigger again.

Mark cleared the mound by six feet this time. My rear flew a foot off the seat. The other snowmobile whipped around. Rolled. Slammed into a tree. The driver was caught under running treads.

Pinging sounds reminded me the game wasn't over. One snowmobile still threatened my daughter.

"Get me closer!" I yelled at Mark's helmet.

He gunned the throttle. Macerated three small firs. Pulled within twenty feet. I was ready. Timed the shot. When the assassin turned, I aimed at the throat. Pulled the trigger. Didn't miss.

Maggie was the epicenter of semi-automatic fire. She leaned around Cliff, half-squatting. Peppered the two remaining snowmobilers trailing Jeff and Becca.

"Get down!" I yelled again.

She couldn't hear me. Doubled over. Dropped from the snowmobile. Rolled into a deep glade. *She had been hit!*

I stopped breathing. Mark cut back to her. Cliff turned. Matthew was closest. He changed trajectory to the glade. Cliff rerouted to the chateau. The last attacker followed Matthew.

I yelled at Mark's helmet. "Matthew's going!"

"Cover him!"

Right.

We crisscrossed between our daughter and attackers. Tried to protect Matthew and her by deflecting shots from them. Became a target. Stayed on the glade crest. Matthew's machine sunk heavily. My vest took another hit. I fell into four feet of snow, buried so deeply I couldn't stand. I fired three shots at the last attacker, who disappeared into the woods.

I staggered up. Saw a machine heading for me. Mark stood on the runners of his, aiming to T-bone the incoming snowmobile. I waited two seconds—an eternity—until certain of my shot.

Semi-automatic fire showered the driver. His body jerked, responding to multiple hits. I dove toward the glade. Didn't roll far in deep snow. Shots continued. The snowmobile exploded, the force slamming me. Then Mark yanked me from a fluffy pile at the bottom of the glade. I searched for my daughter as he dropped me, sidesaddle, on the snowmobile bench.

Matthew clutched Maggie, who waved the Uzi. She had saved my life. He patted the vest in a way that, under other circumstances, would have been wildly inappropriate. She finally shoved him toward his machine, and they began a dash for the carriage house.

I didn't see blood. But we almost nailed Jeff, rocket launcher in his free hand, blasting out the doors to our rescue.

...

We slid in. Two machines stopped by hitting a wall on the far end of the carriage house. Ours was one.

THE BROTHERS' KEEPERS

Matthew pulled his vest snaps open in one motion from collar to waist. We threw our gear and helmets on a large heap.

I demanded proof that Maggie was unharmed. Matthew ran past us and grabbed her. They dashed toward Bashir, who gesticulated madly on the top step.

"Follow Father!" Matthew yelled.

CHAPTER FIFTY-TWO

Cushan Estate, Switzerland

Grace

From the carriage house built into the outer wall, we dropped to a subterranean passage heading east. Our last turn, down a flight of narrow stone steps, led to a metal door with a keypad on its frame. The atmosphere became colder and wetter, and lichen blurred the edges of rocks in the walls. We were nearing the lake. Bashir entered a code, and we rushed onto an underground dock.

Maggie spoke first. "Crap."

Four slicker-yellow submarines hung from sturdy cranes, their dark-glass bubble tops open like clamshells. They resembled catamarans with protruding outer pontoons, and looked ridiculously cheerful. I had seen these, or similar ones, years ago. *The Neiman-Marcus Christmas catalogue?*

Catwalks led to each cabin. The water beneath lapped peacefully. I started muttering. "How did they get here? How do they get out? More importantly, were we expected to escape in these yellow submarines without singing Beatles tunes?"

Matthew conferred with Bashir before brushing past us. He unlocked a cabinet on a far wall, retrieved more gear, and returned to distribute ammunition.

"I won't do it." Maggie stared at the subs.

"What?" Matthew was puzzled.

"Submarines." She stood on my boots, pointing at yellow balls dangling like ornaments.

He looked toward the machines. "Of course not. We can't. The lake is frozen." He reloaded seven bullets in the magazine of my Glock, replacing those I fired during the snowmobile debacle. "Father has a warehouse across the lake. We use the subs to go back and forth in the summer. It's faster than going around, and the dock has a crane." He motioned to the steel arms suspending the subs. "Plus, it's actually a lot more scenic than the speedboats. And safer."

"Who can't snow ski?" He addressed all of us now, ignoring Maggie. No one responded. "Dr. Merrit, with respect, I think you need to stay with Father. He will get you to Rome to join us."

We waited for the theologian's response.

"Of course. I do not want to slow you down," he said humbly.

"I'm not concerned about you slowing us down. I'm worried about you having a heart attack. Cross-country skiing is hard at any age, but few people do it past their sixties," Matthew said. "For a good reason."

"And cameras in the cabin quadrant indicate fog. It will be unpleasant and icy," Bashir added. "You have perhaps forty five minutes until it's too dark to see."

Dr. Merrit stepped to him. "I am honored to stay and help. Go with God's speed, friends."

"Are you telling me we're going to just ski out there with a helicopter overhead and armed assassins on snowmobiles?" Cliff demanded, flinging his arms in the direction of the ceiling. "In fleezing flog? I mean, frog? Fleezing frog?"

"Try *crap*. It works for me," Maggie said, frowning.

"Actually, that's not what we're going to do. Please follow me." Matthew trotted to a door near Bashir, then into a tunnel. "This leads to a cabin a mile from the chateau and . . . " His voice became faint. " . . . change and ski to town from there."

"You think they're not going to attack the cabin?" Cliff shouted.

"The flog, the frog, or the fleeze?" Maggie snipped, running past him and after Matthew.

"I do not think they're going to attack this cabin," came Matthew's distant reply.

. . .

We made quick work of the well-lit passage, jogging it in five minutes. Even Maggie's claustrophobia appeared in check. We clambered up, emerging into a cabin from the American West. *Rustic* was the word. Incongruously, drapery hardware ran along the top of each windowless wall.

As Cliff popped through the floor, he accosted Matthew. "Why won't they hit this?"

Matthew opened two empty cupboards. "Ever heard of Quantum Stealth?"

"Sounds like a video game." Cliff leaned toward the back of Matthew's head.

"It does." Matthew reached toward the drapery rod, pretended to grab something, and shoved.

An entire wall of cross-country ski gear appeared.

Mark stepped to the gear, moved his hands like a mime, and tangled in something. "Fabric," he said. He pulled in the opposite direction of Matthew's shove, and the gear disappeared.

"Quantum Stealth—QS—is a light-bending material developed by a Canadian company in which Father is an investor. They used the cabin as a prototype. Global powers competed ruthlessly to secure the rights to QS, and the company needed someplace neutral to test it."

"MI6 would kill for this," Becca said. "Probably already has."

Mark still moved the curtains back and forth. He had company. Jeff and Cliff felt around the walls, swinging arms to expose more gear, lamps, televisions, and equipment I could not identify.

"They sheathed the cabin two years ago. QS is impervious to night-vision and infrared technology. Reflects surroundings so the cabin, and anything else, disappears." He turned to Cliff. "The jackets are lined in it. Pants, mittens, hoods, ski hats, boots—all invisible. The skis and poles are white, so the only problem there will be our trail. Turn everything inside out. Gear up."

We scrambled. And incrementally disappeared

"Put the hoods and hats on last, once we're outside." Matthew leaned skis against an exterior wall. "The material will protect your faces from the fog, which is becoming ice fog. Droplets hurt. And you can't see through it.

"There's a step, so be careful. Step off, click on your skis, and wait. Once you're out, put on your hood and hat. Goggles, of course. They'll blur your vision a little since there's not much light to begin with, but you do *not* want ice fog bouncing off your eyes." He disappeared as he donned layers of QS. "I'll go first because I know the way."

Cliff hadn't uttered a word since he began playing with the draperies. Jeff's upper body looked like the cabin wall, his head floating in space as he helped Becca with her jacket. Maggie wrapped her jacket around her hips and declared she had finally lost that last ten pounds.

"We're an invisible army." Mark's disembodied voice sounded like a kid's on Christmas morning. "This is incredible!"

"A game-changer," Matthew replied from near the door. "But only if we survive. Let's go."

Outside, white skis jutted as if leaning on a rack—which they were—with matching poles. Glancing toward the cabin, I saw forest. We shoved off, creating sets of parallel tracks lengthening with every slide. Glacial blue, green, dark brown, and deep blue eyes scanned around me as if ensuring QS worked.

Mark, behind me, confessed. "I'm sure it's so highly classified it won't be available to the public in our lifetimes. I still want some."

I agreed, slid unevenly, bobbled, and tried to stay in Maggie's tracks, which I knew she cut for me. The good news was QS hid my spastic movements. The better news was we weren't skate skiing, something I decided to forestall.

"Matthew? Skate skiing in our future?" I sounded worried even to myself.

Jeff translated. "Matthew, that's a Mother Question with one correct answer, and it's *no*. You're doing a good job, Mom. Stay vertical."

"How can you tell?" I asked him. "I am invisible."

"I hope not, Dr. Madison," Matthew said as we pushed into the forest, the incline increasing our cardio. "We don't have a groomed track."

Consistent, rhythmic *swish*es accented by the occasional *clack* of a pole (mine) hitting a ski (also mine) enhanced by mild profanity (mine again) were our musical score. The forest floor was fluffy powder, and better than that in clearings where fog knit into an icy crust. It would all be ice soon, causing skis to stick abruptly, and triggering falls (mine once more). I wished I knew how far we were skiing, and reminded myself to feel for the first gripping tug, accompanied by a grating *crunch*, of ice fog frozen on top of otherwise perfect snow.

I tightened core muscles, centering my weight over my hips, and didn't sway from side to side. I thought about the one-mile meadow loop Mark plowed for me at the ranch, and figured we had come about that far. The repetitive movement was calming, and I hummed—always "Angels We Have Heard on High" when cross-country skiing—to maintain consistent effort.

We sliced through thick pine and fir. Zigzagged down a copse of beech. Crossed two glades primed for avalanches. Skirted a crevice probably containing a spring stream. And bumped over a half-dozen logs. Then we traversed a three-foot-wide, snow-packed bridge spanning a thirty-foot-deep ravine—a charming interlude wearing hiking boots, but terrifying on skis.

Sweat poured down my back. The temperature had to be near zero, which meant my purple face sported a faucet for a nose, while a retro headband covered my ears.

After fifteen glamorous minutes—slow progress uphill—we gathered on a crest at the forest edge, overlooking a meadow in a scene worthy of a Norman Rockwell Christmas card. A wooden barn separated the Cushan estate from the road, and was silhouetted against the sunset. A town nestled in a vale a couple of miles beyond, with a second village five miles farther. I prayed we would stop at the barn or nearest town.

Gunfire began in the direction of the chateau. Matthew's skis, poles, and eyes—the visible parts—attracted my attention as he spoke. "This is the hardest section because we're in the open. Our tracks will lead right to us. We cross the meadow." He gestured by swinging a pole at the farm. "Head for the barn. The van is there." His disembodied voice was less unsettling than the fact that I had to downhill ski. "Father owns the farm. It's vacant. Try not to fall, but hurry."

A chopping noise approached. Rotors. Again.

"Matthew?" I called, my voice rising on the last syllable.

"Hear it!" he replied as he pushed off, down the slope. "Keep going. Father's got our backs."

If there's one thing of which I'm certain, it's that I cannot downhill ski. And that was just too bad. I was going to have to do it anyway.

And Mark knew it. "Gracie, keep your weight forward," he shouted from behind as I watched the young peoples' tracks lengthen. They slalomed to break speed or avoid a hillock, and flew toward the barn.

"Mark, I can't do this." I turned toward him, forgetting he was invisible. "You know I can't."

"You don't have a choice. I'm staying with you." The rotors were louder, meaning a chopper would crest the treetops momentarily. "You have to try, Gracie."

"Mark. I *can't*."

"*Shut up and ski, Grace!*"

My skis slide forward because he shoved them hard.

"Don't rush, Gracie."

Right.

"Choppers! And you tell me not to rush?" My poles whirled like bicycle pedals. I gasped each breath—when I breathed.

"You have to slow down, Grace! Pivot your ankles and weight! Slightly. Like a cross-country turn. Make a slow *S*!" He coached from a few feet behind.

I focused on everything I didn't know how to do. I almost stopped when I turned.

He yelled at me unnecessarily. "This isn't working!"

He was just now figuring that out? "No duh!" I shared Maggie's gift of encouragement.

His mass bumped me as his skis paralleled outside mine. His uphill arm wrapped my waist, and we propelled forward, doubling my speed.

"Do exactly what I tell you. I taught the kids to ski this way. Watch my skis. Do what they do. Turning left now. On left edges. Mindful of ankles."

His skis angled left, a move I tried to duplicate. I ran over his skis while stopping us. My legs splayed out, my rear dangling a foot above the snow. He held me with an encircling grasp under my armpits. I shimmied to stand, succeeding only when he jerked hard.

"Not good. Going again." He pushed off.

We were halfway down the hill, cutting across its face. An explosion triggered my prayer, and the barn door opened. I assumed the kids made it inside.

I tried to survive two more slaloms. The barn was five hundred feet ahead. I would never make it on my own. My stomach started to unknot—too soon.

The slapping rotors were deafening. I heard the high-pitched scream of a snowmobile and wondered, *Friend or foe?* Mark's strong legs pumped, and I came up short. We were on a straightaway now, drawing attention to our destination.

Where my children hid.

"Should we try to draw them off?" I yelled.

"Won't do any good. Tracks."

My right ski shot out with a splatter, quickly followed by the left—*swoosh*—in the opposite direction, resulting in a high Chinese split. Mark picked me up, lunging toward the barn. Twenty feet out, he set me down. I heard a shot, then another explosion.

He threw his body across mine. Skidded us against the barn. Debris sputtered across the meadow. Mounded in sizzling piles. A rotor bounced off the metal roof.

The barn door opened and the van rolled out.

"Here!" Jeff yelled, sliding the door so we could vault inside. I glanced back, at the waving snowmobiler. The passenger held up a small rocket launcher. Bashir had, indeed, covered us.

I started to run to the van as I looked for Mark.

Crimson dots covered the snow in which he lay.

CHAPTER FIFTY-THREE

Cushan Estate

Grace

Mark sprawled on the barn floor. He was nicked in the neck, but conscious enough to argue. We slowed the bleeding with an antiquated medical kit from the glove box, and I prayed for a heavy-footed ambulance driver.

He insisted he was fine. I tried not to pass out.

"I don't believe you *want* to come," Matthew said. Try though he might, Mark was losing this Matthew Inquisition. "You would unintentionally slow us down, and distract us because we would worry about you. Father will have your wound tended. When doctors say you can join us, he'll see to it that you do."

As I knelt next to Mark, tires crunched outside. Matthew ushered Bashir and Dr. Merrit to me, and three strong-looking young men followed them to Mark. They could handle whatever my husband, an infamously bad patient, dished out.

Matthew gestured toward the van as he moved to the driver's side, saying that we needed to leave.

I cut him short. "Not a chance until I know how badly he's hurt." Moving barely out of the way so medics could tend my husband, I felt his hand gently grasp my ankle. After cleaning and dressing the wound, they asked if he could stand. He was gray-green, I assumed from blood loss, and barely able to prop on his elbows.

"I can stand, walk, run, and travel," was his response. "Anything I need to do, I can do."

"You've lost a lot of blood, Mark. You need rest." Dr. Merrit loomed large. "You pulled my slack in Venice. Let them pull yours now. I'll stay with you. Matthew will get them safely to Rome. And we can probably—" he glanced at the medics "—join them in Venice?"

"Perhaps," one replied. "He's built like a bull."

I searched Mark's face until he nodded, indicating I should leave.

"You'll get them to us as soon as he's able?" I asked Bashir. "*But not before?*" My emphasis was unmistakable. Dr. Merrit nodded vigorously.

"Of course, Dr. Madison. I doubt we'll be able to persuade them to stay too long." Bashir's kindness and competence reassured me, as did his power to keep my husband from harm's way—for now.

"Go on," Mark said. "Get to Rome. We'll be in touch. I'll follow as soon as I can."

Getting on my hands and knees to kiss his cheek, I whispered in his ear. "Thanks for the skiing lesson. You saved my life."

"I know I did." He smiled, and raised his voice theatrically. "I've always told you I'd take a bullet for you."

"You don't ever need to prove it again, dear." I straightened, and climbed in next to Maggie. Matthew shut the door behind me, then spoke with his father and Dr. Merrit. While we waited for him, I noticed the young people staring at me, so asked. "What is it?"

"You okay?" Maggie asked gently. "I mean, with Dad hurt?"

"Of course I'm not okay. I want to kill whoever is behind all this. But I'm calm, if that's what you're really asking."

"She's fine," Jeff said to her. "Threatening people with bodily harm."

...

To Rome

Wheels of the silver jet and black van reached the runway simultaneously, the machines paralleling each other to meet at its end. Our few things were transferred as the plane refueled for a quick flight south.

Maggie and Cliff faced me, and Matthew perched on the other side of the seats, close enough to touch. Becca and Jeff were behind me, in single chairs. They worked furiously on her phone, creating a devious plan with MI6, and assuring the BBC rights to an exclusive. Mark and Becca had largely excluded their agencies until this point since Mark was "retired," and Jeff and Becca were on their honeymoon.

I thought it was time to scream for help. Matthew indicated we would wait in Rome for Cyril.

As if reading my thoughts, Maggie spoke. "Where in Rome? Or do we just head to the Catacomb of Priscilla?" She moved to the galley for something to drink, speaking as she passed Matthew. "Anyone want anything?" Responding to requests for club soda (me) and Turkish coffee (Jeff the Impossible), she returned with a tray of options.

Jeff sipped a Nespresso while planting himself on a bolted-down walnut table. Before Matthew could answer Maggie with his choice of beverage, my son addressed our host. "Matthew. Your background is a little complicated. How are you affiliated with Mossad?"

Matthew twisted the water bottle my daughter handed him. Two turns clockwise, two counter. "That's a tough question. Why?"

"I'm trying to understand your behavior."

Matthew inclined his head to acknowledge the request was reasonable, and twisted the bottle several times. "Does that make a difference in what we're doing?"

"It makes a difference in what I'm about to share, and which may save our lives."

Cutting his eyes to Jeff, then to Maggie, Matthew paused before he spoke. "You know the meaning of *sayanim?*" I nodded, fluent in Hebrew. "*Helper* or *assistant*," he translated. "Typically, Mossad's sayanim don't do anything illegal." He paused. "You know enough about my work with Cyril to understand my role is atypical."

"I understood you were his assistant," I said.

"I am. He and my father have known each other for decades, and my family's political history required difficult responses at times. Cyril is part of my earliest memories. When I came of age, I decided I wanted to train with him. He is, in some ways, a mentor. I suspect I am as close to a son as he'll ever have."

Maggie turned pink. I would follow up with her later.

"He actually created a job for me. I've worked with him for almost ten years."

"You seem torn at times," Jeff said.

"I am increasingly torn, but not for political reasons."

No one touched *that* comment.

THE BROTHERS' KEEPERS

"Where is your allegiance, then? Mossad? Your father? I need to know where you stand, whose back you'll have when bullets fly." Jeff arched to place his cup behind him.

Matthew tucked the water bottle between his hip and the armrest before tenting his fingers the Bashir way. "My allegiance is to what's right. Distinguishing between right and wrong used to be easier." He stopped, reached for the water bottle, then stopped himself and put his hands in his lap. "But I won't do the wrong thing for the sake of the Sovereign State of Israel. And I think Cyril suspects as much. My allegiances have—broadened." He looked at Maggie, and her face deepened to magenta.

CHAPTER FIFTY-FOUR

Chateau Cushan

"Flately . . . yes. I know. Coburg . . . in a hospital. Flesh wound through the shoulder." Merrit answered his friend's questions. Bashir, now working at the computer near the windows, had assured him the lines were secure.

"Good . . . Venice. Forget Madaba. That's over. So is Rome. They're checking on something Grace found there. It ends in Venice."

He twirled a button. "Return to *Farmacia Vaticana*—the Vatican Pharmacy . . . Yes. Where we did the stakeout for the priest and the redhead." He listened. "Good strategy. Okay, go there. I think you need a prescription and your passport." He laughed sadly. "I know. We travel with prescriptions now."

He listened again. "Head to Venice. Wait for me. Translate whatever you find. They're on their way. May beat us . . . possibly Ca' Sagredo, but get in touch when you arrive . . . yes, we'd know if she accepted him. I don't think things are going well."

Flately's mind made explosive leaps after earning a doctorate in chemistry from MIT at twenty-five, so the cryptic conversation was enough to direct him. Science was his native tongue, and far more obscure than any of Jeff's idiosyncrasies.

Flately was also the hopeless romantic of MOSES.

"Bring everything you can get through security. Or drive. But get to Venice ASAP. As well armed as possible."

CHAPTER FIFTY-FIVE

Munich, Germany

The professorial gent dined on fish and salad in a tourist bar across from the Munich Muenchen Hbf train station, his hatted, snowy head low as if mired in the fatigue of the very old.

Limping onto the 9:00 p.m. overnight Eurail to Venice after arriving from Coburg at 7:00, he would sleep on the nine-hour train ride. He splurged for a private compartment from funds tucked in the top of a Gold Toe sock held up by a suspender, and received on the Orient Express.

His plan was simple. Take antibiotics to prevent infection in a wound he would redress, and arrive in Venice in time to do whatever was necessary. God willing.

...

Central Rome

A geriatric man left the three-star Hotel Fontanella Borghese, which occupied a former palace overlooking the Spanish Steps.

After Merrit's phone call, during which he shared that no activity was observed at Palazzo McAlex three blocks away,

THE BROTHERS' KEEPERS

he took a cab to the Vatican Pharmacy before heading to the Stazione Termini, the main train station. He ensured he wasn't followed. Changed jackets and removed his hat in the men's room. Emerged as a traveler needing wheels.

He did not board a train.

He thought about the Goth cashier, who watched him from the other side of the glass wall of the AutoEurope kiosk. His bright-red hair glowed under the street light in the triangular, Victorian-era Residenza Cellini, and he knew it was memorable. Then he focused on his task, meticulously checking the contents of each bag.

She had asked if it was safe to lease a car to someone so old. Then why he had so many pieces of luggage. He replied he would drop the vehicle in Catanzaro after attending a family reunion and ignored her more offensive questions.

When she began to stir her *marocchino* to redistribute the espresso, cocoa powder, and milk foam before the drink became lukewarm, he knew she lost interest. She lifted her eyebrows, picked up *Chi*—Italy's premier gossip tabloid—and began picking at the gold stud piercing her bottom lip.

He fled nonchalantly to his vehicle.

Soon, he cautiously steered the rental Peugeot from the asphalt lot. Graffiti and trash, hallmarks of a rough neighborhood, lined the streets. Tourists knew all roads led to Rome, but most didn't know few led *out*. The Roman road system was a challenging gnarl.

He was experienced, however. The car circled the Fountain of the Naiads anchoring the oval Piazza della Repubblica, and the driver exhibited courage worthy of a Roman taxi driver. It then shot southwest, down the Via Nationale, before turning south.

...

Switzerland near the Italian border

The men—one probably American because of stature and cowboy boots, the second whose bulk and gleaming bald head defied nationality, and the third a wealthy Middle Easterner wearing a hand-tailored overcoat—engaged in an animated discussion in ice fog embalming southern Switzerland.

The bald man energetically twisted, with his left hand, the top button of his jacket. He ascended the metal aircraft steps while holding the handrail with his right, and entered the jet.

"I have your word that you won't alert them yet?" The American hurdled the Citation steps in threes, pausing briefly on the last one to speak to the man on the tarmac. When he turned, the bandage on his neck was barely visible above his flapping jacket collar. He appeared oblivious to the storm, although the airport would close in moments because of weather. "She'll be furious I'm leaving so soon. But my place is with my family."

"I would prefer to tell my son now." The Arab shouted over escalating engines as wind from the lake snatched his cap, and the chauffeur abandoned the car to chase it. "I will wait not a minute more than three hours before I call."

The American nodded before ducking inside. The door swiveled shut, and the craft departed a private airport in Agno, four miles north of the Italian border.

Once its wheels left the ground, the Arab slid into the back seat of a silver Mercedes sedan. Before the vehicle passed the gate, heading to a lakeside chateau to finish business related to a security breach, he was speaking into his cell phone.

CHAPTER FIFTY-SIX

Centro Storico, Rome

From a squid-scented corridor separating Roman mansions subdivided into apartments leased to foreigners looking for *la dolce vita,* Laura entered Palazzo McAlex unseen.

Like most former palaces in the Roman Centro Storico, or Old City, her family digs retained a dingy service entrance off the back alleyway. She preferred the dank chasm of stumbling drunks, whimpering addicts, amorous couples, and golf-cart sized delivery vehicles. Tourists never ventured into the unwelcoming passages where the mechanisms of daily Roman life ground on in ways unchanged for decades. Unfortunately, this was the season for pasta in ink sauce, and somewhere nearby, a trash bag held leftovers of the tentacled type. She didn't notice.

As a child, when Da visited Il Papa—the Pope—on business, her father would spirit Aedan and her down the rear stairway to romp in the Borghese Gardens in the next block. She knew the structure like her heart, and could walk the garden paths blindfolded.

Aedan, literally "Son of Fire," was raucous and lively, the ideal heir, the *last* heir, to Clan McAlex. He was important, in ways she did not understand then, because Clan McAlex was an empire on the verge of extinction. It's future rode on his raucous shoulders.

She was his opposite: reserved, and polite as a princess. Make no mistake. She was Scottish royalty by merit of birth, and the siblings were born to their places until Fate changed everything.

Aedan died shortly before their mother. A second marriage to a younger woman regarded as a brood mare ended without issue. Games and visits with Da, who lost interest in the daughter representing loss, stopped as he roiled inward.

Preoccupied with these memories, she felt for the lock that predated her birth by a hundred years, and swiveled the key. Efficiently deactivating, then resetting, the alarm, she knew Agnelli thought her clueless. Noiselessly climbing the central stairs, she shivered when she remembered Aedan sliding down the banister, ignoring years of warnings, and cracking his head on the marble below. She pictured her small self, sitting on the top tread, waiting. Then Da returned with Aedan bandaged beyond recognition. That was the last moment she felt pity.

She wore black, fiery hair tucked fashionably into a newsboy cap in case anyone held residual curiosity about the comings and goings at the shuttered palace. Tomorrow she would join Agnelli in Venice.

Leaving driving loafers on the top stair, she continued barefoot. The McAlex Palazzo, unlike most, didn't surround a courtyard. Da believed the void a security risk. So he built over the private garden to double the size of the mansion. It was farsighted in ways he could not imagine, because this architectural configuration perfectly suited her pursuits. She chose the normal room in the building center—her mother's bedroom. Light within would remain unseen.

Da never visited, viewing the address as just another holding in a real-estate web. Since St. Andrews, she had reconfigured spaces here to suit her. She left computer equipment, which necessitated extra luggage, each time she visited. It joined technology hidden in a locked, seventeenth-century olivewood credenza, her mum's favorite.

After powering up, she read reports from the Swiss Guard she placed in Agnelli's staff. She knew the cleric would head for the Vatican apartment in the Doge's Palace—his habitual hideaway—so recruited a school chum who led tours of historic monuments on the piazza. McAlex compared her friend's input to that from the guard, keeping everyone honest. When this was over, she would kill both. It would not be the first time. Or the last.

Returning her thoughts to Agnelli, he had found the location of the second scroll half because he raced from the archives to book the trip. The tracker her men had placed on Maggie was deactivated days ago, although field reconnaissance reported the family to be at the Cushan estate in southern Switzerland. They had reunited at Madaba. The octogenarian Steele brothers were wounded, with one near death.

She would focus on Agnelli, who would not expect her, and who would lead to the scroll fragment. The advantage of surprise was stronger when operating under the deceptive cloak of Carnevale costume.

Padding down an unlit hallway to Da's study, she tucked her hat in her pocket, letting her hair drop almost to her waist. She tugged her fingers through it. It was her trademark, impossible to disguise. At some point, she would have to cut and dye it to disguise herself.

Groping the liquor cabinet, she poured three fingers of estate-bottled scotch into a two-hundred-year-old Waterford tumbler. The crystal, from an inherited stash, was cool and soft in her hand, well worn by countless sippers of fine malt—men doing business with Da and the Vatican. She wished she smoked, because he always offered Cuban cigars with his whiskey. Opening the box, she rolled one under her nose. It crackled, then disintegrated from age. He should have stored them in a humidor, rather than a plain box.

Da's scope was too narrow. His allegiances were too naïve. His fidelities irretrievably anchored in the past. His offspring were too few.

Swallowing the burning alcohol, she imagined being the end of Clan McAlex. From this, one of four desks controlling an empire without citizens, she would manipulate a global network of influence and trafficking. Direct an organization referred to as Spigot, developed right under Da's nose.

She would prove that she was every bit the leader her brother would have been.

Slinging back the last of the whiskey, she left the glass to create a ring that would destroy a spotless Moroccan leather inlay. Hers was a trail of destruction. First, Agnelli. Then the scroll. Then Da. Finally, at her death, the clan itself.

DAY NINE
CHAPTER FIFTY-SEVEN

Via Veneto, Rome

Grace

"Mossad, CIA, or MI6?" I asked about ownership of the safe flat.

No one answered, but since Cyril provided the address, everyone acted uneasy. We agreed it was our best alternative, but did not drop our collective guard. Becca, Maggie, and I took the bedroom for the first sleep shift after we arrived at midnight. The men worked out who would stay awake, and who would crash on the sofas. Halfway through the short night, we switched.

At 6:00 a.m., we gave Cyril another hour before heading to the catacombs. Cutting free of Mossad was the most dangerous decision of the past eighteen months. *That* was saying a lot.

By 6:30, Jeff did a herky-jerky dance as he paced. Matthew and Cliff comically ignored each other in the twenty-by-twenty study. I tapped my fingers in an aggravating manner. Maggie stepped to the foot-wide side balcony for air, and ignored everyone until Matthew reminded her that fresh air in Rome ended with the pyroclastic surge at Vesuvius. I walked to her, put my arm around her waist, and leaned my chin on her shoulder from behind.

The apartment was off the commercial Via Veneto, reassuringly three blocks northwest of the American Embassy, wedged into the fourth floor of a once-respectable structure. My daughter and I stared at rooftops that scattered down and around like ochre pigeon feathers, which were as prolific as the splattered calling cards the birds left on every horizontal surface. Broken bottles and syringes littered a narrow schism twenty-five feet below our hiking-boot treads.

Laughter from cafes, and vehicular sounds from polluting traffic, drew our gaze toward a sidewalk two buildings over, where umbrellas sprouted in case the weather turned sunny. From the location of a '60s Fellini film to a seedy nightmare in the '80s to the current renaissance, the Vittorio Veneto—its proper name—contained enough human variety to hide us.

Returning to the living room, we found a place at the glass-topped table covered with documents and maps in neat piles, thanks to Becca. Everyone grouped in light from two sets of French windows, duffels and backpacks scattered on parquet floors. Matthew failed to coax flame from the rare wood-burning fireplace, and Cliff took over with Boy-Scout efficiency.

Matthew held a finger in the air, attracting our attention. He walked the room in quadrants, sweeping a small box the size of a cigarette lighter in measured arcs. Then he did something to a phone hidden beneath a faded plastic houseplant. Monitoring the lighter, he checked for listening devices.

"Clean." He sat on a dainty, straw-bottomed chair designed for an Italian matron. "I suggest we summarize, and develop a plan beyond the catacombs visit." He nodded at me as I brought food from the blue-tiled kitchen, then waited for me to sit. "We have a good map of the catacombs, which thankfully is simpler than most. Dr. Madison marked the Margarita funerary vault."

"Matthew, when do we expect Cyril?" Jeff asked. It was almost 7:00.

"Not to be rude, but whenever he shows up." He looked at his watch. "We agreed to give him ten more minutes."

"Okay. Maggie, why are we here?" When Cliff mentioned her name, she sat upright. At his question, she leaned hard against the chair rungs, impaling her shoulder blades. "We really don't know because you haven't told us."

Everyone stared at her, waiting. There was no use delaying the inevitable.

"I've told you," she said, thinking she would try anyway.

"No. You really haven't, dear." I patted her hand, a sign she was in trouble. "We know you suspect a spring. About the karsts and karstic systems. What we don't know is why *you* specifically were kidnapped. Again. What bit of information caused the abduction, Maggie? What was in that paper you were presenting in Marseilles?"

Jeff loudly munched cookies—it was amazing what he could find in empty cabinets—and offered his sister one as I prodded. Resistance was futile.

"And I'd like to know why you haven't come clean earlier," Jeff said. "I figure you have your reasons."

My stomach hurt. The cookies looked at least three years old.

"Today, Maggie," I said. "*Now*."

She took a deep breath. "Yes. Now."

. . .

"You know where the spring *is*?" Cliff loomed over the chair and into her face, so closely his head blocked her view of everyone. He then abruptly leaned back because my hand pushed his chest in a very unloving way.

"Sit," Jeff said to him in a fierce tone. "And the scroll, Maggie?"

"I wanted further proof before speaking, but everything we've done leads me to Venice as well. Particularly the Piazza San Marco. The basilica."

"Where?" Matthew asked respectfully, playing against Cliff's boorish aggression. He was a smooth operator and gentleman, so far. "I don't mean to sound stupid, but obviously you don't think the spring is in Venice."

"I'm not going to tell you yet," Maggie replied, staying ahead of the game while shifting her weight. "But the last key to the spring location, the one that will confirm or contradict my theory, should be on the façade of St. Mark's Basilica. I'm certain enough I don't think we need to wait for Cyril. Especially if whatever we find in the catacombs supports my suspicion."

Shouts from the Via Veneto reminded me of the real world outside the apartment. Matthew put his lips against the fingertips of his tented hands, and I suspected my daughter was thankful to volley into his court. To redirect attention from herself.

After a pause, he began. "I'm not sure why we're waiting for Cyril, actually." He leaned back and crossed his ankles, then his arms over his chest. The double cross position was defensive, indicating conflict. "Other than he said to."

"Maggie." Becca's strength was analytical, so I assumed—hoped—she was processing. I tried to focus despite the weird vibes in the room. "I trust you. Your judgment. How certain are you of the karstic system and location of the other scroll half? A percentage would be helpful."

My daughter-in-law slipped our scroll fragment from her e-reader to the table, where Maggie covered it with her hand, as if willing its millennia to guide her. "Certainly the karstic system exists, although I don't know what kind of shape it's in, or how it's impacted by current water tables. It could be dry, therefore useless. As to the location—" here she paused "—80 percent. If Mama's catacombs visit delivers, then 100 percent. We're coming at it from two entirely different angles, so a confirming cross-reference convinces me."

The clock ticked. Jeff slurped. I strummed.

"So forgive me. Are we looking for the second half of the scroll? Or the water source? Both?" I struggled to understand, because this was vague and confusing.

"I don't really know. The region needs water. If we can find the spring and karstic system, we can reasonably convey water through Judea and the Negev. That pulls pressure off of existing systems and frees water for Jordan, Lebanon, and Syria—the world's most highly stressed drought regions. Ample water also would eliminate a major cause of war and level the political playing field. We know Spigot targets water, and I suspect they'd be happy to ignite war. And the region supplies oil to the globe, reason enough for Spigot to continue to seek control of anything as essential as water." We stared at her. "Control the water, control the oil. And someone wants this enough to try to kill us."

"And kidnap you again." I would not forget *that* detour.

"Yes. The other question is what does the complete scroll show? As far as we know, once complete, it's a piece of history not seeing the light of day since Solomon." She folded her hands to prevent their shaking, and placed them in her lap. "It touches Solomon, Constantine, and Luther. That trio is reason enough for most of Christendom to try to unite the halves."

"And for those persecuting Christians to try to destroy both halves," I said. "Giving further credence to Maggie's assessment of the importance of the complete scroll is the fact that trade from Arabia, Africa, and the East came straight through the Dead Sea valley in Solomon and David's times." I tried to help her with a bit of seminary chitchat. "We know they could have gotten water from the Nabateans in Petra to the east. But it's most likely there were sources then in the valley itself."

"And Timna," Becca said. "Remember the door at the Grossmunster. Munch depicted Luther standing in front of Solomon's Pillars in Timna for a reason. With a river flowing beneath him."

Jeff stretched. "Surrounded by flowers. I need coffee." His irrelevant statement startled me, and I frowned at him. He started toward the kitchen, explaining as he walked. "If we're going to wait for Cyril, I want to be caffeinated. More rest wouldn't hurt. I may have to scale the basilica. And I'd like to remind you that Cyril's time is up, so we need to get out of here."

"But we're not finished," I said.

He made it as far as the kitchen doorway before he spoke. "Actually, I think we could be." He pivoted. Becca joined him, but he blocked her by leaning against the doorframe, one hand on the opposite side. "We have a cleric in the courtyard with an ungodly interest in these windows."

He glared at Matthew for ten seconds. I thought of Cyril, the only source of information about where we were hidden. Finally, Matthew reached for his cell.

"Bayee's arm is long." He called his father.

THE BROTHERS' KEEPERS

...

Forty-five minutes later, as we waited per Bashir's instructions, Cyril had not surfaced. Matthew summarized his father's plan again.

"In twenty minutes, there's going to be a small protest down the Veneto. Merchants protesting high rent, hookers protesting police presence, university students looking for anything to riot about with unemployment at 40 percent. Tourists will mill from hotels uphill, and stop at cafes for a bite at less than five-star prices. Father's arranged a riot and private security to control it."

We consolidated our belongings, discarding anything unnecessary in the sputtering fireplace. Then I hooked my arm around Maggie's shoulder to lean into her.

"You holding up?" she asked.

"Of course," I sighed. "Worried about your dad." I dropped my voice. "Aside from affairs of the heart, how are you?"

"Remembering your role model as the Greek warrior goddess Athena wearing a ratty gardening hat," she said as she shook her head at me. "We have to stop these adventures."

"I'm afraid that ball is in your court, baby. You always seem to start them."

Matthew's voice broke through. "One thing, Dr. Madison. Father said he promised Mark not to call for three hours, but your husband and Dr. Merrit landed at Fiumicino airport an hour ago."

"Is he all right, then? And we won't be here when he arrives." My voice broke. "Roman traffic is impossible."

"Well enough to travel, apparently. Father was contacting the pilot and Mark. They most likely will meet us in Venice now. They'll be more rested. Something Father thought was important."

"So what *are* we doing?" Jeff asked, his and Becca's frowns indicating resistance if they disagreed with Bashir and Matthew's arrangements.

"Some protestors will flood the courtyard, overwhelming the cleric. We have to assume we're watched from the front as well, although we don't know that for certain. Our best bet is the fire escape. We split up, with Cliff and me going out the front to a waiting car. If anyone sees us leave, we'll draw them from you four."

"And we slide down the fire escape?" I asked defiantly, thinking of my height vertigo, a condition that created dizziness. A three-story, exterior-ladder descent was ridiculous. But so were the skis.

"Yes. A delivery van waits to take you to the catacombs. The drivers are a security detail, and know what to do in almost every situation. We'll meet you at the airport after we lose any tails, or see you in Venice. Cyril expects something to happen at the Il Ballo del Doge tomorrow night."

My eyes shifted to Maggie. A Carnevale ball was a shared dream, but not under these circumstances. Did everyone else wonder if Cyril expected an event because *he* was going to create one?

"Timeline?" Becca was ready to move to the bedroom window adorned with the contemptible ladder. "When do we assume you're not joining us, and go on alone?"

"You'll be there in minutes. It's only a couple of miles. Take no more than thirty minutes to see if you can find what you're looking for. You'll have no cell reception, but inform us the moment you surface." Matthew watched through one of the twin French windows. "Getting to Fiumicino takes longer than the flight itself, but the shortest train ride is five hours. We're going out of Ciampino, seven miles southeast, a private-aviation airport Father uses. The bodyguards will take you there from the catacombs."

I reached for our consolidated bag, which Maggie intercepted. The ladder would be rickety if not rusted out. My imbalance and vertigo were problematic. The bag was a dangerous burden.

"Father asked the pilot to file the flight plan indicating we'd take off in two hours. I'd like to beat that estimate considerably. Be in Venice early afternoon." Matthew grabbed his bag. "Let's go."

Cliff followed him as crowd noise and shattering glass—*were they supposed to do that?*—accompanied their departure. We waited for protesters to invade the courtyard.

Becca was tucked behind the left panel of pinch-pleated muslin draperies, discolored with age. "If we are being tailed, our pursuers are very good. I don't see anything."

Less than a minute later, half a dozen people swarmed the confused cleric. We lined up near the window in the other wall of the bedroom, which was hidden from the courtyard by the building setback. Following Jeff, only one body on the ladder at a time, we climbed out and down. Within two minutes, we were wedged in a florist van slightly larger than a trash dumpster, but smelling much better. Jasmine topiaries, pots of forced bulbs, and vicious shrub roses bred to produce attack thorns surrounded us.

Heaven *and* hell on earth.

CHAPTER FIFTY-EIGHT

Catacomb of Priscilla, Rome

Grace
From the second half of the third century through the end of the fifth, a time of intense Christian persecution ending with the fall of the Western Roman Empire, the Catacomb of Priscilla, "Queen of the Catacombs," was the burial ground of choice for Rome's high-ranking Christians. On this day, the catacomb encompassed eight miles of passageways from which we sought to pluck a single daisy.

We entered through the cloister of the Benedictines of Priscilla, offering stolen gifts of potted bulbs to the nuns, thanking them for our unscheduled visit to their subterranean treasure. Fresh air quickly became stale and dusty, and grew colder as we moved into a labyrinth distinguished from its Jewish counterparts by the absence of menorahs. Ignoring burial chambers of seven early Popes and numerous martyrs, and endless *loculi*—rectangular chambers once sealed with stone or plaster—we brushed past a Greek chapel frescoed in Pompeian style, and a *cryptoportico*—covered corridor—from a noble Roman villa.

Margarita's *cubiculum*—worship chamber—was down the fourth major trunk to our left, the second longest in the complex. I pulled Mark's jacket tightly around my shoulders, and prayed my research was correct.

Rome was close to the Mediterranean, on the Tiber River. Unlike caves and tunnels I often inhabited in the Middle East, the air was moist here. Seeping water was problematic for sites such as this, eroding tuff rock soft enough for the chambers to be carved.

I sighed, missing Mark as I scooted through the tight space, my feet illuminated by Jeff's flashlight. Counting sub-passageways—ten right, nine left—I followed the map with a pencil missing its tip, pulled from his jacket pocket. It was the broken half from the American Church. I shuddered, then refocused. We sought the seventh branch on the right, which was, thankfully, supposed to be short. I barreled into it after ignoring a three-inch step.

"Mama!" Maggie's hand shot out. I saw in the peripheral glow the panicked look of a claustrophobic.

"You okay?" I asked.

She smiled. "Are *you*? That's the question." She assessed my feet to see if I was favoring one.

"Yes," I said, wondering if I had twisted my ankle. "We are the gimp squad. Your dad shot, me falling down, the Steeles wounded." I kept moving, scanning while I rocked to prevent ankle lockup. My mouth tasted sour from adrenaline or pain.

Flashlight beams bounced up and down the walls like a misdirected aurora borealis. I listened for noise emanating from the warren in case our security detail, with entirely the wrong body type to be disguised as florists, were dead, thereby making us more vulnerable than usual.

"Can you share a defining feature?" Jeff asked as he and Becca worked the other side. "I know flowers and water, but anything else?" Jeff inherited Mark's limited artistic sensibility.

"It abuts a small room used for worship. Some loculi are too far from anything that could function as a chapel. Stick to the slots to . . ."

"Here," Becca said. "Look at this."

We blasted two dinky flashlight beams at the wall. The top of Becca's slot curved, out of sync in a space full of right angles and straight lines. The most unique aspect was an indistinct row of incised flowers decorating the curve lip. Greek letters, almost erased by time, were carved there.

I could discern the beginning of the name. "M . . . a . . . space . . . g . . . " I read. "Good possibility. Check this out." I crept into the cubby after assuring a level threshold. Our dimming lights spread slowly, revealing mossy greens and celestial blues. More letters from her name appeared in spots, and as I translated—Jeff's language skills weren't this contemporary—I became certain. "This is it."

We studied the first of three frescoes depicting the resurrection of Lazarus in teals and umber. We then discovered a Good Shepherd surrounded by frisky lambs. I held my breath approaching the last, and was devastated to find Daniel *still* in the lions' den, reclining happily among the king of beasts.

I thought about throwing up. "I was wrong." My cockamamie theory had delayed us, my husband and friends were wounded. As I swallowed tears, I made myself stop wallowing. "I am sorry. We need to get out of here, let Matthew and the decoys know there's nothing here. Head to Venice."

Stepping into the passageway, I waited for Jeff's light beam. "Come on. We've seen it. The batteries are running out."

"Not necessarily, Mother." Jeff, riveted in Margarita's cubiculum entry, shone his light above the doorway—on the *inside*. "Look."

I craned around, remembering the ornery little step, and peered at a space Maggie illuminated, too. A figure, resembling Solomon holding court in a well-known Pompeian painting dating to AD 79, hovered over a river. Surrounding the image, a wreath of small flowers entwined—likely marguerites. Most importantly, outside a window behind Solomon rose the distinctly craggy mountains of Timna. Solomon's Pillars.

"Match. But where are the clues?" I asked. Without clues, this boondoggle was useless.

"Here," Maggie said behind us. "Solomon points this direction. Look near the ceiling."

Weak light hit the far end of the barrel vault eight feet away. Four faint horses, eight inches tall, pranced beneath the ceiling joint. They were identical except for the last horse on the right. A nickel-sized cream dot popped from a steel-gray hoof. The ceiling was almost seven feet above us, and I held my breath as Jeff lifted Becca by the waist.

She studied the dot until his arms gave out. "It's a daisy," she said as she hit the floor, generating a dust storm that changed the air from musty to dusty.

I sneezed.

"Too much pasta," Jeff said about the rough landing. "God bless you, Mother. Sorry, sweetheart."

Becca glared at him.

"The Quadriga," I said. "The Horses of St. Mark's above the basilica. Thank you, Jeffrey."

"You mean the reproductions," Becca said. "Those there now are reproductions. You told us."

"Maybe," I replied. "Some respected historians think otherwise."

"Let's go." Maggie's decisive voice drifted toward the exit. "That's exactly where it should be."

CHAPTER FIFTY-NINE

Catacomb of Priscilla

Grace
"But how could Luther know? That fresco was painted a thousand years before he lived." Jeff would not give up. Neither would the maniacal tree peony. The flowers in the van swerving through Rome to the airport were object lessons in God's general revelation of Himself—the fierce, Old Testament personification of YHWH.

"We may never know," I said, breaking off the offending blossom to hand to Maggie. "But we don't know what else he might have found in the cuneiform, or what's on the complete scroll. Maybe something refers to Margarita's tomb? We know the scroll contains some sort of map, and half of it's missing."

"We also don't know if the doge's great-whatever grandson told Luther anything else," Becca said. "Or what's really on that second half. All we have is a map of the Madaba mosaic."

"To quote Mother, that's why they call it *faith*," Maggie said as she pushed the stem through the buttonhole of her hacking jacket lapel. "We need to alert the decoys ASAP."

"Then get to Venice faster," I replied.

...

Venice

Two hours later, a sleek silver Citation owned by an American company with well-hidden headquarters in Switzerland landed at Aeroporto Marco Polo in Venice. When it pulled to park amidst the fleet of private craft bringing well-heeled visitors to Carnevale, six passengers disembarked to mosey to public transport.

The loving couple (Becca and Jeff) acted like honeymooners. The quartet (me, Maggie, Cliff, and Matthew) might have been a mother with her children, or could just as easily have met yesterday. Bashir's bodyguards were sent home by Matthew because we decided we were too large a group already, and expected Dr. Merritt and Mark to join us.

Within half an hour, we rode a chugging Alilaguna ferry, creaking with humanity, toward the Piazza San Marco. Both journey legs were largely silent, our bonhomie diminished when Matthew severed contact with Mossad before takeoff in Rome.

Our group was on its own, "running black" in spy lingo. (My espionage research was paying off.)

The packed San Marco dock meant Carnevale was gearing up again, the afternoon crowds already, or still, looking seriously hung over. A stream of hook-nosed, masked clowns and historically dressed couples flooded Café Florian as we crossed the piazza. Comic/tragic—*tragicomida*—duos were costume-of-choice for this Carnevale, and for every pre-Lenten festival in history.

We headed to an apartment owned by a friend of Bashir's—not as luxurious as Ca' Sagredo, according to Matthew, but directly behind the basilica, so near our target. It was a two-minute walk over only one small canal to the Horses of St. Mark's.

As we slipped through tourists and hawkers, I suspected every masked face belonged to an enemy. I glanced at the Quadriga before bisecting the Lions of St. Mark's, shuddering when I thought of Steven Steele's apartment a few hundred yards away. My heart beat so violently that I heard it in my ears, which might have been a blessing considering ongoing outdoor concerts geared toward a younger demographic. San Marco was party-central, hosting three bands of questionable talent and multi-lingual drunken howling.

I worked to keep up as we turned right on Piazetta dei Leoni. The tight passage in which we moved against a tide rushing to the piazza reminded me that my life was of a salmon swimming upstream.

Our second right ran parallel to the brackish Rio Canonica, a canal we crossed via the Ruga Giuffa Bridge. Seven steps up and down on each side, with a dining-table-sized flat bit in the middle. We moved fifty yards along Ruga Giuffa Santa Apollonia, surrounded by three-to five-story buildings shedding plaster like molting moths. Feeling trapped, my hate-hate relationship with Venice improved when Matthew inserted a key in a husky wooden door. Jeff motioned us inside, and checked to ensure it securely locked behind him.

"Shouldn't we have walked around for a while in case we were being followed?" I was catching on to this spy thing.

"The Carnevale crowds are excellent cover, Dr. M.," Becca said.

Jeff monitored the entrance. I wondered if she placated me. Matthew opened a second door of ornate glass with a decorative metal perimeter depicting ships on crashing ocean waves—exactly the way my stomach felt, despite a strong constitution.

"Cyril probably knows we're AWOL. I texted Dad from the plane," Jeff said. "To let him know where to find us. Haven't heard back from him yet. How long until things become critical?"

Silly me. I thought they had been critical for *days*.

"They're critical now," Matthew said. "We don't wait on either of them."

Jeff and I were last to enter the courtyard of the well-maintained palazzo. In summer, it would have been marvelous. In winter, it cast a ghoulish pall. *Was it because of Mark's absence?* In the past year, I had become more dependent on him.

"The buildings surrounding this garden are unoccupied," Matthew was saying. "We're going to take the side overlooking the canal . . ."

"This is very expensive real estate to be unoccupied," Cliff interrupted.

"It's part of an estate in probate. Tangling over taxes. Until those are settled, no one can do anything with it." Matthew continued to a door in the canal-facing wall. "In Italy, that could take decades."

"Except they loan it out to friends," Cliff said. "This whole situation strikes me as suspect. And too easy."

Matthew's angry face turned to Cliff. "That's right. They loan it to friends. If you have a better suggestion, then by all means share it. Now." He waited while Cliff said nothing. "I suggest we get out of the cold while we can, settle as best we can, and review everything we have. Then go out to reconnoiter and get food. Father said he would have costumes for us." He looked at footprints leading to a stack of boxes. "I trust him to ensure they'll work for the ball, which is high-brow," he said as he ushered us females in first, ever the gentlemen. Jeff followed, leaving Cliff in the freezing courtyard to fend for himself.

"Cliff, it's time to be constructive or shut up," Maggie said sweetly as she passed him.

I swallowed a snicker.

Heavy covers shrouded furniture, mirrors, and artwork, but chandeliers and sconces were unsheathed, their wrappings piled beneath them. Someone had prepared for our arrival.

Exterior shutters were tightly latched, a disappointment because the room was stale. Slats cast hundreds of harsh spears across an unswept floor. Unlike Ca' Sagredo's formal darkness, this interior was a confection—Rococo, if my one art history class four decades ago stuck—in sea-foam green and gilt, which would have been beautiful in sunlight.

"Does Cyril know of your father's association with whomever owns this palazzo?" Maggie's low voice sounded worried. "I know they have a long history, but do they run in the same crowds?"

"I doubt it. The commander is uncomfortable in certain levels of society. And, honestly, unwelcome. This is one." He thought for a moment. "I doubt Father would make that mistake." He sorted and slid beribboned boxes marked with our names. Two boxes remained unmoved. Matthew's and Mark's.

"Where can we try these on?" I did not want to open mine publicly, having a fear of revelatory moments from childhood talent shows at church camps.

Matthew pointed to a hallway. "I suspect there are bedrooms in this wing or the opposite. You should also find a stairway and a kitchen, although the gas might not be turned on.

Once we've confirmed the costumes work, we'll check out the ball site and develop a plan."

"A dark and stormy night . . . " Jeff muttered. "We should look for candles and more flashlight batteries when we're out, and fully charge our phones."

We went one direction, leaving the men to assemble material on which we would base our movements, as well as our investigation of the Quadriga and site of Il Ballo. Ten minutes later, we appeared, dismayed and astonished.

Becca was a gondolier in a tight, striped shirt. Maggie was Annie Oakley, operable six-shooters in each fringed holster. I was Napoleon, with a bicorne hat, long navy tailcoat, and white tights doing *nothing* to hide my womanly hips. The red sash cutting deeply across my chest made me, and anyone else with the gift of sight, think of the mountains Napoleon crossed.

I would ditch the suggestive costume at my first opportunity because it would *not* allow me to blend into crowds. I turned to change back into street clothes.

One day, Bashir and I were going to have a little chat.

CHAPTER SIXTY

San Toma Vaporetto Stop, Venice

Grace

The Pisani Moretta palazzo, setting of tonight's soirée, was evenly covered in stucco matching the peachiness of Ca' Sagredo. I assumed this shade was popular in the Late Gothic period because it recurred in a city obsessed with tradition as it bubbled slowly into the Adriatic. I would have been more concerned with staying afloat—had I not been obsessed with staying *alive.*

Ornate balconies with six peaked arches centered the second and third stories, and were frosted with a buttercream frieze. This flourish confidently drew attention from a dock too flimsy to support several hundred guests. *No one* wanted to swim in the Grand Canal's sewage-infused water if the welcome mat collapsed.

Matthew mentioned that the palazzo, one of few occupied by its original family, had Murano chandeliers unwired for electricity. Thousands of candles twinkled through mullioned glass at night, creating a romantic venue for Carnevale's apex soiree. Maggie looked depressed, and I wondered about his familiarity with the palace and event. Had he attended many?

"We can't get inside until the ball starts at 9:00. Here's the layout." He unfolded a paper, smoothing the creases. "You'll see we're around one bend of the canal S-curve, close to St. Mark's."

We were acting like tourists again, waiting with the crowd at the vaporetto stop in the shadows of Palazzo Morcenigo, where Lord Byron wrote *Don Juan* in the early nineteenth century. The view of the Moretti across the canal was of an impregnable edifice. Becca and Maggie whispered behind me. Then Maggie's hand pushed lightly on my shoulder as she squeezed next to Matthew to ask a question.

"Why is Cyril's impending Il Ballo commotion important when we believe *it* is somewhere else?"

"Doesn't he know where to look?" Becca startled Matthew with her question. He reached for a blue-and-white striped gondolier pole to which the rocking dock was lashed.

"You know, I hadn't thought of that," he admitted without a trace of pride. "I'm, unfortunately, conditioned to accept what he says as truth, and react accordingly."

"Understandable," Maggie said, grabbing a second pole and me. A wake from a racing Carabinieri speedboat rocked the platform. "But I think we should be suspicious of everything. Focus on getting whatever is hidden. Forget Cyril." She tried not to shout over the motor noise. "Although I'd love to go to that ball." She gazed longingly across the waterway.

"Agreed," said Jeff, bouncing a yellow cheese string from his Lampo *panini* that had snarled in his beard. I smelled the fried fish from four feet away—disconcerting while pitching and bucking. "About ignoring Cyril, not attending the ball."

"Did you hear from your dad?" I asked as he took my other hand to steady me. "I'd like his input. And we need to figure out how we're going to pull off the—hoof heist?"

Cliff grumbled. "Operation H Squared."

I was glad he had decided to contribute *something*. His combative attitude was tiresome, yet he knew too much to try to send home, so was in this adventure until the end. I hoped Maggie's rebuke hit home.

Jeff ignored him. "Dad should be here anytime. Said to tell you he was fine."

I didn't believe that and wanted to return to the palazzo to see if he waited there.

Matthew, silent since Becca's question about Cyril, spoke. "I think we address H Squared. We're not here to control a disturbance. Leave Cyril to the Venetian sayanim. We need to focus on what brought us here."

"How?" Cliff asked in a loudly conciliatory tone. "It's on the façade of the bloody . . . "

"Shhhh." Maggie elbowed him hard enough to knock him into the water had he not been leaning against a handrail.

"Sorry. How?" he repeated.

"Let's reconvene at the palazzo, and hope Mark is there to help," Matthew said to the drunken-looking brigade rocking after him from the canal edge.

When my feet hit terra firma, I was relieved. Even if it *was* sinking.

. . .

Mark wasn't at the palazzo, but his costume box was gone. His finger-drawn heart, in dust on the floor, was either a sweet gesture or attempt to distract me from worrying about his wound.

"What was it? His costume?" I asked Matthew.

"I wish I knew," he said. "We didn't open that carton."

"Jeff, text him," I requested. My son was holding endless white robes. "I would have thought he'd want me to see he was okay so I wouldn't bug him about his wound. He's up to something."

"Lawrence of freakin' Arabia," Jeff said, holding the *agal*—braided rope—that held the *kaffiyeh*—headgear—in place. "I get to be T. E. Lawrence."

I took the costume from him and pointed at his phone. He texted.

"That's going to stick out like a sore thumb," was Maggie's reply. "Do we need the costumes now that we're focusing on H Squared?"

"Yes, I think we do," Matthew answered, hesitating only slightly. "To blend in. Vast festivities occur in the San Marco tonight. A *calcio storico* match—Baroque football in costume. Concerts and performances by mimes and musicians. At least two parades. Drunks. And lights, mostly pointed at revelers. But the basilica, Doge's Palace, and campanile will be illuminated. Ideally, we figure out how to get the lights off the basilica so one of us can do his job."

"Or hers," Maggie said. "I don't think we should send just one of us up there, regardless of who it is. He or she is sitting duck."

"Agreed," I said.

"Mother." Jeff's voice interrupted, but he never looked from his phone. I stepped to view the screen. The text from Mark confirmed he was in Venice, reiterated he was all right

"—totally untrue, of course, because he keeps repeating himself," I said—and conveyed that Cyril was at Ca' Sagredo.

Jeff texted.

Come here.

His dad replied.

Not yet.

I grabbed the phone.

This is Grace. I want to see you for myself.

His response was immediate.

Handsome as ever.

He wasn't coming, regardless of my demands. He continued.

I'll find you this evening. Assuming you're hanging out in the piazza?

My turn. In case we were being tapped, I couldn't be specific about my costume to make it easy for him to find me.

Yes. Be careful. Bonaparte.

He finished.

Careful as ever. You too, Gracie. Hi ho!

CHAPTER SIXTY-ONE

Venice

Grace

Hazy dusk shrouded the crowded piazzas, creating a perfect environment for onsite planning and walk-throughs. We donned coats and mufflers or hats found in a hall closet, then split into teams.

Maggie and Becca posed as coeds on a European tour. Cliff and I portrayed mother and son. Jeff, because his coloring was vivid, wore Becca's gondolier costume and full-face mask with wig to accompany Matthew, in matching regalia.

"We figure out how to get to the hoof. Locate as many lights as possible directed at that part of the façade," Jeff reminded us. "I hope we have time to turn them off, or at least, away."

Becca stopped him. "Look particularly at the Doge's Palace. A passageway connects the buildings and according to my phone app for tourists, it's sometimes open later than the basilica during Carnevale." She glanced at her screen. "I think I see a small interior passage on these schematics as well, but it appears blocked."

"The Fondazione Musei Civici di Venezia isn't running tours of the palace tonight, so we have to reach the central exterior balcony of St. Mark's another way. The Doge's Palace will be locked," Jeff replied. "How do we get from the palace to the horses next door?"

"Access to the balcony is through the museum." I had visited years ago on my way home from a dig. "A stairway inside leads to the museum, then it's a straight shot to the terrace. They limit visitors, probably because of forty-two steep and crowded steps." Of course I counted.

"Museum hours?" Jeff asked his bride after nodding to acknowledge my idea.

"Closes at 5:00," was her reply. "Same time today as the basilica, actually."

"Unfortunate," he said. "We might not get those lights off. We also have to address separating the scroll from the hoof. Those horses are what? Bronze, Mom?"

"Almost 100 percent copper," I said. "That's why authorities supposedly moved the originals into the museum, leaving copies on the terrace. The originals were being destroyed by weather. Copper was used because Romans—the horses probably aren't Greek—knew bronze gilding would bind better to high-copper content."

"*Way* too much information," was his encouraging reply.

"Are you sure they're copies?" Becca remembered my comment at the catacombs, about historians disagreeing that the terrace horses were duplicates.

"I'm not. Which creates an ethical dilemma. You can't do anything to destroy the integrity of the original Triumphal Quadriga. If it's survived for two-thousand-plus years, it should survive *you*. Whichever of you assaults the hooves. These are world treasures."

"Mama." Maggie's voice foretold a lecture, and she placed a hand on my forearm, where it crossed the other in a defensive position over my two-pack. "It's about water. Not shared cultural heritage. We should care more about people dying of thirst. We know Spigot will stop at nothing if this map leads to a water source formidable enough to power the Timna mines. I'm sure whomever is up there will be careful. Right?" she asked our façade-scaling division, seeking confirmation for me.

"We will." Matthew said. "I will, Dr. Madison."

"I don't like it, but understand the priority," I said to Maggie. She waited. "Okay. Human desiccation trumps world heritage. That satisfy you?"

She squeezed my arm. "Let's get to work."

"Meet again in an hour," Matthew said. He gathered material accumulated at the chateau and during our flight—schematics for the basilica and adjoining buildings, schedules for Carnevale events, reconnaissance Becca provided from MI6. "Once we've studied the lights and basilica front in person, we'll determine how to get that scroll unseen, and develop a schedule and individual assignments."

He added Maggie's karstic material and our laptops, and locked the stack in a decrepit chest under a window wall. I wondered why he bothered because a hearty blow would shatter the worm-eaten wood. *And why put everything in the only secured space we had, instead of disbursing it?* Before I could ask, I thought of something else.

"But there's another problem." I should have remembered earlier. "The lines. On a normal day, it would take hours—plural—to get to the basilica front door. I can try to use Dr. Steele's name if you'd like. Admission is a huge issue." I checked to ensure my academic credentials were in my wallet as we moved to the door.

"Good idea. But why would two gondoliers want to enter the museum?" Maggie doubtfully looked at Matthew.

"Dr. M. and I will do it." Cliff stepped between Maggie and her gondolier idol, blocking the view. "She can get access for us easily enough, and I have my creds as well. I can discreetly shoot photos, and we can use them to flesh out the details when we return to the palazzo."

"Good for me. And Maggie, please watch for your dad," I said. "He's boasting too much about his health to be believed."

"Will do, Mama." She hooked her arm in Becca's. "I think it's time we practiced collegiate silliness." They exited, blonde and dark heads together like the sisters they were becoming, and strolled out the door, down the Ruga Giuffa Santa Apollonia.

"Come on, Cliff," I said as I took his arm, assuming Venice's most handsome gondoliers would follow. "We don't have much time."

...

Easily blending with tourists gawking sixty feet up at the Quadriga, we paused for bearings and an overview of the space.

"That looks a lot higher than it did the last time I was here," I said to my escort.

"It'll seem higher if Jeff's up there," Cliff replied.

I glared at him. Then surveyed people to the right of the horses, then looked toward the screen covering the left terrace restoration. It would be simple to maim a horse under the screen, but of course, those we targeted pranced on the right.

At the ticket kiosk, I produced my academic IDs, and Cliff made a show of providing his. We explained, in peasant Italian, that we worked with Dr. Stanley and Steven Steele, and needed to reference something in the museum. I hoped it wasn't a mistake to use their names.

After a delay long enough to brew a dozen espressos—nothing happened quickly in Italy—the cashier said a guard would meet us at Porta della Carta, the entrance between the Doge's Palace and basilica.

Apparently someone else tired of forty-two steps. An elevator installed during renovation expedited our ascent into the almost-empty museum. Myrrh—incense used during services in the basilica next door—lingered as a reassuring grace note.

I reminded myself that the peace of Christ was always with me, then unclenched my jaws and fists.

We moved to the banquet hall displaying thirteenth-to-fifteenth century textiles and a fourteenth-century painted altarpiece beautiful enough to bring any sinner to his or her knees. Studied illuminated music manuscripts for five minutes, discussing the theological significance of the Latin lyrics when anyone approached. Cliff took unrelated notes, and photos without destructive flash. After making a show of scholarly intent, we crossed the terrazzo floors to the terrace door.

The wind whipped from the Adriatic, slapping our faces when we cleared the protective bulk of the structure. Everyone must have blown off the terrace because we were alone, and I wondered if we could escape with the hoof then and there. Looking at the piazza below, like Venetian rulers surveying the naval power of their city-state, I noted tourists photographing the horses—and us.

I decided not to steal the hoof during this multinational Kodak moment. With the Internet, I would go viral in seconds.

The rectangular shape of the square was obvious from above, as were Istrian stone pavers that replaced brick in the sixteenth century. The pavers created an illusion of depth, and marked traders' stalls before tourist extravagances replaced the daily essentials sold here.

"Europe's drawing room." In character, I quoted Napoleon, who thought this the most beautiful space in Europe. The violins at the Florian tuned up, their thin cries lacing the wet air. At any moment their dueling partner, the orchestra from Café Quadri, would join the melodic fray.

Two gondoliers slouched against a light pole in front of a hawker's cart, one wearing full mask with hooked nose. A couple of young women flirted and giggled as they passed. I smiled to see them safe, and worried, partially because Jeff was right. It *would* be a dark and stormy night. Mist made every surface slicker, and whipping wind destabilized even the most sure-footed.

Evening softened Venice's sags and creases as we wandered toward the horses, pointing here and there, finally approaching the objects of our desire. Their gigantic size—at least fifteen feet high, with hooves the size of salad plates—was obscured from the ground. I took photos of Cliff standing next to them, then he of me. He zoomed in on the hoof, so I posed longer than necessary.

I slipped off my glove, coddling the bottom like a disrespectful tourist. I groped the seam that joined hoof to leg. Turning as if to study all four horses, I paid particular attention to sixteen hoof seams. Everything looked original and undisturbed.

"I think we should check the ones in the museum on our way out." As I spoke, a gust of wind tossed my hat to the pavers below. A gallant gondolier picked it up, waved it in an arching bow, and hooked it through the slats of a bench. As I watched Matthew, I thought of the triangle between Cliff, my daughter, and him.

"Do you still love her?" I was direct when something important was at stake, unlike the rabbit-trailing Mark.

Cliff survived my sneak attacks at seminary, so the question triggered a half smile instead of surprise or anger. "Yes, but she's torn. I don't know what to do about it. Matthew's ruined it for me."

"Are you certain?" I tried to show respect to this young man whose behavior had deteriorated in the past week. "Are you doing everything you can to win her love?"

"Do you know anything I don't?"

I chuckled as he held the door. "I know a lot of things you don't, Cliff. But she and I haven't discussed her feelings. Matthew is attractive and honorable. A catch. But so are you."

"Does she love him? Or me?"

We paused in front of the statues inside, and I spoke carefully. This important conversation affected at least three hearts, excluding mine. "I honestly don't know."

The look on his face—*crestfallen* was the word—made my heart hurt, and I reached for his arm again. "If I can offer you motherly advice, and this doesn't mean I'm pulling for one of you more than the other because it's my daughter's choice, and I want her to be happy above all things, continue to court her. Don't act angry, unattractive—keyword there—or hurt. You do your cause no good when you're combative. And I know her. She's watching and evaluating everything, perhaps subconsciously. Be your best, Cliff. It's your only shot. And don't worry about Matthew."

He circled around the horses, studying them. "Thanks, Dr. M. I didn't know when I enrolled in grad school that I'd come out with a second mom."

I laughed. "And remember. God is provident. If she's not the one for you, someone else is."

"There's only one Maggie in this world," he said as he photographed horse ankles.

Their seams were even, without signs of recent work. Dust on the display was undisturbed. Even if we didn't know exactly where the scroll was, I was certain no one had looked here before us, so we moved on.

Tourists formed a line at the elevator doors, and we descended into a night becoming bitterly cold.

...

Stepping from the Porta della Carta after thanking the guard, we tugged our coats around us, and popped the collars. We circled right, around the basilica, past the horses and lions (no bears, oh my!), and turned toward the palazzo. There, we would plan the specifics of our assault.

Directly across from us and slightly to our left, Cyril strode from the Gran Café Chioggia, absorbed with bundling against the elements. He stopped in the blazing lights, half hidden behind laughing couples.

I almost knocked Cliff over as I whirled away from the arched colonnade. "Turn!" I spat.

He did, pivoting a swift right, and swinging me with him. I doubt we looked innocent, but probably appeared no more drunk than most. I grabbed my hat as we passed the bench, pulling it down to my eyelids.

"What?" he barked before apologizing.

I walked, although I wanted to run. "Cyril," I hissed, interrupting his courtesy. "Emerged from a restaurant across the piazza. Beyond the hawkers. Don't know if he saw us."

"Should we press on or hide?"

"Probably hide. I don't want to lead him to the palazzo."

"Where?"

"This way," I said, veering left.

We moved toward Gioielleria Missiaglia, a prestigious jewelry shop inaccessible without ringing a buzzer, then cut into a passageway perfect for an ambush. A parade began, and I willed madly costumed participants between the commander and us.

Just before the bridge, I darted up six steps, past a peeling park bench on the left, and into a Burano lace shop. I was right at home, while Cliff waited patiently on another planet.

The proprietress greeted me before disappearing. Burano lace was a dying art because shop staff never seemed to care about a transaction. I looked at doilies and collars, table runners and lace-trimmed napkins. Cliff sat by the door, monitoring the corridor outside.

Cyril hadn't passed, so I nodded for Cliff to place the call. After chatting, he inspected a delicate handkerchief, and found the salesperson.

"Maggie wears these in her jacket pocket sometimes," he explained proudly.

I smiled as he implemented my advice. While the woman rang the purchase—maybe Venetians only sold lace to men?—he said Matthew recommended giving ourselves ten minutes before coming home the long way.

In Venice, that could be a problem because I always got lost, and the long way could result in a tour of Lapland. "It's a good thing this is an island," I told Cliff.

He understood.

CHAPTER SIXTY-TWO

Venice

Grace

"Someone should keep an eye on Cyril," Matthew was saying to Becca and Maggie when we followed Jeff into the room. "Your skills are better used at the ball."

Maggie's face was firm, her eyes narrowed like her brother's. Becca hid her anger better. Jeff shrugged at me.

"I agree with him," Cliff said, handing Maggie the tiny, lilac package tied with vermillion raffia. "We can handle this, and Mark will appear at some point."

"Wounded." I stood dramatically, my hands balled into fists where my hipbones should be. "Not badly, but still wounded. Besides, we don't even know where he's hiding, or why he's not here."

"She has a point," Matthew said as he distributed a diagram. "Several points. In the meantime, please study these. They'll give you an idea of the palazzo layout."

"We need to settle who does what first," Maggie said. "Although I understand about us at the ball."

"The *point* is that you can cover the ball while we start on the hoof." Matthew stood tall and straight, facing her. "It has nothing to do with your physical abilities, but in my *professional* experience, women are more observant than men."

Well, well, well. Wasn't this interesting?

"And you're a crack shot. Like your mother," he continued, nodding at me while referring to my marksmanship when I killed Maggie's abductor in the wadi. "I strongly prefer you return to the piazza to cover us as we retrieve the scroll. By that time, we'll need your skill with a firearm."

She stared at him for thirty seconds. "That's reasonable."

With at least one sigh of relief—mine—we reviewed the diagrams, and he returned with more boxes. "These disguises, which were stacked in a bedroom, are better suited to the evening than a gondolier and western heroine. Maybe the earlier ones were for daily use. You have to be appropriately dressed tonight. It's formal. And you need tickets."

Anyone who could dance the *quadrille* in period costume was welcome to a public ball, but private dances cost more than five hundred euros a ticket, and attendees had to meet dress-and-dance requirements. Of course Bashir arranged our entry.

"It starts in an hour with cocktails and appetizers for VIP attendees, which you are." Matthew handed me three rolled parchments, our tickets. "Next, upstairs to the first floor for dinner. Dancing—*farandollas, minuettos, contradanzzas*—begins at 10:30. You'll be gone before then, so don't worry about being able to dance. At midnight, everyone moves downstairs and the palazzo becomes a disco. We'll be finished long before midnight."

"Or you'll be dead," Becca said.

"Yes." He turned from us to flip through more papers. "If you're there long enough, you get scampi, truffles, and risotto, filet of sea bass, raspberry cake, and a chocolate fountain."

"Oh, chocolate fountains," Jeff replied, his voice sounding envious.

"Don't worry. This meal would be interrupted too," I said. "We're not staying for dinner."

Maggie was in a corner, trying to open her gift discreetly. Cliff walked to her.

"Do you have a plan?" I moved to the table, reading notes in my son's neat handwriting over his shoulder. "I see you're going to move along the outside of the Doge's Palace, cross the della Carta, then onto the right terrace." I felt my jaw clamp at such an idiotic idea. "That's suicide. It's raining. There's fog. The stone is slick. You're sixty feet in the air. I can go on. Your deaths won't accomplish anything, much less secure that scroll half. What's your Plan B? The intelligent one? You're not Spiderman."

"Mom." Jeff began in a tone meant to conquer.

"Don't start, Jeffrey. You know this is impossible," I said.

"Do you have any other suggestions?" he asked, his tone conveying more than a hint of defiance.

I held my tongue about his attitude. "I can request after-hours access to the basilica library for research . . . "

"You know that won't work on late notice. You have to request exemptions like that months in advance." His chin jutted out like his father's when angry.

I stood defeated, glanced at Maggie and Cliff having a quiet conversation, then continued anyway. "Then break in. Becca is a gifted lock picker. Ask Bashir to research the alarm system, but keep your rear off the façade of the palace and the Carta. Reach the terrace in one piece."

He paused. I had a chance, and I was going for it. "Or better yet, take a tour of the Doge's Palace, and slip away to hide until it closes. Or do this with the basilica."

THE BROTHERS' KEEPERS

Becca spoke. "I agree with Dr. M. Your plan sounds great if you're a superhero, but beyond fatal for mortals." Her voice was level and reasonable, unlike mine. "No flying without a cape, Jeff."

Maggie nodded vigorously as she joined us. A lace-tipped kerchief flopped from her breast pocket, just below the wilted peony in her lapel. She blushed when I looked at her, which made me smile.

Cliff inspected his boot toes. "Both buildings are closing," he mumbled.

"Then hurry," I replied. "We'll help get your stuff together. With my credentials, I can access the Palace library up to an hour after the public portion of the building is locked. I'll get you in, and then you're on your own. If we—" I motioned to Becca and Maggie "—discover anything earthshaking, or a reason to call everything off, we'll slip a message in the lion mouth at the top of the Scala d'Oro. Check there before you get in position."

"The lion mouth?" Cliff questioned, his head cocking to one side.

"Venetians weren't loyal," Becca began. "To anyone. The palace is riddled with open-mouthed carvings. Citizens slipped papers containing accusations in these holes, called lion mouths, which then fell into wooden boxes on the other side. Notes went to magistrates like the Condiglio dei Dieci or Inquisitori di State, and punishment was severe, although the offenses were seldom proven. A very efficient ratting system."

I raised my brows at her. I thought she hadn't studied history at St. Andrews.

"It's historic forensics, Dr. M.," she explained.

I nodded, and resumed stating unrelated information as I picked up the phone. "And we'll all be wired. We can keep each other informed. Request backup." I had told the desk clerk I was sending three associates to confirm last-minute research for their dissertations. I assured her that they would be no trouble, and would work quickly because they were on their way to have fun at Carnevale, which I knew she wanted to do as well.

...

Within ten minutes, we were ready.

Becca and Maggie wore panniers—the broad hip hoops that made dresses four feet wide—and squeezed through the single doorframes sideways. I was a thankful Napoleon, knowing my womanly derriere in tight white breeches looked slim next to theirs. This miracle would end too soon.

"I'm not sure where to hide it," Maggie said. "Do you think we should leave the scroll here?" She lifted the heavy lid of the chest in which Matthew stored our laptops and data, inspecting it.

"Where is it safest?" I asked. "I would think . . . "

Shuffling feet caught my attention, and I turned as Matthew, Cliff, and Jeff entered the room. Each carried a backpack, which contained climbing gear, small hacksaws—God forbid they had to use them—night-vision gear, and weapons. Bashir had sent it all, plus other things I couldn't identify. One thing I *could* identify was their Berettas.

Jeff looked pleased with his Lawrence of Arabia costume. I told myself it would work fine, having been sideswiped by less relevant street-strolling drunks. Matthew was still the most handsome gondolier in Venice, a city of men blessed with Italian good looks. Cliff was a Baroque dandy—ruffled collar, knee britches, two-inch heeled shoes, and a dark, split-tailed suit. The powdered wig framed his half-mask perfectly.

"The minute we hide, the girly shoes are history." He grumbled, shoving boots into his pack. "As are the ruffles."

"I honestly don't blame you," Matthew said, throwing his rival a look of pity.

...

We stood at the door, partygoers on the last hoorah of Carnevale.

"You still haven't told me how you're getting the other half of the scroll." They thought I had forgotten. Silly children. "How do you plan to get it out of the hoof?"

Cliff pushed Jeff forward, and Matthew stepped back, leaving Jeff to answer. "Mom, we're planning to hack off the hooves."

"You only need one." The answer dawned on me as I spoke. "You mean the original inside and the reproduction out? Or whatever they are? *Both*?" I asked, my pitch rising.

"Yes. Unless we know we have the scroll from the exterior horse, we're mutilating the interior one as well. I'm sorry." His chin tilted upward.

Hyperventilating, I opened my mouth so quickly my lips made a loud *pop*. "You *will* try to ensure you don't desecrate both unless absolutely necessary?"

"We will try. But our goal is to get that second half, and get out of there alive. Whatever that means. At whatever cost to humanity and our shared anything."

I nodded, defeated.

We unlocked the wooden door. Turning to the young women, I confirmed we would meet in an hour on the dock of Pisani Moretta palazzo after leaving the men somewhere in the Doge's Palace. We were wired and cross-wired. We could communicate unless someone fell into a canal and shorted out the equipment.

No one in our group would be drunk enough to perform *that* classic Carnevale maneuver.

CHAPTER SIXTY-THREE

Venice

Grace

The men were in the palace. The library would hide them until they worked north to the basilica.

Ten minutes later, via private launch along the southernmost reverse *S* loop of the Grand Canal, I arrived at the Moretta dock. Among guests preparing to promenade to the ballroom, a dark beauty in scarlet brocade whispered with a pale creature in midnight blue damask. The latter had a lace-trimmed kerchief in her décolletage, which led me to believe Cliff might have pulled into the lead.

Both women looked gentile, but their panniers held a Walther and a Beretta, while the hastily stitched interior pocket of my bicorne cossetted a 9mm Glock. I hoped it didn't fall on my head, which would hurt and be hard to explain.

I strode to them a confident Napoleon, cut my right hand across my midsection in a bow that triggered one snort and a donkey-like guffaw.

"Manners, ladies," I whispered at my gaudy toe buckles, flashing in the dock lights.

"Well played, Mama," Maggie said.

We crossed the threshold, intercepted a liveried man offering champagne from a tray, and floated up a marble stairway. We were not in a party mood, but needed to look festive.

Becca tried to lean to whisper, but her panniers did the Bump with my non-Napoleonic hips. She almost fell when an acrobat tumbled recklessly down the steps we had ascended. I didn't worry about their balance because the girls were wearing hiking boots under the flounces. The saucy mime traced faux tears down her cheeks before cartwheeling down the hall.

"Dr. M., we really can't do this."

"Do what, dear?" I set the full flute on a tray of empty glasses. The girls did the same.

"Dance the night away."

"Of course not, Becca. We'll be here for fifteen or twenty minutes, try to spot Cyril, then go help the boys." If I had made this plan clear earlier, the young men would never have agreed. "And at some point we need to find Mark. It will be at least thirty minutes before they do anything overtly dangerous in the piazza, so we have time. To save them, if necessary." I looked at Maggie's lace. "You okay?"

"Just dazed and confused."

"Put that aside. We need you whole." I tried to speak kindly, and wished Cliff had waited until our adventure was over for his bid to out-prince the prince.

"I'm all here, Mama. No worries. But if both of them are drowning, don't ask me to choose."

"I am a life preserver, baby." I sighed as the first notes of Pachelbel's Canon floated our way from the orchestra on the *piano nobile*—principal floor of a royal house. The composition would haunt me to my grave.

THE BROTHERS' KEEPERS

Fortunately, the abridged version incongruously transposed into a tarantella. My foot tapped. I loved a spicy tarantella. When the opera singer began—I loathed opera—we sashayed around the perimeter, minding that the girls' skirts didn't graze any candles. Murano glass chandeliers twinkled, and painted ceilings glowed. Becca and Maggie chatted and fluttered fans while packing substantial heat. Napoleon brought a cannon.

Becca saw him first. "Near the palm tree. Under the cherub flying over Marie Antoinette. In front of the *trumeau* laden with pears and cherries." She described almost every painting and woman in the room, but the palm tree was one of four. "Preening," she said, giggling.

Sure enough, the elegantly attired fireplug stood near a mirror, admiring his portly physique as if born to Baroque.

"Don't stare," I instructed while staring. "Our next mission, and we have no more than five minutes because it's black outside, is to identify Mossad operatives. Or Mark. Let's go opposite directions. Pay attention to wait staff, which is where I'd hide an agent. Meet me on the dock in four."

I smelled sea bass swimming from the kitchen to the dining rooms and knew we needed to leave before the dinner seating made our departure obvious. I thought about how little I had eaten in the past week, and didn't know if I had lost weight or just looked trimmer compared to the panniers.

As dancers merged to begin a minuetto, I ducked and wove to the beat. Managed a little Moonwalk. Did a break-dancing spin. Sashayed toward the pier doing Steve Martin's *Walk Like an Egyptian* dance. It was, after all, Carnevale.

Maggie and Becca skimmed the far side of the ballroom. Nodded to men doffing feathered hats. Avoided the potted palms.

I fingered no one as Mossad. Pausing in the doorway to ensure the young women didn't encounter problems, I descended to the dock thirty seconds ahead of them.

My earpiece generated static, then Jeff's voice. "Everything closed. Library clerk left with a guy and forgot us. Will begin H Squared in twenty."

I pressed the medallion on my bicorne, reassured by the shape of the Glock. "In place. He's here." My feed was hidden in the base of a trio of ostrich plumes.

The static stopped when Maggie and Becca joined me. I gestured toward the second water taxi queued. Declined to give the dock attendant our destination. Told the captain to head for the Rialto. We pulled away, indirectly toward Piazza San Marco.

Looking at the palace beyond our wake, I saw a gondolier place a cell phone to his ear. I squinted hard, and thought I saw Cyril exit.

Within five minutes, buildings we had passed were silhouetted in orange. The Moretta was a pillar of fire, according to chatter from the captain's two-way radio. I was sure authorities would blame the candles. And was equally sure they would be wrong.

CHAPTER SIXTY-FOUR

Doge's Palace

"*Buona sera.*" Agnelli bade the guard good evening as he left the Vatican apartment. He followed the route mapped in Rome. A service passageway—unused for decades, so lost to the world—connected the palace to the basilica. Its entry was unlocked this afternoon during a final sweep. Friends in low places helped, as did knowing buildings as an insider.

This same cleric had copied the museum key. Agnelli believed the scroll fragment was in a hoof, but did not know which one. Four horses. Sixteen hooves on the façade.

The skill saw under his robes was charged. While fireworks and drunken antics occurred below, he would detach the hooves until he found the other half. A jet waited at Marco Polo to take him to Saudi Arabia, where anyone was welcome for a price. From there, he would follow wherever the scroll led.

CHAPTER SIXTY-FIVE

Grand Canal, Venice

"Agnelli has the key?" she asked from the water taxi as it followed Commander Abraham ben-Dove Cyril from the Moretti bonfire.

The guard's response to McAlex's question indicated everything went according to her plan. The priest would lead to the scroll fragment before her guard killed him. The guard would bring the fragment to her, and she would eliminate loose ends—he and her college friend. Before she left Venice to implement the rest of Spigot, she would deal with the Madison family. And relieve them of the scroll from the cuneiform she could not switch out in Paris.

Natural resources in South America could help fund global work. There was also money to be made in Greece and Turkey, particularly as radical Muslim groups like the Taliban and ISIS squeezed both countries, and the EU continued its steady assault on Greece.

But those decisions would be made later.

And there was Becca. Laura McAlex had a score to settle.

Heading for the dock of Piazza San Marco, she ensured her pistol was loaded. She returned it to the flap resting on the bubble over her left hip.

She had waited since Aedan's death. She would wait no longer.

CHAPTER SIXTY-SIX

San Marco, Venice

Grace

"I am *so* done with these skirts," Maggie had said while pulling her outfit overhead, revealing midnight leggings and an UnderArmour tank. She retrieved the matching turtleneck from the cup of a pannier. Becca mimicked every motion.

"You girls are going to have a hard time hiding a firearm," I whispered as the craft bumped the San Marco dock. My Napoleon costume didn't billow, and the middle-aged body that bore two children wouldn't attract the attention their youthful bodies would. After all, this *was* Italy.

"With these drunken crowds, I'm unworried about hiding anything, Mama." Maggie pulled rolls of black cloth from a pannier, producing lightweight, calf-length capes with ties at the necks—normal Carnevale apparel. Becca fished three utility belts from her costume.

I shook my head. "Where in the world . . . "

"A hardware store near the palazzo. College girls left to their own devices go shopping," Maggie said as she tied a cape under her chin. "We figured we'd need the belts. The capes came from a tourist joint near a pastry shop."

The family always traveled with UnderArmour in winter, so she didn't need to explain those garments.

"Okay. Any spares?" A Glock in the bicorne might remove my head, so a holster would be nice.

"Of course. In character, even." Becca handed me a belt.

Maggie held a red cape resembling the one Napoleon wore in the Jean-Louis David *Napoleon Crossing the Alps* painting. "It's harder to hide, but note the lining is black. Wear it inside out when you need to hide."

I whirled it on like a toreador, buckled the belt, and hooked the Glock in an improvised holster. I looked pirate-y. "Ahoy there, maties."

"You have an identity crisis, Napoleon. Let's stick to the plan," Becca said.

"I plan to ensure no one gets shot, or falls off the façade of the Doge's Palace or St. Mark's. That's enough for me," I mumbled.

They looked at each other.

"Pretty much our plan, too," Maggie said.

"Then let's go, ladies," I said, walking toward the quay.

Our captain reversed the engines while other passengers boarded. I wondered how he would explain three cubic feet of tangled petticoats and pannier wires in the cabin floor.

DAY TEN

CHAPTER SIXTY-SEVEN

San Marco

Grace

Just after midnight, Becca picked the lock of the two-bedroom apartment above and north of the café from which Cyril had emerged few hours ago. We trusted its owners or tenants were celebrating elsewhere. Its balcony offered a perfect view of the basilica façade, which was easily in range of every firearm we carried. The crimson and orange sky southwest of the piazza confirmed that the Moretta was burning to piers embedded in clay muck at the bottom of the Grand Canal.

"I trust you plan to be ghosts?" I studied the girls' clothing, which would enable them to disappear into the night. "The Moretta fire isn't an accident, you know." Arson upped the danger ante. "As a mother, I have to remind you to be careful." I lay my hand across a knotting stomach. "We can still call the whole thing off."

"I didn't take rappelling class for nothing." Maggie referred to a P.E. credit during undergraduate work in the Rocky Mountains. "Although I haven't used the skills since."

"Nobody marries into this family without knowing how to shoot, fly fish, and mountaineer." Becca smiled, acknowledging the inevitable. "Animal husbandry helps, too."

"Only on Mark's side," I joked nervously, twisting my wedding band. "Okay. I get it. We go ahead."

"So this is our cubby." Maggie returned to business by looking around the trashed room. "Men. Quite a few. At least five." Picking up a pornographic magazine, she continued. "Approaching stupor stage, from the looks of their literary taste. Spending tonight passed out in an alley, if not facedown in a canal. They won't crawl back here until tomorrow. If we need a high-level shot, this is the perch."

"Agreed." I slalomed around laundry to reach the balcony. "How'd we choose this apartment?"

The girls exchanged a glance.

"Research," Becca said.

"She hacked reservation systems of online booking agencies. Searched until she found multiple male names renting a unit facing the basilica." Maggie patted her sister-in-law's shoulder proudly. Becca stared out the window, disengaged from our conversation. "Compared floor plans to choose the best angle."

"Goodness," I replied, not knowing what else to say.

"Not really," Becca said. "Nothing about this adventure, except the possible outcome, relates to goodness. Especially since Laura McAlex is beneath us, staring at those horses."

...

"In place," crackled in my headset. Becca and Maggie heard it, too. Jeff was on the terrace.

THE BROTHERS' KEEPERS

"Ditto," Becca said into the feed. "Ball was a snooze until the palace became an inferno. Interesting development here, though. Scottish heir below, watching the equines. You hidden?"

Muffled discussion preceded his response. "You're certain?"

"With my eyes closed. *Jeffrrrrrey*." Becca's purr was not of the house-cat variety.

His profane exclamation followed. Then, "Company!"

"Who?" Maggie adjusted her night-vision goggles to search the palace facade.

"Cleric ahead of us." Jeff sounded as if he were straining. "Moves stiffly, like an older man."

"Consider even a collar the enemy." I probably said too much if someone eavesdropped. "Remember the priest that preceded the train explosion."

The apartment lights were off. Maggie offered a set of goggles to me. The basilica was lit from below, leaving the terrace floor in shadows. Shadows were good.

The bad news was the horses were brilliantly illuminated, and three forms—balustrades made discerning tough—crouched near the door, invisible to the crowds. Another crawled close to the horses. The loner had to be the priest.

"Let him do the work," I said.

"Will do," Jeff replied.

Maggie nudged me. "Jeff's not in Lawrence's robes. He had UnderArmour beneath as well. He's dressed like us." She must have assumed I would watch for white. "It's probably Agnelli."

Nodding in the dark, I thanked her before I jumped. "More company behind you, Jeff!"

335

A form rappelled from a crenulated roof arch, then tucked into the protection of a setback. Except for the priest approaching the horses, everyone was about to get acquainted.

"I'm tailing the Scot," Becca said as she scooted past us to the door.

"No—" Jeff said from three hundred yards away "—you're not. And on it, Mom."

"You in a position to stop me?" his bride asked.

"Maggie?" he recruited his sister to accompany Becca..

"Pleasure," she said to her brother. "I'm coming too," she told Becca as they left me in the room.

"Mother, you're proficient with that Glock. Stay there and cover us all." My son read my mind.

"Don't worry, Jeff. I'm disinclined to climb." Zooming in, I saw an arm reach for a horse as the terrace party collided, ignoring the priest. The priest wasn't moving much, although fireworks exploding over the basilica interrupted his cover and probably made him more careful. When Jeff engaged the form behind him, the noises weren't pugilistic. "Jeffrey?"

"It's Flately. Merritt sent him. MOSES has crossed the Venetian lagoon."

"Ask him for me if the waters parted," I said, unable to resist. "What's the cleric doing?"

"Power tool," Jeff said as my professor entered the museum. The younger men would deal with the father vandalizing the statue.

In two minutes, the priest's form dropped, and I assumed the hoof was detached. "Downward motion. Should be returning to you," I said to my son. Shifting my vision right, along the terrace, I watched the men disburse, and hoped they hid. The priest crept toward the door. At the Porta, my reunited professors—Merritt and Flately dressed as the Two Wise

Men?—threaded the crowds. They had to be wired to stay near each other because no one could see through the reeling humanity.

Below me in the piazza, Becca and Maggie milled amidst revelers, ten feet behind McAlex. They wore tracking dots visible with my goggles.

I was searching the terrace when the fight broke out. Lights on my building silhouetted men struggling against the pale marble across the piazza. Jostling shadows danced on the mosaic above the altercation, which was framed by a gothic arch. The crowd's attention shifted to the fight, perceived as a staged part of this last night of Carnevale.

Looking down, I could pick out flaming red hair moving toward the basilica. One hand clutched a cell phone to her ear while the other pointed a pistol at the façade. Maggie and Becca closed on her.

I didn't have time to get out and downstairs before something happened. Training my weapon on her, I prepared to drop Laura McAlex before she killed. After my double-murder last year, what was one more?

The men struggled at the balustrade. First one leaned out, then another. How could one old priest fight off three young men? Was he empowered by the un-Holy Spirit? Were they fighting over the hoof?

As I tried to determine what to do, the crowd roared. On the terrace, one man punched the priest's head. I gasped as he fell over the railing. Sixty feet to the pavement. The crowd roared again, and I turned toward the lagoon with them in a human wave.

"Hi Ho Silver, Away!" I whispered.

The Lone Ranger galloped on a white stallion around the southeast corner of the Doge's Palace. He accessorized his gray-blue costume, black eye masque, red bandana, and heavily studded belt with a white Stetson, which he doffed at the crowds. When the light hit the bandana, I realized it was a bandage red with blood.

Then he pulled a six-shooter and shot McAlex, who recoiled and spun, tossing her pistol and cell phone before dropping near the splayed remains of the priest.

The crowd erupted, thinking the shot was a blank.

I knew better.

He whirled the horse on its hind legs to ride toward the island of Murano. I zoomed in in time to watch the splash of a revolver tossed in the Laguna Veneta.

I pivoted to the two fallen bodies. A small shape grappled over them. Four Wise Men approached the ferreting form as it tore through the costumes of the dead. When the shape straightened, I yelled.

"Stop the beggar!" I forgot about my wire, and probably burst more than one eardrum. "He has the scroll!"

I had seen that beggar before.

. . .

"Beg . . . gar! Direc . . . tion?" Jeff ran hard, his breathing labored.

"Got him," Becca called.

"Tailing," Maggie added.

"Where?" Matthew demanded.

"We think brother's," Becca said.

Steven Steele's Antico Privato apartment.

THE BROTHERS' KEEPERS

I could be there in five minutes, particularly since I was already out of the building. My cell vibrated. I fished it out of my utility belt. Mark. I texted.

Privato.

I could barely run, much less type or talk and run, through crowds on rain-slick piazza stone. Sliding into the Calle de Peregrin because of someone's nauseated deposit, I fell against the glass of the Max Mara store, triggering an alarm. Shoving my way to the narrow alley entrance, I pushed through an open door at Antico. The flowerboxes were on the ground, their contents scattered.

Dashing through the plaster-sheathed hallway, I ran to the back room. To the garden. Toward the back-canal gate. And joined five young people on the dock.

Professor Stanley Augustus Steele, PhD., turned at the end of the canal, erratically piloting *The Whinny* under a yellowing safety light.

CHAPTER SIXTY-EIGHT

San Marco

Grace

"He's escaped." I spoke into my phone to Mark. "Via launch."

"Again? Send Jeff and Cliff to the train station. He's probably headed there. Did he get a piece off of McAlex?" Mark sounded fine for someone shot yesterday. "Did you hide your half in the old chest? It was a pile of splinters. I found it when I swung by to show you I was all right, but you had already left."

"Mama," Maggie interrupted.

"I don't know," I said as I dug the toe of my pleather boot into the rug. "Probably. And if the chest was shattered, he has ours, too."

"*Mama*," Maggie persisted.

"We were afraid to bring it with us." I didn't want to lay too much blame at Matthew's feet. "And we've lost the commander."

"He took off in a water taxi. I saw him when I hung a left at the lagoon." From the tone of his voice, I knew Mark grinned inappropriately.

"*Mother*." She pulled the phone from my ear, and I glared at her. She slid the lilac paper from her utility belt, untied vermillion ribbon, and showed me our half of the scroll.

I looked from it to her face. "Game changer, Mark. We have our half."

"What?"

"I don't know anything else, but Maggie has ours." She nodded as I arched my brows, trying to focus on Mark. "It's authentic."

"Stay put. I'm coming to you. Can you call Steele?" Mark started moving because I heard him jingle. *Was he wearing spurs?* "And get Jeff and Cliff back there."

"I can try."

"Tell Dr. Steele what you have. He'll come for it. I'll be there to welcome him. Where are you?"

I handed my phone to Matthew and suggested we return to the apartment across from the basilica. It was the only place that hadn't been compromised, best I could tell. He gave Mark directions only a spy could follow, then texted my professor.

Thirty minutes later, after he changed clothes, took three public waterbuses, crossed four neighborhoods, and ate two paninis—to ensure he wasn't tailed, he said—we hugged. Uncovering his wound, I found it looked good. I asked how he felt.

"Honestly, I think I'm high. Bashir's doctors gave me meds, which I'm taking religiously. I've never felt better. In my *life*."

I searched his face. "You channeling the Lone Ranger?"

"One of my favorite childhood characters," he replied earnestly. "Hi ho."

Jeff and Cliff then told a similarly convoluted tale about their adventure that evening, although they were stone-cold sober.

...

We reconvened at Philippo's.

Matthew had raced for the scroll we thought Maggie hid at the palazzo, unaware Becca and Maggie instead left a copper souvenir picked up while costume shopping. Our thief could not have been a criminal mastermind, because he (or she) grabbed the worthless sheet of metal containing a recipe for *frittura mista* (fried fish).

Matthew arrived five minutes before the huddled form limped up the entrance steps in steady rain, and navigated four passed-out bodies that might have been the tenants of our bolt hole. Jeff and Cliff ensured he wasn't followed. The knock was quiet.

"Grace," Dr. Steele said meekly, hiding behind the doorframe.

I wanted to strangle him.

Mark pulled a chair to the middle of the room after kicking clothing out of the way, indicating my professor was to sit. Just before he dropped, Dr. Steele placed two copper fragments in Mark's outstretched hand. I gave them to Maggie to study.

The second knock announced Two Wise Men. Mark pointed to the sofa.

"Before we get into this, are you stable?" I asked Dr. Steele.

"Stable enough."

I remembered his near-escape, and realized he probably was more stable than me.

"Do you know where Cyril is going?" Mark asked, towering above him with his arms crossed.

"Israel, I'd imagine," was his answer. "I sent him photos of these pieces I took from the woman and the priest. If you have one of the original halves, at least one of those photos was of a fake. He's following that trail."

"So you broke into the palazzo?" I asked. "How in the world did you break into the chest?" Before he could answer, Maggie spoke.

"You're close but not entirely accurate, based on what I see." She looked at the three sheets side-by-side, illuminated by a craning metal desk lamp. "Why don't you tell us why these are so important to you, Dr. Steele? Then I'll fill in the blanks."

He sighed, rolled forward, and settled himself. The Wise Men leaned in.

"We need the short version if Cyril's on his way to Israel," Matthew said.

"Yes. My brother—I need to check on Steven—and I searched for this scroll most of our lives. Before becoming *Steeles* we were *Stahls* in Germany. Distant relatives of Luther. Family lore included the scroll. Steven and I, as boys, played out the story. When he began to see bits in the antiquities press, and I found the half in Wittenberg, we put two and two together. I suspect, if we did research and filed papers, the scroll might actually be ours."

No one said anything, so he continued. "Once we started analyzing the scroll as scholar and antiquarian, and most particularly its depiction, we realized it was much more than an heirloom. Of course, we never intended for things to get dangerous." He looked from me to Maggie. "We would never have jeopardized you." He paused, his mouth puckering. "Things got ugly when someone or something tipped Cyril to this search. Before I knew it, he was in Wittenberg, interrupting the conference, thrusting himself into the picture."

"And whoever it is kidnapped and planted the bug on Maggie?" I asked. The danger seemed so senseless to me that my cheeks burned. And I had to remind myself to breathe.

"To flush us out, and involve your family to speed up the search," he replied. "I have to tell you that I don't know who's behind this disaster."

"So what do you think the scroll depicts, Dr. Steele?" Maggie pitched her head to one side, beckoning me so I could look.

"To us, it was an heirloom. I now know it shows the water source for Solomon's Mines at Timna," he said. "Of course."

"No, it does not," I said, slipping the lilac paper between the important halves, tossing the recipe in the wastebasket, and shoving the parcel deeply in my pocket. "Matthew, is that Citation still available? Can it take us to Ein Gedi?"

DAY ELEVEN
CHAPTER SIXTY-NINE

Ein Gedi, Israel

Grace

The water at Timna might well have been there. But we weren't.

Our *complete* scroll, aside from depicting locations of miracles and long-lost settlements, showed Luther's rose here. Near the Dead Sea, confirming the confusing layout of the Madaba mosaic. In a hydrological system just like the one Maggie had thought ran along karstic lines near Solomon's copper mines.

Ein Gedi, the oasis in Israel where David hid from King Saul, contained two powerful springs, *nahals* David and *Arugot*. Two other springs, the *Shulamit* and Ein Gedi, also irrigated the wadi reserve in which we hiked. For a spot in the middle of a desert, it was watery.

When the State of Israel dedicated this verdant park, they documented every square inch with the detail of a Pharisee. But we thought they might have missed something.

Temperatures were bearable thirteen hundred feet below sea level on this early spring day. We climbed a mile to David Falls, hopped boulder-to-boulder, tight-roped fallen timber, and passed few tourists. Most visitors were in Jerusalem enjoying the pageant of Ash Wednesday in the Holy City.

We left Dr. Steele in a MOSES reunion at the Hallelujah Hotel, with Drs. Merritt and Flately. They compared slips of paper handwritten in Hebrew, which they said they would explain tonight.

Steven was still critical in Germany, and I prayed for him during the last hundred yards of the climb.

The five-hundred-foot waterfall splashed into a basketball-court-sized rock bowl where swimmers normally recovered from summer heat exceeding one hundred degrees Fahrenheit. Plants dangled from dark slashes around the falls, in spots where slivers of rock had detached to create voids perfect for soil pockets.

We enjoyed the spectacle alone, in shade from an olive tree arcing from a crevice high above. Rosemary and fennel, my favorite wild herbs, found similar footholds. I admired the buds on an almond tree, the first species to bloom each spring, knowing it would be a pale-peach pompom in a week or two.

"It should be *here*." Maggie pointed at a cracked wall tucked behind an outcropping the size of a school bus. I knew most people gazed at the waterfall, never looking from its beauty. But our goal was in the other, less-observed, direction.

"What are we looking for?" Matthew asked. Before we left Jerusalem, where we spent the night, he had announced Cyril searched furiously in Timna, harassed by representatives of the Israeli Antiquities Authority and Mekorot, Israel's National Water Company.

Maggie forcefully stated they deserved each other. She assured us he wouldn't find much water there because the scroll indicated the spring lay several miles northeast. I believed MBM

Hydrology would pursue this resource, and was concerned that she would stay in the Middle East—in danger.
 I also believed Matthew had abandoned Mossad to pursue my daughter. Cliff obviously maintained courteous attention to ensure he was not forgotten. His lace-trimmed handkerchief never left her pocket.

...

We searched the cliff side, uniform in the swirling way of wadis and slot canyons around the globe. Reaching for a gnarled stem of a rosebush, I dislodged a bract with my fingernail, and nipped the bud tip to force it open. The immature blossom was simply white, with four petals.
 Identical to the depiction of Luther's Rose.
 "Here," I said. "Look at this." I pointed the flower at the plant.
 "How is this significant?" Jeff asked. "I mean, I see the resemblance between the flowers, but the story is a lot older than this plant. And I thought we were dealing with daisies."
 "One rose bush in Germany is said to be more than a thousand years old. Even when no one cultivates them, roses spread. This might not be the original plant, but there's a good chance one with this genetic code has been nearby for thousands of years." I stopped and thought. "The other wild roses I've seen in Israel are pink."
 We stared at the blossom. Then Cliff and Matthew began climbing the slick-rock formation, comparing plants and stems. I pointed to suspects whose growth resembled the sprawling shape of a rosebush. The men surveyed the wall thoroughly, but

eventually dropped, defeated, with greater respect for David's legendary athleticism.

"Maybe Luther's rose was modeled on this one, and we need to look from that perspective, instead of *back* in time?" I motioned for Maggie to join me, and turned her toward the rock face. "Notice the cracks?" A swing of her ponytail indicated she did.

"They're everywhere," she began. "But roses are hardy. The cracks where the root system is spreading . . . "

"How?" I pushed. Everyone clumped around us and tried to catch up. "How do roots spread? Access water?"

"Obviously, water percolates . . . " she started to say.

"Through rock, Maggie?" I kept pushing.

"Yes." She paused. "But probably not this type of rock. And there's not much water here. I see your point." She paused again. "How *do* they get the water to survive up there?"

We stood in a deep rift, surrounded by vertical crags in one of the driest regions on earth.

"You're the hydrologist," I hugged her waist.

Jeff guessed. "They look like an airplane."

"Or a dove," I replied, shaking my head. "I'd love to discover what is behind this wall of rock. Or on top of it."

"Maybe streams of living water? The dove has been symbolic of Christ since His time," Matthew contributed.

"What are you suggesting, Mama?" Maggie walked to inspect the cliff closely.

"Could there be a cavern behind this wall, baby? Could Ein Gedi have been part of a karstic system? The Dead Sea and Jordan Rift Valley are part of the Great Rift Valley running from Africa into Europe. Only the Jordan River feeds the Dead Sea after Northern Israel and Jordan drain it for agriculture. Where does the water sustaining the roses come from, or go?"

THE BROTHERS' KEEPERS

Maggie giggled.

"I don't have a brioche," Matthew said as he nudged her.

"You can owe me, Matthew." She pivoted to me. "You might have something. The scroll specifically points here for a reason. Let's start with that small cave." She pointed to a hole about two hundred feet above the waterfall, toward the top of the wadi, then scampered up the rocks. "Mountaineering, anyone?"

Becca squinted. "If it's a dove, then the beak points to it," she said, motioning toward an animal path running near the entrance. "If we can connect to that path, you can probably get to the cave, Dr. M. Although I'm sure all these caves were picked clean in the 1940s and '50s, after the Qumran discovery down the road. And I think we're seeing what we want to see with the dove shape."

"We might be. And sometimes people miss things," I said doubtfully.

I am not the scampering type, so managed, with a lot of help, to enter the cave thirty minutes later.

The cave was large and deep, without signs of vandalism or camping. We began to explore. I peeked outside when I heard hooting, and saw Israeli Defense Force personnel sunbathing and swimming, their semi-automatic weapons scattered on flat rocks.

"I don't think there's anything here, but I enjoyed the climb," I said sarcastically. I peered over the top of my sunglasses at friends and family. "Thank you for this adventure, Maggie. More importantly, everyone agrees we don't discuss any of this until we know more? I'm ready to go back to Jerusalem."

"That's the most powerful Mom Look of Death I've ever seen," Jeff said before becoming louder. "I promise. My sister will investigate?"

"Yes. Quietly," she replied.

"I'm clueless, Dr. M., and happily leave hydrology to my sister-in-law," Becca said.

"We're sworn to silence," Matthew replied, nodding at Mark.

"Agreed," Cliff said. "Let's give Maggie time to do her work."

I rolled my eyes at my daughter.

"You have the makings of a great spy, Gracie," Mark laughed as he spoke.

He saved me as I tumbled, still vertical, over a rockslide on my way toward the sunshine beaming outside the cave mouth. I kissed him, a romantic delay that saved my life.

Mark yanked me from the opening when a deafening *rumble* and choking cloud of dust announced the rockslide that sealed the cave. We fell in a heap, knocking over Jeff and Becca. When the earth stopped, we sat. Stunned.

"Does anyone believe in coincidence?" Maggie asked. She looked around, as if trying to find an escape. "Crap."

"No. Not at all. You all right?" Matthew answered, assisting me as I stood. He looked at us, we looked at each other, and Mark and I nodded that we were okay.

"Good to see everyone's calm," Mark said. "We need to stay that way."

"I left my adrenaline in Israel last year, so you can count on my being unperturbed." I kicked a rock, hurting my toe. "I have nothing left."

"I think it's time to explore the depths of the cave," Jeff said, taking Becca's hand.

Turning to Maggie, I pointed at her. "Do you think it's safe to go down there after an earthquake?"

"If I thought it was an earthquake, I'd say no. All things considered, I say we go for it because I'm pretty convinced it was *not* an earthquake."

"Your professors know we're here, and are experienced enough to search if we don't return for dinner. They know Ein Gedi, and will recognize a fresh rockslide and footprints." Mark took my other arm as we worked—and work it was—more deeply into the mountain. "They'll come looking for us."

"Thank you," I said to the man still trying to encourage me. "So shouldn't we stay here?"

"The air is awfully fresh," Jeff said. "For a cave."

"I was thinking that," Matthew said.

"I'm thinking most people would stay near the mouth, waiting to be rescued," I replied, interrupting their discussion of fresh air. "But we're not most people, I guess."

Maggie patted my arm. "We are most definitely *not* most people, Mama. And I'm wondering if this is—and this is a stretch, so don't anybody hold me to it—part of the karst you proposed at the waterfall."

"That would make me very happy because then it would *go* somewhere," I replied. "I repeat, shouldn't we stay here if you think my professors will come to look for us?"

"Assuming it wasn't natural, whoever caused that rock slide will be waiting outside too, Grace. I think we can afford to explore a little, and move away from what used to be the mouth," Mark said, finally answering my question.

We picked along. Slid on the seats of our pants. Dropped after dangling in a short human chain. Dropped again, but further. Stepped after ensuring boulders were stable. Tried not to trigger another slide that would cause more problems. Dropped a third time. Used very colorful languages, some dead, from around the globe.

Along the way, an occasional slit between rocks illuminated caverns we traversed, and rockslides we scaled. Most of the walls were smooth, polished by flowing water. At the least, Maggie said, we had found another historic source of water for the Dead Sea.

We spread out a bit once we reached a level stretch. Cell phone flashlight apps revealed a floor as smooth and sandy as a beach, but crusted in spots with the white mineral crystals that fringed the Dead Sea.

"Looks natural to me," I said. "Not a cistern or manmade waterway."

"Agreed," Maggie said. "Looks more and more like a karst."

"More fresh air?" Matthew asked, sniffing.

"I believe so," Maggie replied.

"Maybe we're close to the end," I said. "I'm talking about the hike, not life." No one laughed, which was good because I was serious. I steered Maggie twenty feet ahead of the group, out of earshot. "Assuming we survive, what are you going to do?"

She wasn't coy. "I have no idea."

"Do you have a favorite?"

"Yes. Depending on the day of the week. I am, for the first time in my life, fickle."

"Wow." We navigated a rock fall silently, then I continued. "Maybe a break is in order. Come to the States. Run MBM. Leave them here. Matthew working for Bashir. Cliff running the dig." Focusing on our futures helped me believe we would actually *have* them.

She nudged me, and pointed to sunshine ahead. "I've already decided. I'm giving myself a year off, hoping time helps me choose." Her voice was weary. "I'm coming home."

Quick footsteps behind us indicated our team was about to pass us in a race to the light.

"If someone thinks they trapped us, and we don't know where this opening leads, we probably shouldn't just pop up," I called to them.

"Kind of like picking off prairie dogs at the ranch," Jeff said, remembering a less-savory chore that honed our shooting skills. "Whack a Good Guy."

"Although if they knew that cave led to an old waterway or karst, they would have tried to dispose of us another way," Mark said. "But you have a point, Grace. Let me ease out first."

Maggie stroked the walls. "A lot of water here. For a long time, long ago."

"Makes sense, given the view," Mark said. "I think we're fairly well hidden. Take a look, Maggie." He hoisted her just high enough so she could peep outside.

"A Dead Sea sinkhole," she informed us as he set her down. "This system once led into the Dead Sea, but after it dried up, it was compromised by a sinkhole. The water was long gone by then."

"Stupid for us to walk along the shores within yards of Highway 90. We'll be spotted," Jeff said as Becca nodded. He referred to the road that linked northern and southern Israel, and paralleled the Dead Sea. "And we won't know by whom."

"And access to the sinkholes is restricted because they're dangerous, and the earth is so unstable. If whomever trapped us doesn't see us on a seaside stroll, then Israeli authorities will.

I don't want to answer their questions, which would eventually attract Cyril's attention. We need to wait for dark." As Maggie slid down the wall to sit, she checked the time on her cell phone. "Nightfall in the hour. Makes sense sinkholes would appear near a karst. The infrastructure is compromised."

"She's as bad with this geology stuff as Jeff is with languages," Mark grumbled.

"I didn't bear and raises idiots, Mark. And I want to see." Mark obliged by lifting me, and I found myself face to face with an ibex nanny and twin kids. Beyond the fabled beasts, the turquoise Dead Sea lay a few hundred yards away.

"I'm confused," I said as he sat me down, looking at the bodies that had settled comfortably on the sand. "How do Spigot, the priest, and Agnelli fit together? I thought Spigot ended last year, when al-Jafar, Rosenthal, and David Spiedel died beneath the Temple Mount. Where do all these horrible people keep coming from?"

"Remember, Cyril said Mossad continued to watch Spigot and the Steeles," Jeff replied. He turned to Matthew. "And probably us as well. What else do you know?"

Matthew didn't answer immediately, and I assumed he was determining what to share. "He thinks it's a syndicate. Much larger than what we uncovered last year. Very well funded. Global. With a lot of fingers in the environment."

We waited for more.

"That's really all I know."

"And what about Laura McAlex?" Becca asked.

"She's the wild card for me," Mark said. "I had the rest of this figured out, but she blew a substantial hole in my theories." He cringed, and I knew he remembered shooting her. "She was about to hurt Maggie and Becca, so I had no choice but to kill her."

I squeezed his hand. "You saved our girls."

He nodded at his boots. "I didn't do much of the violent stuff for the CIA."

I glanced at Maggie, and she cleared her throat before kindly attempting to change the topic. "I told Mama I'm going to the States for a year. I need to supervise MBM from the corporate office. Try to figure out how to manage our crazy growth. I've been offered an adjunct professorship at Colorado School of Mines, too, leading a research team for the year. It's only a few miles from headquarters. I'm probably going to take it."

Matthew and Cliff's faces revealed nothing.

"I'd love to have you close by," Mark said.

"As would I," I smiled, excited at the thought. Becca and Jeff were London-based, and it would be grand to have a child close to home.

"It's for the best," she said. "Away from this Spigot nonsense."

"If we get out of Israel alive," I said, leaning into Mark.

"Count on it, Gracie," he said, laying his arm over my shoulders.

We waited for the passage of time.

I was glad my schedule was light for the coming year. My only commitments were in Greece and Turkey in the fall, monitoring for UNESCO a dig near the enormous Gobekli site.

Perhaps she could join me for a little peace and quiet among the ruins.

ONE MONTH LATER
CHAPTER SEVENTY

Doncon Castle, Scotland

The bandaged form in a chintz-infused bedroom had not spoken since the medical helicopter landed next to the castle loch a week ago. Edinburgh doctors took over from the best London had to offer, and confirmed she remained in a coma. They warned her father to expect brain damage, and a grim future for his only living child.

During a medical intervention of massive proportions, her headful of flaming curls had been left on a surgery floor.

But in her childhood bedroom, in a castle deep in the silent moors, she replayed redirecting her associates from Timna to Ein Gedi. Right before she was shot.

Her mind was very much alive, delighting in her revenge in Israel.

THE BROTHERS' KEEPERS

A READERS GUIDE

QUESTIONS FOR BOOK CLUBS

1. The title of this book, *The Brothers' Keepers*, refers to Grace Madison's determination to protect her beloved professor, Stanley Augustus Steele, PhD. To what lengths would you go to protect someone? Do you think Grace is crazy? Why or why not?

2. *The Brothers' Keepers*, like *When Camels Fly* before it, is about "doing the right thing." Cite a situation in which you chose to do the right thing despite personal cost. Was it worth it?

3. Grace and her husband, Mark, are working to rebuild their marriage. How hard do you think it is to try to fall in love again? Is marriage only a commitment or covenant? Which is most important: love or commitment?

4. How do you think society's perspective of marriage differs in the three generations—young adults, Boomers, and mature adults—depicted in the *Parched* series?

5. Which of the characters in *The Brothers' Keepers* can you relate to, and why? Do any seem incomprehensible?

6. Do you want Maggie to fall for Cliff, the all-American as loyal as a golden retriever? Or Matthew, the handsome foreigner exuding danger, and bringing different cultural expectations to the table? How important is common ground? Or what common ground is most important?

6. In *The Brothers' Keepers*, Mark seems more comfortable with the independence Grace developed in *When Camels Fly*. How would your spouse react if you decided to pursue a vastly different career after your children were grown? Would he or she be supportive, or threatened?

7. Grace raised children, built a family, and has a career. Maggie has sacrificed her own family life for her career. Can a woman "have it all," or is that lifestyle a myth? How does contemporary Christianity support or discourage the choices Grace and Maggie are making?

8. In Genesis, we're told that man and woman are created equally in God's image. What attributes of God do you see in characters in *The Brothers' Keepers*? Are they stereotypic?

9. Laura McAlex exhibits some nasty personality traits as the villainess of the *Parched* series. But we learn about her background in *The Brothers' Keepers*. Does her history evoke your compassion? Do you think she can change and be redeemed? How does she differ from male villains?

10. Are you comfortable with a villainess? Do you respond to Laura McAlex the same way you would respond to a villain?

11. Do you know vigorous octogenarians? Talk about the traits of the Steeles, Merrit, and Flately. What can you do *today* to prepare to live actively and joyfully for the rest of your life?

DEFINITIONS

These are the author's definitions. Some of these terms have multiple meanings, and in those cases, only those appropriate to the book are offered.

Academie français — leading French authorities on the French language (French)
Al fresco — "to fresh" (Spanish), referring to outdoor dining
Aqua alta — a phenomenon of temporary flooding in Venice (Italian)
Arrondisement — neighborhoods into which Paris is divided (French)
Aurelian — Roman emperor from AD 270 to 275; built the Aurelian Wall in Rome
BRAFA — Brussels Antiques and Fine Art Fair, a pre-eminent show of antiquities
Barrista — coffee maker (Italian)
Bayee — father (Lebanese)
Bergère — low armchair (French)
Bienvenue — welcome (French)
Boisserie — exquisite wood paneling (French)
Bonne nuit — good night (French)

Banzai — "ten thousand years," but used as a war cry by Japanese in WWII
Brasserie — relaxed restaurant (French)
Café au lait — coffee with hot milk (French)
Café crème — coffee with hot cream (French)
Cappa magna — great (red) cape with trailing train used by cardinals
Cappuccino — espresso, hot milk, and steamy foam (Italian)
Carabinieri — Italy's National Military Police
Chianti — red Italian wine
Cloche — close-fitting, bell-shaped hat wore low on the forehead (French)
Contradanzzas — country dances (Italian)
Crème fraiche — a soured cream with high butterfat content
Danke — thanks (German)
Demilune — half circle
Disputatio pro declaration virtutis indulgentiarum —Luther's Ninety-Five Theses (Latin name)
Djellabah — a loose-fitting, traditional Berber robe with long sleeves; unisex (Arabic)
Doge — honorary Venetian ruler
En masse — as a group (French)
En route — on the way (French)
Entrée — enter (French)
Espresso — staggeringly strong coffee (Italian)
Farandella — a version of the conga line from Southern Italy
Gare du Nord — large train station in Paris
Grazie — thanks (Italian)
Guten abend — good evening (German)
Hausfrau — housewife (German)

Hercule Poirot — famed Belgian detective created by author Agatha Christie
Isha — call to last Muslim prayer of the day (Arabic)
Kaffiyeh — cotton head scarf worm by some Arab men (Arabic)
Kinneret — also *Kinrot*, the Dead Sea (Hebrew)
Krav maga — the pre-eminent self-defense protocol in the world (Hebrew)
La dolce vita — the sweet life (Italian)
La Serenissima — the Serene (Italian)
Lampo — famous sandwich shop in Venice
Lancia — type of automobile manufactured in Italy
Lutherdenkmal — large Protestant Reformation monument in Worms, Germany
Lyria SAS — subsidiary of the French National Railway
Macchiato — espresso drink with a small amount of steamed milk (Italian)
Mais non! — "but no!" (French)
Marocchino — the Italian version of a mocha coffee drink (Italian)
Merci — thanks (French)
Minuettos — an historic French dance for couples
Momento, por favor — "a moment, please" (Spanish)
Mossad — Israel's Institute for Intelligence and Special Operations
Nahal — stream (Hebrew)
Non sequitur — illogical conclusion or statement (Latin)
Ostracon — pottery scrap (Greek)
Pain au chocolat — bread with chocolate or chocolate-filled croissant (French)
Panini — pressed and griddled Italian sandwich
Par excellence — better than others (French)

THE BROTHERS' KEEPERS

Plat du jour — special of the day (French)
Puces — literally, fleas, but in this instance, flea market
Quadrille — dance for couple in square formation
Rosa rugosa — perennial rose with heavy thorns (Latin)
Rue — street (French)
S'il vous plait, une kir royale — "if you please, a kir royale" (French)
Sayan — plural of sayanim (Hebrew)
Sayanim — helper or assistant, a civilian who works with Mossad (Hebrew)
Sayonara — goodbye (Japanese)
Shalom — peace (Hebrew)
Shar Pei — a deeply wrinkle Chinese dog breed with a short, rough coat
Shawarma — meat roasted on a spit (Arabic)
Thesentur — door to which Martin Luther nailed his theses (German)
Trumeau — a painting in a frame inset into a wall, usually above a door (French)
Un café, per favor — "a coffee, if you please" (Italian)
UNESCO — United Nations Educational, Scientific, and Cultural Organization
Vaporetto — water taxi or waterbus (Italian)
Viva la bourgeoisie — long live the middle class
Z-SCANS — a scientific method
Zucca — pumpkin (Italian)

ACKNOWLEDGEMENTS

The Brothers' Keepers is in your hands after the tireless work, endless encouragement, and unbridled enthusiasm of a team of readers, editors, agents, geologists, theologians, hydrologists, and artists. Each one transforms my mental wanderings to keep me on track, and I thank them.

I'm delighted that the caravan from *When Camels Fly* mounted up for *The Brothers' Keepers*. My acknowledgements again begin with the inimitable DiAnn Mills: friend, mentor, and author extraordinaire. My literary agent, Mary G. Keeley, continues to forge new territory by my side, and I applaud her courage every step of the way. Editors Jamie Chavez and Ginger Kolbaba polish my writing to a professional gleam, and tease out the story I imagined. New to the team, beta reader Ann Rosenwald deserves a special nod for her meticulous attention to detail and inquisitive mind.

Most of all, I thank my family: Ranchman for his patience; Bear for his dedication; Bird for her insight, and the trail of chocolate fingerprints across *When Camels Fly* and *The Brothers'*

THE BROTHERS' KEEPERS

Keepers. Our household creed is, "From those to whom much is given, much is expected." I am blessed in abundance with these three.

Camel up!

A NOTE FROM NLB HORTON

Dear Readers:

Thank you for joining Grace and her friends and family on their Reformation adventure. It's a delight to researching the facts that pepper my work and to travel to the locations that appearin these books. Then I get to share my tales with you, which is the very best part!

I would love to know what you think. Please consider posting a review on the website of your choice: Amazon, Barnes & Noble, iBook, Kobo, or Goodreads. *Your reviews really count, and they really matter.* Reader reviews enable authors to continue to share stories by generating credibility and recommendations to other readers. Your thoughts and opinions trigger the media engines that provide exposure for our work.

You are the reason I write. Your reviews keep me writing.

You also might want to take a look at the website, **NLBHorton.com**. News about the *Parched* series appears there, and I'll be sharing previews of the third book soon. You'll also

THE BROTHERS' KEEPERS

find photographs of locations from the manuscripts—although I reserve the right to twist them to suit my stories.

I am sincerely honored you're sharing Grace and her family with me. Please stay in touch!

NLBH

NLB HORTON

After an award-winning detour through journalism and marketing and a graduate degree from Dallas Theological Seminary, NLB Horton returned to writing fiction. She has surveyed Israeli and Jordanian archaeological digs accompanied (*twice!*) by heavy artillery rounds from Syria and machine gun fire from Lebanon. Calmly (*not!*) tossed a tarantula from her skiff into the Amazon after training with an Incan shaman. Driven uneventfully through Rome. And consumed gallons of afternoon tea across five continents. Life is good.

She is a member of the venerable Explorers Club, founded in 1904 as a multidisciplinary professional society of explorers and scientists. From the Rocky Mountains, she writes, cross-country skis, fly fishes, gardens, shoots sporting clays, and researches ideas for the next novel in the Parched series.

Her first novel, *When Camels Fly*, was released in May, 2014. *The Brothers' Keepers* is her second. The third in the series will release in the fall of 2015.

If you've enjoyed *The Brothers' Keepers*, don't miss NLB Horton's first novel, *When Camels Fly*.

Made in the USA
Middletown, DE
11 November 2014